WRATH
OF THE
APPRENTICE

BRENT SNYDER

WRATH OF THE APPRENTICE

Copyright © 2025 Brent Snyder

PROMINENT
BOOKS

5830 E 2nd St, Ste 7000 #9983
Casper, WY 82609
USA

The jail cell in Yelliton held the most famous criminal of all time. Kaistam-Laq had been detained in the jail for the past four years. After his run in with the healer Tÿr'Ynyn he was in ruin and disgraced. She had him beaten and had seen to his disastrous fall. He sat in his cell and plotted against this girl healer with his whole being. He would have his revenge.

His days were spent in solitude. No one came to visit. No one was allowed in to see him. None of his trusted followers were allowed near the jail. If any of his followers were found near the town, they were rounded up and moved to jails in neighboring villages. Yet he had a plan. He would not spend the rest of his life in this cell. He would escape and be free once more.

Kaistam-Laq's power had not waned since he had been incarcerated. If anything, his powers had grown. Now, if only he could be allowed to get to his staff of power. He had magiqal powers, but the staff amplified them by a hundred times. All it would take is a weak-minded guard or a dishonest one, and he would be free in an instant. The only issue with that was that guarding him was a position of honor and it was taken very seriously. Swaying anyone from their duties would be very difficult indeed.

Laq had been busy in his cell while he had been locked up. He had been planning and plotting on how best to get back at the healer. She had seen him go from a brilliant sorcerer to a ruined man in just moments during their fight four years ago. How she had bested him was still a mystery to him. She was not more powerful than he and she was not remarkable. She was only a healer after all. The thought of it made him furious and made his resolve grow with each day.

Unfortunately for the sorcerer, he was locked in a high security prison that also had a magiq dampening spell put on the whole complex. No magiq could be performed inside the prison by guards or prisoners. This was to ensure that no escape could happen. The only person who could perform magiq in the complex was the warden. This was a highly protected secret that only one guard knew about, and he was sworn to secrecy when he took the job. He was the guard that was the personal bodyguard of the warden, and he was privy to all the secrets of the jail.

The jail cells were constructed of four feet thick rock and the bars were made from tyrin, a metal that is corrosion resistant, and impossible to cut without magiq. Since magiq was impossible to use in the jail there was no worry about cutting the bars. The cells were for all intents and purposes, impossible to escape. Each cell had a bed roll to sleep on and a hole in the floor for doing one's business. Other than that, the cell was empty and had no comforts at all.

The jailer was a strict disciplinarian who took his job very seriously and did not stray from the rule book. He did not succumb to the begging nor whining of prisoners. He went by the rules and followed them to the letter. There was no mercy. If you did the crime, you did the punishment, it was as simple as that. The warden had no family nor friends so he couldn't be influenced by someone threatening his loved ones. He was tough as nails and loved his job and was very good at it.

The jail had fifty cells, and all were high security. No criminal who came here spent less than four years in the infamous jail. Most who came here spent the rest of their days in the jail. It was reserved for the worst of the criminals on the conjoined planets of Peyda Kirin and Peyda Noirin. The jail sat on the shift in the middle of the planets where it was easier to access. Yelliton was a jail community and everyone that lived there knew of the high security prison. The building itself looked more like a medieval fortress than a prison with battlements and towers surrounding it.

Luckily for the residents of the peaceful village of Yelliton, the prison was located on the outskirts of the town, and no one was allowed near it ever. Guards kept unwanted visitors away from the huge building with magiq and the use of ranged weapons like ballistae and trebuchets. The guards arming the weapons were incredible shots and took no survivors. If there was an attack on the prison, the goal was to quell it immediately and forcefully. Along with the large weapons. There were many bowmen situated along the battlements. They too had orders to shoot to kill. There had never been a breakout of the prison and they intended for that record to stand forever.

Kaistam-Laq had a plan. His plotting had turned from a mere hobby to a full-on obsession. He was certain his plan would work. No one had ever escaped from the prison, and he was hoping that this would be the flaw that helped him to escape; their arrogance. He was of the opinion that anything was possible with enough planning.

He had the time to do the planning, now he needed the manpower. Now was the time to do his recruiting. He would build his new crew back to his perfect number of seventeen. That was the number he believed in and that he trusted. That was his magiqal number.

He would begin recruiting immediately and he would not use any of his old crew. They had disappointed him and essentially landed him in prison to begin with. None of them deserved a second chance. That was if any of them still lived. Since he had been locked away, he had gotten no word from any of his old crew. None of his old loyal people had come to visit him. They were now dead to him and if he found any of them, he would make them pay for their betrayal.

The first place he would recruit from was the prison he was locked in. There were many prospects that he found acceptable. There were thieves and cutthroats and there were also magiq users that had been locked away for using their skills for their own gain. All qualities that he found to be useful for his purposes. The magiq users would be the first to be recruited into his fold.

Now, how to get messages to them? He would have to be cautious and use those who were easily bribed. The jailor was too honest, but those that worked for him could be persuaded. He was certain about that. There were some corrupt guards in the prison who would do anything for a bit of cash, and cash would not be an issue. Once he held them under his sway, he would have his staff of power back in his possession and then things would fall into place.

The first thing he needed to do was figure out how to get messages to the other prisoners. He had no money with him but getting it once he was out would not be an issue. He had plenty at his disposal. He would begin with the guards. Which were corruptible? He would have to spend time with each of them to find out. He would need to find personal details on each of them to find what he could use against them. That meant, he swallowed disgustedly to himself, he would have to learn their names. Things he didn't excel at. He barely remembered the names of his own crew, and now he'd have to learn the names of people he detested.

He decided there and then that he would begin the laborious task of learning the names of the guards and learning about each and every one of them. He would have to be careful how he did this and not just jump in with both feet. That would raise too many eyebrows. He would have to do this slowly and cautiously.

That night he sat in his cell and listened to the conversations of the guards. He could only get bits and pieces of it, but from the conversation he was able to ascertain the names of the two guards. Javyn and Hader.

It wasn't much but it was something. Now to put the names to the faces. There were eight guards that kept watch over the section that Kaistam-Laq was in. He now knew two of their names. Luckily for him, he had a good memory for names.

He waited until things were settled down and not much was going on and then he called out.

"Javyn."

It took a few moments but then a face appeared at his cell. It wasn't who he was expecting, but now he knew who to put the face to. The man was dark haired and tanned with brown eyes and a bewildered look on his face.

"Did you just call my name prisoner?"

"Um yes, do you think I might get some water?"

"Don't ever use my name again, I am called guard!" the guard called Javyn admonished.

"Of course. Now may I have some water?"

The guard grumbled but walked off to get the sorcerer some water. He was definitely displeased that he knew his name.

Now he would wait until the time was right to find out who Hader was. He would probably be dressed down the same way for using the guard's name, but he would know it and that way he would be able to get more familiar with them. He was certain that the more familiar he became with the guards, the more they would let down their guard and he would then find a way to escape this hell hole. He might not be able to use magiq here, but he had other charms at his disposal. He was very charismatic, and he could get his way with almost anyone if the situation was right. He just needed to make sure the situation was in his favor.

The guard returned with a ladle of water for the sorcerer, and he drank it down quickly. It was all done without the exchange of any words. The guards had all been warned about the sorcerer and his tricks. He was clever and he could manipulate any situation to his advantage. The guards had all been trained not to speak to the prisoners unless they really had to.

The guard who returned with the water was not Javyn. It was someone else.

"Thank you." The sorcerer said. "Your name is Hader, correct?"

The guard stared in shock. He neither denied nor answered the question. He simply turned around and walked away.

Hader wondered how the prisoner had learned his name. He was visibly shaken as he walked back to his station. He didn't like the fact that the sorcerer knew who he was. It was something he would be bringing up to his supervisor.

Kaistam now knew the two guards by name and face. There were still many more he had to learn the names of, but it was a start. He would need to keep his ears open. Now it was time to build a rapport with them. This made the sorcerer sick to think of. He hated these people for keeping him locked up, but he would need to learn to be friendly to them in order to escape.

One thing the sorcerer wished was that he had some kind of contact with anyone other than the guards or jailor. It was going to make recruiting very difficult if he couldn't talk to people or at the very least write to them. All of his correspondence was monitored with an eagle eye so he would need to come up with a way to contact people without raising suspicion. He would need a code that couldn't be broken.

He had already tried to write to some of his followers who had ended up in other prisons around the land, but none had returned his letters. Either the letters were being stopped at the jail here or they were being stopped at the other prisons. Whatever the case, it was making the sorcerer angry and when he got mad, bad things tended to happen to people around him.

There was one way that prisoners could communicate with each other in the prison. They would bang on the walls with rocks or other objects that they smuggled in from the outside. The prisoners had a whole language made up of percussive smacks and bangs of rocks hitting the walls in certain rhythms.

It took Kaistam-Laq several months to learn the language but eventually he picked it up and was able to communicate enough with the other prisoners. This of course was frowned upon by the guards, but either they didn't know or care about it. In most cases they just thought the prisoners were being noisy and they told them to stop. The guards didn't actually spend that much time in the actual jail, they spent most of their time in front of the place. They would make their rounds every so often but spent as little time as they had to in the actual cell area.

The prison communication system was how Kaistam-Laq would recruit his new team. At least in part. He would be able to find the magiq users and the most dangerous people in this prison and get their loyalty. The promise of money would win them over. He had plenty waiting for him when he got out. There were vast amounts of money all over the land, hidden in places that only he knew of. He trusted no one with his wealth and so he kept that information to himself.

The prison was put under a magiq dampening spell every day by the warden. This was to ensure that no magiq would be allowed to happen in the prison. The warden, a man called Challum Vandess was a magiq user of some great importance in the land and was charged with making sure that none of these high security prisoners escaped. He was a gruff man, six feet and seven inches tall, and did not tolerate failure from anyone, himself included. When he learned that he would oversee Kaistam-Laq's detention, he was thrilled to have the opportunity to show his talent for his job. He had no family so he could not be blackmailed or have them used against him. He had very few friends and those he called friends were kept at arms-length.

Kaistam-Laq had a plan for escape, but it would take a bit of luck and a lot of help from the other inmates for it to work. The first part of the plan had to do with the jailer. Kaistam had to prevent him from performing the dampening spell on the prison. Somehow, he had to interrupt the daily routine. Then, he would have to rally the inmates to riot. During the riot he would get to his staff of power. Once he obtained his staff, it wouldn't matter how many dampening spells the prison had on it. He would be able to make a speedy exit with the staff and a new crew. At least part of one.

His staff wasn't even supposed to be here. It was supposed to have been destroyed when he was captured, but greed and power had taken over the people that were supposed to have destroyed the staff and now they had possession of it. The sorcerer knew that his staff was close, he could feel its power. Power that only something that magiqal could produce.

That night he began to put his plan into motion. He began to recruit people into his crew. He asked what people were in for and if they could do magiq. If they couldn't do magiq they were not even considered. He found several people the first night. People that would fit the mold he was looking for. To his surprise, there were more than just men in this prison. Dangerous women were also kept here. As none of the inmates mingled with one another it was safe to do this.

As night fell Kaistam used the inmate messaging system to find out who was in the cell closest to him. He found out that it was a man called Renner-Van who also had a sister in the same prison, and she was called Ollis-Van. Both could do magiq and both were in for murder. Quickly Kaistam-Laq told Renner of his plan to recruit a crew. Just as quickly, the murderer agreed to join the sorcerer. Within minutes his sister followed suit. Kaistam had his first two followers.

The sorcerer continued to recruit into the night. He found that there were five others in the prison that also fit the mold. By the end of the night, he had recruited those that would be his closest colleagues. Two more women called Sioran-Oh and Valis, and three rough and brutal men called Morin, Jeris, and Levin-Ghee. All of the new recruits could do magiq, and all were in the prison for murder. They would serve his purpose well.

Kaistam-Laq now had seven of the seventeen he needed for his crew. He would continue to recruit from prison when he found a person that was worthy. If he didn't find anyone else in prison, he would wait until he was free and then recruit in earnest.

It was the following day when rumors spread through the prison that the warden would be leaving the prison to collect a new prisoner. This was huge news because the magiq dampening shield that he kept on the prison would be weakened when he was away. It was only strong as long as he remained on the grounds. The secret that he alone kept the spell in place was not as secret as everyone thought.

Kaistam figured the new prisoner must be of great importance if the warden himself was going to collect them. The warden didn't ever leave the prison, so this person was a huge deal. As big as the sorcerer himself.

This was the time that the sorcerer and his lackeys would make their escape. The warden would be gone, and the prison would be at its weakest. There would still be magiq in place to protect the prison, but it would be weak and if the sorcerer and his followers all put their magiq together they should be able to overcome the security that was in place. Once Kaistam-Laq got hold of his staff they would have no problem escaping.

The following morning came and immediately Kaistam could tell that the warden had left the prison. The normal magiq that protected the site was definitely lessened and attitudes were different. The guards were not as disciplined, there was more joking and fooling around.

This is the time to strike, the sorcerer told himself. Through the inmate messaging system, he told the inmates to prepare themselves to attack. Their magiq wouldn't be as effective as it could be, but it would have to do. Together they would be able to escape. The first cell to open was the sorcerer's. Once his was open he would be able to open the others as soon as he had his staff.

The sorcerer had been saving a bit of powerful magiq for his escape. He hoped it would work. He hadn't been able to do it with the warden here, but with him gone, he would try it. he would try to teleport to the outside of his prison cell. It was only a couple of feet, but it was extremely difficult magiq to perform without his staff. He doubted that anyone else in the prison could even come close to doing it. The issue was going to be the tyrin bars of the jail cell. Would he be able to pass through them?

Through the inmate messaging system, Kaistam-Laq had prisoners call to the guards from cells that were located far from his so that there were no guards near his cell when he tried this magiq. Alarms were sure to sound. At least he was certain that they would. No one had ever tried to escape before so there was no precedent for this.

He waited until the guards were all occupied elsewhere before he tried to teleport. He concentrated on moving just a few feet forward. It wasn't difficult magiq, but without his staff and in the dampened prison it was going to be a challenge.

Kaistam-Laq closed his eyes and used every but of magiq he possessed to teleport. He held his breath and waited for a second before opening his eyes. When he finally opened them, he was delighted to see that the bars were no longer in front of him. He turned around just to be sure. Yes, he had done it, he had moved outside of the jail cell.

Now to find his staff. He knew it was kept in the warden's office under lock and key. He would need to get to the office and get to the keys to free the other prisoners. Then he would have enough magiq at his disposal. He told Renner-Van to have the other inmates keep the guards busy for a little while whilst he went on the search for his staff and the keys.

The other prisoners had the guards running back and forth all over the other end of the prison. This gave Kaistam plenty of time to reach the warden's office. It was locked but with a little magiq he was able to remove the door. Inside he found a large chest that was locked with several locks. He knew right away that this had to be his staff. The sorcerer looked around the office for any keys and located some in an old-fashioned desk. They were on a large ring like all jailers keep their keys on. He did however notice that there was one that looked like a master key for the prison.

Unfortunately, none of the keys fit the locks on the chest. In fact, as he looked at the locks on the chest, he noticed there were no keyholes. These locks were magiqal and would have to be opened with magiq.

He returned to the jail cells and opened the ones of Renner-Van and Ollis-Van. They hugged briefly and then went on to follow their new leader.

"I'm going to need help opening a chest in the warden's office." He told the brother and sister.

The pair nodded and followed him to the office. They took stock of the situation. The locks were definitely going to require magiq. The locks were made of tyrin as well, so this was going to be tricky. Kaistam felt that if all three of them casted their magiq at the same time they should be able to force the locks open. Kaistam, was after all, more accomplished at magiq than the warden.

"Should we try to remove the locks, or should we just blow the chest apart?" Renner-Van asked.

"We must be careful, the item inside it is too precious to destroy. I do not wish it to be harmed. We must try to destroy the locks first and if that desnt work then we will try something else. We must hurry though!"

The three of them set out to destroy the locks on the chest. There were two smaller locks and one larger one in the middle.

"Concentrate your energy on the top lock." Kaistam-Laq told the siblings.

The three sent spells at the top lock and after a minute there was a sizzling sound, and the clasp broke, and the lock fell off the chest. The sorcerer pointed to the bottom lock, and they did the same to it. The middle lock proved to be a bit more difficult. It seemed like they wouldn't get the center lock off at all but after three straight minutes of casting spells, the clasp sizzled and the lock fell away as well.

The brother and sister were very interested to see what was in the chest.

"Stand back!" the sorcerer shouted. "Anyone who touches it is dead!"

The siblings halted in their tracks. Kaistam bent down and opened the chest. He pulled out his staff of power. He could feel the magiq flowing through him.

The staff was an extension of him. It was a part of him, and it felt good to have it back in his possession after so many years. Now to locate the other five that had sworn their allegiance to him. He turned to his two new followers and asked where the others were kept. They led him through the prison to the other's cells.

He instructed each inmate to stand back from their door as he removed it from the frame. Even with the magiq dampening spell in place, it was no match for the sorcerer and his staff of power. Eventually, the guards heard the commotion and came running to see what was going on. Kaistam-Laq disposed them in no time at all. They had yelled for him to stop, and he turned and blasted them off their feet and out of existence. One moment they were standing and shouting at him and the next, they had been blown to bits by the most powerful staff on the planet.

Kaistam-Laq slowed only to memorize the faces of his new crew and then he and his new followers left the prison. They didn't stop to rescue any of the other inmates. They left as quickly as they could to get as far away from the prison as was possible. The sorcerer had no issue with killing, but if he could keep the death toll down it would be better in the long run. Right now, the plan was to get out of Yelliton and as far away as they could get. The area would be swarming with law men looking for the fugitives before night fall, and Kaistam had no intention to be anywhere near the area.

"We must leave this place now," the sorcerer told his crew. "They will be looking for us almost immediately. There is no time for long goodbyes, we must leave now."

"What about supplies?" asked Levin Ghee, the muscle-bound killer that Kaistam-Laq had freed.

"We get them as we move. We take what we need, and only what we need. There is not going to be room for luxuries right now. They will come shortly. What we need now is to find some horses to get us out of town. Renner and Ollis, I am putting you in charge of finding us horses. We will meet on the outskirts of town in two hours."

The siblings nodded at the sorcerer and ran off to find horses as he continued to delegate jobs. Things like finding changes of clothing and getting food. Some of the others got down and kissed the blue earth. They had been in the prison for many years and were so glad to be out.

"There will be time for that later," the sorcerer told them. "We need to get out of here now!"

Right now, Kaistam-Laq had a score to settle, and he wanted to dish out some long-awaited revenge. He had been plotting his revenge on the healer Tÿr'Ynyn every day since he had been incarcerated in the god-forsaken prison. She had taken away his freedom and now he would take her life.

Tÿr'Ynyn was just waking up when she heard the shrill shriek of the säqyr wyvern. This meant that Sëvyq was on his way with a message from Vennex. Her mother and father only used the little wyvern in case of emergencies, so she sat up and rubbed the sleep from her eyes. What could possibly constitute an emergency on such a fine morning?

Tÿr got out of bed and walked to the opening of the cavern. The suns were shining brightly this morning as she made her way to the plateau outside of the cave. She waited for the little wyvern to arrive. The black speck in the sky got larger and larger as the creature neared. Tÿr could see the wyvern's wings beating furiously as it flew towards her.

Rævii the shift fox was there too, to greet her friend as he flew in. The two creatures were as close as any two creatures could be, and the little fox missed the wyvern when he was in Vennex.

The little wyvern sped up to the plateau and landed very ungracefully. He practically flipped over on his head as he came to a halt. Tÿr walked over to the wyvern and opened the little tube on his neck. There was a piece of rolled parchment inside. She unrolled it and read.

Clinic has been destroyed. Sorcerer has escaped. You are in danger!

Tÿr blanched. How had the sorcerer escaped a maximum-security prison? Her parents hadn't mentioned if anyone was injured. She knew she would need to get to Vennex as soon as possible. She also knew that her parents wouldn't want her to come back. She needed to see what kind of damage was done to her clinic. First, she would need to get a message to Varanus. He would know what to do.

She wrote out a quick message to her mentor, rolled it up, and placed it in the tube around Sëvyq's neck.

"Take this to Varanus." She told the little wyvern.

He let out a little squawk and then took to the air. She and Rævii stood and watched him fly off into the distance. He would have the message to Varanus within the next hour or two. Her mentor was off on a gathering expedition. He was collecting herbs and other items that would be used in medicines and salves for the clinic.

Tÿr'Ynyn hoped with all her being that no one was in the clinic when it was attacked. The note had not said anything about casualties. She also hoped that her parents were clever enough to get out of town. The sorcerer had already used her parents to get to her several years before. He was evil and Tÿr knew he was not above doing something like that again.

There were things to do around the cavern. Tÿr set out to get some of the chores done before she heard back from Varanus. She was certain that he would be returning sooner than expected because of the attack. She had to take inventory of the medicines in the cooling tunnels and that would take her several hours to complete. She figured that she better get started on it now while she was thinking about it.

The healer was in the middle of inventory when she heard the squawk of the säqyr wyvern returning to the cavern. He hadn't been gone as long as she had figured he would be. Rævii ran to the entrance of the cavern to greet her friend when he arrived, her tail was fluffed out in excitement.

The little wyvern arrived with a non-elegant landing. He flipped a couple of times before coming to a halt. Tÿr walked over to him and opened the tube around his neck to take out the note that was inside. It was a short note from her mentor.

On my way back. Don't do anything rash!
V

Tÿr took the note and crumpled it up. She knew that Varanus must be close by if the little wyvern had already returned. He hadn't been gone that long before she had gotten a response. The healer continued to take inventory of the medicines in the cooling tunnel. She was finishing up on the poultices and salves when she heard the flapping of her mentor's wings.

Varanus came flying onto the plateau gracefully and landed next to the healer who was waiting for him on the ledge. The wyvern had grown significantly over the past few years. He was now close to forty feet long, not including the spikes on his tail. His scales shone a gorgeous lustrous blue green with flashes of purple and orange when the suns hit them just right.

"Do we know how the sorcerer escaped?" Varanus asked his apprentice.

"No," replied Tÿr. "I only received a message from my da and it said that the clinic was destroyed and that the sorcerer had escaped. That's all I know."

"Okay, we are going to have to find out what is going on in Vennex.

"I agree. We need to see how bad the damage is and if there were any other casualties."

"I suggest that you get ready to go then, I'd like to leave as soon as possible." The wyvern told her.

Tÿr ran into the cavern to grab what she would need or a quick trip to Vennex. She didn't know exactly how long they would be gone but she didn't plan on being gone for more than two days. She got the harness out of the cavern and helped to get it on the wyvern. The newest harness was leather and was very comfortable for her and the shift fox to ride with. It had a saddle that fit over the back of Varanus in such a way that she could sit comfortably for hours without going numb in the lower regions.

They were ready to go in a short time and were in the air and flying to Vennex as quickly as they could move. There was no time to waste. The people in Vennex needed them and they needed to see what was left of their clinic.

Luckily Danior and Gordian were still training and were not in Vennex at the time of the attack. Tÿr didn't like to think what would have happened if they had been at the clinic at the time of the sorcerer's attack. He was ruthless and showed no mercy to anyone. Týr was certain that he would have used the boys to get to her had they been there.

The trip lasted only a short while, Varanus was able to ride an air current that got them there in no time flat. Týr was taking in the damage from the air as they spiraled into the field outside the clinic. The damage looked extensive. The walls of the clinic were no more. They were literally blown off the building and in rubble around the area. The roof was laying in pieces on the ground. Týr felt sick as she assessed the damage.

The wyvern and the healer landed near the remains of the clinic. They walked around the site and took in the damage from the attack. Things were scattered everywhere. Medicines and potions and salves were laying all over the ground. Some were salvageable, but many were lost, smashed beyond saving. The sorcerer had really done a number on the clinic.

"How did the sorcerer escape, Varanus?"

"I am sure we will hear how in the near future. The important thing is that no one here was injured."

"Look at all of this destruction." Týr said sadly.

"You must go to your parent's house to make sure they got out in time." Varanus told the girl.

Tÿr turned to go, but Varanus stopped her and told her to climb on his back. He didn't want her to go alone. The two flew off together and landed outside of her parent's house. There was still blue-black smoke coming from the chimney.

"Mom, Da!" Tÿr burst into the little cabin. There was nobody inside when she got there, although there was still a fire in the hearth, so her parents had not been gone that long. The kettle was still on the fire which meant that her parents had left in a hurry. They must have heard the commotion at the clinic and left immediately. There was no sign of a struggle so they must have left on their own.

The silence was suddenly broken by the shrill cry of the familiar sound of the säqyr wyvern. Sëvyq had returned to the cabin for some reason. Tÿr ran over to him and opened the tube on his neck. There was nothing inside.

"Why would he show up here?" Tÿr asked her mentor.

"He lived here with your parents, and he returned here because he probably considered it his second home." Varanus told her.

Tÿr found a piece of parchment and scribbled a quick note to her parents. She asked them to stay away from Vennex until she told them it was safe to return. She also asked them to let her know where they were. She needed to know how to get in touch with them in case of emergencies. As soon as she was done writing she rolled up the parchment and put it in the tube and then sent the little wyvern off to find her parents. He took off with a little shriek and was gone.

The säqyr wyvern was only gone for a few hours before he returned to Tÿr and Varanus. He landed with a thud and a flip and Tÿr ran to greet him. She opened the tube around his neck and took out a piece of parchment and read the message from her father:

We are travelling now. Don't know where we are going yet. Will let you know when we arrive.

Tÿr breathed a sigh of relief. Her parents had gotten out of town and were on their way to someplace safe. She was grateful that they had not run into the sorcerer. He had been a formidable opponent and she didn't look forward to facing him again. From what she could tell, his powers had grown even stronger. He had escaped from a supposedly inescapable prison, and he was destroying everything in his path.

Tÿr got the little wyvern a bit of meat to eat after his numerous trips back and forth between her and her parents. She wanted to make sure his strength was kept up in case he had to go out again.

Varanus wanted to go back to the clinic and begin the clean-up. It was going to take many man hours to clean up the wreckage of the building. Tÿr climbed back on Varanus's back and the two flew back to the clinic. She felt a lump in her throat as she saw the wrecked building again. It made her sad and angry to see debris strewn everywhere by the destruction caused by the sorcerer. She vowed there and then that she would have her revenge. This was something that could not go unpunished.

It took a week to sort through the wreckage and find all the medicines that were still viable. They had lost over three quarters of their supply. Salves and poultices, pills and other medicines lay wasted on the ground. Tÿr was able to collect some of the rarer medicines. For some reason they had not been damaged. Of the rarest medicines, Tÿr transported them daily back and forth because they were too valuable to leave at the clinic. Many of them needed to be stored in the cooling tunnels overnight so they came home with Tÿr nightly.

It had been over a week and Tÿr still hadn't heard from her parents. She decided to send a quick note to them and make sure that they were okay. She wrote out a short message and placed it in the tube around the little wyvern's neck. Varanus instructed him to go in Cmok, the wyvern language. The säqyr wyvern took off with a shriek and was gone.

Tÿr was still going through all the medicines that they had collected from the wreckage of the clinic. She was busy repackaging them in new bottles and relabeling them. She had been using her parent's abandoned house as a makeshift clinic for the time being. She had included this information in the letter that she had written to them. They had written back and told her that it was fine to use, and she could continue to use it until they returned, or she built a new clinic.

She and Varanus had contacted the builder's guild in town to see about constructing a new clinic. They gave the specifications, and the guild quoted a price that was acceptable. The construction was to begin immediately and in a new spot. The new clinic was going to be closer to the town center and easier for all of the people to access. It was also going to be at least twice the size of the previous clinic. There would be three large bays for the wyverns to be able to observe, the former clinic only had the one. There would be several more rooms to see patients in as well. Once Danior and Gordian returned from their training, they would also take up offices in the building. The boys were almost done with their training, as they had been put on an advanced course of teaching due to their quick learning aptitude. What normally took twenty years of studying was taking them less than five. They were absorbing knowledge almost as fast as their friend Tÿr'Ynyn did.

Tÿr couldn't wait for the boys to be finished with their training. She missed being with them. This was the longest that they had ever been apart from each other. They used to spend every day together, and now it had been several years since they had spent more than a couple days together. Tÿr had been able to go visit them during their training, and the boys had taken a couple breaks from their learning to come and see their friend. Now that they were coming up on the end of their training Tÿr was getting anxious for it to be over. She couldn't wait for the days where they would all be together again.

It was a few days later before Tÿr heard anything back from her parents. She got the message back from her dad when she and Varanus were out watching the builder's guild breaking ground for the new clinic. The clinic was going to be huge compared to the former one. There were many townspeople gathered around as well. It was exciting to see the beginning of the new clinic taking shape. There were many builders working on the project as they wanted to get the clinic built as soon as possible. Without a clinic in town, the more serious cases had been shipped to neighboring villages which was bad for some of the people who really needed immediate treatment. Tÿr could only do so much in the makeshift clinic building they were using.

The message from her dad said that they had reached their destination and were safe. They would be messaging them more when more information became available. Until then, Tÿr shouldn't worry.

Of course, Tÿr was concerned for her parents, but she tried not to worry too much. Her dad would tell her if anything serious came up or was cause for concern. If she really needed to know where her parents were, she could have Varanus find out from the little wyvern. He knew where they were after all.

The next months flew by as the clinic was raised. The walls went up quickly once the ground was cleared. Before Tÿr knew it, the clinic was finished, and she and Varanus were moving into it. The building was huge and very nice. It was by far the largest and most elegant building in the town. People from neighboring villages came from all around to see the new clinic of Vennex. The three large bays were an engineering masterpiece. The doors could be raised and closed with a switch that could be used by both human and wyvern alike. The operation theaters were of the highest standards and the most recent advances in medicine. The clinic was the best in the land if not on the planets and Tÿr was incredibly proud of it.

Varanus had contacted some of the wyverns from his home island and asked them to stand guard on the clinic for some time. Ghra'zhenn, the paragon of the wyverns had agreed to let four of the older wyverns come to the village and keep it safe while the sorcerer was at large. He felt it would be best to have some type of protection in the village for the next few years, or until the sorcerer was apprehended again.

Tÿr had a celebration for the wyverns that showed up to guard the clinic. The whole town showed up to show their support. Tÿr's cousin Sämir even showed up for the event. He too, like her friends was being trained as a healer. He was not as advanced as her friends and would probably take close to the twenty years that it took most everyone else to complete the training. Tÿr was pleased to see her cousin. He had really become a pleasant person. Which was ironic because her uncle and aunt had been so despicable and nasty. They unfortunately had come to a nasty end at the hands of an assassin. The very same assassin that her aunt had hired to kill her husband.

The celebration was meant to last a day and night, but the town was famous for their parties, and it ended up lasting for three days and nights. Much dragon fruit was consumed by the wyverns and wine and ale flowed freely among the townsfolk. Tÿr and the brothers drank more than they intended to, but since it was a celebration, they allowed themselves to indulge a little.

The next morning following the festivities, Tÿr's head was pounding, and she was certain that the boys were in the same boat as she was. Danior was the first to get out of bed and he looked rough. His hair was standing in every direction and his clothes were all rumpled from sleeping in them. Gordian heard the noise of his brother stirring and got up shortly after.

"What's with all the noise?"

"Don't shout!" Danior said as quietly as he could.

"I'm not shouting," Gordi said just as quietly.

"I'm never drinking again!"

Tÿr laughed at the brothers. Her head was aching too, but she found the brothers very amusing this morning. She was so glad to have them here with her. It had been so long since they had spent this much time together, and she didn't know how long it would be before they would again.

"When do you boys have to go home?" Tÿr asked.

"We don't really have a schedule." Danior told her.

"So can you stay a few more days?"

Danior looked in Gordi's direction. Gordian cocked his head in thought.

"I suppose we could." He said.

"We don't really have that much going on." Danior reiterated.

"Well then, it's settled, you'll stay with me for a few days and we can drink some more wine." She said with a grin.

Danior groaned loudly.

"Our training is almost complete." Danior told Tÿr. "We only have a few more months left before we are done."

"You'll be coming back here to open your offices then?" Tÿr asked.

"If that's okay with you."

"I would love it." She told him.

"Who would have thought that we would all be healers?" Gordi asked.

"I know, I never would have believed it." Danior said.

The brothers got out of bed slowly. They were in bad shape from the celebrations of the past few days. Tÿr put on a kettle and made some qafi for all of them. Qafi always seemed to help with a night of drinking.

The boys were enjoying their cups of qafi with a few eggs that Tÿr had managed to find. It would make for a decent breakfast. She also cooked up a few strips of wild hog meat for each of them and she had a loaf of crusty bread to share with the boys. The only thing missing was a few fox cherries. She wished she had time to go scavenging for the boy's favorite fruit. Instead, they would have to make do with a pear from the tree outside of her cavern.

As she was cooking, she gave the shift fox a few pieces of hog meat to nibble on while she waited for the meal to be finished. Rævii gobbled up the meat and waited for her meal, drooling the whole time.

"It's coming, it's coming." Týr told the little fox.

She threw a couple pieces of pear down to the furry creature. It wasn't what she wanted but she didn't turn her nose up to it. She ate it quickly and was ready for more. Týr was always amazed that the little fox wasn't fatter than she was. She ate so much food yet stayed small and fit. Of course, she was always busy doing something.

With breakfast ready, the group sat down to eat. Rævii was right there among them at the table. The boys ate like they normally did. Ravenously. Týr smiled as the boys finished their meals. She would miss them when they left, but they would be back again before she knew it. Time had gone by so quickly. She sometimes had trouble believing that it had been that many years since she had become a healer. Four years had passed in the blink of an eye. Her cousin was now well on his way to becoming a healer as well, and she planned on him coming back to the clinic to work one day as well. It would be a long time before that happened, but he knew that he was welcome to come back there when his training was over.

Sämir was training in the healing arts but he had shown no aptitude in magiq. He couldn't perform even the slightest bit of magiq when the wyverns had put him through his paces. He had however, shown great potential as a healer in basic healing, and he was exceptionally caring. This is where his specialty would lie. He was not the only healer that could not employ magiq. In fact, most healers couldn't do any magiq. Tÿr and the brothers were the exceptions to the rule, and this is what made them great healers. This was why the wyverns had taken such an interest in them.

Sämir was doing very well in his studies. He was quick to learn the remedies and recipes for making medicines. Tÿr knew he would make a fine addition to the clinic when he was finished with his studies. She received updates on his progress from the wyverns. She also received updates on the brothers as well. They were almost done with their courses. They had done accelerated courses in medicine and also in magiq. Danior was proving to be better in the medicine and Gordi excelled in the magiq. The boys complimented each other in everything that they did.

Tÿr was trying to figure out what she and the boys were going to do with themselves for the next few days. She thought that maybe they could go out on a day trip into the woods. The clinic was running itself right now, and there were wyvern healers watching over it for the time being in case there was a tough case that needed to be diagnosed. Týr could afford to take a day or two off right now. Besides, she would have Varanus with them. He would go with them in case something came up. He would fly back and forth between the clinic and the camp site each day to make sure everything ran smoothly.

After discussing it with the boys, Týr decided that they would go off into the woods for one of their famous camping trips. They packed a bunch of food and sleeping mats and were ready to go a short time later.

"You're sure that you can handle the clinic while I am away?" Týr asked the wyverns.

They assured her that they would be fine and sent her and the boys on their way. The boys brought some fishing lines to try to snag some fish while they were out so they could have something different for a change. Týr brought her famous salt bag with herbed salt for the meat that they caught along the way.

It took them most of the day to hike into the woods near the river where they would set up camp. Each of them had their duties to perform once they got to their campsite. They had camped so many times before that they had a routine down to a tee. Týr prepared the fire and Gordian got the beds set up and the fish snares set. Danior waited for them to bring back any fish to be fileted. He was in charge of fileting the fish as he had gotten so good at it. He was fast and never left any bones in them. In the old days they would have just roasted the fish on pointed stick over the fire, but now the had a metal grate that they could set up over the fire and cook on like a camp stove.

Gordian came back with several fish to be cleaned, and Danior set off cleaning them as quickly as he could. Tÿr had a roaring fire going and by the time Danior had finished cleaning the fish, the fire had settled to a bed of hot coals for them to cook over. The fish didn't take that long to cook, and they were eating in no time. None of them realized how hungry they were until they actually sat down to eat.

"Does anyone need any more herbed salt?" Tÿr asked.

"I can't believe that you remembered to bring that with you." Gordian told her.

"I bring it everywhere I go." She replied. "I like to have it on everything I eat."

"It does make things better," Gordi agreed.

"Now, wouldn't it be perfect if we could find some fox cherries for a snack?" Danior chimed in.

Tÿr and Gordian got up and went to the edge of the stream.

"There are sure to be some around here somewhere." Gordi said.

The two of them began to look up the stream and sure enough, there was a huge bush of fox cherries just up the stream from them. Tÿr went back and got Danior and led him back to the bush so he could eat his fill of the little round fruit. The trio of campers ate until they couldn't eat another cherry and then they went back to the campsite and talked until it got late and they got tired.

The three suns of the conjoined planets never really went down on this part of the planet but it did get dusky and so it did make it a bit easier to sleep for the campers. The suns, though not completely set, were lower in the sky at this time of day and it seemed that it was darker though it wasn't much. The smallest of the three suns was almost hidden by the horizon at this point, but it would soon rise again in another hour.

The campers awoke early the next morning and were ready to go exploring. They planned to head toward the mountains though they wouldn't get as far. They only wanted to hike around the area and see what they could find like they used to do when they all lived in Vennex four years ago. They would use the time to show each other their magiq skills as well. Performing little feats of magiq to impress each other was something the friends liked to do.

Gordian would always do some fantastical magiq that impressed the others. Tÿr was amazed by how much magiq her friend could do. Danior's skill was more in healing than in magiq and he struggled to do more difficult spells but still was able to perform basic magiq. It thrilled the trio that they could perform magiq now, when only a few years before they were just average kids growing up in an average village.

The three friends were having fun trying to impress each other when they herd the flapping of wings. They looked up in the direction of the noise and saw Varanus flying down to meet them. He landed near the trio and folded his large wings.

"Is something wrong?" Tÿr asked him as he walked up to greet them.

"No, there is nothing wrong." He said shaking his huge head. "I just came to check on you."

"We are fine."

"We are just practicing our magiq" Danior told the wyvern.

"Do you think it wise to be doing magiq with the sorcerer at large again?" the wyvern asked.

"We aren't doing any big spells." Tÿr interjected.

"I would be cautious doing any magiq until he is captured." Varanus told the group. "It is like a beacon leading him straight to you."

"I didn't think about that." Tÿr admitted. "Should we not use magiq to heal?"

"Healing magiq is different. It will confuse the sorcerer. He will probably think that it is wyvern magiq. It's when you use other magiq that he will notice." Varanus explained.

The trio agreed not to use any more magiq and the wyvern flew off to watch out for any trouble. The campers spent the rest of their time exploring the countryside, collecting herbs and other things for their medicines. They spent one more night in the forest before heading back to Tÿr's cavern. The rest of their time together was spent preparing medicines and poultices and other medical supplies.

Kaistam-Laq felt a jolt through his staff. Magiq. Someone somewhere was performing magiq and it was in his best interest to find out whom. The last time he felt this much power he ended up in prison, and he had no desire for a repeat performance. He would find out who this magiq user was. If it was who he though it could be, it would be even better. He could have his revenge after long last.

He would be calling his crew together to search out this bit of magiq. He now had a crew of seventeen cutthroats and magiq users at his disposal. Renner-Van and his sister Ollis would be in charge of the day-to-day details to help the sorcerer as he led the charge on finding this magiq user. He was certain that it had to be the healer he had dealt with over four years ago. It was possible that it was wyvern magiq, but he knew deep down that it was the healer.

The gathering of the seventeen was an occasion without pomp. Kaistam-Laq called the meeting of his trusted assassins to discuss the apprehension of the magiq using healer. She was to be brought to him to be assimilated into the fold. She would make a powerful ally if she could be turned this time, and he did not intend to fail again. If she could not be persuaded to join him, she would be destroyed.

The table was situated in the center of the tent with Kaistam-Laq at the head and Renner and Ollis-Van sitting at either side of him.

"We are only concerned with the capture of the healer. I want her alive!"

There were murmurs around the table.

"Anyone who harms the girl will answer to me and will be punished most severely."

All of those gathered around the table knew what this meant. The punishment would most certainly be death. Their leader did not tolerate failure at all. None of them had ever served under him before but they knew of him by reputation. He was a very strict disciplinarian and did not accept apologies.

"If there is more than one magiq user?" A tough looking ruffian with a baneful stare called Levin-Ghee," asked.

"I want every magiq user that you come across. Even if they can only conjure a bird. Any magiq!" Kaistam told them. "None of them are to be harmed."

The meeting only lasted for five minutes. It outlined the plan to capture the healer. None of the people at the table asked any questions after. They understood what needed to be done and they didn't need to ask a bunch of questions. Their leader had made things perfectly clear, and he always got his way.

Each pair of the crew had instructions on where to go. They were to spread out over the planets and search for the healer. They were to go to every town that they came across on their trek across the land. Kaistam told them to acquire horses when they could and go out with great speed to find the healer. Anyone that got in their way was to be eliminated with prejudice. Kaistam would keep three of his crew back with him, Renner and Ollis-Van and a female that the sorcerer had taken a liking to called Xanuc. She was tall and dark skinned with long dark hair and bright green eyes. She had a narrow face with a narrow, pointed nose and full lips. She was pretty in a non-conventional way. She was also a vicious killer. Kaistam had found her in a tavern working as a confidence woman. She was swindling people for their money and other favors.

Xanuc had killed over twenty people. Most of them were because of debts. She didn't beg for her money when someone owed her, she simply took their lives, and their money. She had amassed quite a large amount of money by the time Laq had recruited her. He hadn't had any problems recruiting her, he simply promised her more money. She wasn't interested in power or fame, but money was something that she lusted after. Kaistam-Laq promised all his crew a large amount of money to join him.

Despite the fact that he had been in prison for several years, the leader of the new sect of murderers and thieves had hidden a lot of money away for when he got out. He knew that he would need it to recruit a new team of followers. It went to show how feared he was, because his former team knew of the money and didn't touch it. Each one of them knew of the consequences for disloyalty.

It was rumored that one of his former crew had searched him out and demanded that he compensate him for his losses over the past few years. Laq had laughed at the former member of his team and then used his staff to kill him as a monition for anyone else thinking of extorting money from the sorcerer. It was also rumored that there was one that came to him and he let him go to spread the news that he was a sadistic killer and not to be trifled with. Nobody really knew what the truth was other than that Kaistam-Laq was a cold-blooded murderer.

The person that he had let go was called Cyllus and he went throughout the land telling everyone that would listen that Kaistam-Laq was a brutal murderer and that he should be feared above anyone else in the land. He had gotten away with his life somehow and he spread the word of the sorcerer's treachery. Of course, this cursed him with a death mark. If he ever came across the sorcerer again, he would most assuredly be killed outright. Kaistam-Laq did not treat traitors favorably. To his knowledge, Cyllus was the only remaining member of the sorcerer's former crew of seventeen. The others were either in prison or dead.

Kaistam finished his meeting with his new crew with a pledge of loyalty. Each of the new members had to pledge their loyalty to the sorcerer and his rule. If any of them had not, they would have been eliminated on the spot. Once that was completed, he sent them out on their mission. The pair of members who came back with the healer would be rewarded handsomely. If they killed the wyvern that accompanied the healer there would be a bonus for them as well. They were to use any means necessary to detain the healer and bring her in. The spike of the wyvern's tail would be proof of its death and would garner the bonus money.

A wyvern's tail spike was worth so much more than money to the sorcerer. It would be used in potions. The spike of a wyvern's tail was extremely hard to come by as they usually only came from a dead wyvern, and wyverns lived for many hundreds of years. Many alchemists tried to sell things claiming that there was wyvern tail spike in them but more often than not it was something else. The tail spike was extremely hard to obtain. If someone did have a real tail spike, it was usually given freely at the time of the wyvern's death with its permission.

One of the most common uses for the tail spike was a potion used for poisoning a person. It was completely untraceable. The spike could be ground down to such a fine powder that the drinker of the potion never knew that they were drinking it. It was flavorless and odorless and was usually put in some type of liquor or ale although it could be put in water or milk. The potion had no specific name but was usually called something like liquid death, or quick death, as it killed in just minutes. It was not a potion that was freely sold on the market as it was illegal to possess.

Once the meeting was over and the crew broke up into their small groups to go out into the land, Kaistam retired to his tent to think. He had many things on his mind. He wondered where the healer could be and if she would be alone. He also was thinking about what he would do if he came upon the healer and the wyvern together. They would prove to be a daunting pair of adversaries. He had already faced the healer once and the meeting had landed him in prison. He had been there until his recent escape. He had no plans to repeat that again.

He had also been thinking about the ramifications of incurring the wrath of the wyverns. He felt that he could deal with a lone creature, but he wasn't certain how he would fare if he was faced with two or three or even more. He knew for a fact that the healer spent her time in the presence of at least one wyvern.

What the sorcerer didn't know was that Tÿr'Ynyn had been adopted into the wyvern clan and was considered one of their own. Nor did he know that she had undergone the process called intercalation which in essence had linked her to the collective wyvern mind of the dynasty. The process had also made her more powerful than the sorcerer himself. He did not understand this because this was a closely guarded secret. One that could put Tÿr's life in jeopardy should the wrong people find out. People like Kaistam-Laq. There were also certain wyverns that would not have looked favorably upon the revelation. So Tÿr had only told her close friends, the brothers, her cousin Sämir, her mum and da, and the wyverns from the dynasty that Varanus and Ghra'zhenn belonged to. Anyone else would have been a liability.

As he sat in his tent, the sorcerer fiddled with some of his magiqal devices. Some were whirring silently while others were spinning noisily. There were gadgets that puffed smoke and others that projected pictures of people on smokey screens. The clicking and clacking of some of the devices was almost deafening in the tent. Eventually the sorcerer waved his hand and all of the equipment stopped working. The smoking and whirring came to a standstill. He needed silence to think.

He walked over to his scrying mirror and sat down at the table it was sitting on. He drew a glyph across the surface of it and the symbol glowed for a moment before fading to black. The mirror then began to shine. Kaistam willed the mirror to show him the healer.

"Show me the girl!" he said to the mirror.

The mirror remained blank.

"Show me the position of the healer." He tried.

Nothing.

The sorcerer tried asking the mirror twenty different ways to see where the healer was, but it refused to show him anything more than his own reflection. He became frustrated and almost smashed the mirror. He roared out in exasperation.

"Is everything alright in there, Master?" came the voice of Ollis-Van.

The sorcerer stopped for a moment.

"I am fine." The sorcerer spat angrily.

The woman knew better than to press the issue and left him alone to rage on his own. She had heard of his anger and knew that he was unstable at the best of times. She returned to her patrol of the area.

The sorcerer tried other means of divining the location of the healer and none of them worked. He concluded that she must have a powerful bit of magiq protecting her. He determined that it must be wyvern magiq because nothing this strong could be human based. He was so frustrated by the time he finished conjuring spells of detection and pinpointing a target that he was ready to murder. Luckily no one came into his quarters to bother him. He went to sleep with an empty feeling, knowing he had failed in his task.

The next day didn't start out any better. He had checked in with all of the teams out in the field looking for the healer. He used the scrying mirror to speak with them. They all had small versions of a scrying mirror that they carried with them to allow the sorcerer to communicate with them. None of the teams had found any evidence of the healer anywhere on the planets yet. Of course, they had only been gone a couple of days, but the sorcerer was not a patient man and he expected results.

He was close to raging at the news that there was absolutely no information about the healer. No one seemed to know anything, and if they did, no one was talking. What upset the sorcerer more than anything was that he didn't know what he should do next.

It was on the sixth day that the first bit of useful news came in. The team that went into the town of Vennex had information that the healer had been there recently. The old clinic had been destroyed by the sorcerer, but a new one had been built and the healer had been seeing patients there recently.

"Do you want the new clinic destroyed?" a short stocky lackey called Dannus asked the sorcerer.

"No! We will use it as bait. Stake out the clinic and watch for the healer. Do nothing to spook her. Do not give away your affiliation to me. You are to observe only and report back to me when she returns." The sorcerer told him.

"Understood."

"Do not fail me!"

The crew member looked at his partner and shivered. He was now on edge. His boss was obsessed with this healer, and he would do anything to catch her.

"Did you get all that?"

"I heard it." the other lackey called Melic said.

They both looked at each other with concern written all over their faces. They knew it would be difficult to stake out the clinic in a town as small as

Vennex. Everyone knew each other in a town that small so they would have trouble blending in and keeping a low profile. Luckily the sorcerer had given them enough money to spend so they could spend a good deal of their time in a tavern drinking and listening for information. Drunk people tended to talk too much and very easily. Perhaps they could find out where the healer lives. That would be worth a bonus from the sorcerer for sure.

Kaistam had to decide whether or not he wanted to go to Vennex. He decided against it in the long run because he was set up centrally and didn't feel like hauling his whole entourage that far. He preferred that they bring the girl to him. Once subdued, she should pose no issue, at least that's what the sorcerer felt. His people were powerful magiq wielders and two of them against a single girl would be no contest. She was just a healer after all.

Melic and Dannus resigned themselves to spending time at the local tavern in Vennex for the next period of time. It was hard to say how long they would have to do this but this is what they signed on for so this is what they would be doing. They had plenty of money to drink with and they spent their nights in the forest outside of town.

The tavern they decided on was called The Axeman's Hood. It was a dark and seedy place where a rough crowd hung out. The pair sat at the grungy bar most nights and listened for any news of the healer. The barman didn't complain that the pair sat there all night as they kept buying drinks. He was happy as long as the money kept pouring in.

Most people avoided the pair at the bar. They seemed to have a certain look about them and it said to keep away. Every once in a while, a drunken patron would approach them and they would chase them off by telling them to leave in no certain terms. On occasion they would have an issue with a really drunk person coming up to them and not getting the hint. That is when they would take them outside and have a little talk with them. This only happened once or twice, and then they got the reputation of being a bit antisocial. After that no one really seemed to bother them.

The biggest issue they faced was boredom. They sat in the tavern for literally hours upon hours at a time without so much as a word about the healer. They wondered if any of the others were having any luck but didn't care to ask the sorcerer about the progress of their companions.

It was on the seventh day of sitting there that the small scrying mirror around the neck of Melic began to vibrate signifying that the sorcerer wanted to talk. Melic quickly ran out of the tavern to speak to his leader.

"Yes?"

"What progress have you made?"

"We have heard absolutely nothing about the healer." Melic told the leader. He could see Kaistam-Laq's face darken at this news.

"I have paid you to go out and find news of the healer and you have nothing for me? Not one whisper?"

"No Sir, we have heard nothing. If anyone knows anything here, they are not talking."

"Perhaps you are asking the wrong questions. Do I need to come there and ask them for you?"

"No sir. We will do better in the future."

"I expect you will." Kaistam said oozing sarcasm in every word.

Melic expected the worst but was relieved that it didn't come. The scrying mirror went dark, and he stood there for a moment before going back into the tavern. He told his partner what had just taken place.

"We cannot fail!" Melic told Dannus. "I cringe to think what will happen if we do."

The other man nodded his agreement.

Many miles away Kaistam-Laq checked in with each of his teams. His mood did not improve with each meeting. None had any new information to report other than they hadn't heard anything of the healer, and no one seemed to know where she was or lived. The best information that they did have was that her parents had been seen leaving the town of Vennex following the destruction of the first clinic, but that was weeks ago. They had been seen travelling toward the city of Morioh near the border of Peyda Noirin several weeks ago if the information was to be trusted. The sorcerer didn't know what to believe.

All of his crew knew that he was not pleased with their lack of progress. They were worried about telling him that they had no new information, but they knew it was better to let him know the truth than to make something up. Their leader was not a patient man, nor did he deal with lying very well. None of them had been with the sorcerer very long but they had all heard the stories of his wrath, and none wished to incur it.

Tÿr'Ynyn was getting back into the swing of things after her few days of relaxation with the brothers. People began lining up at the new clinic to be seen early in the morning and the lines continued throughout the entire day. Most of the issues were basic and didn't require extensive healing. There were, however, some issues that did require magiq and Tÿr was excited to heal those people. She was so glad that she knew magiq and that she could employ it so easily.

The brothers went back to finish their training which would only take a couple more months to complete then they would be full healers like their friend. They had decided to do an accelerated program which would finish their training in a few years instead of the normal twenty that it usually took. It was an intense program that required them to learn things faster than normal and this required magiq.

The clinic was bustling with sick and wounded people as Tÿr ran from room to room healing people. The wyvern Varanus was on site to help if there were any cases that were too difficult for Tÿr to handle. Tÿr had four assistants from the village to help direct people to their rooms and clean up after. The operation ran very smoothly as the healer did her job throughout the day.

There were some cases that required all of Tÿr's knowledge in healing to minister to. People who had been traveling and had gotten rare foreign diseases. Then there were those people who had only broken an arm or a foot and simply required her to use a bit a magiq to mend it. It was the rarer ailments that were tricky to heal. Tÿr had to go to her medical journals several times to search up some of the symptoms and treatments. For the first time in a long while, Tÿr was truly happy with her life.

This is how Tÿr's life went on for the next three months. Every day was busy and each night she flew home to her cavern to sleep.

"Varanus, things are going so well. Maybe I will take a day or two off and go see the boys. They are getting ready to graduate and I need to be there."

"I don't see where that would be a problem." The wyvern said.

"I hate having to close the clinic for those days though."

"The people will understand."

"I guess. Do you think we could have one of the wyverns see patients while I am gone?"

"I can ask if there is one that will do it." Varanus said.

The clinic was large enough to accommodate a wyvern healer so Tÿr resigned herself to going to see the brothers graduate. She would have a wyvern healer in charge of the clinic while she was gone and Ghra'zhenn would be around to assist should there be the need. This made her feel a bit better about going.

Tÿr went to pack. She had Varanus take her to her home in the cavern. She quickly packed her sleeping roll and a few days' worth of clothes. When she was ready, she climbed on the wyvern and the two of them flew off to meet the brothers. It would take them a day to get there if the winds were in their favor.

Tÿr forgot how much she didn't like flying. Although the trip was fairly smooth, the rise and fall of the wyvern's wings as they took off always made her feel like she could fall off at any time. She gripped the harness tightly as they rose into the air. The wind buffeted her, so she lay low against the wyvern to keep from being thrown about. She really hated flying this far but she really wanted to see the boys. Rævii was snuggled deep in her pouch on the front of Tÿr. The little fox didn't like flying either.

The winds were at their backs the whole flight so it went quicker than they thought it would. About halfway through the day the wyvern landed so Tÿr and the little fox could have something to eat. The healer was grateful to be back on the ground, as was the fox. It scampered around the area while Tÿr got them some lunch to eat. Varanus went off to hunt for his meal while the other two had theirs. Tÿr had brought some dried meat and some pears to snack on. The fox sat patiently while the healer got her some food as well. When they had eaten enough, Tÿr cleaned up the remains of their lunch and prepared to get back in the air. Varanus had found a small wild boar and had made a quick meal out of it. The travelers were back in the air in less than an hour, and with the favorable winds, the healer figured that they would be with the boys in just about four more hours.

The three suns of the conjoined planets beat down on the travelers as they winged their way to their destination, a small town called Jaansport. It was the nearest to the training area that the boys had been using. They had been training out in the woods in tents where they could be free from distractions and disturbances of the town.

The wyvern that was training them was the same one that trained other wyverns. Her name was Qaren'a and she was old and very strict, but fair. She rewarded good behavior and was quick to correct bad. She had sharp eyes, and her knowledge was immense. Qaren'a was over seven hundred years old. She had deep blue scales that luminesced with the colors of the rainbow. The spike on her tail was over six feet long and she was nearly fifty feet long herself.

As Varanus neared Jaansport he let out a loud shriek. Tÿr assumed this was to let the other wyvern know that they had arrived. She was very excited to see the brothers again. It hadn't been very long since their last meeting, but she treasured every moment with the boys. Since they had been gone, it felt like a piece of her had been missing. Now they were graduating from healer school and were doing it several years sooner than most anyone else ever had. Tÿr being one of the exceptions.

They would have one of the best medical clinics on the planets. There would be three magiqal healers which was something that no clinic on the planets could say they had. It was unusual to have one, but three was unheard of. They would be able to heal so many people from so many villages. Tÿr had even suggested that they might even travel around to heal those that couldn't get out of their homes. They might even travel to far away towns that didn't have medical services at all. Now that there were three of them, the possibilities were endless.

Varanus and Tÿr began their decent into Jaansport just as one of the suns neared the horizon. It was still too early in the year for it to dip below the skyline. It never got dark on this part of the planets. There were always at least two suns shining.

As they neared the blue ground, Tÿr could see the boys and their teacher standing outside waiting for them to land. Gordian was waving up to her as Varanus made a large circle and came into land smoothly next to the boys. Tÿr got down from her mentor's back and ran over to hug the brothers.

"Oh my gosh, I've missed you!" she said as Danior gripped her in a huge bear hug.

"We've missed you too!"

"I can't believe you're graduating already."

"I can." Gordi said. "It feels like we've been studying forever."

"But you guys are graduating so fast. You did the courses almost as quickly as I did them."

"We had a good teacher." Danior added.

Qaren'a said that the boys were very good students and that they learned faster than she had ever seen any other students before. She told Tÿr that the boys had learned the magiq for healing faster than any wyvern that she had taught. Tÿr could tell that the wyvern was very impressed with the brothers.

Tÿr was impressed with the size of the wyvern. She was almost as large as Ghra'zhenn. She was older than he was but not quite as big. Females didn't get as large as males as a general rule.

Where are you planning on staying while you're here?" Danior asked.

"I am going to stay in Jaansport I think, and Varanus is going to stay out here with Qaren'a." Tÿr told him.

"Don't you have a sleeping roll?"

"I do, but I don't want to bother you, if you are still finishing up your lessons."

"We are done." Gordi said. "How about a camping trip?"

"Do you think we have time for that?" she asked Varanus.

"I believe we can make the time."

"Okay. It's settled, we'll have a camping trip then." Tÿr told the boys.

Both boys were very excited at this. They hadn't taken their friend out in the woods here, so they were anxious to make the trip. Varanus agreed to take Gordian into Jaansport for a few bottles of wine for their trip. He would also pick up some food while he was there. Jaansport was a decent sized town that had many shops, and, in the end, all three friends decided to go into town to go shopping. They all had a bit of money and decided that they didn't know what they wanted and probably wouldn't know until they saw it. The wyverns offered to fly them the short distance into town, but they opted to walk instead. The trek only took them an hour.

Tÿr was surprised by the size of the town. She pictured Jaansport to be about the size of Vennex, but it turned out to be larger than Yelliton. It was an actual large town, bordering on the size of a city.

The friends were loaded down with food and wine on their way back from town. Varanus met them halfway back and took their packs back for them. The walk into town had done them a world of good to boost their morale as they were all looking forward to a drink of wine later that evening.

It took them another hour to walk back to the camp. They took their time, chatting and catching up on the events of everything that had gone on since their last time together. Tÿr told them all about the new clinic and how things would work once they came back to Vennex. The boys would each have their own office in the clinic, and they would each get their own patients. Tÿr had been telling her patients to be prepared to see the brothers when they returned. She just didn't have enough time to see everyone in town anymore. She and Varanus were the only healers in the area right now and they were so busy that they hardly knew what to do. The boys would definitely be a great help when they joined the team.

The graduation ceremony was a small intimate affair. The brother's mom couldn't travel all the way to see it which disappointed the boys. She just wasn't well enough to come this far. The only ones in attendance were Tÿr, Varanus and Ghra'zhenn. Tÿr's parents wanted to come but her father was busy at his shop and couldn't leave. Her mother didn't feel comfortable coming all this way by herself. They did send a nice gift for the brothers. Tÿr's father had made each of them a desk for their new offices. They were exquisitely carved, and each had the boy's initial carved on it. Tÿr had gotten a similar desk when she had graduated. It was destroyed when the sorcerer demolished the first clinic.

"I can't believe we did it." Gordian said after the ceremony.

"I can't believe it's finally over." Danior told the small group.

"Congratulations, young masters," Varanus told the boys. He and Ghra'zhenn had been talking to Qaren'a.

"You have done incredibly well, and you should be very proud of yourselves." Ghra'zhenn told the brothers.

The boys were both extremely pleased with themselves. They had never imagined that they would be healers, and now they also knew magiq as well. Both boys had acquired walking sticks that they had fashioned into magiqal staffs, similar to the one Tÿr'Ynyn had. Danior also used his as a cane to find his way around. It helped him to be more independent. He was able to get around most any place he went by himself now. It was as if he almost had a sixth sense.

When the ceremony was over the boys gathered their things for their camping trip. The three friends set out for the woods. Varanus went with them for part of the way until the trees got so close together that he didn't fit between them. Once the forest got that dense, he bid the campers goodbye and went back to stay at the camp with Qaren'a and Ghra'zhenn. He told them that he would remain there until they returned.

The three walked into the forest and found a spot to camp. It was fairly open and they quickly built a fire so they could cook their food. All of them were getting hungry after their long walk. The area was shaded and the sun didn't really reach down to them so it was nice and it would make for good sleeping as the planet never really got dark this time of year.

The campers all decided to have roast owl and some berries that they had found along the way. The berry bush had plenty of fruit so they were going to return the next day for some more. Fox cherries were a treat for all of them as they didn't get them often.

Tÿr thought that her fox would have loved some of the cherries, but she had decided to leave Rævii back with Varanus. The little fox probably wouldn't have been any trouble but Tÿr didn't want any distractions while she was out in the woods. She intended to have a good time and she didn't need to worry about another creature. If she drank as much wine as she thought she was going to, she would have enough trouble caring for herself.

As soon as their dinner was over, the boys brought out the first bottle of wine. It was gone before the three of them knew it. The second and third bottles disappeared just as fast. By the time they reached their fourth bottle, none of them were feeling any pain. There was a lot of laughing going on and the stories that the boys told of their training had Tÿr giggling. The stories got sillier and more ridiculous by the minute and before long the trio were laying back on their sleeping rolls, eyes closed, and trying to keep the world from spinning away from them. Eventually they all succumbed to the effects of the wine, and they were out cold.

In the morning they all awoke at about the same time. A symphony of torment playing in their heads. Luckily Tÿr had thought ahead enough to bring along a headache remedy for them and she gingerly got up to prepare it for each of them. It took a while for it to work, but before long they felt a bit more human.

"I am never drinking like that again." Gordian said.

"Yes, you will. You say that every time you drink." His brother teased.

"My mouth is so dry. What do we have to drink?" Gordi asked.

"Wine."

"You must be joking. Doesn't anyone have a waterskin with just water?"

"Here, drink this." Tÿr told him. She poured him a small cup of wine.

"I really don't want wine." He complained.

"It will help, I promise." She told him.

He drank it down and made a face.

They roasted some meat and ate which helped to settle their stomachs. By the time evening rolled around Gordi was ready to open another bottle of wine. Tÿr and Danior were a lot more cautious about their consumption this evening. Gordi still drank like it was a contest. He was ready for bed an hour or so before the other two. Tÿr and Danior sat up and talked for several hours while they sipped on their wine. They kept adding wood to the fire and saying that it was getting late, but then they seemed to find something else to chat about. By the time they both fell asleep, Gordi was snoring loudly. Tÿr wondered if she would be able to fall asleep, with all of the noise coming from Gordian, but she went out like a light as soon as she shut her eyes.

Morning came quick for the campers. Tÿr got up before the boys and made the headache remedy for all of them so it would be ready for the boys when they awoke. Gordian would definitely need it, she doubted that Danior would, but she made enough for all of them just in case. It wasn't like it would hurt them to take it.

When Gordian got up Tÿr handed him a cup of the remedy. She didn't need to ask if he needed it, she could see from the look on his face that he was hurting. Danior wasn't in that bad of shape. He drank his down and was fine in a matter of minutes.

"So, what are we going to do today?" He asked.

"Nothing until this headache goes away," his brother replied.

"You'll never learn, will you?"

"I can't help it; the wine was going down way too easy last night."

"We are running low on wine." Tÿr told the boys.

"There's no problem. I picked up a bottle of cane rum when I was in town. I've been saving it for later. Now seems like a good time to crack it open." Gordi told them.

"You really are asking for it, aren't you?" his brother quipped.

"What can I say, I like a drink occasionally. Once I'm healing, I won't be able to drink so I might as well get it out of my system now."

"You seem to be doing that very well." Tÿr joked.

"I've made it a hobby."

The three campers were going to walk around the forest and see what they could find, but they got talking and ended up staying at the campsite the entire day. They were all surprised when it was late in the afternoon and they were hungry.

"Let's fix something to eat so we can get on with the rum." Gordi said.

They had kept the fire burning the whole time they were talking by using fallen qyrry wood that they had found around the area. It was a very strong, dense wood that burned very slowly. Qyrry was what all three of the healers had chosen for their staffs. The boys still hadn't completed their staffs to their liking. Tÿr brought hers wherever she went. It was a powerful magiqal artifact that she often used in her healing process. The boys still had to attach crystals and and chose headpieces for theirs.

Tÿr's staff had a pair of wings surrounding a crystal on the top of her staff and it was very powerful. It served as a conduit in her healing process back at her clinic. When she used it, the headpiece would glow, and the power would transfer from her through the staff into the injured or sick person or creature.

Tÿr also had one other thing that the boys didn't have and might not ever. She had gone through a process called intercalation. It was a process where heated crystals were inserted under her skin from her wrist, up her arms and down her back. It was another boost to her already huge amount of power. Very few people were ever chosen to go through this process as it was very dangerous and only offered to people that the wyverns trusted beyond all else. Many people who had tried the process had died in the past due to its violent and painful nature.

"Have you guys figured out how to finish off your staff yet?" Tÿr asked the brothers.

"I want mine to have a large quartz crystal set in an open metal orb at the top," Danior said.

"That would look nice," Tÿr agreed.

"I think I want mine to have a serpent wrapped around it with a piece of citrine at the top under the serpent's head which is raised up to strike.

"Nice," said Tÿr. "Have you collected the metals for it yet?"

"We have. That was part of our training."

"Yeah, I had to do it too," Tÿr told the boys.

"Did Varanus help you with yours?"

"Yes, he helped melt some of the metals with me. Mainly he was there to instruct me on the folding of the metals. We used several."

"We will use our forge for it," Gordian told her. "it's the last thing we need to complete. Technically we are done with our courses, we just need to construct our staffs now. Qaren'a told us we would do this after we graduated."

"If you need help sculpting yours Dani, I'd be glad to help."

"I might take you up on that," her friend told her.

The three campers got through the bottle of rum and chatted about how the boys finished staffs would look and work. Tÿr explained how much she used hers when she was in the clinic. She told the brothers that they would probably use theirs as much as she did. It was an invaluable tool and almost as important as the medicines and tonics that she used. Often, she wouldn't need medicines and alternative traditional things used by other healers. She could utilize her staff to heal or mend the body and the people didn't require any further treatments. Soon the brothers would be able to do this as well.

When the bottle was gone Gordi suggested that they open the remaining wine so they wouldn't have to carry it back when they left the next day. Against her better judgement Tÿr agreed to it and they consumed the last two bottles of wine. She sipped at hers as she was already feeling the effects of the rum. By the time the wine was gone they all were feeling no pain. Tÿr knew she would pay for it in the morning, but since it was their last night in the woods, she didn't care.

The conversations got silly and finally Tÿr felt herself drifting off.

"I'm going to get some sleep boys."

"I am too," Danior agreed.

"Yeah, it is late," Gordi said.

The three climbed into their sleeping rolls and fell asleep within minutes.

Morning was a lesson to the campers that they shouldn't mix their drinks. All of them had headaches that made them swear that they wouldn't drink like that again. Tÿr made them all a headache remedy and they all gulped it down quickly.

"Never again." Gordi said.

"You say that every time," his brother told him.

"I mean it this time."

"I've heard that before," Tÿr responded.

The trio waited for the remedy to work for them before they decided to head back. Varanus and Qaren'a would be waiting for them. Tÿr wasn't certain how long she was planning on staying with the brothers. The clinic was in good hands while she was gone, but she missed her patients. She would need to get back before too long and then the brothers would join her shortly after.

The trip back took longer than they planned. None of them were walking quickly after the night before. Luckily the remedy had worked, and their heads weren't pounding any more. They were all glad that they had their staffs to lean on while they walked back. Tÿr knew that she still had a long trip to get home after they returned to the camp where Varanus and the other wyverns were. She wondered if Ghra'zhenn would still be there or if he had gone back to Ẏkkynnÿk Island.

When they returned to camp, they found Varanus talking with Qaren'a, but there was no sign of Ghra'zhenn.

"I trust you had an enjoyable time." Varanus said to them as they walked up to the wyverns.

"It was very nice." Tÿr told him.

"Yes, we had a great time." Gordi told him.

"How much wine did you bring back?" Varanus asked.

"Umm, none." Gordi said with a grimace.

Varanus chuckled. "Now I understand why it took you so long to get back.

"Where is Ghra'zhenn?" asked Gordian.

"He had to get back to the island, he has business to attend to." Varanus told him.

Varanus asked Tÿr is she wanted to leave now or if she wanted to wait until tomorrow. She told him she would prefer to wait one more day if that was agreeable to him. He told her that it would be fine and that they would leave first thing in the morning then. Tÿr told the boys that she would help get things together for them to craft their staffs. The boys had already chosen the actual staff part, but they hadn't sculpted the headpieces, nor had they chosen they crystals for them.

Varanus and Qaren'a told the trio that they would be happy to fly them out to a place they knew where the boys could look for crystals for their staffs.

When the three were ready, they climbed on the wyverns, and they lifted off towards a mine known for its crystals. The trip lasted about an hour, and they touched down on a small mountain to the east of Jaansport. The mine was old, and it had been abandoned many years before. Qaren'a knew that there were still crystals here though, all of the gold and other metals had been mined out of the place, but they had left the quartz and citrine and other crystals that weren't so valuable.

The three humans went into the caves with their tools and looked for signs of crystals. Tÿr used her staff to light the way while they went deeper into the mine. About fifty feet in they found signs of crystals on the floor of the cave.

"This looks like a good place to start." Tÿr told the brothers.

Danior felt around on the cave floor for any pieces of crystals that he thought he might like to use. It took him a little while before he found a piece half buried in the floor. Tÿr went over with a pick and helped to dig it up. It was a perfect specimen. It measured about nine inches long and was double terminated. It would look great on the top of his staff surrounded by the open orb.

It took Gordian a while longer to locate any citrine. The crystal was rarer and harder to locate. Eventually he found a piece, but it wasn't exactly what he was looking for. He did, however, realize that he had located a vein of citrine and then he found several more pieces. After taking several pieces out into the light, Gordian chose a piece that had three points on the top and it combined into one at the bottom. It would be perfect for what he wanted. It was medium yellow and very clear.

When the boys had collected their crystals for the tops of their staffs, they found smaller pieces to be incorporated into the bodies of them. Once all the crystals were collected, the trio climbed back on the wyverns and were winging their way back to the training camp.

Upon landing at the camp, the trio decided that they would relax the rest of the day. Tÿr wanted to be rested up for her long flight back to Vennex. The brothers got right to work on their headpieces. Tÿr helped to sculpt Danior's with him as he needed a bit of help to get the orb even. When they were pleased with the look of it, they let the clay dry. Gordian's snake took a while longer to sculpt but eventually he was happy with the design. Both boys would be melting their metals and pouring their headpieces the next day. Tÿr could tell that the boys were excited to be finishing off their staffs. They had worked so hard to come this far.

When night rolled around the trio decided to turn in early. Tÿr had her long trip home the following day, and the boys had a day of metalwork. Gordian suggested that they open a bottle of wine but Tÿr told him she would pass. In the end, they all went to sleep early while the wyverns sat out and talked. Wyverns were famous for having long conversations that could last for days.

Tÿr was up early and she and Rævii got ready to leave. The boys had a lot of things they needed to get done so Tÿr wanted to let them get to it. She would see them soon enough as it was. They would be following her to Vennex in a couple of weeks, once they had finished their staffs and doing other things that they wanted to do since they graduated. As soon as they got to Vennex they would be starting at the clinic with Tÿr. They already had a small cabin out back of the clinic to live in. Their old cabin was lost with the destruction of the old clinic.

Tÿr had offered to let the boys to live in the cavern home with her but they had opted for a cabin in town. That way they could visit their mother at night if they wanted to. Tÿr had a new larger cabin built for them. The boys were excited to get back and check out their new home. They still hadn't seen it as it wasn't finished when they were in town the last time.

The healer had many things to do once she got back to her home. First she unpacked and tried to relax a bit but there was so much she wanted to get done. The first thing that she wanted to do was to find out where her parents were. She still hadn't gotten any word back from them since they had gone into hiding. She decided to write a quick note to them and have Sëvyq deliver it. He would be able to find them, and she would feel better knowing that they were safe.

Sëvyq was in his house by the clinic and Tÿr attached the note to the tube on his neck and sent him of to find her parents. He took off with a shriek and flew away to the west. Tÿr didn't know if that was in fact the direction her parents had gone or if he was going the long way to get to where he had to go. He was clever and she knew he wouldn't want to lead anyone to her parents on purpose. He was extraordinarily fast and the likelihood of anyone being able to keep up with him was doubtful.

The next thing Tÿr wanted to get done was replacing her old medicines. From time to time, the old stock would need to be replaced with new, so she would need to make new oils, tinctures, balms and other things that she used at the clinic. She told Varanus that she needed to make a trip out to the country to harvest herbs for the medicines. Varanus told her that they could go the next day if that was satisfactory to her. She agreed so she spent the rest of the day at the cavern cleaning out the old medicines that needed to be replaced, and making a list of herbs and minerals that she would need to make her new stock.

Varanus went out hunting that night so he could feed and be prepared for a day of flying all over the country. He caught a large wild boar and made a quick meal of it. He wouldn't need to feed for the next few days.

Tÿr worked into the night and was ready for her new inventory when she got it prepared. Luckily, she didn't need to throw out too many things, because much of her present stock was fairly new and fresh.

In the morning Tÿr was ready to make her flight around the countryside. She planned on it taking all day. Trips like this usually did. She got her harness ready and then her and Varanus set off. They flew to a spot where the herbs were prevalent and thick, and she was able to harvest many that she needed in one spot. She made labels for each of the herbs that she harvested so she didn't mix any of them up although she usually could tell each herb by sight.

At lunchtime Tÿr ate some dried meat and had some mulled wine that she had brought with her as a treat instead of having to try to find water. After she ate they got back to the search for the rest of the herbs that she needed. The only minerals that she would need could be found on the shore of the Ajenti River so they saved that for the end of the trip. By mid-afternoon, they had collected everything that they required so they began the journey back to the Ajenti and then finally home.

Tÿr was happy to return to her cavern that evening. It had been a long day, and she was ready for a rest. Her backside was aching from riding so far and she was glad to finally be off of the wyvern. She thought it would be nice to try and figure out a way to make a saddle that would make flying more comfortable. She was certain that there was a shop in the village that could help her with that. She would check when she went into town the next time.

A couple days later she was hanging up the herbs to dry when Tÿr heard the familiar cry of the säqyr wyvern returning. She ran outside of the cavern to greet him. Rævii was right at her heels. The little fox was excited to see her friend. The little wyvern landed less than gracefully but managed not to flip over this time. He walked up to Tÿr as if to tell her that he had an important message for her.

Tÿr opened the tube on his neck and took out a small piece of parchment. It was in her dad's handwriting, and it simply said:

We are safe and in Londstäc. Send word
when it is safe to return home.

Dad

Tÿr knew that Londstäc was on Peyda Kirin and a good distance from them. They must have travelled a long while to get there. Londstäc was a large city with a large population which would make it difficult to locate them. The healer took the bit of parchment and threw it into the fire so nobody else could read it. It made her feel better knowing that her parents were safe and secure far away from the trouble that was brewing.

Tÿr went to bed fairly early that night. She wanted to be up and ready for the clinic the next day. The boys would be joining her in a week, and she wanted to make sure everything was ready for them. Their mother had sent a message to her to let her know that they were ready to come home and get to work. Tÿr was excited to have the boys back. It had been a while since they had lived in the same town. They had been training and before that, she had been.

As she lay in bed trying to go to sleep, Tÿr wondered how her cousin was doing. Sämir still had a long time to go in his training. He had only been at it for a short time, but the wyverns had told her that he was doing very well. He too would come back to the clinic to work when he was done with his studies and training. It would be perfect to have a non-magiq user as a healer at the clinic for some of the older people in Vennex. Many of them just didn't trust magiq and didn't want anyone who used it to heal them. This put Tÿr in awkward positions sometimes because she wasn't able to heal certain people because they refused her help for fear of her magiqal skills. Even at death's door, these people would refuse her help. She had to send to neighboring towns for their healers, and by the time they had gotten there, it was too late.

The younger generation was not so finicky and was glad to accept Tÿr's help most of the time. There were exceptions to the rules in each case. Some of the older people embraced the new healer with open arms. Others were just plain stubborn.

The next day Tÿr was ready to get to the clinic. She wanted to make a couple stops on the way. The first was at the leather shop. She was going to see about getting a saddle made for her, especially for long trips. She also wanted to go to the tailor's shop and see about getting some matching tunics for her and the brothers. That way they would all match and people would be able to tell that they were healers when they came to the clinic. They would also spare their own clothes from getting soiled in case of accidents at the clinic. Tÿr wished her dad was still in town because she could use some furniture at the clinic too. For now people would have to stand and wait or use the few chairs that they did have. She could also use new exam tables, but for now she would get by with what she had.

At the leather shop, the man took measurements of Varanus and said he could design a whole new harness with a saddle for Tÿr and at a decent cost. He took measurements right then and said he'd have something ready in less than two weeks. Tÿr planned on giving the man a generous tip if he could get it done in a reasonable amount of time. The tailor also said that they would have no trouble making tunics for the healers. The boys just needed to stop by when they got to town to get measured, and they would be able to get them done in a week.

Tÿr went on to the clinic from there. There was already a long line of people wanting to be seen. She got right on and began to see the patients. There were many easy ones to deal with and she was able to get most of them out quickly. Varanus was there to help with the tougher cases. By the end of the day, Tÿr was worn out and ready to go home. The next day was just as busy.

"I'll be so glad when the boys get back," Tÿr told Varanus.

"You are doing a fantastic job. The people love you and you treat them with dignity, just like your predecessor."

"Varanus, I don't know how long I'll be able to keep up this pace."

"I can always bring in another wyvern to help if you need."

"I'll be fine until Danior and Gordian return," she said.

"As long as you're certain." The wyvern told her.

She cleaned up the room and prepared to leave the clinic for the night. She was tired and needed to get some sleep. It was then that a woman came walking up to the clinic just as they were closing the doors. She was obviously panicked. She was carrying a young girl covered in a blanket. The girl was sobbing quietly.

"I'm sorry we are closing." Tÿr told the woman.

"Please, you have to help me." She said, "my daughter fell and hurt her arm."

Tÿr stopped what she was doing. She could see the desperation in the woman's face. She opened the door back up and led the woman into an exam room.

"Let's see what we have here." Tÿr said.

The lady took the blanket off of the girl and Tÿr could see that the little girl's arm was clearly broken badly. It was discolored and hung at an odd angle. Tÿr stifled a small gasp and told the lady to lay the little girl down on the exam table.

Tÿr had to figure out how she wanted to proceed. She needed to heal it the quickest and most pain free way that she could. She went to her cupboard and got out a liquid made with octyfoil majoris, a plant that was a powerful pain remedy. She gave some to the little girl who coughed and sputtered when she drank it but got enough to begin to feel its effects. Tÿr then explained that she was going to heal her with magiq and the mother, though a bit reticent, agreed.

The healer got her staff and used the power from her staff to mend the bones in the little girls arm. The girl whimpered but was under the influence of the pain medication, so she managed well. The arm went from being at an odd angle to straightening out with a slight popping sound.

In just a few moments the arm was mended, and the little girl could move it without any pain.

"What do we owe you?" The mother asked the healer.

"Pay me whatever you can afford." Tÿr told her.

"We aren't wealthy," the mother told Tÿr.

"Just pay me what you can." Tÿr repeated.

The woman pulled out a grubby little money bag that had very little money in it and began to give Tÿr half of what was in there. Tÿr told her that one silver piece would suffice, and that she should keep the rest for her family.

The woman looked into Tÿr's eyes and a tear rolled down her cheek.

"Thank you. They told me you were kind, but I didn't realize how generous you were too."

Tÿr'Ynyn smiled at the lady and told her to keep her daughter safe. Then she showed her out of the clinic.

Varanus was standing by to help clean up if she needed him, but it was an easy case to fix and there was no real clean up to be done.

"Another satisfied customer," Tÿr told her mentor.

"I can tell. Now let's get this place closed and get you home. You need to rest."

"Yes, I do." She agreed.

The pair locked up and headed home to the cavern to rest for the evening. Rævii was very happy to see Tÿr when she returned. She practically jumped into her lap while she was still standing. The little fox was almost purring when Tÿr began to pet her.

Varanus told the healer that he was going to go out in search of food and, he would be back to take her into town in the morning. Tÿr waved to him as he flew off and she went down into the cooling tunnel to get something to eat so she could relax for the rest of the night.

When Tÿr returned from the cooling tunnel she was surprised to find Sëvyq back in the cavern. She went up to him to see what message he had for her, but the little wyvern scampered away from her and went to play with Rævii.

"Come here!" she told the little creature, but he only wanted to play with the fox. Tÿr finally caught up with him and opened the tube around his neck. There was nothing inside.

"Hmmm? Why did you come back?" she asked him.

He just squawked playfully and went back to his little furry friend. Tÿr figured that it would be fine for him to stay there with her in case she needed to send a message off to her parents or to the boys. It was just strange that he decided to come back on his own.

That night the three of them sat around the cavern and relaxed. The little creatures played together until they got tired and then they went off to go to sleep. Tÿr took this time to read some of the medical papers that Ghra'zhenn had given her. There were things she wanted to brush up on. Things that would help to make her a better healer.

This was the routine for the next two days. Work and then she came home to the medical papers. The critters were eager to see her when she first got home but that was only because they were hungry. Once they were fed, they went back to playing and whatever it was that they did.

On the third day she decided to see how the boys were doing. She jotted a quick note to them and sent Sëvyq off to deliver it. Poor Rævii didn't know what to do without her friend there. Tÿr called the little fox over to her and held her on her lap while she read the last of the papers. The fox ended up falling asleep while Tÿr petted her. Tÿr fell asleep soon after, holding the fox and the papers.

Varanus woke her up the next day.

"Are you ready to go to the clinic?" He asked.

"Yes, just give me a few minutes to get ready."

Tÿr hadn't meant to fall asleep in her chair and was stiff from sleeping in it. She walked around the cavern for a few minutes to loosen up.

Once she was ready, she climbed on the wyvern and the two of them lifted off towards Vennex. It only took them fifteen minutes to get there, and there was already a line forming at the clinic.

"Well, let's get started," Tÿr said.

She opened the clinic doors and let the first people into the waiting room. When they were done at the clinic, she planned on going to the leather shop to see how far they were with her saddle. She was anxious to see how it looked.

About halfway through the day the säqyr wyvern returned to the clinic with a note to Tÿr from the boys. She was surprised that he had returned so quickly. The note read that they were on their way back and should return home in two days' time. This was great news because Tÿr was so busy at the clinic and help would be appreciated. She really needed them to be there with all of the people coming through the clinic.

When the clinic was closed that evening, Tÿr and Varanus made their way over to the leather shop. The owner was pleased to tell her that he was finished with the saddle. He brought out an ornately designed saddle that Tÿr fell in love with immediately. The saddle was stitched with leather cord and then it was also decorated with a vine and flower design. It was beautiful and Tÿr was so pleased with it. She asked the owner to show her how to position it on Varanus, and once she saw it, she had it memorized for the next time that she would have to do it. She wouldn't use the saddle on the short trips because it took too long to get it on, but for the long trips, she would use it to cut down on discomfort. Tonight however, she would use it to fly home on, just to see how it felt.

Tÿr paid the owner the rest of his money and thanked him profusely for his excellent work. The owner looked like he would burst with pride by the time Tÿr left the shop.

"Okay Varanus, let's try this out. Is it comfortable?"

"It is just fine," the wyvern told her.

Varanus spread his wings and the two of them took off for home. Tÿr was surprised at how comfortable the saddle was. It was padded for comfort. It was like sitting in a comfortable seat, Tÿr thought. There was support for her back and the reins felt nice in her hands. Not too large, it was perfect. She couldn't have been more pleased with her purchase.

Tÿr had to admit that it was the most comfortable flight she had ever taken. When they touched down at the cavern, she noticed that she didn't feel uncomfortable in the least. She was very happy that she bought the saddle and was even looking forward to taking a longer flight.

Tÿr spent the next couple of days busy at the clinic as there were many people that needed her services. She was looking forward for the boys' return. They should be there at any time, and they would be able to get right to work.

That night she got back to the cavern and was met with a surprise. Danior and Gordian were waiting inside when she arrived. She knew something was up right away because Rævii didn't run out to greet her when she landed with Varanus.

"Where's Rævii?" Tÿr asked her mentor.

"Maybe she's sleeping."

"She's in here." came a familiar voice.

"Danior?"

"Yup. It's us. Surprise!"

Tÿr dismounted the wyvern and ran into the cavern. Sitting inside were both boys. Danior was petting Rævii and Gordian was nuzzling Sëvyq. Both boys broke into a huge smile when Tÿr ran in. The boys got up and gave their friend a big hug.

"How did you get home?" Tÿr asked.

"Qaren'a. She's out hunting right now." Gordi told her.

"Speaking of food…" Danior said.

"We have plenty. What do you want?"

"How about wild hog of some sort?" Danior suggested.

"Sounds great!" Gordi agreed.

"Okay. Wild boar. We have ribs and steaks and roasts."

"Whatever cooks the fastest." Gordi said.

They settled on steaks and Tÿr had a fire going quickly to cook them on. The boys wanted theirs on the rare side so they could eat sooner rather than later. Tÿr got the steaks cooked and they all sat down to eat and catch up. The boys had stories to tell Tÿr about things they had been through in their training.

"So, are you guys ready to start up at the clinic?" Tÿr asked the brothers.

"Yeah, we're ready." Danior told her.

"We are anxious to see patients." Gordi said.

"Good, there have been a lot of them lately." Tÿr told them.

"How about a night at the pub before we begin?" Gordi suggested.

"Do you really want to go out drinking?" Danior asked his brother.

"I could use a sip."

"Well, maybe if we don't stay out too late." Tÿr agreed.

The trio waited for Qaren'a to return from hunting before they went into Vennex. Varanus and Qaren'a brought the three into town and waited for them near the clinic. The plan was that they would have a couple drinks and meet the wyverns back there.

They decided on The Tarnished Anvil, an old pub that they sometime visited in their youth. It was a respectable tavern with a jovial barman. He was happy to see the trio again and quickly filled their glasses with cane rum.

"Only one or two tonight, Paten." Tÿr told the barman.

If he was disappointed, he didn't show it. The pub was full, so he was busy and having a good night.

The trio sat at the bar and talked about the boys' training. Tÿr told them what to expect at the clinic. She explained that she still took livestock as payments for those who couldn't afford cash. The boys would figure out those people once they had been there a while. The boys asked Tÿr about her parents and how they were doing. Then they finished their drinks and decided to call it a night.

When they returned to the cavern, they were tired and went to bed. Tomorrow was going to be a busy day, so they wanted to get a good night's sleep. Rævii went to sleep with Tÿr which was unusual because she usually slept on her cushion. Tÿr noticed that the säqyr wyvern had taken the cushion for the night, so that was why the fox was eager to sleep with her. Tÿr didn't mind, she liked when the fox decided to snuggle with her. The boys used the cots that Tÿr's dad had built for her several years before. The wyverns went to sleep in the woods nearby.

When morning rolled around, the friends got up and had a quick bite to eat before heading off to the clinic.

As usual the clinic had a long line around it and there were many people waiting to see the healers. Gordian commented that he was surprised at how many people there were. He counted seventy before they opened the doors.

"Is it always like this?" he asked Tÿr.

"Yup. We're always busy." She told him.

"Well, let's get to it then," Danior said.

Tÿr opened the doors, and the day began. There were so many people that needed their services. The boys healed with the help of Varanus. Varanus didn't really do much more than watch them. He just wanted to be on hand in case they should require any help. Qaren'a stayed nearby as well.

The day flew by for the healers. Before they knew it, it was almost time to close the clinic.

"It feels like we just got here, and it's almost time to go." Gordian commented.

"That's how it feels almost every day." Tÿr told him.

"So, how did we do?" Gordi asked.

"You performed masterfully." Varanus told him.

"Thanks, I didn't want to screw anything up."

"You won't, as long as you remember your training." Qaren'a told him.

"The cleaning crew will be here in a few minutes," Tÿr told the brothers.

Tÿr had hired a crew from Vennex to come in each night to clean the clinic and make sure everything was ready for the following day. They were proving to be an invaluable part of her crew.

The three got ready to leave the clinic and head home for the night. They were tired from the busy day that they had just finished. Tÿr suggested that they have some roast boar when they got home, and that seemed agreeable to the boys. Tÿr wanted to let her parents know that she was well and that things were fine, so when they returned to the cavern, she wrote them a short letter and had Sëvyq take it to them. She didn't want them to worry about her.

Sëvyq was all too happy to deliver the message for her. He practically nuzzled her over as she tried to get the letter into his tube around his neck.

Once the letter was secured in the tube, the little wyvern took off and headed towards Tÿr's parents. She wasn't exactly sure where they were other than in Londstäc.

The trio ate their roast boar for dinner that evening and went to bed fairly early. It had been a busy day and everyone was tired. The three of them spent a little time talking about some of the cases that they had during the day. The boys were shocked by the number of people that were sick or hurt and needed care. Tÿr told them to expect that many people every day. She told them that many of the people that they treated came from neighboring villages because they preferred the care, they received here in Vennex. It made the boys proud to be a part of the Vennex team.

elic and Dannus sat at the Axeman's Hood and waited for their leader to contact them. They had been watching the healer's clinic for the past few days and were certain that the female healer was there. There were also two others that they could tell. Two male healers and now two wyverns. They were certain that Kaistam-Laq would want to know this information. They had tried to contact him earlier, but he was busy doing something and told them that he would contact them in an hour. Neither of them knew how their leader would take this information. They were certain that he would want to know about it, but how he would respond was another matter altogether.

Exactly an hour later Dannus's scrying mirror that he kept around his neck began to vibrate. Kaistam was trying to contact them. The pair quickly exited the tavern and went someplace where they had some privacy.

Dannus took the mirror out and the face of their leader materialized.

"Why have you kept me waiting?" he asked.

"We had to get somewhere with some privacy your grace."

Kaistam-Laq nodded and then continued. "What news do you have for me?"

The pair filled their leader in on the activities at the clinic, telling him about the two wyverns that had taken up residency. Kaistam was very interested to know what they were doing there. He told the two men to try to find out what was going on and to report back to him in a week. Then he told them that he would be traveling to Vennex in the near future. That they should have a report of everything that has gone on in the town ready for him when he arrives.

When the two had finished telling their leader everything that had happened in Vennex, he told them that they had done well, and then signed off.

"That went better than I thought it would." Melic told his partner.

Dannus agreed. "I was worried that we didn't have enough information for him, but now he's coming here. We better find something out before he gets here."

"Maybe we should visit the clinic as a patient." Melic suggested.

"What are we going to say is wrong with us?"

"We could fake an illness."

"She might see through that." Dannus said.

"What if one of us got hurt?"

"How?"

Before Dannus could even blink, Melic pulled back and hit him with everything that he had. There was a loud crack as his jaw cracked.

"Oooow, you broke my jaw." Dannus said, holding his face.

"Well now we have a reason to get you into the healer tomorrow."

Dannus's face was already turning purple and beginning to swell.

"Let's head over to the healer's clinic so we can be the first in line tomorrow." Melic told his injured partner.

Dannus was feeling light-headed from the pain. He knew that he was in for a long night. He and his partner walked over to the clinic and waited outside. It was nearly midnight, so they would be there for the next seven to eight hours before the healers showed up. Dannus convinced Melic to go in search of some octyfoil majoris. It was an eight lobed leaf plant that was used for pain relief. If he could find some in the woods surrounding the village, it would bring some relief to Dannus until he could see the healer in the morning.

Melic finally got sick of listening to Dannus complain and agreed to go in search of the plant. He left his partner sitting at the side of the clinic and went off to find the octyfoil. Melic was gone for about an hour before he returned with a handful of the plant.

Dannus grabbed a bunch of the leaves and stripped them from the stalks and pushed them into his mouth. It hurt more than anything he had ever done before. Trying to chew was a new exercise in agony. Moving his mouth even a little bit sent jolts of pain through his head.

Dannus managed to chew the leaves enough to unlock the soothing juices of the plant. After about an hour some of the pain began to diminish. It was far from gone, but it was better. Now, he just needed to continue chewing these leaves every hour to keep the relief going until he saw the healer.

Morning seemed to take forever to arrive. Dannus got little sleep. His face was swollen and purple and green from the bruising. Luckily for him, Tÿr arrived early to the clinic that morning. He heard the flapping of the wyvern's wings as the healers arrived. There were already people queued behind him in line to see the healers, but after waiting there all night, Dannus was the first to be seen.

Melic made himself scarce for the appointment. He had bruised knuckles from where he had punched his partner in the face. He didn't want to have to explain his bruises to the healer.

"What have we got here?" Tÿr asked as Dannus limped into the clinic.

"I had a bit of an accident."

"What happened?"

"I got hit in the face," Dannus said.

"With what?" Tÿr asked.

"I'm not certain. I have been chewing on octyfoil to relieve the pain. Can you fix it?" He asked not wanting to give away too much.

If Tÿr had more questions, she didn't ask them. She gently put her hands on his face and drew on her powers of healing to fix his face. Her arms began to glow under her bracers and the man felt the bones begin to knit themselves. The pain subsided and he could move his jaw without the intense discomfort.

"How did you do that?" He asked.

Tÿr smiled and simply said that it was all part of being a healer.

"Can you all do this?" Dannus asked.

"We all do what is required of us," Tÿr said deflecting the question.

"How much do I owe you?"

Tÿr looked at the man for a minute and then told him her fee. He immediately reached into his coin purse and paid her without complaint.

There is something about this man that is unusual. Tÿr thought to herself.

This healer is very powerful. I wonder if the master knows what he's getting into? Dannus thought.

"Please be careful." Tÿr told the man as she opened the door to let him out of the room.

Dannus nodded and walked out. He got out of the clinic as fast as he could, he needed to find Melic and let him know about the healer. Dannus found his partner near the Axeman's Hood. He was just walking into the tavern to have a drink to pass the time.

"Melic!"

Melic swung around to see who was calling him. He had his hand on his hunting knife at his belt.

"Oh, it's you. You look better."

"No thanks to you."

"We needed to get in close to the healer and you did. What did you find out?" Melic asked.

"She is very powerful. She healed me without breaking a sweat." Dannus told him.

"We can use magiq." Melic reminded him.

"Not the way she does. It comes very naturally to her. She doesn't have to work at it." Dannus said. "Plus, her arms did something I've never seen before. They almost looked like they were glowing when she healed me. It's been forever since I've been to a healer, so I don't know if that's normal or not."

"Glowing?" Melic asked.

"Yes, almost like they were on fire."

"I've never heard of that before." Melic agreed. "That is definitely worth mentioning to Kaistam-Laq."

"Were you able to find anything else out while you were in there?"

"Nothing." Dannus said. "She had me in and out so fast that I didn't have a chance to do anything."

"Laq isn't going to be pleased." Melic said.

"He's going to have to understand that she got me in and out so fast that I didn't have a chance to do anything. Surely, he'll understand that, right?"

"I wouldn't be so sure." Melic said shaking his head. "He isn't known for being understanding and forgiving."

"At least we know we have the correct person."

"That's true," agreed his partner. "We can keep an eye on her from now on. We can see where she goes and follow her."

The two made plans to stake out the clinic and follow the healer when she left that night.

Melic and Dannus sat outside the clinic all day long and waited for the healer to emerge. When she and the boys finally did, they prepared to follow them. What they weren't prepared for though, was the fact that the healers were all flying away together on the wyverns. They ran for a short distance, but they couldn't keep up. It was obvious which direction they had gone, but there was no way to determine their final destination.

"There's no way we will find where they went," Dannus told the other man.

"I agree, let's just go back to the pub."

The men turned around and walked back to Vennex. Both of them were thinking that their leader was not going to be pleased that they hadn't gotten any information on the healers. They hoped he would be understanding and appreciate that they had figured out which direction she had gone when she had left the clinic. It wasn't much but it was something.

The two returned to the Axeman's Hood and went in to begin their night of drinking and waiting until the clinic opened the next day. By now the barman recognized the pair of them and got them their usual drinks. A glass of ale and a shot of cane rum. They were used to the cane rum and the ale was good and strong too. It didn't take too many rounds to get them drunk. The golden rum and dark ale went down quicker with each round they bought. On the third night of their inebriation, Dannus happened to look up and see a familiar face as it walked in the door of the pub.

The blood ran out of Dannus's face as he saw Kaistam-Laq stride into the pub. The leader of the assassins did not look pleased to be there. He wore a scowl as he approached the two men sitting at the bar.

"Is this what you've been doing the entire time you've been here?"

"Dannus glanced at Melic and said, "we have been watching the healer but she has gone for the evening."

"Where does she go?" Laq asked.

"What exactly have you been doing while you've been here then?" Laq drawled.

"Well, they fly in and out on wyverns, so it makes it very difficult to follow them."

"You have access to horses do you not?"

"We do sir, but they fly…"

"Excuses, that I don't need. I need solutions. How are we going to find the healers?" Kaistam-Laq asked.

"What if we used our own wyvern?" Melic suggested.

"Are you suggesting that we go to that foul snake, Nagarr Zmaj?"

"Well, it might be useful…"

"Nothing that creature ever does is useful to anyone but itself."

"Surely there is another wyvern we could turn to."

"I prefer not having to turn to the wyverns at all. I don't trust them." Kaistam said dispassionately.

"How are we going to track them to their home? They fly and we can't keep up, even on horses." Dannus added.

"You leave that to me." Their leader said smoothly. "I believe I may have a plan that will work."

Kaistam turned and exited the pub leaving the two drunken lackeys wondering if they should follow or continue drinking. In their drunken stupor, they remained behind and continued to drink the rum being offered to them by the barman.

The sorcerer went outside and looked for the two other assassins that he had traveled with. He had told them to blend in and try to keep out of sight as much as possible. The three of them had tents set up outside of town and were going to stay there until this business with the healer was finished. Kaistam wondered if he brought enough of his assassins with him, but he was certain that this time Renner and Ollis-Van would be able to remove the healer threat with his help. They were the best assassins he had ever worked with and they should be able to make easy work of this one female healer.

Kaistam stopped walking and looked behind and noticed that the other two hadn't followed him out of the pub. He rolled his eyes and turned to go back and retrieve them. Drink had addled their brains and he was at his wits end with the pair of them.

He marched into the pub and walked up to the two drunken idiots and grabbed them by the back of their shirts and yanked them off of their barstools.

"Idiots!" He spat. "We are leaving!"

The two men could barely keep their footing as he shoved them out the door.

"Were you waiting for an invitation?"

"Uh, we thought that you wanted us to…"

"To what? Continue your sottish quaffing of ale?"

"Um…what?"

"Never mind. You need to get yourselves sorted out and be ready to work. We have things to do, and you better be up to the challenge. I don't pay you to be incapacitated."

"Um, yes sir, Kaistam."

With that said, the leader of the assassins turned and led the men away from the village to the area where the tents were set up in the forest. The two drunk men could barely keep up with the sorcerer and the other two assassins that joined them as they made their way through the village.

"Is everything okay?" Renner-Van asked the sorcerer.

"It will be once these two have sobered up. Tomorrow we go looking for the healer's home."

"But she flies…" Dannus started to say.

"I am aware of that. You told me once. I haven't forgotten that already." Kaistam-Laq said sarcastically.

"If she flies, how will we follow her?" Melic asked.

"We will be prepared. We will go in the direction she comes from in the morning and travel there tomorrow. We will then wait for her to cross over us and follow her as she nears her home and do it again the next day if we need to. Eventually we will come to her home.

When they reached the forest the sorcerer went into his tent and told then others that he was not to be disturbed. His marquee was actually a tent in a tent, and his tent was much more luxurious and elaborate than the others with an inner and outer sanctum. The outer sanctum was where his books and instruments and other apparatus was stored. The inner sanctum was where he slept and meditated. It was very elaborate with a four poster bed that had to be carried everywhere that he went. The entourage that travelled with the sorcerer was large. All of his books and instruments had to go everywhere with him, and everything had to be packed and moved in a particular way.

The sorcerer slept very lightly that night. He wanted to be up early the next morning to be moving as soon as possible. It was still light throughout the nighttime so they would have no trouble seeing to get things packed up and moving in the morning. Kaistam had the whole group up and moving at a time most people were still dreaming in their beds. They had the camp packed and ready to go in record time. They knew that the sorcerer wanted to get moving and it didn't do to keep him waiting.

Kaistam had Dannus and Melic point him in the direction of the healer's home. He moved the convoy in that direction and they would travel out as far as they could until they would need direction. They would wait to see the healer fly over them and then follow her the rest of the way.

The convoy waited the entire day for the healers to fly overhead and finally in the late afternoon it happened.

"Two wyverns coming overhead!"

Kaistam watched them fly over and followed them with his eyes as they flew past.

"They must have a den in the mountains." Laq said to his entourage.

"We can make it there by morning." Renner-Van said.

"We'll need to ride all night." Agreed his sister.

The sorcerer moved the convoy towards the mountains, and they began their long trek. The terrain was rough and rocky and needed to be traversed slowly. Now the sorcerer understood why the healer flew.

The carts had trouble with the rocky ground and had to be dislodged several times during the trip. This caused many delays that didn't please the sorcerer.

They finally reached the mountains by the morning and many of the carts had to be left behind. Kaistam-Laq was not pleased to have to leave so many of his carts and people behind. He still had four assassins with him and that would have to be enough. The rest of his crew had been left behind and would be joining him shortly. Kaistam hated not having his normal seventeen together but the situation dictated that he come with just the two siblings to gather the other two assassins from Vennex and now they had this mission to do. He could have waited to attack, but he wanted to catch the healer by surprise.

In the morning, Kaistam and company were camped near the foot of the mountains and they were waiting to see where the healer came from. There were lookouts posted all over to keep a watch for the healer to come flying past. The sorcerer knew that they had to be close to the healer's home. The plan was to wait for her to fly out and then they would go out in search of her home and ambush her when she returned that night.

Ollis-Van was looking up to the west and she saw the healer and her wyvern emerge from the cavern on the side of the mountain. Then the second wyvern with the boys came from behind and the pair took off for the village. Ollis reported to her boss where she had seen the wyverns and the location of the cavern.

As soon as the wyverns had flown off, the convoy moved toward the cavern. Kaistam instructed the assassins to scale the cliff to enter the cavern. Kaistam himself levitated up to the entrance. There they waited until the healers returned that evening. Rennner-Van was left outside as a lookout to watch for any sign of the returning wyverns. Around dinnertime the familiar flapping of the wyvern's wings filled the air.

The assassins were poised to strike when the first wyvern landed on the ledge of the cavern. Gordian and Danior got off of Qaren'a who took back off and walked into the cavern. The assassins sprung into action and attacked. They grabbed the boys and hauled them to the edge of the cliff as Tÿr'Ynyn was still coming into land. Kaistam-Laq strode out of the cavern as Tÿr tried to figure out what was going on.

"Tÿr'Ynyn, you have one chance to join us and one chance only. If you choose to ignore us the consequences will be drastic."

Tÿr was still trying to figure out what was happening. Then as if to prove their point, one of the assassins shoved Gordian off of the edge of the cliff and he plummeted down to his death. Tÿr heard him scream and then he was silent. Her stomach lurched as he went over the edge.

"NO!" Tÿr screamed.

She gathered her magiq and attacked the assassin holding Danior. A bolt of energy shot from her hands and hit the lady square in the chest. She toppled backward and fell over. Tÿr attacked again. this time at the assassin that shoved Gordi over the edge. She hit him in the head and his head snapped back and he fell over. Then she readied her attack at the sorcerer who was preparing to attack as well. Their bolts smashed into each other and caused a huge explosion of energized matter.

Two more assassins emerged from the cavern. Tÿr recognized one of them from the clinic.

"Danior! Behind you!"

Danior turned and cast energy bolts in the direction of the cavern hitting one of the assassins. He dropped immediately. The other tried to take cover but Tÿr had already taken aim at him and struck him in the back as he turned to run back in the cavern.

The sorcerer walked to the edge of the cliff and jumped off. He fell for a moment and then floated the rest of the way down. When he hit the ground, he cast a vanishing spell on himself and disappeared.

Tÿr told Danior to go back into the cavern and then dove Varanus to the ground to try to help Gordian. When she got to the fallen brother, he was not moving. She could tell from the angle of his body that he was already gone. His face was frozen in a horrifying death mask. Tÿr moved over and closed his eyes. Tears fell down her cheeks. Tears of rage.

She lifted the body onto Varanus, and they flew back up to the cavern. Tÿr saw the bodies of the assassins laying on the ground around the entrance of the cavern. Anger like none she had ever felt before flooded through her. She wanted to push them off the edge to pay for what they had done to her friend.

"We need to get Qaren'a back here." Varanus told Tÿr.

Varanus opened his mouth and shrieked loudly. Moments later a response came back through the air.

"Qaren'a is on her way back." Varanus said.

"We need to take his body back to his mother." Tÿr said.

Danior came from the back of the cavern. He walked up to Tÿr.

"They killed him, didn't they?" He asked somberly.

Tÿr reached out and took his hand. A new batch of tears ran down her face.

"We will make them pay. I promise."

"What am I going to tell my mum?" Dani asked with tears in his eyes.

"What do we do with these…" Varanus couldn't bring himself to call them people.

Tÿr's first reaction was to kill them outright, but they were defenseless right now and she wanted them to pay for what they had done.

"They need to be in prison." Tÿr said.

"I will travel and get Ghra'zhenn. He can help transport these repugnant beings to the prison in Yelliton. But first we need to get you back to Vennex and the boys back to their mother. We need to get some kyskÿzha potion and dose them up to keep them sleeping for a while."

Tÿr went to her supply shelves and got the potion. She opened the mouths of the fallen assassins and poured the potion down their throats. She made sure to give them enough to sleep for a long while so she and the wyverns could tend to their business. Then she dragged them to the edge of the cliff. She didn't want them in her home if they did happen to wake up. If they stumbled off the edge in a drug induced state, she wouldn't lose any sleep over it.

Tÿr felt a lump in her throat as she thought about the conversation she was going to have with the boys' mother. This was not something Tÿr was looking forward to. Death was always difficult, but when it was someone close to you it was even harder.

Danior flew with his brother to Vennex and Tÿr flew behind them on Varanus. They landed outside the boys' mother's home. She could tell that something was wrong immediately. She came running out to Qaren'a and Danior who was staying with his brother's body.

Mëyan Suttÿr, the boys mother stopped dead when she saw the body of her son draped over the wyvern.

"Danior?"

"Mum. There's been an incident…"

"NO!" She wailed.

"Mum, try to understand…" Danior tried to explain but his mother was having none of it.

She ran up to her dead son and held him in her arms, sobbing. Danior tried to comfort his mother.

Then she turned on Tÿr.

"You!" she pointed at the healer, "this is all your fault! You took my sons away from me and now he's dead."

Tÿr felt like she had been slapped.

"Mum! That's enough. It's not Tÿr's fault. We were ambushed and they killed him without any warning. There was nothing we could do."

"It was her; she took you away from me and now Gordian is dead."

Danior just shook his head and went to hold his mother. She collapsed into his arms. She wept openly as he held her. Danior held back tears as his mother cried into his chest.

Tÿr turned around and headed to the clinic. She was going to go to sleep in the clinic tonight. She would have Varanus go back to the cavern and tend to the prisoners. He and Ghra'zhenn would transport them to Yelliton to the prison there. Then Tÿr would begin the search for the sorcerer. He had mysteriously vanished during the fight. He had simply jumped off the edge of the cliff and disappeared. Tÿr knew that he would be back though. He wasn't finished with her.

When she got to the clinic she found a bed and laid down. She was so tired and the emotions were flooding through her. Tears and sobs threatened to break through at any moment. The harder she tried to keep them back the more they came at her. Eventually she broke down and cried. She cried for Gordian and for Danior who would not have his brother anymore. She cried for their mother who had lost a son. Then she cried for herself. Finally, she couldn't cry anymore and she drifted off to sleep.

When she woke in the morning she hoped that it had been a bad dream, but then she saw where she was and knew that it wasn't. People were already lining up at the clinic to be seen. Tÿr thought about keeping the clinic closed for the day, but then she figured that work would be the best therapy.

What surprised her the most was when Danior came walking into the clinic just before she opened the doors for the public.

"What are you doing here?" she asked.

"I have to work. I can't just sit at home with her and think about it all day. I think working will do me good."

"That's kinda what I felt. I couldn't just sit at home and think about it."

"Then shall we open?"

"I guess we better. We already have a line." Tÿr said.

Tÿr went to the doors and opened the clinic for business. Danior busied himself with patients to keep his mind off of the loss of his brother. It was late afternoon before the wyverns returned. They informed Tÿr that they had taken the prisoners to Yelliton prison and they had been incarcerated. The wyverns also told Tÿr that they had searched the area around the cavern for the sorcerer, but there were no signs of him.

News of the loss of Gordian was talked about at the clinic as the people waited in line to be seen. Tÿr didn't know how they knew about it, but someone had obviously said something. She was glad when the last patient walked out the doors. She needed to get home and get some rest. She hadn't slept very well the night before. Danior had mentioned that he hadn't either.

The two healers went to visit Danior's mother before they went back to the cavern. She was still distraught, but she had calmed down enough to have a coherent conversation. She had quit blaming Tÿr for Gordian's death as well. Mëyan told the two healers that there would be a funeral in two days' time. Tÿr said that the clinic would be closed on that day out of respect for Gordian.

They left the house of Danior's mother and flew back to the cavern. Tÿr told Danior that she would look after him like his brother used to do. He smiled at her and told her that she didn't have to do that.

"I want to Dani. We are more than friends, we're family and I will look after you until I no longer can or you leave me."

"Well, then, I guess you're stuck with me." He told her.

She hugged him closely. "You know I love you, right?"

"I do, and I love you as well. Now enough of this lovey crap. Let's eat!"

"I agree," she chuckled. "What shall we have?"

Deep in the forest around the mountains Kaistam-Laq ran away from the cavern. He wasn't about to go back to prison. It was a small sacrifice to have to send a few of his people away. But sometimes you lost people. He would worry about setting them free once he got back to the rest of his company. That, or he would have to find four more men to join his group of assassins.

The sorcerer made his way back to the horses and the crew and had them tear down the tents immediately. He was not going to waste any time getting out of the area.

"Faster!" he bellowed to the crew.

They were working as fast as they possibly could but that wasn't fast enough for the sorcerer. He wanted to be gone. He knew that if the healer came back and found him there would be a showdown and he wasn't ready to face her. He wanted to be a full strength. That meant seventeen men, and he was four short at the moment.

Within the hour the tents were packed away, and the convoy was on the move back toward Yelliton. They had fellow crew members to break out of prison.

The funeral for Gordian was a whole village affair. Everyone from the magistrate to the lowliest person showed up to pay their respects for the fallen boy. Tÿr was surprised at how many people there were in the village. The funeral took place in the middle of town and the magistrate presided over the proceedings. It was a very formal affair for someone of Gordian's humble status. It just went to show how much the village held the healer in esteem.

The boy's mother sat through the funeral stoney faced. She had obviously done her mourning in private and didn't want to cause a scene. She listened with pride as the magistrate praised her son for all the good, he had done for the village. Then he presented her with an additional honor. They named that day after Gordian, and it would be celebrated for years to come.

After the funeral they had a burial at the town cemetery and Gordian's body was laid to rest in an elaborate crypt. It was a crypt that was used for important people in town. Magistrates, heroes, and other important people. Everything was taken care of by the village because Gordian was killed during his fulfillment of duty. His mother was humbled by the treatment her son received.

Danior and Tÿr sat at the funeral and burial with the boys' mother. When the proceedings were over, she hugged both Danior and Tÿr and went back to her home. The two healers went and found the wyverns who had also watched the ceremonies. They were ready to get back to the cavern and try to get back to a normal life, if that was possible. Tÿr mounted Varanus and Danior climbed aboard Qaren'a. Together the wyverns lifted off and headed back to the mountainside cavern.

When they arrived the säqyr wyvern and shift fox were waiting for them by the entrance of the cavern. They must have heard the wyvern's wings and come running out to see the passengers. Tÿr and Danior climbed off of their rides and went in to give the little guys some love. Rævii jumped up into Tÿr's lap the second she sat down. Sëvyq was close behind. Danior nuzzled the little wyvern while Tÿr petted the fox.

The humans spent an hour with the critters before Danior mentioned that he was getting hungry.

"Yeah, I am too." Tÿr agreed.

They decided on wild boar steaks and got a fire going. Before long there was meat for everyone. Tÿr made enough for the animals and fed them first. She and Danior ate after the other two had been fed. She picked some pears from the tree outside of the cavern since she didn't have any time to get anything else. She seasoned the meat with some herbed salt and remembered how much Gordian had liked the salt. She smiled to herself.

"Gordi would have really liked this," Danior told her.

"That's exactly what I was just thinking." She replied.

They sat and reminisced about the old days when they used to go out camping in the woods. How they all had their jobs and how Gordian used to catch more fish than they could ever eat. He never liked to throw any back. He also had the bad habit of drinking a bit too much and falling into the stream while he was fishing. The two of them sat and laughed about that.

"What would you say to a bottle of wine?" Danior suddenly asked.

"I think I would enjoy that." Tÿr said.

She went off to the cooling tunnel and brought back a bottle and two cups.

"Here you go," she said, pouring Danior a cupful.

He took it and the two toasted his late brother.

"I'm really going to miss him," Tÿr admitted.

"Yeah, I don't know what I'm going to do without him."

"I already told you, I'm going to take care of you from now on."

He got teary-eyed for a moment and then took a drink.

"You know that's going to be a full-time job some days."

"I can handle it. Besides you're family."

Danior smiled. He knew she was right. She was as much a sister to him as Gordian had been a brother. They just weren't blood related.

The nights were beginning to get darker as the planets got farther away from the suns. In another hundred or so days it would get even darker. The darkest that it got on this planet. Peyda Noirin was always in the shadow and always darker. The 965-day year was long and mostly spent near the suns. Only as the planets were farthest from the suns during their revolution, did it get darker.

Peyda Kirin and Peyda Noirin, the conjoined planets did not rotate like most planets did. Instead, they wobbled a bit as they made their trip around the tri-suns. They did however, spin very slowly, like a drill, but the movement was so slow that it was barely noticeable. They only made one revolution every thirty days.

The shift was the section of land that connected the two planets together. It was the most habitable place. Peyda Kirin was a desert planet and Peyda Noirin was a planet covered with oceans and islands. Though there were people that survived on both of the planets, most of the population lived on the Kirin-Noirin shift. The shift had a temperate climate and was heavily forested.

The two friends sat and drank the bottle of wine and then went back for another.

"Only one more." Tÿr insisted.

"Yeah, it's probably best. We have a long day tomorrow."

"Here's to you and me." Tÿr said.

"To us." Danior said. "I love you Tÿr."

Tÿr blushed. She was glad Danior couldn't see her.

"I love you too." She reached forward and kissed him on the cheek.

Danior put his hand to his cheek as if to save the kiss for later.

Tÿr finished her cup of wine in one big gulp and told Danior that she was going to go to bed.

"Do you need me to get you anything before I go?"

"Nope, I'll be fine."

"Okay, then I'll see you in the morning."

"Night Tÿr."

Tÿr went to her cot and laid down. She had drunk more than she had meant to. Her head was spinning a bit, but she fell into a deep sleep soon after she laid down. Danior went to his cot soon after and lay in his cot thinking of the past couple days. He thought about how much he was going to miss his brother. Luckily, he still had Tÿr. He didn't know what he would have done without her. Then he thought about what he had said to her. He fell asleep knowing that he truly loved the girl sharing the cavern with him. Would he ever be able to tell her the honest truth? He doubted it, but she had told him that she loved him back and that would have to do for now.

Morning came quicker than either of the two would have liked. Danior was awakened by Sëvyq nudging him gently with his head. Danior felt around to see what was causing the disturbance. He felt the little wyvern's head bumping his side.

"Hey, what do you want?"

The little wyvern chirped and soon he was joined by Rævii who joined in by licking the boy's hand.

Tÿr heard the little commotion and woke up to see what was going on. She saw the two creatures waking Danior up in their own way. She was surprised that Rævii wasn't over by her waking her up. She wondered if the little creatures could tell that something was wrong and that Gordian wasn't coming back. A sixth sense or something. Whatever it was, Danior seemed to be enjoying it. He was all smiles.

Tÿr got out of her cot and walked out to the ledge. Varanus and Qaren'a were already there.

"I trust you slept alright?" Varanus asked.

"I did, thank you. And yourself?"

"I slept very well."

"Good morning Qaren'a," Tÿr said to the other wyvern.

"Good morning young mistress."

"We'll be ready to go in a little bit," Tÿr told the wyverns.

"There is no rush." Varanus told her. "We are ready whenever you are."

Tÿr went back into the cavern to get ready. When she got in there, Danior was already up and dressed.

"The wyverns are ready for us whenever we are ready to leave." She told Danior.

"I'm ready whenever you are."

"Okay, let me get the critters something to eat before we go and then I'll be ready."

Tÿr got the säqyr wyvern and the fox some leftovers from the night before and then she was ready to go. The two creatures were happy to have some food to eat. They ate it quickly and then went to their beds.

"I can't believe it you wore yourselves out eating." Tÿr joked.

The pair of them left for the clinic and arrived a short time later. When they had opened the clinic and began seeing patients, Danior could tell that something was on Tÿr's mind. She seemed to be a bit distant, like she had something on her mind. When they had a small break, Danior said something to Tÿr about it.

"What's on your mind? You seem to be somewhere else today."

"It's nothing."

Tÿr, you can't pull that on me. We've known each other too long. I know you have something on your mind. What's up?"

"We'll talk later."

"We have no one to see right now, tell me."

"Okay, I've been thinking that I'm going to go after that sorcerer. He needs to be stopped and I don't think he will until he kills me. He has a vendetta against me ever since he landed in prison and I think he meant to get me instead of your brother."

Danior listened to her and nodded.

"I think you may be right. I'm going with you." He stated matter-of-factly.

"No!"

"Is it because you would have to watch over me?"

"You know that isn't why." Tÿr told him.

"I have just as much to lose as you do, and I have a bit of a grudge now." He told her. "I'm going with you."

"But Dani, I don't know where we would even look or when we would be back. If anything happened to you, your mother would never forgive me."

"Then we go to my mother and tell her what we're going to do."

Tÿr didn't like the idea but finally agreed to it.

They agreed to visit his mother after they were done at the clinic that evening. The rest of the day passed by quickly and they finished up with their last patients.

"Let's get this over with." Tÿr told her friend. "What do we do when she says no?"

"We'll cross that bridge when we come to it," Dani said.

They closed up the clinic and went to Dani's mother's house.

Tÿr was right about her not being thrilled about Danior going after the sorcerer, but she understood why he was going to do it. in the end, she gave her blessing and made Tÿr promise to bring her boy home no matter what. Danior asked his mother if she would mind watching the two creatures of theirs while they were gone. They would need to be fed and let out to do their business. She agreed to look after them while they were away. Tÿr promised to return her son and then the two of them bid her farewell.

"That went better than I thought it would." Danior admitted.

"Yes, it did." Tÿr agreed.

They told the wyverns of their plans. At first they were skeptical but then they understood that the humans were going to go with or without them so they agreed to take them on their quest.

"We will need to stop in Yelliton to let the healer know that they will be getting our patients," Varanus told Tÿr.

"Will you explain to Sëvyq that he will be staying with my mother?" Danior asked Varanus.

"Yes, I will take care of it. I will also tell him to keep Rævii safe."

The wyvern talked to the säqyr wyvern in their language, Cmok, and the little wyvern seemed to understand perfectly what was going to happen. He chattered back to Varanus and the larger wyvern told Danior that the little wyvern was concerned for his safety. Danior put his hand out and the smaller wyvern came up and nuzzled it.

"He knows that you are going away and that you will return to get him. Now you just have to make sure that you return."

Danior smiled and told him that he would be back even if it killed him.

Tÿr didn't smile at that. The loss of her friend was still too fresh in her mind. She was on a mission now, and she was going to make the people who killed her friend pay. Her and Danior might be outnumbered, but the others didn't have two wyverns on their side.

Tÿr thought about writing her parents to let them know what she was doing but by the time she sent the säqyr wyvern to find her parents she would have lost too much time. The sorcerer had not gotten that far ahead of them and with the ability to fly, she hoped to be able to catch them up quickly.

Tÿr and Danior were ready to leave. They loaded up the wyverns with their belongings and then they took off. They flew high and fast and used the air currents to glide on. Tÿr and Varanus took the lead and Danior followed on Qaren'a. They flew for most of the day, and it wasn't until Tÿr began to get hungry that she even thought of landing. She yelled out to Varanus, and he signaled that he had heard her and began to descend to the ground. When they finally landed, Danior asked why they had landed.

"I'm getting hungry, and I figured you would be too." Tÿr told him.

"Well, now that you mention it."

"It's settled then, we'll eat."

"What do we have to eat?" he asked.

"Mainly dried meat. We might be able to find some fruit around here. I also have some bread. If we don't eat it all, we'll have some for a couple of days. Oh yes, I also brought some cheese."

Danior opted for some meat and cheese and a bit of bread. He told Tÿr not to worry about trying to find any fruit. Maybe they could find some tomorrow. He would be fine without, today.

The pair sat and ate their meal while the wyverns went out and hunted.

"We've come a good distance so far today. How much farther do you want to go yet?" Danior asked her.

"I don't know. I was thinking maybe we could stop for the night."

"I wouldn't have any problem with that."

"We could get up early and start earlier tomorrow." Tÿr suggested.

"That sounds like a good idea. My backside is sore. I don't have a nice saddle like you do."

"You should get one when we get back, it's worth every penny."

"Maybe if we stop in Yelliton for a while I can get one made."

"Maybe we will stop there for a bit. If Kaistam-Laq goes into Yelliton it could take us a while to find him there. I don't think he is the type to stay out in the wilderness for very long. He strikes me as the type of person that needs to be around others."

"You might be right." Danior said.

They rested for a while before flying on to Yelliton. The flight was uneventful. They landed outside of town and walked in the rest of the way. The wyverns stayed in the forest outside of town and gave the humans a whistle that only they could hear in the case of an emergency. Danior and Tÿr carried the whistles around their necks on a bit of cord.

Yelliton was a large town with many businesses and establishments to visit. There was even a leather shop that could make a saddle for Danior. He and Tÿr decided to stay in town long enough for the shop to construct a saddle for him. Together they walked back out of town to fetch Qaren'a so the leathersmith could take her measurements for the saddle and bridle.

The wyverns accompanied the two humans into town, and there were curious looks from the townsfolk. Many had never seen a wyvern before. By the time they reached the leathersmith, there was a crowd that had gathered.

Tÿr was a little concerned that the sorcerer might turn up and there would be too many casualties. Her fears were laid to rest when no assassins nor sorcerer showed up. They were able to get the wyvern's measurements and a promise that the saddle would be completed in three days' time.

The four of them walked around town and got some supplies that they would need for spending the nights out in the woods. Tÿr led Danior around town and they decided to go to a pub after they had done their shopping for the day. They chose a pub called The Dry Dock. It was a small pub with a highly polished bar and an old barmaid. She poured them each a glass of cane rum and an ale. She was very generous with the rum.

"Drink it slowly, there's a lot in that glass." Tÿr told Danior.

"Good, I need a stiff drink."

The two sat and nursed a couple drinks before they decided to head back out and join the wyverns at the campsite. Tÿr's head was spinning as she left the pub.

"I think I drank a bit too fast." Danior told her.

"Yeah, I was thinking the same thing. We should get back and get something to eat."

The two walked back to the campsite and Tÿr built a fire to cook over. They had some type of meat to cook and some bread and cheese to have with it. Tÿr was hesitant to open a bottle of wine with their dinner but figured that they didn't have anything to do the next day. She and Danior finished the wine with dinner and then they fell to sleep.

Tÿr awoke to find Danior snuggled up against her. He must have moved during the night, she thought to herself. She turned and gave him a hug while he continued to sleep.

In the morning the two of them walked back into town and spent the day looking through the shops and eating at the food stalls. The wyverns decided to stay in the forest to keep from worrying the citizens. People still weren't used to seeing wyverns on a regular basis.

This was what the pair of them did for the three days it took to complete the saddle, and on the third day, they returned to the leather shop to check on the progress. When they arrived at the shop the owner presented them with a beautifully made saddle. Tÿr described how beautiful it was to the blind boy and he smiled as she told him about the intricate stitching and the superior craftsmanship.

The two of them told the owner that they would return in an hour with the wyverns so they could have it fitted on Qaren'a properly. That way Danior could tell how to do it. Tÿr explained to the owner that Danior was blind and asked if he would mind showing him how to adjust the saddle on the wyvern properly. The owner was happy to help so the two of them went to fetch the wyverns.

The wyverns and the humans returned and hour later and the owner showed Danior how to place the saddle on Qaren'a. She too was impressed with the craftsmanship. She commented on how comfortable the saddle was. Danior thanked the owner for the wonderful work and then he suggested that they give the saddle a try.

Tÿr already had her saddle on Varanus and so the two of them mounted the wyverns and they lifted off for a test flight. They flew around the town and then out into the country. Danior rode in the saddle like he had always owned it. When they landed an hour later Danior had a big smile on his face.

"That was great. No sore area on my backside." He told Tÿr.

"They're wonderful, aren't they?"

"It was well worth the money, that's for sure."

"I say we rest for the night and then get up early to begin our search again." Tÿr suggested.

"That sounds like a plan."

"I think we should begin right here in Yelliton. If the sorcerer is hiding here, I want to catch him unaware. I don't want him to have his whole crew together when we face him. It will be so much easier to take on four of them than twenty."

"I agree." Danior said. "Where should we begin?"

"I think we should hit the pubs. People tend to talk when they've had a bit to drink. Maybe they've seen him or someone in his band of assassins."

"The pubs are just my style," Danior laughed.

"I knew you wouldn't have a problem with that." Tÿr smiled.

"We will fly around the town and watch for anyone leaving," Varanus told the two healers. "But I'm afraid that the sorcerer has many tricks up his sleeves and can probably cloak himself. We may not be able to see him if he leaves. That is if he is even here."

Tÿr nodded. "Thank you Varanus, Qaren'a."

The two wyverns took off to begin patrolling the skies.

"Let's eat and get some rest," Tÿr told Danior.

"Okay." He went to their supplies and pulled out some bread and cheese and a bottle of wine.

They sat and ate in silence. Both were thinking about the loss that they had experienced and also about the huge mission they were getting ready to undertake. Tÿr was not going to put the sorcerer back in prison again. She was out for blood this time, and so was her companion. They wanted revenge for the death of Gordian, and they would have it by the time this adventure was over. Failure was not an option.

The two of them talked about the good times they had with Gordian and Danior got choked up when they talked about continuing the mission without him.

"I really miss him" he said to Tÿr.

"I do too, but we have to stay strong for him. We must do this to make sure he didn't die in vain."

"I will make that sorcerer pay!" Danior said.

"We both will."

They finished the bottle of wine and decided to call it a night, though they still chatted a little more.

The wyverns returned from their patrol having found nothing of the sorcerer.

Tÿr asked Varanus to tell them about Ÿkkynnÿk while they were chatting before they went to sleep.

"You know Ÿkkynnÿk means thunder mountain in the human tongue." Varanus started. "It is a warm place, much warmer than it is here. You have visited before so you know what it is like."

"I know, but what was it like to grow up there?" she asked.

"Ah, it was peaceful when I was young. We lived in harmony with one another. Even the humans seemed to accept us for what we were. There were exceptions to the rule of course, but for the most part things were good and my childhood was excellent. My teachers were very patient with me as I didn't learn magiq as quickly as other wyverns did, but my magiq grew strong and I became powerful. Soon I could do magiq that rivaled my teachers. That's when they brought me to…"

That was all that Tÿr heard of the story. She was so tired that she fell asleep and Danior was right behind her. Varanus looked down to see the sleeping humans and shrugged.

"They were very tired," he told Qaren'a.

"It was a very long day." She agreed.

The two wyverns stood guard over the humans as they slept.

In the morning Tÿr woke before Danior and found the two wyverns sitting where they had been the night before.

She remembered that Varanus had been telling her about his home and that she had fallen asleep.

"Oh Varanus, I'm so sorry, I fell asleep while you were talking last night."

Varanus just chuckled. "You aren't the first to drift off while I was talking."

"I'm so embarrassed." The girl said.

"Don't be. You were tired and needed to sleep. I wasn't saying anything important anyway."

Danior began to stir as the wyvern and girl talked.

"Is it morning already?"

"It is master Danior." Qaren'a said to him.

"I don't even remember what we were talking about last night, I was so tired I fell right to sleep. Did I miss anything important?"

"Nothing." Said Varanus.

"How late did you stay up Tÿr?" he asked the girl.

"Don't ask."

Varanus and Qaren'a both chuckled.

"What'd I miss?" Danior asked.

"I think I fell to sleep before you did." Tÿr told him.

"You know what sounds good to me?" Danior asked. "A pipe. We haven't had a pipe together for quite some time. Did you bring yours with you?"

"I did. I almost forgot that I had it. That does sound like a wonderful idea."

They both got up and went to their packs, and got out their pipes and some pipe weed. Tÿr's pipe was a gift from her father, it had belonged to her grandfather. Danior got out his pipe and they sat and enjoyed a pipeful in the morning sun.

Tÿr coughed a bit as she pulled the velvety smoke in for the first time. It was something that reminded her of her father. He always had a pipe while he worked in his shop. He usually didn't smoke in the house because it drove her mum nuts. Tÿr didn't smoke a pipe until fairly recently, but she thoroughly enjoyed it.

Kaistam-Laq led his crew toward Yelliton. He was on a mission to break his leaders out of prison. Renner-Van and his sister Ollis were imprisoned there along with two more of the crew. They had gotten themselves caught at the healer's home when they attacked and now, they needed to be freed. This was not a stop that the sorcerer had planned on making but he insisted on a crew of seventeen and he did not feel that it was time to go out recruiting new people.

He had broken out of the Yelliton prison before so he figured that it would be easy to break out his associates. He would have the help of the rest of his crew so he wouldn't be doing it by himself this time. He figured he would walk into the prison and incapacitate the guards and set his people free. If that didn't work, he would destroy the prison and walk away with his people. Either way, he was going to get his people back. Thanks to his superstitious nature, he wouldn't be doing anything more until he retrieved his incarcerated comrades.

The group cleared a hill and saw the prison in the distance.

"Split up," Kaistam told the group.

The group split into four smaller groups and headed off in different directions around the prison. When they reached their destinations, they sat and waited for the signal from their leader. None of them knew what that signal would be, but they were told they would know it when it happened.

Kaistam knew they would have to get in and out quickly. The prison itself wasn't huge so they could get through it fast. The issue would be that their magiq would be of no use once inside. He didn't know what would happen once the walls were breached, if the magiq would work then or not. He had to assume that it wouldn't. Still, he carried his staff of power with him and the others had their weapons.

The sorcerer waited until he was certain that everyone was where they were supposed to be. Then without warning he sent a magiq beam of energy into the back wall of the prison. The wall exploded into a ball of fury and dust. What was left was a gaping hole.

"Now!" he yelled.

The assassins poured through the hole in the wall where there was chaos. Guards were running around trying to find out what was happening. The assassins with Kaistam-Laq were knocking down the guards and disabling anyone that wasn't a prisoner. There was yelling and screaming coming from all around.

"Find our people!" He yelled over the din.

He strode through the chaos, slamming anyone that dared come close to him. Guards were releasing crossbows at the intruders, but the bolts were going wide and pinging off the walls. The assassins found that they couldn't use magiq in the prison, but the sorcerer was able to use his staff as it was a very powerful magiqal item. He shot beam after beam at the walls, blowing holes into the thick stone.

"We've found them!" one of the assassins yelled.

Kaistam-Laq turned and walked in the direction of the call. Soon he came upon the imprisoned assassins.

"Stand back!" he ordered.

He blasted the bars off of the hinges. Then he moved to the next cell and did the same thing. When the four were released, he turned, and they all walked out the huge hole in the wall. Any guard that tried to stop them either was knocked out or lost their life. The assassins didn't stop to see which. Most guards were left cowering behind the walls inside. The whole operation had only taken less than three minutes.

Other prisoners were yelling to be set free, but the sorcerer ignored their pleas and left them in their cells. He was only worried about freeing his people and no one else.

As they made their getaway, several guards had gone to the roof with crossbows and were trying to hit them, but now the entire crew had magiq at their disposal. The bolts from the crossbows were sent flying wildly in every direction by the assassins' magiq. They had horses waiting for them and were off before any of the guards could give chase. The alarm sounded, but it was too late. The assassins had escaped.

Kaistam had the crew ride toward the town if Yelliton. It was large and it would be hard to find them there. They wouldn't stay there, but it was a good place for them to get lost. He could hear the wailing of the alarms as he rode away from the prison. He was pleased to have his seventeen members together again.

"We are going into Yelliton he told his crew when they had stopped. We will not all ride in together. They will be looking for a large group of us, so we will ride into town in groups of twos and threes. We will split up and stay in different inns and meet up outside of town in two days' time. By then they will surely have thought that we have left the area. Keep your noses clean. No fighting, no thieving, no nothing!"

He looked at each of the crew members as he spoke. He wanted to make sure that they understood that he was very serious.

"Renner, Ollis, you are with me." The sorcerer said.

The brother and sister moved to join the sorcerer.

"We will be staying outside of town," he told them. "Too many people will be looking for us."

"What about us?" Melic asked, pointing to himself and Dannus.

"Keep your heads down and stay out of trouble," the sorcerer told him.

Melic looked like he wanted to say something else, but Kaistam gave him a look that said that he was better off keeping it to himself.

Kaistam-Laq and the brother and sister rode off, leaving Melic and Dannus standing there alone.

"Can we go to the tavern?" Dannus asked.

"I don't see why not. He didn't say we couldn't."

"Then let's go get a drink."

The two mounted their horses and rode off toward Yelliton. Both of them looking forward to a glass of ale and some rum.

When they reached the town two hours later, they left their horses on the outskirts and walked the rest of the way in. Horses tended to draw attention to people, and they didn't want that. Both were dressed as working-class citizens to complete the disguise. They both carried lachtrys daggers under their cloaks. Lachtrys was a midnight blue stone that they could magiqally mold into any shape they chose. It made incredible dagger and knives.

Kaistam-Laq had made certain that each of his assassins had a piece of lachtrys to carry with them. Most of the assassins formed it into daggers with a long thin blade. Lachtrys could be morphed into anything and then be morphed back into a blade almost instantly, which is why it was favored by Laq's assassins.

The two of them wandered around town before settling on a tavern called The Cutthroat's Den. A seedy looking place that catered to the lower-class citizens of Yelliton. It was a dingy place with dirty tables and a grimy bar. This didn't matter to the two assassins. They only cared about blending in with the people in the tavern. They sat down at the bar and each ordered a large glass of dark rum.

The barkeep, a pudgy old man who was as grimy as his bar, brought them their drinks and took their silver.

"New in town, eh?"

"Mind your business old man." Melic told the barkeep.

"No need to be rude." He retorted. "Just trying to make conversation."

"Go bother someone else. We'll call you when we need you."

The barkeep shuffled off to tend to his other customers and continued to wipe the dirty bar top with an even dirtier rag.

Dannus and Melic finished their rum and called for another. The barkeep brought them another in a semi clean glass.

"That'll be two silver pieces each." He smiled. He was missing more teeth than he had.

The two paid him and settled down to finish their drinks. Luckily the pub was not the kind of place where people were overly friendly, so no one came up to them, trying to start a conversation. The barkeep's prices seemed a bit steep, but the privacy that the pub afforded the assassins more than made up for the prices.

This went on for two days and they did nothing but drink more and more rum and ale. When the two days were over, they collected their horses and headed back out to meet up with the other assassins and their leader.

Kaistam-Laq was not pleased about having to have gone back to rescue part of his crew from prison. He was fuming that he had to break into the very place that he had been incarcerated just months before. He had not planned on ever seeing the infernal place ever again. Now he was behind in his plans, but he would adapt. He prided himself in the ability to adapt and overcome any obstacle that presented itself.

Right now, Kaistam was waiting for his crew to reform. Most of the group had come back together but he was waiting for a few of the members to return. He was not a patient man, but he had told them two days and the time limit was not yet up. The sorcerer was pacing impatiently as he waited for the rest of the crew to return.

When they had all returned, Kaistam-Laq told them that they would be moving to the town of Jaansport. They would be going there to stock up on some magiqal items that the sorcerer couldn't find any other place nearby. Things that would take place in rituals that were considered dark and dangerous.

The trip would take them over a week to complete and they would have to cross a mountain that was inhabited by the ill-tempered wyvern Nagrr Zmaj. The wyvern and the sorcerer had a history of feuding that was legendary. Both had nearly killed the other, and the sorcerer was not looking forward to facing the wyvern again. He was confident that he would emerge victorious with his crew of assassins behind him. The wyvern was enormous though, and very powerful. It would be best to avoid it if at all possible.

As the sorcerer was explaining the forthcoming trip, the assassins had questions for him regarding the wyvern. Questions like, what to do if the wyvern attacked, and what if there was more than one wyvern now. Kaistam answered their questions matter-of-factly.

"You will kill them. Then we will harvest their organs." He said simply.

If anyone had any more questions, they kept them to themselves.

Kaistam-Laq moved the crew out and they began their long trip to Jaansport. The sorcerer and his entourage were an impressive sight as they travelled across the country. Kaistam rode at the front of the procession and Renner and Ollis-Van brought up the rear, keeping an eye out for any unfriendly pursuers.

The crew traveled for five days before the mountain came into view. The mountain, which was actually a huge mountain with three peaks, almost a small range, loomed up ahead of the group. Kaistam-Laq called the group to a halt. He pulled out a spyglass and looked in the direction of the tallest peak. The sorcerer was trying to determine of the wyvern was in residence at the present time or if it was away hunting.

He did not notice any movement on the peak, but that didn't mean anything. The wyvern could have already spied them approaching and was lying in wait.

Despite the enormous size of a wyvern, they were ambush predators, and they were very quick. By the time their prey realized something was wrong, it was usually too late. Luckily, Kaistam-Laq knew that the beast lived on the peak and knew to be on the lookout for it.

When they reached the mountain, the suns were dropping behind the peaks, and although they wouldn't be setting all the way, it made it dusky out. Shadows grew long on the ground and the crew moved slowly through the trail on the mountainside. They did not want to spend the night on the mountain, so they were going to press on and travel through the night. The hopes were to make it over the mountain by the next day and then they would rest on the other side. With any luck they would avoid the wyvern and be long gone before it realized that they had been there.

As they cleared the peak, the unmistakable shriek of a wyvern split the evening air. Kaistam readied his staff and the others prepared to fight. The assassins scanned the sky for signs of the creature, but the wyvern was clever and stayed in the glare of the suns. As it neared the caravan, the shrieks died down and the beast went silent.

The assassins began to shoot energy beams into the air, but the sorcerer waited. He would wait for the beast to show itself before he attacked. He was not prepared to waste energy on useless shots going wide and missing the creature. He planned on downing the wyvern as soon as it got near enough for a clear shot.

Without warning, the beast swooped in and attacked with bursts of fire from its open mouth. Round after round of fireballs struck down at the caravan. The assassins scattered to avoid being hit. When they found adequate cover, they fired up at the wyvern, but their shots only bounced off its thick hide. Still the sorcerer waited to attack. The wyvern wheeled round and began another run on the caravan. The assassins had taken cover under wagons and carts and were firing up at the wyvern as it neared but as before, none of the energy bolts had any effect on the beast. As it neared, the sorcerer stepped up and raised his staff. An enormous burst of blinding power shot out and hit the wyvern directly in the upper body. The wyvern slowed, shrieking in anger.

The assassins took this as a sign and began to shoot crossbow bolts and more energy up at the creature. Some of the energy blasts tore at the wings of the wyvern, ripping holes in the membrane and causing it to scream in pain. The beast had to flap its wings harder to keep aloft. It shot more bursts of fire down at its attackers.

One of the assassins ran out to attack and left the cover of the wagon he was hiding behind. The wyvern took the opportunity to dive and snatch the attacker by the head and lift him off the ground. With a snap of the head, it flicked him down its throat. The assassin screamed and then was silent as he disappeared down the wyvern's maw.

The other assassins and the sorcerer shot beam after beam at the wyvern. Eventually the wyvern had been dealt enough damage and flew away to heal. The damage was already done though. Kaistam-Laq was down an assassin, but the wyvern was heavily damaged. The sorcerer considered it a major victory for himself. The first thing he would need to do though, was find a replacement for his deceased assassin. All activities and operations would cease until he found a replacement. He needed to have seventeen in his crew, and he could not proceed until he had filled the empty position.

Seventeen was a magiqal number for the sorcerer and he adhered to it like it was a religion. From the number of rings he wore to the number of people in his crew, everything had to equal seventeen. Each shelf in his tent contained seventeen books. If the books were too large, he would find a book that fit. He was very serious about the number, and nothing would change his mind. When an operation took place, it more often than not happened at seventeen past the hour. The wheels of his wagons all had seventeen spokes. It was a number he was fanatical about.

Kaistam-Laq had to be cautious on his trip to Jaansport now. He had to make certain that there were no altercations nor any incidents requiring a full team. He was down a man and until he could find a replacement, he would not feel comfortable doing anything. His team knew this and though many didn't share his feelings, none of them were brave enough to say anything to the contrary. At least not to his face.

Tÿr and Danior made their way through the streets of Yelliton. Danior used his staff to guide him as he walked. Tÿr also carried her staff, and both got looks from the crowd as they walked through town. The wyverns stayed out at the camp but were in earshot of the whistles that the humans carried. One blow on the whistle is all it would take to bring them in to aid them.

The pair hit every pub and tavern they could find in town. There was no sign that the assassins had ever been there. No one had seen any of Laq's people, or if they had, they didn't realize it. Kaistam-Laq did not brand his people nor did any of them have any distinctive markings that they knew of. None of the new group of assassins were Imbröttiös which would give them hairy faces and no earlobes as easily recognizable features.

It wasn't until later in the afternoon that their first break came. The pair passed by a group of the town's law officials and overheard them talking about a prison break. The two of them slowed and listened closer to the conversation. Things like sorcerer and assassins were mentioned, and then they heard that the prison had suffered its second breakout in just a short time. Everything was spoken in hushed voices, but the two healers managed to overhear everything that was said.

"Did you hear that?" Danior asked Tÿr.

"I did. They're having trouble keeping their prisoners."

"That means that the sorcerer is back to full strength again. This is just the beginning."

"I agree. We have to find them quickly and stop this madness. I wish we knew where they were headed." Tÿr told him.

"I doubt they were headed back toward Vennex. Maybe they left the shift altogether." Danior offered.

"If they left the shift, they're probably going toward Peyda Kirin. I doubt they'd go toward Noirin."

"Yeah, they would need boats and a lot of them." Danior agreed.

The pair continued their search through the town. They would spend another day there and then they would move on. They visited every pub and tavern and rundown drinking establishment. They questioned every barkeep and landlord that they came across to see if there had been any newcomers to their establishments recently. The owners of the drinking establishments didn't have much information for the healers. A couple of them told Tÿr that there had been strangers in town, but they didn't have much insight to give them beyond that.

Details were sketchy at best. If anyone had seen any of Kaistam-Laq's people, they weren't talking or didn't realize it. His assassins were not marked like other assassin sects. Many had tattoos or brands that unified them and made them easily recognizable. Kaistam-Laq did not want his people marked for easy identification. He felt it was easier to conceal oneself without marks of identification.

They continued to walk around town and listen for any signs that the assassins had been there. Danior had a keen sense of hearing and could pick up things that Tÿr might miss. Despite this, they heard nothing of the assassins while they were in town. After spending the entire day looking for signs and listening for any clues, they decided to move on.

Tÿr and Danior made it back to the campsite and told the wyverns that they had no luck in town. The wyverns suggested that they move on toward Peyda Kirin. The healers packed their belongings and loaded them on the wyverns. They decided to wait until the morning to take off for the nearest town, but Varanus convinced them to leave that afternoon. That way they could get a good jump on their pursuit of the sorcerer and his assassins.

"I say we head to Görne," Tÿr suggested. "It's the next decent sized town we would come to on our way to Peyda Kirin."

"I agree," Varanus said. "Maybe someone has seen the sorcerer passing through. He travels with a large entourage. Someone, somewhere is bound to have seen them."

"From there we should go to Alaëndäl and then Athöl and Voora."

The wyverns were loaded and ready to go. Tÿr and Danior rode side by side on the wyverns and though they couldn't really hear each other with the wind blowing in their faces, the wyverns could communicate with each other. The wyverns were much louder when they spoke, and their voices carried over the wind. Danior and Tÿr trusted the wyverns to lead them where they needed to go. The humans simply told them their final destination and the wyverns got them there.

They flew throughout the day and arrived in Görne in the early evening. Even though it wasn't dark out, the two flyers were tired from their trip. The wyverns needed to rest as well, they had flown a great distance and needed to find something to eat.

Görne was not a huge town, but it was bigger than Vennex and Yelliton combined. It had several pubs and taverns, and the two humans would be visiting all of them while they were here. If Kaistam-Laq had come through town, someone would remember him. The sorcerer was not someone that one forgot easily. He was flashy and gaudy and extravagant, and he traveled with an entourage that people wouldn't be able to miss.

Varanus doubted that the sorcerer was staying in town anywhere. He traveled with a massive tent and didn't need the services of an inn. His entourage also traveled with tents and camped with the sorcerer. They had a mobile town that they traveled with. It also made it more frustrating for the healers, because there were so many people in the sorcerer's crew that they felt they should be able to find them easily.

Görne was a bustling town with many taverns and shops along a long strip of roads that led into town. The houses of the residents were scattered on the outskirts. The town was a fairly modern village compared to Vennex. The buildings had tiled roofs instead of straw or wooden shingled roofs. Most of the buildings were made of mud bricks instead of wood. It was a thriving metropolis.

The people of Görne were friendly toward strangers and were not afraid to talk about any that had wandered through town. Tÿr and Danior spent a day and a half in pubs talking to the citizens, asking them if they had seen any unusual strangers passing through town lately. Tÿr described the sorcerer to the people she talked to and warned them about him should they ever come across him or his assassins. Most people seemed receptive to her advice and thanked her for her warning. She and Danior agreed that Görne was a very nice place to live.

Unfortunately, no one had seen the sorcerer. Either he hadn't been through town, or he had been in disguise. Tÿr had a feeling that he hadn't been through town because he caused chaos wherever he went, and most people noticed the incredibly tall sorcerer.

Tÿr and Danior walked all through the town and found no one that had seen the sorcerer nor any of his crew, but there was someone in town who knew of Kaistam-Laq. She was an old woman who owned an herb and tonic shop, and she had dealings with the sorcerer before. He had come through the town several years before and had stocked up on several herbs and other unusual things that she sold.

Tÿr thanked the old woman for her information and asked her to let her know if the sorcerer came by again. She gave the woman a small green stone sphere that she could use to signal her if the sorcerer came through town again. All the woman would need to do is pass the sphere through a flame and it would heat a similar sphere that the healer had and she would know that the sorcerer had returned. It was a simple way for her to send a message to someone or vice versa.

There was one more shop in town that they had yet to try. It was a magiqal shop. They sold magiqal items like wands and scrying mirrors and crystal balls. Things that a sorcerer might need at some point. Not every town had a shop that specialized in items like these. Tÿr thought there was a chance that they might have seen the sorcerer. When she walked through the open doors, she was hit in the face by a cloud of thick incense smoke. There were things in jars used in rituals and things used for dark magiq. This was exactly the type of place the sorcerer would visit.

The proprietor of the shop was a wizened old man barely five feet tall. The way he was stooped over, he didn't stand even four feet tall. He walked with a walking stick and was older than the oldest person Tÿr had ever seen. He had a beard that almost touched the ground.

"He's older than dirt," Tÿr whispered to Danior.

"He might be old but he's not deaf." The old man said to the two.

Danior giggled at this.

"I'm sorry," Tÿr said to the old man, "we are looking for someone and were wondering if he may have come in here recently."

"Who might that be?" the old man asked.

"We are looking for a sorcerer." Danior added.

"Kaistam-Laq." The old man said knowingly.

"Yes." Tÿr told him.

"Why would you want to deal with him?" the old man asked.

"He had my brother killed." Danior told him.

"Well, he hasn't been in my shop."

"Do you know if he's been in town?" Tÿr asked.

"I keep to myself, and don't pry into the business of others. I have no idea if he's been in town, but I can point you in the right direction."

It turned out that the right direction was a shop in the next town called Athöl. The wyverns flew them to Athöl and they found the shop that the old man told them about. It too, was a magiq shop. The proprietor, another old man who could have been the other's twin, told them that he hadn't seen the sorcerer for a very long time. He also told them that it was a well-known fact in these parts that the sorcerer often frequented an establishment in the next village over. Tÿr and Danior thanked the old man for his information and left his shop, hopeful that they might find something out in the next village.

The next village they came to was a place called Alaëndäl. It was a larger village than Athöl with many shops and buildings down a main road. They found the shop right where the old man said it would be. They told the proprietor who they were looking for and immediately the owner got silent. He seemed frightened to say anything regarding the sorcerer or his associates. It took them several minutes to even find out that Kaistam-Laq had not even been there for many years. The owner was too frightened of the sorcerer to give any information regarding him or his business. Tÿr had to assure him it was in the strictest of confidence but in the end, he refused to say anything.

"Seems the sorcerer has people too frightened to say much of anything." Danior said.

"He must have some kind of hold over these people." Tÿr agreed.

It was the same no matter where they went in Alaëndäl. No one was willing to speak of the sorcerer. Even the mention of his name was met with hateful stares and cold shoulders. Tÿr figured that the sorcerer must have done something very bad to these people to cause such issues.

"I guess we move on to the next town. No one here is willing to talk." Tÿr told Danior and the wyverns when they had reunited.

"The next town is Voora," Varanus told them.

"Have you ever been there?" Danior asked.

"I have, it is a very small village, much like Vennex only it's on a small lake."

"Maybe we'll have better luck there." Tÿr suggested.

"Perhaps," Qaren'a agreed, "but it seems like this sorcerer has covered his tracks and doesn't wish to be found."

"Are you suggesting that we give up?"

"Not at all," the wyvern said. "I believe it is going to be a very hard and long hunt for the sorcerer. He appears to have disappeared into thin air, but everyone makes a mistake sooner or later."

"Well, on to Voora then," Tÿr said.

Voora only was only an hour's flight away. Tÿr could see the lake as they were coming in to land. It was a beautiful looking town with idyllic homes scattered here and there around the lake. She hoped that they would have better luck gathering information on the sorcerer here than they had in the previous town.

The people of Voora were very curious to see the wyverns landing outside of town. Many gathered as Varanus and Qaren'a landed near the lake. Despite their curiosity, they were friendly and very helpful. Some of the older residents even remembered the time that Varanus had visited. Sadly, for the healers though, none had seen the sorcerer nor any of his assassins.

As it was getting later in the day, Tÿr suggested to Danior that they go to the tavern for a meal while the wyverns hunted. As usual, he was hungry, so they walked to the tavern to grab a quick meal. At the tavern they had a meal of fried fish and chips. Something that neither of them had ever tried before. They both really enjoyed it. They were used to frying their fish in a pan but they had never had it with breading.

When they were done eating, they met back up with the wyverns and decided to camp at the edge of town. Tÿr was beginning to feel like this was going to be a lost cause. She knew that finding the sorcerer was going to be difficult, but to go from town to town without any news of him was getting disheartening. She would not give up as long as Danior wanted to continue the search though.

"What is the next town?" Danior asked the wyverns.

"I believe it is Klaandÿn," Qaren'a said.

"That is correct. It is a larger town than Voora and maybe we'll have better luck. For some reason I believe it is on a direct path to the city of Jaansport. If there is a city to get lost in, that is a city that the sorcerer will choose I believe," Varanus said, "but it is still prudent to check out the towns on the way."

"Well then, on to Klaandÿn," Tÿr said.

"We should be able to make it by nightfall." Varanus told them. "It's not that long of a flight."

The healers mounted their saddles, and the wyverns took off for the town of Klaandÿn. They flew low and fast which pleased Tÿr who preferred to stay low. There were some shouts as they flew over farms, skimming treetops and dodging taller buildings. Many of the people they flew past had never seen a wyvern before, let alone two.

They reached the town of Klaandÿn as the three suns lowered on the horizon. It still was not time for it to be dark yet, but the suns did turn red as they came close to setting. The planets were in the process of wobbling just enough to turn the shift to face the suns during the day and the night. When the planets turned back just a bit, the shift would experience darkened nights and days again, not totally dark but a constant twilight.

Instead of going into town that night, the healers decided to stay on the outskirts and wait until morning. They were tired and wanted to get some rest. Tÿr told Danior that she was so tired that she wasn't even going to eat. Danior had some cheese and bread and ate while Tÿr laid down. They chatted as he ate but then Tÿr fell asleep.

"Varanus, do you think we will ever find the sorcerer?"

"I think we have a good chance." The wyvern told him.

"I just don't want to ask Týr to do this if there is no chance of catching him." Danior said.

"She is fully invested in this search with you, young master." Varanus declared.

"I just don't want her to waste her life on a fruitless search."

"I truly believe we will find Kaistam-Laq. It may take us a while, but in the end, I have a feeling that he will make a mistake and that will be his downfall. People like him are always over-confident with their capability. He overestimates his cleverness and that will contribute to his demise."

This made Danior feel better about their mission. It gave him a new hope and a renewed sense of calling. He would face the sorcerer and he would emerge victorious.

Danior drifted off to sleep after the encouraging words from Varanus. He dreamt of his brother and of times they used to have. They were happy dreams, but when he awoke in the morning, he missed his brother even more. Gordian hadn't been gone that long, but the hurt was still fresh. He was glad that he still had Týr with him. If anything happened to her, he didn't know what he would do. He reached his hand out to feel for hers. When he found it, he squeezed it gently.

Týr stirred. "Good morning," she said.

"Good morning."

"What's up?"

"Just missing Gordi a bit."

Tÿr brought his hand to her mouth and kissed it.

"I know what you mean. I miss him too."

"I was just worried about something happening to you." Dani said.

"Don't worry about me. I'll be around forever. Besides, I've got to look out for you." She told him.

"And I will look out for you." He replied back to her.

She squeezed his hand.

"We can find an inn in town and eat something there. That way we don't waste any more time out here." Tÿr suggested.

"That sounds good to me." Danior told her.

"We will stay outside of town and wait here. We will hunt during the afternoon, but one of us will stay close enough to hear your whistle should you need us." Varanus told them.

"We will be back later this afternoon," Tÿr told the wyverns.

The two healers walked off toward town. Danior held Tÿr's arm in one hand and his staff in the other. Tÿr carried her staff as well. The two healers looked out of place as they walked into town. They were dressed in their normal garb, the clothing of Vennex folk which was very different from the clothing the people of Klaandÿn wore. The clothing that the locals wore was long and flowing whereas the clothing that the people from Vennex wore was tight fitting. The colors of the locals were more subdued, but the clothes of the people from Vennex were much brighter. Needless to say, Tÿr and Danior stuck out when they walked into town.

"People are staring at us." Tÿr told Danior.

"Why?"

"We look out of place."

"They'll get over it." Danior said.

People stopped and stared and pointed at them, but Tÿr kept walking. She just smiled at the people and looked for the inn. There were two in town, and she headed toward the larger of the two.

The inn grew silent as the two healers walked in. They found a table and sat while the patrons inside stared at them. The proprietor, a handsome lady, came over to them and asked what they would like to eat. Tÿr told her that they would take two breakfasts, and she shuffled off to the kitchen to place the order. If the lady found the two out of place, she never showed it.

Breakfast came to the table a little while later and there was more food than the two of them could possibly eat. The portions were huge, and even Danior couldn't finish his. When they were finished, Tÿr paid the lady and gave her a nice tip on top of the fee. The lady thanked them profusely and told them to come back any time.

When they came out of the inn, there was a crowd gathered outside.

"I smell trouble," Tÿr muttered to Danior.

"Why, what's up?"

"Get your whistle ready."

Danior reached into his shirt and pulled out his whistle. Tÿr did the same.

A tough looking man stepped forward from the crowd.

"What is your business in our town?" he asked gruffly.

"Just passing through." Tÿr told him.

"What's his deal?" he asked pointing to Danior.

"He's blind."

"Doesn't he speak?"

"He does." Danior said.

"He's a wise ass then." The man said.

"Look, we don't want any trouble. We came here to eat, and we intend to leave here just as we came. Peacefully." Tÿr told the large man and the group that had gathered.

"I noticed that you haven't paid the tax for passing through our town."

"Tax? What tax?" Danior asked.

The brute chuckled. "Everyone that passes through my town pays me a fee."

"That is ridiculous." Danior said.

"I happen to know you paid the innkeeper her fee, now you can pay me mine."

Some of the others began to move around the two of them. Obviously mates of this brute. Tÿr held her staff at the ready but knew that they were outnumbered.

"Whistle." She whispered to Danior.

Both of them put their whistles in their mouths and blew.

The brute laughed. "What do you think you just did? Your whistles don't seem to have worked." He took a step forward.

"Stay away from her." Danior told him.

"Or what little man? You're blind and it doesn't look like you're in a position to give any type of order."

Danior turned to the large man. He had called on the power of his staff. The top of it began to glow. The man paused for a moment.

"What kind of magiq is this?" he asked.

A couple more of the crowd stepped forward to join the man.

"Dani, there are more." Tÿr whispered.

"How many?"

"Three."

Tÿr lit her staff too. The man took another step back.

Then Danior heard what he had been waiting for. The flapping of wings. They were still a little ways away, but they were on the way. He blew on the whistle again.

The large man laughed. "Boy your whistle doesn't work."

"No, but this staff does. One step closer and you will find out how well."

The smile left the man's face. He was no longer in the mood to joke around. He was mad and now the boy had made him look foolish in front of his people and friends. The man decided that the threat wasn't real and stepped at Danior and Tÿr. A mistake he would regret almost instantly.

"Now!" Tÿr yelled.

Both healers let a bolt of energy fly at the brute at the same time. Danior's hit him in the chest and Tÿr's hit him on the forehead at the exact same time. He flew backwards and landed on his backside in the dirt. He sat there stunned for several seconds before trying to get back up. His cronies had stepped back, they were not anxious to tangle with something that could do that to them. Some more of the crowd moved in on them. Apparently they figured that they couldn't attack all of them at the same time.

"Put your weapons down." Someone yelled to them.

"Do not relinquish your staffs!" came a voice from above.

The crowd looked up and the blood drained from the faces of the men who had come after the healers. The two wyverns were descending on the crowd, and they didn't know what to do. Varanus and Qaren'a dropped down in front of the men who had come after the healers. Their bravery had melted away and they ran as fast as their feet would move them. The large man that had tried to intimidate the healers in the first place backed up slowly.

"Why are you harassing these two people? They are healers and are of no harm to any of you."

No one said a word. The wyverns sat and stared around the crowd. When no one responded at all, Varanus told the healers that it was time to leave. They climbed aboard and then they were gone.

They flew for a good portion of the morning before they stopped for a rest. Tÿr wanted to get down and walk around for a bit. That is when Varanus told the two healers that they would be passing over a mountain, and that there could be an issue. "We will be entering the domain of a wyvern called Nagarr Zmaj. This wyvern is powerful and not friendly toward humans."

"Couldn't we go around the mountain?" Danior asked.

"We could but it would take us out of our way by a day or more." Qaren'a told him.

"It would be best if we just flew straight through as fast as we can. We may need to fly higher than normal." Varanus said.

"If you think that is best, then we will do it." Tÿr said. She did not look forward to flying that high, but she looked forward to an encounter with a rogue wyvern even less.

The humans grabbed a quick lunch and then they were ready to get back in the air. The wyverns figured that they would hit the mountain with three peaks after dinner. They hoped that Nagarr Zmaj would be done hunting when they passed over. They hoped he would be in a den by that time.

Flying high had its advantages. There was less flapping and more gliding. Tÿr enjoyed the gliding times despite the heights that they were approaching. Danior loved flying and was very good at it. He was a relaxed flyer and with his saddle he was able to decompress from the stresses of the day and just fly. He had no worries up here, he let the wyvern take charge and he went where it led him.

Tÿr was a bit more nervous as she flew. She never realized how heights bothered her until she got up on the back of Varanus. When she was on a mountain, at least she had the ground under her feet. Up here there was nothing between her and a long, long drop. It made her stomach tie in knots, and her feet tingle.

As evening approached, the three peaks of the mountain appeared on the horizon. Varanus began to descend and Qaren'a followed. The wyverns brought the party to land with the mountain still off in the distance.

"Why did we land?" Tÿr asked.

"We need to fly over the mountain lower than we were. The air currents up high are strong and will buffet us more than if we stay low. I just wanted to prepare you because we are going to be flying low and fast. We also run the risk of a confrontation with Nagarr Zmaj. If this happens, let Qaren'a and I deal with the wyvern, you stay back and try to remain hidden if possible."

They got back underway and were near the mountain in no time. The wyverns increased their altitude, and they began to ascend the mountain. Varanus went to fly between the highest and the middle peaks. A roar from below split the air.

Varanus veered to the left and dropped down. Qaren'a followed him closely as they dove toward the side of the mountain. In just moments the wyverns had landed and were scanning the sky for Nagarr Zmaj.

"Get to cover!" Varanus barked to the healers.

The two humans ran to a crag in the side of the mountain. It protected them from an attack from above, so they were safe for now.

Another bellow sounded. And another. Tÿr risked a glance out of the protective overhang. She saw a huge wyvern swooping down to attack Varanus and Qaren'a. The wyvern was larger than Varanus and she noticed that his wings were in bad shape. They had been damaged in a fight recently. That was its weak point.

Tÿr stepped out with her staff and aimed at the Nagarr Zmaj. A beam of energy shot from the head of the staff and ripped through the wyvern's wing. It glanced around to see where the attack had come from, but the healer had stepped back under the overhang.

The wyvern shrieked with fury. It attacked Varanus with a ball of fire from its open mouth. Varanus managed to dodge the fireball and called one up of his own. He shot fire at Zmaj who was hit on the hind quarters. It did no real damage as a wyvern is protected by thick skin and armored scales. The place to wound a wyvern is its wings.

Tÿr shot another blast from her staff and another energy bolt shot through the wyvern's wing, tearing an even larger hole in it. The wyvern was having an issue flying now.

"Get out of there!" Varanus yelled.

Tÿr grabbed Danior and the two of them ran from the overhang towards another crag in the side of the mountain. This left them wide open for a moment. The rogue wyvern noticed them running and began to come after them. Varanus amped up his attacks on the wyvern and blasted him with two huge balls of fire. Qaren'a hit him in the left wing, tearing a new hole in it. The two wyverns had accomplished what they had set out to do, distract Nagarr Zmaj. This had allowed the healers to escape to a new recess in the rocks.

"Why do you attack me?" Zmaj bellowed.

"You attacked us." Varanus replied.

"I thought you had come back to finish me off."

"We have not been here before." Tÿr said.

"Do not lie to me."

"She speaks the truth. Who attacked you?" Varanus asked Nagarr Zmaj.

"A powerful magiq user and a band of assassins."

"Kaistam-Laq." Varanus said with disgust. "We are on a quest to find this sorcerer and bring him to justice."

"Well, he has passed through here. I thought you were him coming back to finish me off. He left here several days ago. He is headed toward Peyda Kirin."

"Perhaps we can help you," Varanus told the wyvern.

"How can you help me?"

"I have the best healers in the land, they can help to mend your wings."

Nagarr Zmaj was very leery. He obviously didn't trust many people or anyone for that matter.

"I will heal in time." He told Varanus.

"Please let us make up our misunderstanding. We can do this and then leave you in peace."

After a bit of persuading Nagarr Zmaj agreed to let Tÿr and Danior tend to his wounded wings. He was cautious about having them use their staffs to heal him, but in the end, he allowed them to get near enough to touch him and mend his wings. They put their hands on his wings and with the aid of their staffs, the tears in the wings began to mend. It took an hour but when they were done, his wings were whole again. The ragged looking wings had no more holes in them and were strong once more.

"You are welcome to visit my mountain at any time." He told the healers.

"And you are welcome to visit us in Vennex at any time too." Tÿr told the wyvern.

"You are superb healers, both of you."

"Thank you Nagarr Zmaj." Tÿr told him.

"We must get going now. We have to try to catch the sorcerer. If he is moving on to Peyda Kirin, we should try to catch him before he reaches the planet." Varanus said.

"Hopefully we can reach him by the time he makes Jaansport." Qaren'a said.

"That would be ideal." Varanus agreed.

The wyvern's wings had healed and looked good and strong to Tÿr. She was satisfied with her work and Nagarr Zmaj had full movement. The healers bid the wyvern goodbye and then mounted their rides and took off toward Jaansport. Varanus and Qaren'a stayed low against the mountain until they cleared it, and then they climbed higher where the currents were less violent.

It was getting late when a small town appeared below the travelers. Varanus began to descend toward the town and Qaren'a followed behind him. It took them several minutes before they reached the town and landed just on the outskirts near a pub. Several people standing outside of the pub saw them land. They moved forward to see what was happening as they landed.

Tÿr could tell that many of the people that had gathered there had been drinking quite a bit. Some held each other up as they stood there. Others sat down as soon as they landed. Most everyone was just curious to see the wyverns. It was obvious to Tÿr that none of the people gathered there had ever seen one before.

Tÿr walked up to the crowd that had gathered there and asked if the magistrate was around.

"I am the magistrate here in Fendish." A man said, walking out if the pub. "What business do you have with me?"

"I am actually looking for your healer. Could you point me in the right direction?"

"I'm afraid our town has no healer." The magistrate said.

"Where do your sick go then?" Tÿr asked.

"We go into Jaansport if we need healing," he told her.

"Isn't that a long trip?"

"That's where the healer is." He said simply.

"We are healers," Tÿr told him, pointing to Danior and herself. "If any of your people are in need of healing, we would be willing to see them."

"What's going on?" Danior asked her.

"I'm trying to make an ally." She whispered.

"I will spread the news," the magistrate told them, "You may use our town hall for an office."

"We will begin in the morning and end at evening time." Tÿr told him. "We have a schedule to keep to, but we can spare a day here to help you. May we join you for an ale this evening?"

The townsfolk were happy to have the healers in town and glad to buy them a glass of ale. Tÿr and Danior told them about the sorcerer and their quest to find him. The citizens were outraged about what had happened to Danior's brother. They also vowed to keep an eye out for Kaistam-Laq and his crew. Tÿr gave the magistrate another of her little spheres and told him to pass it through a flame if he came across the sorcerer. Instead of a green one, this was a small blue one. That way she could keep track of them. She still had two more spheres that she could give out, but she wanted to make sure they went to the right people.

The healers asked where the best place to spend the night was, and the magistrate pointed them to a small inn.

Tÿr wanted to get their belongings to the inn before they had a drink. She and Dani got settled in at the inn and then headed out for a drink or two. The wyverns were still at the pub answering questions for the people. They were fascinated by the large creatures as none of them had ever seen a wyvern in person.

Neither Tÿr nor Danior had to buy a drink that night, the people of Fendish were happy to buy them round after round. When Danior's head began to spin, he told Tÿr that he needed to go back to the inn. She agreed with him and they made their apologies to the people who were sad to see them go, but they understood that they were going to be up in the morning healing them.

In the morning the two healers got their bags and headed to the town hall. There was already a line there when they arrived. Varanus and Qaren'a also went to help with any cases that they might not be able to manage. Luckily, there were none that day. Most of the cases were minor illnesses. There were a few broken bones that needed to be mended and other than that, it was basic medicine. Tÿr felt good about being able to help the people of Fendish. The people were very grateful to have the healers in town.

When they finished with the clinic, they decided to go back to the pub. They would spend one more night in Fendish and leave first thing in the morning.

They rose early in the morning and got their belongings together. The magistrate was there to send them off. He thanked them again for their assistance with the sick. Tÿr and Danior told him that they were happy to help and then they took off for the town of Jaansport. Varanus figured that they would be traveling most of the day. The wyverns flew high and fast and rode the air currents whenever they could.

By late afternoon, the large city of Jaansport came into view. It was a sprawling city that wrapped around a river. It had large buildings everywhere; unlike the smaller towns the healers had been to recently. Despite the late hour, there was activity everywhere they looked.

People walking around, horses pulling carts and wagons here and there. There were stalls selling wares everywhere they looked. The city was a bustling metropolis and right through the heart of it ran a crystal-clear river.

The wyverns sat down outside of town so the healers could walk in. They had a lot of area to cover and many shops to visit. If the sorcerer had been here, they would find out and hopefully find where he had gone. If he was still here, Tÿr would have to prepare herself for a showdown between herself and him. Every time she thought of what happened to her friend, she felt rage like she had never felt before. She would have revenge for Gordian, and it would happen one day soon.

Tÿr lead Danior through the streets to the first shop. It was a shop that sold magiqal supplies and items for making potions. The owner said that the sorcerer had not been in the shop recently, but she would keep her eyes open for him. Tÿr gave her one of the spheres that she could use to alert her if he came into the shop. Tÿr had one more sphere left to hand out.

The two healers spent the day going from shop to shop asking for information on the sorcerer. Many people had rumors that he was near, but nothing solid. They knew that he was supposed to be in the area, but none of them had seen him, or if they had, they were too frightened to say it. Kaistam-Laq instilled fear wherever he went, and his assassins were just as bad.

The healers began to feel like they were not getting anywhere. They had been to every magiq shop in the city and they were getting ready to hit the pubs and taverns. The wyverns suggested that they try some of the seedier places. The smaller, out of the way pubs. They told them that maybe the sorcerer wanted to stay out of sight and visited some of the smaller places. Tÿr didn't think that was Kaistam-Laq's style. He was flashy and liked to be seen.

People were not eager to talk about the sorcerer. He had them frightened and it was evident that they were going to be a challenge. Some of the people in the pubs talked more when they had been plied with alcohol. Still, no one seemed to know where the sorcerer was. Eventually one person suggested that they go to the healer in town and check with him. He might have information about the sorcerer.

Tÿr and Danior left the pub and looked for the healer's clinic. It was located in the center of the town. There were several people standing in line to be seen, so the pair of them queued up and waited their turn. It took them an hour to be seen but the information they received was well worth the wait.

The healer told them that Kaistam-Laq had indeed been in the city. He had been through Jaansport just recently. In fact, he had been through the area just a day or two before them and had caused chaos in his wake. The healer did not get into details, but he did mention that more than one person from town had gone missing. This, Tÿr guessed, was why no one was talking. Fear that the sorcerer would come back.

Tÿr asked if the healer could tell her who had disappeared. He told her that he knew of two people and that he could put her in touch with their families but not to expect much from them. The families were so scared of the sorcerer and retribution from talking that he doubted that they would say anything to Tÿr. Still, Tÿr had to try.

When Kaistam-Laq arrived in Jaansport he and his assassins entered the town in disguises. Even though they wore disguises, most everyone in town recognized the sorcerer immediately. He stood head and shoulders above most everyone else in town, and he still carried his staff of power. That was one thing he refused to travel without.

Most all of the citizens in town gave the sorcerer and his entourage a wide berth. They avoided him at all costs. But the vendors in Jaansport were another story. They were happy to see the money he flashed around and spent at their establishments. He was extravagant and spent money on things that the citizens normally did not. Things like fine linens and jewelry. He bought new blankets for his horses, and a gold hilted dagger with a large emerald in the pommel that he now wore at his waist. He bought a new set of robes that were blood red and stood out wherever he went.

As he walked down the streets of Jaansport people stopped and stared at him. He was a sight to behold with his staff which was seven feet tall and topped with a serpent bent over a large ruby. His red robes billowed out behind him as he strode down the streets, a royal purple sash at his waist, and the same blood red colored leather boots. He was not hiding anymore; he was there to intimidate. His entourage walked close behind him, all carrying weapons ready to kill at a moment's notice. All it would take is one word from their leader.

Kaistam-Laq was not ready to kill yet. He was in town to recruit. He was still down a member of his crew, and he needed to fill the spot, quickly. He sent his people out to the taverns and pubs to begin the tedious task of finding a new assassin. They were to observe people to see how they acted in a crowd.

Renner and Ollis-Van found a woman that was proficient with short blades. She could throw a knife as well as wield it in a combat situation. She could also use a sword. When she was presented to Kaistam-Laq, he accepted her immediately. The new assassin was called Deljaa-Elck and she was happy to join the crew.

The new assassin was given a task to perform. Assassinate a person in Jaansport. It could not be just anyone either. It had to be a city official or someone of importance. Renner-Van and his sister would be witnesses to the affair and report back to the sorcerer. Then and only then would she be allowed into the crew.

Deljaa-Elck accepted the task and set off to accomplish it immediately. Renner and Ollis followed in her shadow. They stayed a short distance away from her but close enough to observe everything that she did. She moved like a fox, swift and light on her feet. She was agile and fast, and the councilmember that she snuck up on never saw her coming.

The man was alone, walking home from a day at the council, he had books and scrolls under one arm and a walking stick in the other. Deljaa-Elck struck fast and hard. She hit him from behind and slit his throat before he even knew someone was with him. He dropped his belongings to bring his hands up to his neck, but it did no good. His lifeforce oozed out between his fingers. He tried to yell but he couldn't find his voice. The assassin stepped in front of him and watched him die. She snatched a gold necklace from his neck as proof that she had killed him.

Renner-Van and his sister stepped out of the shadows and joined the other assassin.

"You have done well." He told her.

She nodded in acknowledgement.

"Come, let's go meet our master," Renner said.

The three left the body in the street and turned to go back in the direction of the town center.

They found Kaistam-Laq in town and the brother and sister told him of the woman's expertise. She gave the sorcerer the necklace that she had taken from the body. He was enthusiastic and wanted to see her work firsthand. She agreed and she and the sorcerer left the brother and sister to go out on another killing mission.

Kaistam stayed hidden while the assassin looked for her next victim. To prove her worth, she brought him back to where she had killed the councilmember. There was now a small crowd gathered around the place. A few law officers were there telling people to move on and that there was nothing to see. Of course, that just made people more curious.

A single officer was walking back toward town and that is when the assassin took her cue to attack. She ran up behind him and before he knew what was happening, she slit his throat with a quick slice of her dagger. He tried to yell but she had cut through his voice box and windpipe. The officer dropped to his knees and died right where he was. The assassin ran back to join the sorcerer. Together they hustled away from the murder site. As they moved away, they heard a scream signaling that the body had been found.

Kaistam told the assassin that he had seen enough to be impressed with her work. He told her that he would be honored if she joined him. Deljaa-Elck paused before answering, and then told the sorcerer that she would be pleased to join his crew.

Kaistam-Laq had been holding his staff at the ready in case the assassin declined his offer. Had she declined, he would have had to destroy her, which would have disappointed him. Such talent was rare.

Together they walked back to join the other assassins. Kaistam had already made his mind up and had chosen Deljaa-Elck as the replacement. He did not need to see any more candidates. She was fast and deadly and that was what he needed in his crew. Renner and Ollis joined them on the walk back to join the others. As the four walked down the street, people parted and moved away from them.

Kaistam-Laq strode through the streets with his assassins behind him. The seventeen were now complete and he was ready to begin his search for the healer once more. He had gotten his supplies in town now and he was ready to carry on with his mission to destroy Tÿr'Ynyn. He knew if he did not destroy her, that she would eventually be his downfall. What he did not know was at this very moment she was searching for him.

Together with his assassins he would go back to his encampment. He needed to use his scrying mirror to try to find the location of the healer. It hadn't worked in the past, but he was confident that his magiq was stronger now and that he would be able to seek her out. He was at full power with his team now and being at seventeen provided him with powerful magiq.

The four of them got back to the sorcerer's camp and Kaistam-Laq went into his tent and told them he was not to be disturbed. He retrieved his obsidian scrying mirror and put it on the table in front of him. He sat down after lighting incense and the circular candelabra. He began to scry on the mirror, trying to find the healer. He drew a glyph on the mirror with his long fingernail. It glowed orange before fading away. Then he drew another. The mirror sparked and sputtered, and smoke rose from the surface.

"Show me the healer!" he shouted to the mirror.

Nothing happened.

He drew another glyph across the mirror. This time he held his hand over the surface of the mirror and small sparks of lightning shot between his open hand and the mirror.

"Show me the healer!" he almost screamed.

Then the mirror swirled with a hint of a shadow. The sorcerer looked at it closely, trying to see what it was showing him. He was frustrated because the picture was distorted and unclear. He put his hand back over the mirror and more sparks shot from his palm.

"The healer! Show me the healer!"

The image on the mirror got clearer but it wasn't the one he was hoping for. It was a male face. Not Tÿr'Ynyn. He came close to smashing the mirror, but calmed himself down. He breathed in the incense and chanted to himself. Kaistam knew the face in the mirror but couldn't place it off the top of his head. It would come to him.

If the mirror wouldn't show the healer, perhaps it would give her location. Again he drew glyphs across the surface, and again it sparkled alive. He watched as a scene appeared before him. It looked to be a tavern. Of course, it could be any tavern in Jaansport or in any town on the shift or on Peyda Kirin. The sorcerer felt defeated right then.

The thing the sorcerer had to do now was to visit every tavern and pub to find where the healer had been. There was a time restraint to work with, because he didn't know how long she would be in Jaansport if in fact she was here. He couldn't send any of his people to search because none of them had seen the mirror nor the scene of the face in it. He did send his people out in search of the healer, but he had a feeling that they would all come up short. None of them had ever dealt with her so none of them had ever seen her.

By the end of the day, the search came up short. No one had found the healer or her companion. The sorcerer decided that they would move on to the planet from there. It would be another long trip, but he had exhausted all of his resources here in Jaansport. Maybe Peyda Kirin would pan out for him.

The sorcerer figured that the murders that his new assassin had committed would raise red flags soon so he got out of town with his crew and got moving toward the planet. If any of the crew was against the idea of moving on, they kept it to themselves. Disagreements with the sorcerer never went well.

The new assassin, Deljaa-Elck fit in with the others on the team. She pulled her own weight as far as the move went. She helped with the tearing down of the tents and the packing up. She was there for all of it and she volunteered to keep watch as they rode out. The others were impressed with how well she fit in with the crew. It was as if she had been with them the whole time. The sorcerer couldn't have been more pleased with his choice.

Deljaa-Elck too, was pleased at how the crew was making her feel like family. They had gone out of their way to allow her to join in their activities in the organization.

Renner and Ollis-Van had already asked her if she would like to be a part of their tent group. Normally the brother and sister didn't share their tent with anyone, but they found the new assassin to be charismatic and very skillful and they wanted her with them. She was happy to have found friends this quick, and readily accepted the offer to be tentmates.

Renner-Van and his sister rode with the new assassin in the front of the procession. They were constantly scanning the horizon for trouble, but it remained open and desolate. In ten hours of riding, they only passed a few people and there were none that posed a threat to the small caravan. They passed a few traveling vendors and some weary travelers like themselves. Most were poor travelers, not even worth their time to steal from. Kaistam-Laq made sure to tell the crew to avoid any conflicts if at all possible. If it wasn't possible, get it over as quickly as they could and try not to let many people witness it. Yes, they were assassins, but there was no reason just to kill people for being in the wrong place at the wrong time.

The brother and sister took this time to try to get to know the new recruit. As they rode, they asked her questions about her past. Things like where she was from and what she had been doing for the past year. Deljaa-Elck was happy to answer their questions because she knew they were probably getting answers for their boss. She told them that she was originally from a town on the planet of Peyda Noirin, the ocean planet; that she had come to the shift when she was very young. Her parents were both dead, and she had been on her own for over ten years. She managed by stealing and doing odd jobs when she could.

The new assassin told the siblings that she had been in the care of an older gentleman but when he got inappropriate with her, she killed him and left the ocean planet to come to the shift. She hadn't been back since, nor did she want to go back. She told them that she made her first kill when she was only eleven years old. From then on it just got easier. Until this very day, she sold herself out as a freelance assassin to whomever would pay her fees.

Renner asked her if she could perform any magiq. She replied that she was afraid that she couldn't. She did ask if that would be a problem. Renner told her that they would work with her to try to teach her basic magiq to aid in her assassinating skills. Things like making her blend into the background of a scene, or allowing her to disappear altogether. Renner told her that neither he nor his sister could do that yet, but it was something they were working on. They did have the ability to melt into the background and become unseen. Only the sorcerer could completely disappear. He was teaching the siblings the magiq to do that, and then they would teach others in the crew when they learned it. They did know things like sleight of hand which came in useful when dealing with merchants and other salespeople that they were cheating out of their goods. They also used this talent on the street corners by running confidence games. It didn't make much money, but when a person ran the bets up, it could bring in a little fortune. Then they would have to run before the constabulary arrived.

Most people didn't complain about the assassins because they knew that their leader was the famous Kaistam-Laq. They knew that if they did complain there would be more trouble than they wanted to deal with. There was only one other assassin sect that was feared more than Kaistam-Laq's Murtair Amagii, and that was the Amsälja Vrasës. They were the most feared in the land and most people only discussed them in hushed voices.

They had only been traveling two days when the sorcerer pulled the caravan to a stop. He had been scrying the night before and the mirror told him that the person he sought would be seeking him. He thought that they should slow things down and wait to see what happened. If the healer was seeking him, he figured that they would be close behind. He posted guards behind them for several miles. Then when the healer appeared he would nab her and destroy her once and for all.

Tÿr and Danior left Jaansport to go to Peyda Kirin. Tÿr discussed it with the wyverns and Danior and they all figured that if they hadn't found the sorcerer in any of the towns that they had passed through, he must be on the planet. There was no other explanation, he must be on Peyda Kirin.

Towns were far apart on the planet and water was scarce. The desert planet was a harsh climate to live in and Tÿr and Danior had to adjust to survive there. Their clothes were not made for a warm climate like Peyda Kirin. Their clothes were tight fitting, and the desert people wore loose, billowing clothing.

Tÿr and Danior landed late in the day in a town called Villsen. It was the first town they came to on the planet. The town was not large, but it had a population of over two hundred and a very nice tavern. The pair spent a couple of hours in the tavern having a meal and a few drinks. It was a nice way to wind down the day. Varanus and Qaren'a spent their time hunting in the desert for anything they could find.

When the pair was done at the tavern, they went out to find the wyverns. Varanus and Qaren'a were at the edge of town, waiting for the healers.

"Did you find enough to eat?" Tÿr asked Varanus.

"We ate our fill," he replied.

"Are you sure? We could always get you something here in town."

"I am certain." He told her. "Qaren'a?" He asked the other wyvern.

"I am fine." She said.

"If it is okay with you, I think we will stay in town tonight," Tÿr told the wyverns.

"I have no issues with that." Varanus told her.

Tÿr and Danior gathered a few things they would need for the night and then went back into town. They found the inn and took a room. It only had one bed. Danior offered to sleep on the floor but Tÿr told him not to be ridiculous.

"We are small and can share it."

"Only if you're certain."

"Of course, I am."

The two got settled in their room and laid down in the bed.

"I've never shared a bed with anyone before," Tÿr told Danior.

"You get used to it. Gordian was a cover hog. I used to wake up freezing my butt off."

"Well, I will try not to do that." Tÿr told him, chuckling.

"If you do, I'll just snuggle up with you." Danior stated simply.

Tÿr blushed. She was glad her friend couldn't see her face.

Danior pulled the covers up over the two of them.

"Goodnight." He said.

"Goodnight."

Tÿr reached over and kissed Danior on the forehead.

It was his turn to blush.

Both friends lay awake for quite some time before falling asleep. They were both thinking about their mission and each other. They hadn't been this close to each other before. The funny thing was it wasn't that uncomfortable. This was the first time that either of them had thought of each other as more than just a brother or sister figure. Eventually sleep set in and they got a good night's rest. In the morning they were snuggled up together like they belonged there.

Danior was the first to wake in the morning. He woke up with his arms around Tÿr. He tried to move away from her without waking her, but without success.

"Hey," she said to him as he rolled away from her.

"Hey."

"Sorry if I crowded you last night," he told her.

"You were fine." She said. "I didn't steal the covers, did I?"

"No, I don't think so. I fell asleep and slept pretty hard."

The two made small talk as they got ready to leave. Both were surprised at how comfortable they were with each other. Of course, they had been friends their whole lives so it wasn't that big of surprise. Neither mentioned the fact that they woke up in each other's arms though.

They went out to find the wyverns where they left them. Varanus commented that there was a glow in their faces that wasn't there before. Tÿr glanced at Danior who was blushing. She was sure that there was red in her cheeks too. Neither said anything about it.

"Okay, where is the next town in our search?" Danior asked the wyverns?

"I believe the next town we will come to is Cänbry." Varanus told him.

"What do we know about it?" Tÿr asked.

"I'm afraid I don't know that much about Cänbry," Varanus started. "I do know it has a sister city called Callidon down the Auritar River from it. It is a very small river which is rich with fish and other wildlife."

"How far away is Cänbry?"

"We should be able to reach it in about eight hours or so."

"Do you think we'll find the sorcerer?"

"I think we'll find him eventually. He is used to hiding, and I don't think he is looking forward to a confrontation with you." Varanus told her.

"I'm not looking forward to that confrontation either." Tÿr admitted.

"I want him dead." Danior said with very little emotion in his voice. "He killed my brother, and he *will* pay for it."

"Dani, I will make him pay for Gordian." Tÿr told him.

"I know you will. I love you for that too, but I want to be the one that kills him. I want to do it for Gordian."

"Then I will help you to do whatever it takes." Tÿr said.

Tÿr felt a deep kinship for Danior right then. If anything happened to him, she didn't know what she would do. Losing Gordian was hard but if she lost Dani she would be devastated. He was her rock as much as she was his.

They got packed up and were ready to head off for Cänbry. They flew high and fast on the currents and the trip took eight hours just as the wyverns had predicted. They landed outside of the town and the two healers walked in. It was a lot different from Villsen. Where Villsen was dry and desert like, Cänbry was green and full of life, an oasis in the desert.

Cänbry, it turned out, was a thriving farming community built in the middle of the desert. They raised cattle and Zea tricasia a wetland food that everyone ate back in Vennex. Tÿr was looking forward to having some Z-Tri, as it was called, when they found a place to eat. Back in Vennex most people ate it for the morning meal, but in other places they ate it for any meal. Tÿr hoped that this was one of those places. It wasn't especially flavorful, but with some fruit or meat cut up in it, it was quite tasty. She knew Danior would enjoy it too.

They found a pub on the edge of town and entered. They got some odd looks at first, but mostly people ignored them. They seemed to be happy to be ignored by the newcomers. Tÿr and Danior found an empty table near the bar and sat down. The barmaid, a young girl, came over to take their order. They both ordered a glass of ale and a bowl of Z-tri with some wild hog strips and pears in rum syrup.

As soon as the Z-tri came they tore up the strips of wild hog and put it in the bowl with the mash.

"This takes me back to Vennex," Danior said.

"Yeah, to mum's kitchen." Tÿr said, nodding.

"I hope we get back to see them."

"We will."

"We aren't on a wild goose chase, are we?" Danior asked.

"It might seem like it sometimes, but we need to do this. We need to finish this and stop the sorcerer. Kaistam-Laq will continue to hurt people if no one stops him." She said.

They continued to talk about how they were going to defeat the sorcerer and his crew of assassins. They knew they were vastly outnumbered but with the help of the wyverns they had a shot.

"Do you want to stay in town or camp out with the wyverns?" Tÿr asked Danior.

"It doesn't matter to me. We can share a room again if you'd like." Secretly Danior was excited to be sharing the room with Tÿr again. He'd never say anything, but he enjoyed the last night they spent together.

When they were done eating, they went back to find the wyverns and let them know that they would be staying in town again. The wyverns were agreeable to this, so the two healers walked back into town to find an inn to stay in for the night.

They found the local inn which was a small run down place, but it was clean so they got a room and once again there was only one bed. Danior's heart leapt at the thought of sharing the bed with his friend again.

"We could get separate rooms if you'd be more comfortable," Danior told Tÿr.

"Don't be silly. We can share a bed again. I'm fine with it if you are."

Danior got a smile on his face.

"What's that smile for?"

"Am I smiling?"

"You are." She said, smiling back.

"I didn't realize that I was." He fibbed.

"Well let's get to bed," Tÿr said, "we have another long day tomorrow."

The two climbed into bed and got situated. Tÿr pulled the covers over them and said goodnight. Danior hugged her and then turned back over on his back. He was smiling again. He really enjoyed spending time with Tÿr, even if it was to hunt down a murderer.

When morning came, Danior was the first to rise. He rolled over and remembered that he was sharing a bed with Tÿr. He lay still trying not to wake her. He knew she was tired, and she needed her sleep.

Tÿr woke up a short while later.

"Hey, how long have you been up?"

"Not long." He told her. "Where are we heading next?"

"I think it's a town called Callidon. It's just down the river from here."

"I'm thinking we'll have some fish tonight then." Danior suggested.

"You're already thinking with your stomach?" Tÿr asked.

"Of course, I am. You know me."

The two got up and went to find the wyverns. They found them at the edge of town.

"Good morning young masters." Varanus said to the healers.

"Good morning." Danior replied back to the wyvern.

"Are you ready to move down the river?" Varanus asked.

"We are." Tÿr told him.

They were packed and left soon after. A short flight later and they landed in Callidon. It was a very similar town to Cänbry. There were many docks with fishermen out fishing on them and there were also many farms speckled around the town.

The healers went around the town and asked if anyone had seen the sorcerer. He had not been in town in a very long time. In fact many of the younger people didn't even know who the healers were talking about. The older generation knew of the sorcerer and were not pleased to hear the name. Kaistam-Laq was a name that was synonymous with torture and hatred.

"How about grabbing something to eat," Danior suggested.

"You and your stomach." Tÿr teased.

"Hey, I'm a growing boy."

"Yeah, yeah," she smiled.

The two found a pub that served a nice fish fry up and Z-Tri with fruit. It was a nice meal and the two were incredibly full when they left the pub. Tÿr suggested that they go for a walk after their meal. Danior agreed to this so they walked up and down the river. Instead of holding her arm like he normally did, he held her hand.

Tÿr watched the fishermen cast their nets in the water and pull them back out loaded with fish. There were fishermen all up and down the river. The rest of the river was surrounded by Z-Tri farms. There were a few shops in town, shops like a net mender, and a farm equipment store, a blacksmith and of course a general store. There were two pubs and an inn.

The pair walked around the town and then headed back to find the wyverns.

"I think we will spend the night out here," Tÿr told Danior.

"Sounds good to me."

"Did you find any new of the sorcerer?" Varanus asked.

"Nothing." Tÿr told him.

"Perhaps we have gotten ahead of him." Qaren'a offered.

"That is a possibility." Varanus said.

"What do you suggest we do?" Asked Tÿr.

"Maybe we should stay put for a few days. If the sorcerer is behind us, we can catch him unaware and attack him before he has a chance to organize his crew."

"Agreed." Tÿr said. "We need to come up with plan of attack."

"I want to be able to help." Danior said.

"We will find a way to let you." Varanus told him.

"I want to be the one to destroy the sorcerer. He had my brother killed so I want revenge on him."

"Just don't waste all of your energy on him. You have more important things to do than spend your days hating that man."

Danior nodded.

"I swear I will help you get revenge on him." Tÿr told her friend. "I want to see him fall too. He took Gordi from me as well."

"Let's get set up for the night." Danior said.

"Do we want a tent, or shall we sleep under the stars?" Tÿr asked.

"There's no need for a tent." Danior told her. "We will be fine under the stars. "It doesn't look like rain, does it?"

"No, it's perfectly clear out. We should be fine."

The two got out their bedrolls and prepared themselves for bed. It was early but they were both tired. They had no place to be in the morning, so they slept in. When they finally woke in the morning, they went to the pub for a late morning meal. They both had a bowl of Z-Tri and wild hog strips with a glass of dark ale. It was comfort food for them, and they enjoyed it immensely.

When they were done eating, they walked around town some more. Tÿr found a magiq shop and so the two of them decided to look around. There were wands and other things that weren't magiqal at all. Things that were sold as magiqal items, but held no magiqal properties whatsoever. Tÿr was amused by the shop's owner trying to sell her potions that were probably just colored water or rum.

On the way out of the shop, Tÿr noticed a grimoire that was handwritten and bound in leather. It, unlike the other books, had a magiqal aura around it. In fact, it was the only thing in the shop that show any signs of being magiqal. Tÿr walked Danior over to the book and picked it up. Immediately, she could feel the power coming from it. The book was not large by any means, but it radiated power.

Tÿr showed no emotion to the shop owner as she brought the book to him.

"How much is this?" she asked.

"Ten silver pieces." He told her.

Her heart leapt. She had no idea what was in the tome, but she knew she had to get it before it fell into the wrong hands. The healer quickly got out ten silver pieces and paid the man. She had no idea if the man knew what he had, and by the price he charged her, she guessed he didn't. She grabbed Danior by the hand and practically dragged him out of the store.

"Whoa, what's the rush?" he asked.

"Come on, let's go," she said.

"What's up?"

"I just found a magiq book and I want to get back to the wyverns to read it," she told him.

"A real magiq book?"

"I think so."

What was it doing with all the other books?" he asked.

"I'm not sure, I just know it's old and it feels special. Here, see for yourself." She handed the book to him.

He took the book, and a shock went through his body.

"Gaunts!"

"Yeah," she said. "I felt it too."

"What are we going to do with it?"

"I need to see what's in it." she told him.

She practically dragged him back to the wyverns. Luckily, he was just as eager to find out about the book as she was.

They got back to Varanus and Qaren'a and Tÿr showed the wyverns the book. Varanus agreed that it needed to stay out of the wrong hands.

Tÿr opened the book and the first thing she noticed was that it was written in another language. There were various diagrams and pictures drawn in it.

"Varanus, can you make any of this out?"

Varanus studied the text and gasped.

"What is it?"

"I can't believe it?" he said. "This book is over three hundred years old. It holds some of the most vile and dangerous spells on the planets. This grimoire comes from the planet Peyda Noirin, from one of the remote islands where they practice magiq as a religion. It is best that we found this book so no one else can use it."

"Is there any spell that we could use against the sorcerer?"

"We must be cautious, but there may be." Varanus said. "I will have to research this book and find out."

"What language is it written in, Varanus?" Tÿr asked.

"It is an ancient variation of Cmok, the wyvern language, back when some humans still spoke it," the wyvern told her. "I haven't seen it for many years."

Varanus spent the night reading the grimoire. He became more concerned with each page he read.

"This book can never leave our hands. If it fell into the wrong hands, it would be devastating. It gives instructions on how to create zombies, the living dead. Beings that will serve you without question, that will do your bidding and call with just a simple command. Imagine the army that Kaistam-Laq could raise with this book."

"It is too frightening to imagine." Tÿr agreed.

"This book must stay close to us forever. Or it must be destroyed if it is possible." Qaren'a said.

"I am not certain that it is even possible to destroy such a book." Varanus told them. "Let's try to destroy it now."

Tÿr was apprehensive but sat the grimoire down on the ground and stepped back. Varanus's neck swelled and glowed. He shot out a burst of fire at the book. It appeared to have some sort of shield protecting it because the fire never touched it. The flames burned the ground around it, but the book was left untouched.

"It is as I feared," Varanus said, "it is protected by powerful magiq."

Tÿr picked up the book and began to rip out a page. Before she even finished, the page magiqally mended itself.

"I can't even remove a page." Tÿr said."

"This grimoire is protected by old magiq and it will not allow it to be destroyed. It is more powerful than my magiq which means it is older than me." Varanus told them.

"How are we going to get rid of it then?" Danior asked.

"We must keep this book from the sorcerer at all costs." Qaren'a said. "If it falls into his hands, he could raise an army that would be unstoppable."

"Is there a place we could hide it?" Danior asked.

"It is possible that it could be protected on Ÿkkynnÿk. We would have to fly to Thunder Mountian and put it in the vaults there. That would mean backtracking a great deal, but to keep the tome safe it would be worth it." Varanus told them.

"Then I guess we are going to head back to Thunder Mountian?" Tÿr asked.

"It is the only logical conclusion."

"How long will that take?" Danior asked.

"We should be able to make it in about four days. If we get a good tailwind maybe a bit sooner." Varanus told him.

Tÿr wasn't looking forward to the long flight, but at least she had the saddle now so it would be much more comfortable than it used to be. She wondered where the sorcerer was. She was not looking forward to their next confrontation. She knew that one of them would most likely not be walking away from it. With a little bit of luck, and her skills, she would hopefully be able to defeat the sorcerer once and for all. He and his assassins had terrorized the country for too long and they needed to be stopped.

The four of them set off for Thunder Mountain flying high and fast. Qaren'a took the lead with Danior on her back. Varanus followed closely behind. Tÿr did not like flying so high but closed her eyes and held on tight. They had a long trip and the sooner it was over, the better.

The sorcerer had stopped the group for the night. He wanted to try to scry again. He went to his tent and told Renner and Ollis-Van that he was not to be disturbed. He pulled out his obsidian scrying mirror and sat it on the table in front of him. He sat down and let out a sigh of frustration. He had been unsuccessful so far and he didn't hold high hopes that he would be successful this time.

With a wave of this hand, he lit his circular candelabra and then he lit some incense that would aid with scrying. He breathed in the fumes and then drew a glyph across the mirror. It glowed orange and placed his palm on it. Then he drew another and did the same. The mirror flickered to life. It showed faceless people, which frustrated the sorcerer. He needed to see the healer. Then it showed him something that he didn't expect. It showed a book.

"What's this?"

Kaistam-Laq stared at the mirror. He tried to figure out what he was looking at. What was this book? He could tell from the cover that it was a magiq tome and that it must be powerful. Immediately he felt pulled toward it.

"Why does the healer have this book?" he asked himself. "Surely she doesn't know the power she holds."

He watched as the pages turned. He couldn't make anything out, but from what he could tell, he had to possess this book. If the healer had it, it was one more reason to find her. His mission had just become that much more important. Kaistam knew that a showdown with the healer would result in heavy losses on both sides, but he had to have that book. The power he would possess would make him unstoppable.

The sorcerer sat and watched the mirror for several hours, staring into its depths despite the fact that it didn't show any details of the book. Where had she gotten this book? Were there more like it? He finally paced up his mirror and got his crew ready to travel again. There was no time to waste, they needed to get back on the road and find the healer.

The assassins were just setting up camp when they got word to tear it down and get ready to move again. There was grumbling all around but none where the sorcerer could hear. Even Renner-Van was curious as to why they were leaving right then. He knew better than to question his boss though.

The assassins had their gear packed up and ready to go in record time. They knew that Kaistam-Laq was ready to go and none of them wanted to be the reason that he had to wait.

Kaistam drove them hard and fast, he was not about to lose this book. They traveled day and night for two days before he called them to a halt. Many of them were so tired that they could barely stay up on their horses. When they dismounted, most of the assassins didn't even bother to set up their tents. They just slept in the open near their horses.

Kaistam set up his tent so he could scry. He had to know more about the elusive book. He sat up scrying during the night hours and still got no farther that he had been before. His frustration was beginning to get the best of him. His crew was apprehensive to approach him because of his tendency to snap.

It was late in the afternoon before the assassins finally got underway. The sorcerer spent all of that time on his mirror. He saw the book but the images were foggy and each time he thought he was getting close the image would go hazy again. It was as if the book did not want to be seen. This book was powerful, and he knew that he must get it from the healer. He would take it no matter what he had to do.

They had only traveled half a day before he called them to a halt. He was becoming obsessed with this book and he wanted to find out more about it. He would try a different approach. Instead of trying to see the book, he would try to find out about it with the help of the spirits of the mirror. He spent another night talking to the mirror, asking it questions, to reveal answers about the book.

The mirror shimmered and showed the book once again and then it opened. The pages were not clear at first, but then with some help of the spirits, certain pages became discernable. There were no words, but it showed images, armies of the dead rising. Kaistam became euphoric at the images he was seeing. These images showed him unlimited possibilities. An army at his command.

His desire for this book grew even more. He would kill for the book, and he didn't care about the repercussions. With an army of the dead at his command he could rule the world. There was no army on either planet that could defeat him.

The assassins took this time to try to catch up on sleep. The sorcerer had been pushing them hard these past few days. Even Renner-Van and his sister were getting weary though they showed no signs to the others. They had to appear strong so none of the others thought them weak and tried to take advantage of them.

The sorcerer did not confide in the brother and sister about the grimoire that he had seen in the scrying mirror. He was concerned that if they found out about it, they would want it for themselves. The book was already making him paranoid, and he didn't even possess it. It was a power he would not share with anyone.

The assassins moved on from their place as quickly as their horses would go. They didn't understand the rush. Kaistam-Laq was driving them at a frenzied pace. The horses were tiring, and they needed to be rested but the sorcerer pushed on. He told no one of his mission and this was causing morale to dip among the assassins, though none of them dared to say anything for fear of retribution.

Renner-Van and Ollis began to discuss what was going on in hushed voices. They were trying to figure out what the sorcerer was up to. He had them traveling at an incongruous rate of speed. They really wanted to speak up, but they knew the consequences would be dire if they did. It was a case of biting their lip and saying nothing to anyone. Things like this had a way of finding their way back to the sorcerer.

Kaistam spent his time of resting, on his mirror. In fact, he spent all of his free time on it. The mirror never showed the healer, but it did show places now. Places that Kaistam-Laq was not familiar with. He was certain that it was not on the shift though. From the places the mirror showed, it appeared that they were in the desert which could only mean one thing. The healer was on Peyda Kirin.

Mostly the mirror showed the book which made the sorcerer want it even more. He didn't know what all it contained but he knew that he must have it. If the healer had it, she possessed a weapon that could potentially defeat him, and he could not allow that.

As he continued to lose sleep, he became more and more erratic. He pressed the team on with less rests and more miles per day. The crew was bone tired, but still no one dared complain. Assassins braved sleep while they rode, dozing for a few seconds here and there when they thought no one was watching them. If anyone attacked now, they would be in danger.

Finally, it got so bad, and the sorcerer was so upset and tired that he finally stopped the caravan. He had to rest, and no one complained about it. Renner and Ollis-Van pulled the caravan to a halt and had them pitch camp for the night. The assassins all slept where they were. They didn't pitch tents or pull out sleeping gear, they simply lay down on the ground and slept.

The sorcerer stayed on his palanquin and didn't leave it for the entire time they rested. He slept with his chin on his chest. There were always two assassins guarding him at all times. Since they were all so tired, they took one hour shifts instead of the normal three. This allowed everyone to catch up on sleep.

The crew was up and ready to go the next day, but the sorcerer remained asleep. No one dared wake him and risk his wrath. He slept the entire day and into the night. The crew remained anxious, they didn't know if they should wake him or let him sleep. In the end, they let him sleep.

He finally woke the next day and seemed fine with their decision to let him sleep. The crew was feeling better too. They had gotten a chance to rest and relax a little while their master slept. Their horses also had a chance to catch up on a much needed rest.

By the sorcerer's thinking, they had at least five more days before they hit Peyda Kirin. He figured that they would catch up to the healer sometime soon after that. They couldn't be that much farther ahead of them.

The one thing that the sorcerer hadn't taken into consideration was that the healers were on wyverns, and that they were flying when they traveled. They could cover a much larger distance than the sorcerer could. In his blind eagerness to get the book, he seemed to forget that the healer was traveling faster and farther every day than he was.

The procession began to move again. Kaistam took the lead with Renner and Ollis-Van alongside him. He pushed the crew again, trying to make up for lost time. They rode over the shift quickly going through town after town without stopping. Every town that they passed through breathed a sigh of relief when they passed through without stopping. The Murtair Amagii rode on for three days straight without more than two or three hours rest each day. On the fourth day, they noticed the climate changing and were able to slow down. They were coming up on Peyda Kirin.

"We are entering the desert planet. The healer is somewhere on this planet, and she has something that I will be taking from her. She is not to be harmed until I get what I need. The person that causes her harm will answer to me." He told the crew as he addressed them before they entered Peyda Kirin.

"Is there something specific we should look for when we find her?" one of the assassins asked.

"You will bring her to me!" he said sharply.

"And if she fights?"

"You will disarm only. If any harm comes to her before I get what I seek, the person who causes it will pay with their life." He said simply.

It was a sign of how much the assassins feared the sorcerer because no one else asked another question. They had their answers, and they knew what had to be done.

"We will now split into teams and go out onto the planet. Renner and Ollis, you are with me." Laq said.

He wanted the strongest and best of the assassins with him. Kaistam-Laq made certain to surround himself with the biggest and strongest people he could find. He wasn't much of a fighter, so he hired others to do it for him. Renner and Ollis were his best two assassins and he made sure that they were near him at all times. That didn't mean that he couldn't fight when he was cornered, he just preferred to have someone else do it for him.

He told the teams that they would meet back at this place in two weeks' time. They all had small scrying mirrors that they carried around their necks. If any of them came across the healers, they were to observe, but not engage. They were to let the sorcerer know where they were and then he would join them. The crew would then assist the sorcerer in the capture of the healers. Kaistam had the power to deal with the healers by himself, but he wanted the crew with him in case anything unforeseen happened. The healer was powerful and full of tricks herself, and the sorcerer wanted to have back up when he dealt with her.

This was a setback that Kaistam-Laq had not foreseen. He wanted the book and he wanted it now, but he had to find a way to deal with the healers first. Where had this book come from and were there more like it? It was hard to believe that they had found it lying around in a book shop. Tomes like this were usually kept by magiq users, and not the type that the healer usually dealt with. Nothing about this made any sense to the sorcerer.

Before he and the siblings went anywhere, he would scry some more to find out if there were any more books of power like the one possessed by the healer. He told Renner and Ollis to get some rest while he went into his tent and began to scry.

He used different glyphs this time as he spent his time in front of the mirror. He drew one over the other, each glyph fading into the next. The fiery orange symbols sparked and then faded as he continued to scry. The mirror finally showed another image of a book that was quite like the book that the healer possessed. The cover was almost identical except there was writing on this cover. Writing that the sorcerer could not read.

The sorcerer grabbed a piece of parchment and scribbled down the words from the cover of the book. He would need to do some research to find out what it said. He folded the parchment and slipped it into an inner pocket of his robes. He wanted to make sure that he didn't lose it. If there was another book of magiq out there, he had to find it. He would travel the entire planet of Peyda Kirin, and Peyda Noirin if he had to. This book was the key to defeating the healer, he was certain of it. If he was able to possess both of the books, no one would be able to oppose him. Unlimited power was what he craved.

Kaistam-Laq continued to scry as the image of the book faded.

"Show me the location of this book," he said aloud.

The mirror's image changed to a view of water, roiling, and churning. It showed a lighthouse on an island in the middle of an ocean of deep blue water. The waves were beating down on the island, one after the other. Thirty feet tall waves that would literally tear a boat apart on the jagged rocks that surrounded the small island.

This was where the book was. Peyda Noirin; the water planet. The sorcerer was certain of it. His mirror didn't lie, nor had it ever been wrong before.

"But which island?" the sorcerer asked no one in particular.

Kaistam-Laq grabbed another piece of parchment and quickly sketched a picture of the lighthouse. It was a unique lighthouse, and he wanted a picture of it for later reference. The lighthouse was not a normal looking lighthouse. It was black and had two towers instead of the normal one. When the sorcerer was finished with this sketch, he folded it up and put it with the other piece of parchment in his pocket.

"What is this book doing on an island in the middle of nowhere?" the sorcerer asked.

"Show me the island!" the sorcerer told the mirror.

He held his hand over the scrying mirror, and it began to spark and smoke and then a hazy image of the planet came into view. The magiq of the mirror highlighted a group of islands on the back side of the planet. It didn't show the specific island but it did show the cluster of islands that it belonged to.

Kaistam was elated to know where he had to go, but it was a long way to travel. They would have to turn around and go back in the direction they had just come from. Not only that, they would have to wait at least two weeks to go, because the whole crew was split up right now. With a mission such as this, Kaistam had to have his seventeen together.

If anyone was confused about the orders from the sorcerer, they didn't say anything. When he suddenly turned the caravan around and headed them back in the direction they had just come from, there were puzzled looks but no one said anything.

Renner and his sister discussed the sudden change in direction quietly between themselves, but not loud enough that anyone else could hear.

"What is going on?" Ollis-Van asked her brother. "We've just turned around."

"I'm not sure." He told her.

"Should we ask Laq if he's certain that we're going in the correct direction?"

"It is probably best that we don't."

She nodded in agreement.

"Perhaps if we go together." He suggested.

"That might be best." She agreed.

The two of them rode up to the sorcerer's palanquin and prepared themselves.

Kaistam looked up to see the siblings approaching. "Yes?"

"We noticed that we have turned around and are heading back in the direction we just came from…"

"Do you have an issue with that?" he asked silkily?

"Uh, no. No problem." Renner said.

Kaistam glared at them for a moment before looking away.

Renner-Van felt his blood go cold. He and Ollis turned and went back to their place in the front of the procession.

Kaistam moved the procession forward again. They were headed to the shift and then on to the water planet. He still didn't have any idea how they were going to reach the island, but he knew they were going to get there somehow. They would have to charter a ship of some sort, possibly two. It was not going to be an easy voyage. The water planet was a vicious place covered in wave after wave of dizzying height. Some of the larger tidal waves traveled the surface of the entire planet at incredible speeds. The waves could wipe islands off of the map. Only the bravest of people lived on the islands in the ocean, and only on the larger islands.

There were two small continents in the middle of the ocean. Technically they were just big islands, surrounded by smaller ones. The riptides surrounding islands were treacherous and many people had died in them. How Kaistam planned on getting close to the lighthouse was still a mystery. The waters were rough and only experienced sailors would be able to get the crew to their destination.

Kaistam needed to find the best port to hire experienced captains for his chartered boats. He would talk to Renner and Ollis and ask them where they suggested. They had been all over both planets and would probably have a suggestion for him.

The four flew high and fast in the currents of the wind. Tÿr wasn't a fan of such heights but she knew that it had to be done. They had to get this book back to Ÿkkynnÿk where it would be safe in the vaults of Varanus's home. For all she knew, the sorcerer already knew about it by some dark means and was coming after it, which made this trip even more important. They could not let the sorcerer get this book at any cost. It couldn't be destroyed so it must be protected.

It had been a long trip so when the wyverns began to descend, Tÿr breathed a sigh of relief. She knew they would be on the ground in less than an hour. She watched as the ground rose to meet them. The mountain of Ÿkkynnÿk appeared in front of them in the Keltainyn sea. Tÿr's grip relaxed as they grew lower in the sky.

Varanus gave the signal that they were arriving. This time Tÿr was prepared for it. In the past his shriek had frightened her, making her almost let go of her tether. Now she was used to it and had anticipated it.

She heard the response from the ground. Another loud bellow from the paragon most likely. Tÿr was anxious to see Ghra'zhenn. It had been a while since she had seen the leader of the wyverns. There were others she was looking forward to seeing as well, but this was going to be a short trip so she didn't know how many they would have time to visit with.

When they landed the wyverns gathered around them and greeted them in the wyvern tongue, Cmok. Tÿr tried to respond as best she could in their native language. The wyverns soon switched to common tongue out of respect for Danior and Tÿr.

Danior greeted Ghra'zhenn as if he was his paragon. The wyvern was very fond of Danior and pulled Varanus aside after greetings were finished. He and Varanus seemed to be having a very serious discussion. Tÿr talked to several of the wyverns as they were old friends now. They asked how Danior was doing since the death of his brother. Tÿr told them that he was doing okay, but that it was hard for him. Gordian's death had hit him very hard, and he was suffering.

Danior spent his time talking to some of his old friends as well. Some of the younger wyverns that he had gone through training with, were there and so happy to see him. He told them what had happened to his brother and the wyverns also vowed that if they ever came across the sorcerer or his assassins, they would exact revenge for Gordian. This helped to ease some of the pain Danior still felt.

Glædi'Lann was still the deputy paragon on Ÿkkynnÿk and was one of the first to greet the four as they landed. Another to greet them right away was Krÿ'zhed. Danior and Tÿr remembered him as the wyvern who had cooked them an incredible meal when they had been there before.

Varanus was still talking with Ghra'zhenn in low tones when Tÿr approached them.

"I didn't get the chance to say hi yet." Tÿr told the paragon.

"Greetings young master Tÿr." Ghra'zhenn said.

"I hope I am not interrupting anything," she told them.

"Actually, we are discussing Danior, and you have something to do with it."

"Oh? How's that?"

"We think he might be another candidate for intercalation. What do you think? Do you think he would even be interested?" Varanus asked.

Tÿr unconsciously moved her hands to her arms. She felt the bumps going from her hands to her shoulders.

"I think," she started, "that is something only he can answer. I honestly don't know how he would feel about it."

"Then," the paragon said, "I believe we should ask him."

"He would be the only other human on the planets with this power." Varanus told Tÿr. "You and he would be unique, and possibly targeted if this information ever gets out."

Tÿr looked around for Danior and spotted him talking to the deputy paragon. He seemed to be having an animated conversation with her as the three approached him.

"Your friends approach." Glædi'Lann told Danior.

Danior turned and cocked his head to try to determine who it was.

"Hello Tÿr, Varanus." He said.

"Hello young master." Ghra'zhenn said.

"Oh master. I'm sorry, I didn't hear you."

"Don't apologize." Ghra'zhenn told him. "Varanus and I have something we would like to speak to you about when you are finished talking here."

Glædi'Lann took the hint and told Danior that she had to go.

"What's up?" Danior asked when the other wyvern had gone.

"We have a question we would like to ask you. Something very serious to consider." Ghra'zhenn told him.

"Okay."

"You know what intercalation is. We were considering you as a candidate for it."

"Really? You think I'm ready?" Danior asked.

"Both Varanus and I agree that you are ready. The question now remains, do you feel that you are ready to accept it?" Ghra'zhenn asked.

"I feel that my healing is where is should be." Danior began, "but to receive an honor like this, I am not certain that I deserve it. This is usually reserved for people who are outstanding and …"

"It is reserved for people like you. People who are humble and will use the power for what it is intended to be used for. That is why Tÿr was chosen. That is why you have been chosen. If you accept, you will be only the second person in a long, long time to have the honor."

"Will you give me some time to think about it?" Danior asked.

"We will give you two days, if you think that will be enough. Then we would like to perform the ceremony."

Danior agreed to this. He asked Tÿr to take him to the edge of the island and let him sit there by the water. He said the sound of the waves on the shore were soothing and helped him think. He sat there overnight and did some deep thinking and when morning came he had reached his decision.

Tÿr found him in the morning and he asked her to take him to the wyverns.

"You're going to do it, aren't you?"

"You know me too well." He smiled. "I think I have to."

"That's exactly how I felt." Tÿr told him.

Tÿr led Danior up to the wyverns and he gave them his answer.

"When do we start?" Danior asked.

"We would like to begin as soon as possible." Varanus told him.

"Could we begin as soon as tomorrow?"

The wyverns looked at each other and nodded.

"Tomorrow would be fine." Ghra'zhenn told him.

"We will begin as soon as you wake." Varanus explained. "We will prepared everything and be ready for you when you get up in the morning."

"I suggest you get a good night's sleep, because this is going to be an ordeal that you will never forget." Ghra'zhenn told Danior.

Danior brought Tÿr aside and asked her, "Is it really as bad as all that?"

"Oh my gosh, yes." She told him. "I have never experienced pain like it before or since."

Danior swallowed hard.

"Are you nervous?" Tÿr asked him.

"Very."

"The best advice I can give you is to try to get a good night's sleep and then chew on the leaves they give you. They help to dampen the pain but only a bit. They also put some stuff on to help I think but I was so out of it that I don't remember much. I only remember pain. Intense pain."

The two friends walked around the island for a bit before they turned in for the night. Tÿr tried to take Danior's mind off the procedure by talking about old times and things they used to do as kids. Of course, this brought up Gordian which opened another batch of memories, but at least it got Danior's mind off of the upcoming ordeal.

The two slept next to each other near the site where they would be doing the intercalation. Danior had trouble falling asleep but eventually dozed off. He had dreams of things that he could not remember when he woke up in the morning, things that made him feel uncomfortable and anxious. He awoke early and nudged Tÿr to wake her.

"What? What is it, are you okay?" she asked.

"I'm just a bit nervous. Can you tell me anything else to expect?"

"Honestly the most important thing to remember is to relax."

Varanus and Ghra'zhenn were approaching the healers.

"It is time, Master Danior." Ghra'zhenn said.

"Wish me luck." He said to Tÿr.

"Good luck, you'll do fine. May I watch the process?" Tÿr asked the wyverns.

"That is up to Danior." Varanus said.

"I don't mind if it is alright with you and Master Ghra'zhenn.

"You may watch but you will have to stay back, and not interfere no matter what happens." The paragon told her.

"I'll stand back and watch from a distance for a while, but then I will probably go and talk with the others," she said.

"That is acceptable. Now let us begin. Danior if you will come to this bench and lay face down on it we will begin. We will start with your left arm and go up your arm to your shoulder and then the same will happen with your right arm. Then we will start on your back and work our way down to your tailbone. It will take approximately two days, maybe less depending on how you handle it. When you are done you will have something called kÿrkÿll tÿgymyst, also know as reptile skin. It is a great honor to have and you will be only the second person in many years to have it.

"Is there a reason that we are doing this in your home and not out with the other wyverns?" Danior asked.

"Not everyone believes that humans should have this power. Most of our dynasty has no issue with it, but there are a few who take exception to it. We will keep this secret until you are healed."

Varanus gave Danior some leaves and told him to chew on them. The healer took them and began to chew. Almost immediately he could feel his throat begin to go numb and his head to spin.

"This feels odd?" Danior told the wyverns, is this normal?"

"What are you feeling?" Varanus asked.

"My throat is going numb and my head is light. It is spreading down my body."

"It is normal and that is what you want. It is all the relief we will be able to give you."

Varanus poured a sack full of tiny crystals into a stone bowl. When he was ready he breathed fire into the bowl, heating the crystals until they glowed red. He pulled one from the bowl with his clawed hand and held it at the ready.

"Prepare yourself. May I have your left arm please?"

Danior held out his arm. He was in a type of trance. Varanus took the crystal and positioned it for insertion. "We begin." He said.

The first crystal was placed in Danior's arm and he almost screamed in pain. The crystal slid in and instantly cauterized the small wound. The smell of burnt flesh wafted through the air. Danior tried to grit his teeth. He knew this was just the beginning. The second crystal went in just the same way. And the third. By the fourth, Danior was in such pain he began to sweat uncontrollably.

"Help me Tÿr!" He pleaded.

"I am right here. You are doing fine." She told him, not knowing whether he heard her or not.

Ghra'zhenn held Danior down while Varanus inserted crystal after crystal. The ordeal lasted all day and night. By the time Danior's arms were done, he had slipped into unconsciousness. Varanus had now begun to insert the crystals under the skin of Danior's neck. This is where the true pain began, but luckily for Danior, he was already unconscious.

Hour after hour the wyvern worked on the healer. He had to continually heat the crystals up to make sure they slid in easily and cauterized the wound. Tÿr watched the whole ordeal, she couldn't take her eyes off of the process. It was both horrifying and fascinating. She thought back to her time when she went through the process. It was the worst pain she had ever endured. She too had passed out a short time into the process. She wasn't sure anyone could go through it without passing out.

Tÿr was tiring quickly as the ordeal was coming to an end. She moved closer to the bench as Varanus slid the final crystal into the area above the tailbone.

"Are you done now?" She asked.

"The process is complete. We wait for him to awaken. Could you fetch that bowl of herbs from the table and bring it over here?" Ghra'zhenn asked.

Tÿr went to the table and brought the bowl over to the bench. There was a brush made of grass in the bowl that Varanus used to mop Danior's back. The herbs had a cooling quality and the healer began to wake up.

"Welcome back." Ghra'zhenn said.

"It's over?" Danior asked.

"It is over. You did splendidly."

"My back is on fire."

"I am going to put a salve on your back in a minute. It will help to take some of the burn away. First, we need to see if it worked though."

"What do I need to do?" Danior asked.

"We need you to perform some magiq. Most anything will suffice. I will fetch your staff."

"I'll get it," Tÿr volunteered. She ran over to the side of the cavern where Danior's belongings were and got his staff. She handed it to him gently. He took it gingerly and stood up. His back was throbbing, but he wanted to find out if the intercalation had worked or if it had all been for nothing. He didn't know what he would do if he had spent two days of torture with no result.

"Don't worry it won't hurt." Tÿr told him.

"Okay, good. I'm not sure I could take anything else."

"We will have you do something simple. Light the top of your staff." Varanus told him.

Danior concentrated and then the orb on his staff began to glow along with his arms and back where the crystals were inserted.

"Is it working?" he asked eagerly.

"Turn around." Tÿr told him.

She gasped as she saw how he glowed.

"Oh my."

"What?!"

"You're glowing."

"Me?"

"It has worked Master Danior. You are now an honorary wyvern. Welcome to the dynasty!" Varanus said.

"Thanks!" he told the wyvern.

Tÿr walked up and gently kissed him on the forehead.

"Thank you for not hugging me." Danior said gratefully.

They walked out of the cavern together. Danior still had no shirt on. His skin was too raw to tolerate it. Ghra'zhenn called the wyverns around. He felt that now was the proper time to announce the addition to the dynasty. Some might not be too pleased with it, but none would challenge him here on Ÿkkynnÿk.

"I wish for you to welcome our newest addition to the dynasty. This is our brother Danior who has just gone through kÿrkÿll tÿgymyst."

There was muttering throughout the dynasty. Many of the wyverns came forward to get a glimpse of Danior's back and arms. The younger ones especially crowded forward to see. This was something that most of them had never seen before, the older wyverns included, other than Tÿr's. Now they had two healers with reptile skin. This was an unprecedented event.

Glædi'Lann asked if Danior could demonstrate his new powers for the dynasty.

Danior cocked his head toward Varanus questioningly.

"Go ahead young master but let me have everyone step back."

Varanus told everyone to stand back before having Danior call down a bolt of lightning. The energy bolt came down from the sky with a loud crack and shot out in all directions from the healer for fifteen feet. The wyverns all began to speak in awe of this feat. Tÿr was impressed as well. She had never tried to do that, but now that she knew that she could, she would have to remember it for the future.

"Holy smokes Dani, that was incredible!" Tÿr told her friend.

"Yeah? I didn't even know if it would work. I just tried it and it happened."

"We are going to be unstoppable. That sorcerer is going to be sorry he ever heard the name of Gordian. We will make him pay for killing Gordi, you know that, right?"

"I do." He told her.

"Kaistam-Laq is still very powerful," Varanus told the two healers. "He must be dealt with cautiously. If we are to defeat him, we must outthink him and his band of assassins."

"He is not expecting us to have such powerful magiq at our disposal, is he?" Danior asked.

"I do not think he is, but we are outnumbered. We must think smart and be cautious."

"We welcome any suggestion you and Ghra'zhenn might have." Tÿr said.

"Well, we did one of the first things that we could to keep him from raising an army of the dead. We have sealed the book away, but now we have to worry if there are other books and if he can find them or if he even knows about them. With his scrying mirror, I have no doubt that he already knows about our book, he may even be trying to figure out how to get to it right now. My fear is that there are more books like this out in the world and that he knows of them."

"So should we be trying to find these other books too?" Tÿr asked.

"It might be a good idea. Wyverns have ways to divine as well. Perhaps we could find out if there are more books of power out on the planets. If there are, we could possibly beat the sorcerer to them and hide them away in Ÿkkynnÿk."

Varanus and the two healers were gathered in his living quarters. The wyvern was preparing to search for any books of power that might be out on the planets. They needed to find them before the sorcerer did. Varanus told the healers that he had a scrying mirror that they were going to use. It was a huge square piece of obsidian, smooth as glass. The wyvern carefully took it off of a shelf and brought it to the floor of the cavern. The three of them gathered around.

"Tÿr, I would like you to do this." He told the healer.

"I have never done something like this before," she told him.

"I will walk you through it."

"First you will draw the seeing glyph." Varanus said. He drew the glyph on the mirror and it glowed orange.

Tÿr followed his lead and did the same. The glyph burned bright under her finger.

"Now we draw the future glyph." Varanus drew another glyph and it glowed again.

Tÿr drew this glyph as well.

Varanus wiped the mirror blank and told her to draw both glyphs together and place her hand upon them when she was finished. She did this and then the mirror began to glow.

"Now, think of what you wish to see."

Tÿr concentrated on the book. She wanted to know if there were more. Over and over, she asked if there were more books.

"Now take your hand off of the mirror and watch it." The wyvern instructed.

Almost as if a cloud rolled away, an image began to take shape. Another book.

"Look," she said excitedly.

"Yes," Varanus said, "this is a different book. It comes with a warning. It says not to use the book of the dead with out this book because you cannot control the dead without it. It also says that there is another book and only with it can the dead be destroyed."

"So, we need to find all three books?"

"We must find them in order to keep Kaistam-Laq from getting them. If he were to get them, he would be able to create an unstoppable army."

"But he would need all three books though, right?"

"He could raise the dead with our book, he just couldn't control them. Therein lies the problem." Varanus told her.

"Where do we even begin to look for these other books?" Týr asked.

"I will do some scrying myself to try and find that out." The wyvern told the healer.

Danior, who had been quiet up until now asked, "So will we ever use these books to destroy the sorcerer? Wouldn't they help us?"

"We can never use these books. They are evil and can never be used."

"But if they are so powerful, wouldn't they help us?"

"They might, but I believe they are just too dangerous. It will take some research to find out about them. We will have to talk to the paragon." Varanus told Danior.

"I just thought that it would be better if we had them instead of Kaistam-Laq." Danior said.

"It is better if we have them, I'm just not certain they can be used for good," the wyvern said.

"What we need to do, is find out how to destroy them. If we can do that, no one could use them. Then we would be safe, correct?" Tÿr suggested.

"If we could do that, it would be for the best. Again, it will all hinge on what Ghra'zhenn has to say about it. He is wise and might have some suggestions about the books and how to proceed from here.

"I am going to go speak with the paragon and tell him of the situation. I will find out how he wishes us to proceed. Are you prepared for a fight? This could mean a battle if the sorcerer knows of these books which I have a feeling he might."

"We are ready to fight." Danior said. "I want revenge for Gordi."

"We all want that, Young Master." Varanus told him.

Varanus went out to find the paragon.

"Tÿr do you really think the books are as dangerous as Varanus says they are?"

"I do." She said, "But there has to be a way that we could use them for good."

"That's what I was thinking."

"Then we must find a way to use these books. There has to be some information out there that tells something about them."

"Sounds like we're going to be doing a bunch of research." Danior said.

"Why don't we go outside and get some sun," Tÿr suggested.

The two healers went outside, and the suns beat down on their faces. The warmth felt good on their skin after being in the cool cavern. Tÿr took Danior's hand and led him around the island. They soon found Varanus and Ghra'zhenn talking in hushed tones.

"They must be discussing the books," Tÿr told Danior.

"What do you think they are saying?"

"I don't know, but I bet we are going on another journey to get those books." Tÿr told him.

"I bet we are too."

"Where do you think they are?"

"Nowhere close is my guess."

"Yeah, mine too." She said.

"I just wondering where we are going to have to go. I'd kinda like to see my mother before we go if that's possible. I want to check on her and see how she's doing."

"I'd like to see my mum and da too," Tÿr said.

"Maybe we can make time for that. We are on Peyda Kirin, your parents are in Londstäc, we could stop in and see them." Danior suggested.

"That would be nice." Tÿr agreed.

"Then we'll talk to Varanus about it."

When Varanus was finished speaking to the paragon the two healers approached him and told them of their plans. He told them that it would be fine if they made a detour to their parents since they hadn't seen them for a while.

"When do we leave?" Danior asked the wyvern.

"I would like to leave as soon as possible." Varanus told him. "We can head to Londstäc first and then make the trip back to Vennex to see your mother. Then we will get underway to finding the books. We have a long journey so if you and Tÿr are ready I would like to leave within the hour."

"That would be fine." Danior told him.

Tÿr and Danior gathered their belongings and prepared to leave.

The flight to Londstäc took four hours. Varanus landed them outside the city and they all walked in. The city was larger than Vennex and they had to ask several people to get directions to Tÿr's parents' home. When they arrived, her mother was in the kitchen cooking and her father was at the kitchen table having a glass of ale.

"Tÿr, is it really you?!" her mother exclaimed.

"We thought we would come for a visit since we were close by." Tÿr told her.

"I'm just cooking dinner; can you stay for a bite?"

"I think we can." Tÿr said.

Her mom stopped what she was doing and walked over to Danior and gave him a hug. "I'm so sorry to hear about your brother."

"Thanks," he said with his voice full of emotion.

"So what are you two up to?" Tÿr's dad asked.

"We can't really say Da, but we are on an important mission. We will be gone for quite a while."

"Can you say where you're going?"

"All over." Tÿr laughed, avoiding the question.

"Okay, well be careful out there!"

"You know us, we're always careful." Danior said.

"Uh-huh."

"Where are Rævii and Sëvyq?" Tÿr asked her mum.

"Oh, they're somewhere around here." She said.

"Tÿr called to the shift fox and in a moment, she heard some scurrying from the back room. The little shift fox came running out to greet her. She almost purred as Tÿr petted her. Sëvyq came running out behind the fox. He too was happy to see the healer. She spent a few minutes with each of them before she told her mum that she had to go let Varanus about their dinner plans.

Tÿr went out and let Varanus know that they were going to be eating there. He told her that he and Qaren'a would go hunting then while they ate. Tÿr went back in to join her family and answer the questions that they were bound to have.

Elmky made a stew of some unknown meat that Tÿr and Danior really enjoyed. Tÿr didn't ask what type it was for fear that she might not enjoy it as much after the fact. Danior had three bowls of the stew and her mother was worried that she would run out of it, but as usual she had made so much there was tons left over.

The home that Tÿr's parents were living in here in Londstäc was much larger than their home back in Vennex. They offered Tÿr and Danior a bed for the night which they readily accepted. It had been a while since they had slept in a comfortable bed. Each healer had their own bedroom which was nice for both of them. They got a night of uninterrupted sleep. In the morning they woke and had breakfast with Tÿr's parents and then they got back on their way.

Tÿr's family went with her and Danior to see them off the next day. Tÿr's mum and dad thanked the wyverns for watching out for the healers and keeping them safe. Varanus assured them that Tÿr could take care of herself. Everyone got hugs from everyone and then the humans got on their saddles and the wyverns took off for Vennex. Danior was really looking forward to visiting with his mother. He knew she was lonely and would enjoy the company. He didn't know how she would feel about seeing Tÿr again, but he would tell her that she would have to get over it. He was going to be with Tÿr for a while if he could help it.

The flight to Vennex took six days. They fought the air currents the whole way back so the wyverns ended up flying lower and slower than they would have liked. Tÿr and Danior were buffeted as they flew so they tried to stay low on the wyverns' backs.

Danior practically dragged Tÿr back to his mother's cottage. His mother answered the door and her face broke into a huge smile when she saw her son.

"Oh, my boy, have you come home?" she asked.

"Just for a short visit. We have some business that we have to tend to." He told her.

Her face fell for a second but then she smiled again. "Well let's get you something to eat."

"We aren't here to trouble you mum," he told her. "We wanted to stop in to say hi for a short visit before we go on to Peyda Noirin."

"Peyda Noirin?!" she exclaimed. "Why would you need to go there?"

"We can't really say." He told her. "We have some business that needs to be taken care of so we can defeat the people who killed Gordi."

Her face tightened. "You are going after the sorcerer, aren't you?"

Danior looked down.

"Tÿr'Ynyn don't you let anything happen to my only son!"

Tÿr looked directly in her eyes and told her that she would bring her son back alive and that she would defeat the sorcerer with the help of her son. She didn't know if any of what she said helped, but the woman didn't say anything else about it.

"Well let me make you two something to eat."

"Seriously Mum, you don't have to."

"It's no trouble. I don't get many visitors. I want to do this." She said.

"Well, okay, if it's okay with Tÿr."

"Sure. I'd be happy to join you."

From that moment on, Danior's mother treated Tÿr like a member of the family.

They sat and had a meal of roasted fowl and Z-Tri and a big glass of ale. Dani's mum offered to refill their glasses, but the two healers told her that they really needed to get going. They had a long trip ahead of them and they needed to get started. She hugged them both and sent them on their way. Tÿr was pleased that the visit had gone so well. The last time she had seen Dani's mother she had not been so friendly. She had blamed Tÿr for Gordian's death.

Tÿr and Danior found the wyverns outside of town and told them that they were ready to set off. The wyverns suggested that they get some supplies before setting off. Things like food and ale and other various things they might need while they travel.

"You don't need to get much, but maybe a little food and ale in case we end up away from a town for a night or two." Varanus suggested.

Tÿr and Danior hit the shops and got food, drink and some medical supplies that they thought would come in useful on the trip. Tÿr also got some wax and cloths to polish her and Danior's staffs. She thought they would look nicer if they were polished and shiny. Just before they left town, Danior suggested that they get some more pipe supplies. They were running low on pipe weed.

"Good idea, I think I'd like a pipe tonight," Tÿr said.

"Me too."

They made a quick detour to the tobacconist and stocked up on pipe weed. There were a nice collection of pipes there but nothing as nice as the one Tÿr had. Danior had an old one that was ready to be replaced, so while he was smelling different pipe weed, Tÿr thought she would surprise him with a new pipe. She surreptitiously bought it while he was occupied with the weed and slipped it in her pocket.

This will be a nice surprise for him tonight, she thought.

They ended up getting four different types of pipe weed. They were anxious to give them all a try later that night.

"We'll have to stay up half the night to try them all." Tÿr said.

"That's okay, I love a good pipeful." Dani responded.

"Me too. Me too."

They returned to the wyverns on the edge of town and told them that they were ready to go. Varanus and Qaren'a were ready, and they took off as soon as the healers climbed aboard. The trip back was higher than the trip there. They flew high and fast and made good time. By the time it got late, the wyverns decided it was time to land and get some sleep. Danior and Tÿr were ready for a break. They had been flying for nearly six hours and they needed to rest too. They were hungry and their backsides were in need of a rest.

The healers built a fire which Varanus lit for them and they cooked some sausages over it. When they had finished eating Tÿr presented Dani with his new pipe.

"What's this?" he asked.

"Just a little something I got for you." She told him.

He opened the little box and pulled out the pipe. It was a qyrry wood pipe that had been polished to a high gloss.

"Oh my, this is too much," he said.

"You needed it, yours was old and I saw this one and though it would be perfect for you."

"Thank you so much." He almost got choked up.

Dani got up and gave Tÿr a great big bear hug.

"You are welcome. Now let's break it in!

They filled their pipes and sat back for an after-dinner smoke. Danior said that it was the best smoke he had ever had. Tÿr smiled and thought it was about the best money she had ever spent. The two of them sat up later than they had meant to, trying each of the pipe weeds. They both agreed that the one flavored with rum was the best. There was a cherry flavored, and a vanilla, and a straight pipe weed. They were all tasty, but the rum soaked one had the best flavor. They would definitely be buying more of that one on their next trip to Vennex.

"Maybe we can get my Da to send us more when we run out," Tÿr suggested.

"That would be great." Danior agreed.

Danior moved closer to Tÿr. She looked at the wyverns and smiled. She was almost certain that she saw Varanus smile back at her.

"This is nice." She said.

"I really do like a nice pipeful." Danior said.

"I mean it's nice being here with you, silly."

"Oh, yeah, I uh, yeah." Danior didn't know what to say, but his face turned bright red.

"That's the first time I ever heard you at a loss for words," she teased him.

"You just took me by surprise." Try it again.

"Nope, you lost your chance." She said.

"Aw man." He pretended to pout.

"Don't do that, it's ugly."

"Sorry," he said.

"Don't apologize either.

"Is there anything I can do to please you, your highness?" he asked sarcastically.

"I can think of something."

"Yeah, like what?"

Tÿr lean forward and kissed him on the mouth. She sat back again.

Danior turned bright red once more.

Varanus and Qaren'a both took their cue to go and hunt.

Danior reached out and took Tÿr's hand. "How did you know I wanted to do that?"

"Lucky guess." She said.

The two sat, holding hands for the rest of the night. They fell asleep that way and woke up in the morning still holding hands. For the first time in her life, Tÿr felt comfortable with a boy as more than a friend. She wondered if he felt the same way, but she was pretty sure that the feeling was reciprocated. This was not something that she had anticipated. There were a bunch of feelings going through her mind at the moment. She shook her head. She needed to concentrate on the mission, not this, but she couldn't help it.

The wyverns returned in the morning and nothing was said about the night before. Tÿr and Danior had an unspoken understanding that something had happened, but neither was ready to discuss it yet. They would wait until the time was right. Both were pleased with the happenings of the previous night, they just wanted to take things slow and as they came. Neither could think of a better mate.

Everyone was ready to leave and so they took off for Peyda Noirin. It was going to be a long journey. They would have to fly high and rest only for short periods of time. The islands could be treacherous at this time of year. When the planets were on their way farthest from the suns the waves were perilous. Some of the waves were literally hundreds of miles long and over thirty feet high. They could roll over and decimate small islands.

The trip to Peyda Noirin took four more days to reach the edge of the planet. The edge of the was marshy and wetlands and there was little space to camp. They had to make camp without lighting a fire because there was no dry wood to burn. Luckily the weather was still warm, and they didn't really need a fire. Unfortunately they were in the swamplands though and the insects were bothersome. Small biting insects attacked them while they slept. Varanus told them that they would be away from the marshlands by the next day so they wouldn't have to deal with the insects.

In the morning the two healers woke up with several dozen insect bites all over their bodies.

"What the heck?" Danior hollered when he woke up. He was scratching at the bug bites.

"Oh my." Tÿr said. She too was scratching at her skin. "I think I have some stuff we can use on these." She said rummaging through her bag.

Tÿr found a salve that she gave to Danior to try.

"Put some on your arm and see if it works," she told him.

She helped him rub some of the salve on his arm. He waited a few minutes and decided that it worked.

"This stinks to high heaven." He said.

"But if it works," she said, "it will be worth it."

She put some of the salve on her arms and found it to be soothing so she rubbed more on Danior's other arm and on his face and neck where he had been bitten. She finished rubbing more on herself. The salve did stink but it really did help. She would have to remember it. There were bound to be other applications they could use it for.

"Whew, it really does stink, I hope it goes away after a while. Luckily, we aren't going to be around anyone today." Danior said.

"I think we will get used to it after a few minutes." Tÿr said.

"Worst case, we can wash it off when we land tonight."

They got situated and were ready to go. The wyverns flew them high and fast for a while but then dove down and flew lower to avoid the air currents that were buffeting them. The wyverns flew for most of the day and then they found an island to land on. The island was larger than most of the others they had seen. They chose it because the chance of a rogue wave wiping it out was less than if they stayed on a smaller island. This island also had a bunch of dead trees on it which provided firewood for their campfire that night.

Tÿr and Danior roasted sausages and had a bottle of wine for their meal that evening. The planet was already dark being on the back side of the suns. It would remain dark the whole year as it didn't rotate. This made for perfect sleeping. Tÿr and Danior had never slept in the dark outside before. They lit a fire and sat back and enjoyed the darkness together.

"Hey Varanus, will you be able to see alright to fly us in this dark?"

"I can see equally well in the light and the dark," Varanus told Danior.

It amazed Tÿr that Danior knew it was dark out. He almost had the senses of a sighted person. Sometimes she thought he could hear better than she could, but she just realized that he paid better attention than she did. He managed to find his way around places after being there for just a short time. His memory was incredible. Tÿr was always amazed by how he managed to get around. Many people didn't even realize that he was blind.

They sat up and talked into the night like they used to do. Eventually they were so tired that they fell asleep in the middle of a conversation. The wyverns both chuckled at this. They were listening to their conversation and then suddenly it stopped.

"They were tired." Varanus told Qaren'a.

"It's been a long day." She agreed.

The two wyverns curled up and went to sleep next to each other. They too were exhausted from the long flight.

In the morning Varanus woke first and then woke everyone else. It's about time that we get going. We have a long journey left, and I'd like to make a place called Skerry Cove. It is an inland lake town on an island about a day's flight from here. There are only about fifty people that live there and they are extremely wary of visitors. I have been there and know the magistrate. He will help us with food and lodging for the night.

The four got underway and they flew hard to reach Skerry Cove by late afternoon. The town was very small, only about six buildings in the actual town. Varanus landed them on the outskirts and the four of them walked in. People stopped and stared at the wyverns and healers as they entered the town.

They were greeted by the magistrate and his entourage.

"Varanus, is that you?"

"Magistrate. I'm glad you remember me."

"How could I forget you? Who else have you brought with you?"

Varanus made introductions all around.

The magistrate was ecstatic that there were healers on the island. His island didn't have any healers and if they needed healing, they had to sail to distant islands in the sea which was treacherous.

"Would you mind seeing a few patients while you are here?" the magistrate almost pleaded.

"Of course, we will." Tÿr told him.

"Have them come to your town hall tomorrow morning and we will treat anyone that shows up," Danior told him.

"That is very generous." The magistrate said. "Please eat and drink at our tavern tonight as my guest."

Danior and Tÿr followed the magistrate to the tavern and the wyverns went out to hunt. The healers were treated to a huge feast and were stuffed when it was over. Danior complained that he hadn't eaten that much in his whole life. Both he and Tÿr were miserable from eating so much. They thanked the magistrate for his hospitality and then told him that they needed to get some sleep. There was only one small inn in the town. It had three rooms and two were taken, so Tÿr and Danior had to share a room.

"You take the bed and I'll take the floor," he told her.

"Don't be silly, we can share."

Danior got a funny feeling in the pit of his stomach. He was going to be sharing a bed with the woman he was in love with, at least he thought he was.

What he didn't know was that Tÿr was having the same exact feelings herself.

They both climbed into bed and said goodnight. Tÿr snuggled up to him and he put his arm around her. They were so dead tired that they fell asleep like that in about five minutes. Neither of them moved the whole night and they woke up in the same position in the morning.

Danior kissed Tÿr on the cheek in the morning when she woke up.

"Good morning." he said.

"Good morning."

"How much farther do you think we have to go?"

"A couple weeks probably." She answered.

"Is Peyda Noirin really that big?" he asked.

"Yeah, I think so."

"I hope we beat the sorcerer to the book." He said.

"We will. We don't even know if he knows about it."

"Can I tell you something?"

"Of course." She told him.

"I just wanted to tell you…" he stopped. "I mean I just wanted to say…"

"I already know Dani. Me too." She said.

Danior looked relieved.

"So, what now?"

"I don't know, I've never been…you know."

"Yeah, me either."

"Let's just play it by ear."

"Okay, good plan," he smiled.

She took him by the hand and led him from the room. The two went to find the wyverns so they could get back to their journey. Danior admired how soft her hands were for the first time ever.

Kaistam-Laq was driving his caravan like a madman. He wanted the book from his vision in the scrying mirror and he wanted it as soon as he could get his hands on it. The longer he waited, the more of a chance someone else could stumble onto it. They had at least twelve days left to get to the water planet at the rate they were traveling. He didn't know if the horses could keep up the pace but he meant to find out.

Renner and Ollis-Van were becoming concerned with the sorcerer's erratic behavior. He was driving the crew hard and they were tired. They knew better than to say anything to anyone other than themselves. If word got back to the sorcerer, there would be trouble.

The crew stopped in every small town they came to for food and supplies. The sorcerer was paranoid about running low on anything. This proved to be a good thing for the crew because it gave them a chance to rest for short periods of time. The assassins were tiring quickly due to the traveling schedule, so any rest was welcome. The horses also needed the rest for water and food.

Kaistam-Laq was still obsessed with the book in the tower and used his mirror constantly. He wanted to rush but yelled if the palanquin got to rough to scry. The driver of the horse drawn palanquin was careful to keep it steady and as quick as he dared.

They traveled day and night sometimes. It made it difficult on the team but Laq wanted this so much that he was willing to risk the crew's welfare.

After an all-nighter Renner risked asking if they could rest for a few hours. He caught the sorcerer in a decent mood and the sorcerer halted the group and had them rest for six hours before moving on again. This did a lot to help morale for the time being. Still the assassins were very tired, and many were ready to desert.

After the short rest they were back on their journey to the water planet. Once they got there the sorcerer would have to charter two ships to take them to the island. Either that or he would have to leave half of the crew behind, and with his obsession with the number seventeen, the likelihood of that was slim.

As the days wore on the horses grew wearier and slower. This did not please the sorcerer. He was in a foul mood with everyone. The only ones he tolerated were Renner and Ollis-Van. They were able to calm him down a bit and he stopped his ranting for the time being. Still, he told them that he was surrounded by fools and idiots, and no one cared about his plans. They explained that the horses were tired and needed to rest. He calmed down enough to rest another day and a half. This gave him time to use his mirror without being jostled all over the place.

The sorcerer, after the short rest, was ready to get back on the road. They were now only five days out from the water planet. This made the sorcerer want to drive the crew even harder. He wanted to reach the dark towers and retrieve the book. He was certain that others must know about it, and he was not prepared to share it. This was his find, and he was not about to let some second rate magiq user find and get this book before him.

The crew began a series of traveling all day and night and then resting for six hours. Then they got up and did it all over again. By his figuring, Kaistam felt they would reach Peyda Noirin by the third night. This was much more acceptable to him.

Horses began to drop from exhaustion. The sorcerer made the assassins walk then. The procession slowed because of this but they kept the same regimen, traveling day and night and then resting. When they came upon a town, they commandeered horses or paid very little for them. This helped to speed things back up a bit. Still, they were slower than the sorcerer wanted them to be.

Eventually the procession reached the water planet. They came to the port town of Seaward where the sorcerer was going to charter the ships to take them on to the black towers. Kaistam-Laq sent his crew to get some rest while he set out to charter the ships. The captains he found wanted a good deal of silver to take them to where Kaistam described. Since he didn't know the exact location, they charged extra.

The crew found a tavern and had a few drinks but they were so tired that they went and found rooms at the local inns and just went to sleep. They were to meet the sorcerer on the next day at noon at the docks. Renner and Ollis spent the night with the sorcerer at a small inn that was near the dock by the ships.

In the morning the crew slept late and got to the docks at the last minute. The sorcerer was waiting for them to arrive. Everyone showed up at the same time because nobody wanted to be the last one there.

The sorcerer chartered two ships to take them to the island, *The Harridon Barque* and *The Savage Bateau*. Both were huge ships that were equipped to handle the waters of the seas they were going to travel. The captains were experienced in the seas of Peyda Noirin and had been all around the planet. Kaistam felt reassured by the experience of the captains.

The sorcerer and the assassins all got loaded on the ships and they were ready to sail. They weighed anchor and then they were off. The seas were choppy and the winds were strong and the ships moved quickly into the depths. The captains were very experienced in dealing with the seas like these and they moved the ships skillfully between some of the smaller islands they came to. As they got out into the deeper waters, the seas rolled, and the ships were tossed but the skill of the captains prevailed. As they got out past the islands the waters smoothed out. The winds stayed steady, and the ships began their course toward the island with the black towers.

The waters began to swell as they moved farther out to sea. The ships were tossed about on the seas like corks. The assassins began to feel the first signs of seasickness. Even the sorcerer felt the effects of the roiling seas. Kaistam-Laq began to wonder if this trip would be worth all of the trouble they were facing. His crew were all sick and couldn't function, and even he was ill, but his resolve was still strong.

As the voyage progressed the seas got worse. The swells reached thirty feet and the clouds rolled in. Rain began to pour down on the ships and winds tore at the sails. The salt spray burnt the eyes of the crew as they made their way to their cabins.

Kaistam remained in his stateroom and used his mirror to check on their progress. He wanted to make certain that the mirror was still in the towers. The mirror no longer showed the towers in its depths, it only showed the book with the strange writing. Kaistam tried to figure out the words but had no luck. He had no books that had the ancient language in them. He thought it might be an old dragon-like language but couldn't be certain without more research and he didn't have all of his resources at his disposal.

The ships had to stop at the inhabited islands to resupply, which took time that the sorcerer didn't have. He wanted to be at the island of the dark towers sooner rather than later, but it was taking longer than he anticipated. He grew frustrated in his stateroom, but he didn't leave it to show his frustration to the rest of the crew. He kept to himself and ranted to no one in particular. On occasion, Renner-Van would pass by his stateroom and hear him raging inside.

The ships were following the shoreline of the larger islands but when they were no longer in their path, they headed back out to the open sea again. Every once in a while they would come across a stray island and sail around it, but the stayed mainly out to sea.

The weather had settled down and the waves were not as bad as they had been. There were still fifteen foot swells which tossed the ship back and forth, but it was much better than the thirty foot swells they had dealt with during the storm. The winds had calmed to just a gentle breeze which pulled favorably at the sails. The ships cut through the waters with the skill of the captains behind the wheel.

The first signs of trouble came when Captain Black, the captain of The Harridan Barque, felt a sharp bang on the hull of the ship. His first guess was that they had hit a reef, but then it went away. Then a few minutes later, BANG!

The crew all ran out of their rooms to see what they hit. They ran to the deck and were greeted by large tentacles writhing over the side of the ship. Immediately they drew their swords and knives and began to hack at them. Slashing and stabbing at the dark green appendages. The ship lurched as the beast pulled at it, trying to drag it down into the depths. Three more tentacles shot from the water and grabbed the deck.

The crew of the ship ran to the crossbows attached to the bulwarks and began to fire into the tentacles. Bolt after bolt struck the long green tentacles causing them to spray dark green ichor all over the deck. The crew slipped and slid, and they defended the ship.

One long tentacle snaked its way to the mizzenmast and grabbed hold snapping it off at the base. The mast came down nearly crushing several sailors beneath it. Several lanterns were knocked over and started small fires that needed to be put out. The crew were running around from side-to-side hacking at tentacles and putting out fires. The captain had all he could do to keep the ship afloat. Finally, the beast had enough, and it gave up. The tentacles slid back into the water and the crew could see the hulking beast swim away into the depths.

The crippled ship was drifting aimlessly in the sea. The other ship, The Savage Bateau, came around and threw them a tow line so that they could tow them to the nearest harbor to fix the broken mast. This was not in the sorcerers plans and he was furious that they needed to stop to fix the ship. He ranted to the captain that he needed to follow a set schedule, but the captain explained that they couldn't go any farther without the mast.

Two days later, the two ships pulled into the harbor town of Skandor's Reef. It took another three days to fix the mast on The Harridan Barque. Kaistam-Laq was anxious to get underway as soon as the mast was fixed. He never let the crew leave the ships while they were in port.

With Skandor's Reef behind them, they headed back out to the open seas. The winds were in their favor and they began to make up for lost time. The ships cut through the waves like a knife through soft butter. Kaistam-Laq began to think that luck was with them for the first time in a while.

The ships passed into dark water, and it became choppy again. The captains kept the ships steady and moving swiftly. The assassins stayed in their rooms as they remained sick from the motion of the waves. The sorcerer was in his stateroom scrying and becoming more frustrated by the minute. The mirror didn't show the book, it only showed the dark towers, causing the sorcerer to wonder if the book was still on the island. He had come this far so he had to follow through.

They sailed for three days without stopping through the choppy waters. The sorcerer was anxious to reach his destination, but they needed to stop for supplies again. The galley needed to be resupplied and they needed more fuel for the lamps. The nearest port was a place called Valerai Landing so they pulled into port for a short stop overnight. This was the first time the crew was allowed to disembark for some time. They all practically ran to the tavern. The sorcerer remained behind on the ship to scry and try to divine the location of the book.

By morning the crew stumbled their way back to the ships to continue the journey. They were still drunk from the night before. Luckily for them the sorcerer hadn't left his room to see them stagger back to the ships.

They weighed anchor and headed back out to sea. The favorable winds put them back on course and they were on their way to the island with the dark towers again. Captain Black led the way with the Savage Bateau following close behind. They sailed hard and fast as the sorcerer wanted to reach the island as quickly as possible. He offered the captains a large bonus to get them there quicker than anticipated.

Tÿr and Danior flew for almost a week to reach the island of the dark towers. When they saw the silhouette of the towers in the distance, they hoped that they would have an easy time retrieving the book. The wyverns began their descent to the island by circling it in large, slowly abating orbits. They wanted to make certain that there was nothing on the island that was unwelcoming. When they were sure that there was nothing unfriendly waiting for them, they finally landed.

The healers remained on alert. They didn't know what type of traps that were waiting for them, so they prepared themselves for anything. They both walked with their staffs charged with energy. Tÿr led Danior forward towards the towers that loomed above them. There was a feeling of dread that emanated from them.

"This place feels bad." Danior told Tÿr.

"I know." She agreed. "I wonder what we will find inside."

"Do you think the towers are cursed?"

"I'm sure we will have to get through some traps that have been set for us."

The wyverns followed the healers to the towers.

"We will not be able to follow you inside," Varanus told them. "We will fly to the top and see what we can see from up above. There is no roof so we might be able to see inside and help you find the book."

The wyverns flew up to the top of the first tower. As they neared the tower glowed an eerie green color. They could not get close to the tower, but they could go above and look down into it. After a few moments they landed back near the healers.

"The book must be in the second tower. It is covered and we couldn't see into it. There is nothing in the first tower except a winding staircase which wraps around the tower all the way to the top. There are no floors, there is nothing except strong magiq protecting it." Varanus told them.

"How do we even get in then?" Danior asked.

"This is where your training comes in." Qaren'a said.

"Use your instincts, your intellect." Varanus told them.

Tÿr and Danior continued to walk to the second tower. They came to the door in the side. It was protected by a seal of magiq. Tÿr looked at the symbol above the opening. It was one she had never seen before. An eye with an arrow piercing it. She could see an eye symbol through the opening on the far wall.

"Do you suppose we have to shoot an arrow into the eye?" she asked Varanus.

"I believe it is something more involved than that. Besides, we have no crossbow nor bolts."

"What about throwing a knife into the eye?"

"You can certainly try it. I seem to think that it is something else though." The wyvern said.

Tÿr took a knife from her waist and tried to hit the eye on the wall. The knife didn't even make it through the barrier. It simply bounced off and fell to the ground. Tÿr picked it up and put it back on her belt.

Danior spoke up. "What if it doesn't mean putting anything in the eye?"

"What do you mean?" Tÿr asked.

"What if it means that you don't use your eyes at all. Put me by the door," he instructed.

Tÿr took his hand and led him to the opening. She told him to walk straight forward. He inched his way forward, hands out reaching for the doorframe. Nothing stopped him. He continued forward and entered the lower level of the tower. He turned around when he was inside.

"Now you try." He told Tÿr.

The girl closed her eyes and put her hands out. She moved forward at a snail's pace, shuffling her feet. Danior held out his hands, reaching for her. Tÿr walked forward until she felt her friend's hands. She opened her eyes and found herself inside the tower.

"Okay, first obstacle overcome." She shouted out to the wyverns.

"Just be careful there are bound to be more." Varanus said.

Tÿr noticed that there were steps missing on the staircase.

"There are missing steps, Dani, I should probably go up alone."

"Are you sure that they're really missing?"

Tÿr grabbed a handful of dirt from the ground on the floor and threw in on the missing steps. Magiqally the steps appeared under the dirt. She walked up and tested one with her staff. It felt strong underneath it.

"Do you want to go with me or stay down here?" She asked Danior.

"I should probably go with you. You might need me."

Tÿr led the way up the stairs to the second landing. The second floor was completely empty except for a pilar which was positioned in the center of the room. There were no more stairs going up from this area. Tÿr took another handful of dust and threw it where the stairs should be. There was nothing. She could see the third floor above her but there were no stairs available to get there.

Tÿr described the room to Danior.

"There have to be stairs," he told her. "We just have to figure out how to make them appear. I think it has to do with the pillar.

Then Tÿr notices holes all round the circumference of the room. The holes were about the same size of the pillar. Tÿr figured that it was possible for the pillar to fit into one of the holes. That was the only thing she could think of. Unfortunately, there were about forty holes in the floor and the ceiling above didn't give and indication of where the steps were. The ceiling appeared to float on nothing.

Tÿr and Danior went to the pillar and dragged it to a random hole and carefully lowered it into it. The pillar was heavy and dropped in with a loud thud. Nothing happened. They tried to lift the pillar out of the hole, but it was to smooth to get a good hold on and they couldn't grab it. They tried and tried for a few moments, and finally gave up.

"We should use our staffs." Danior said. "We can lift it using the staffs and put it in the next cavity. It will make it so much easier than trying to push and pull it."

Tÿr liked the idea so she used her staff to make a beam of energy to grab the pillar and lift it to the next hole. Nothing. Then she moved it to the next, and the next. Finally, after moving it half-way around the room, it fell into a hole across from the one they started on and there was an audible click. Then there was a grating sound as stairs slid out of the wall. They were narrow, wide enough for only one person to walk up.

Tÿr told Danior that she would go up to the next level alone. She didn't know if he would do well on the next level. The stairs were narrow, and they didn't know what was in store.

"You might need me again." he told her.

Tÿr didn't want to put him in danger, she cared too much for him.

"I can take care of myself," he said. "Don't worry about me."

But Tÿr did worry as they walked up the stairs. She went first and held Danior's hand as best she could. They reached the floating landing and noticed there was one more floor above them. It was a partial floor with stairs going up both sides.

"There is one more floor." Tÿr told Danior. "Stay close to me."

They had their staffs in one hand and held hands with the other. Slowly they climbed the stairs. They were hypervigilant as they ascended the staircase. As they neared the top, Tÿr could see the plinth on which the tome sat. The plinth was covered with a blue energy shield of boiling plasma, under which the book sat.

"The book is here." She told Danior.

"Let me guess, we can't just walk off with it."

"It doesn't look like it. It is in an energy field of some sort. I don't think we'll be able to just reach in and get it. We need to find a way to dampen the force field."

Tÿr tried putting her staff in the forcefield and immediately it began to smoke. She pulled it out.

"Well, that didn't work." She said.

"What's burning?" Dani asked.

"I tried to put my staff into the force field. It didn't work." She told him.

"Can we use the staff to lift it out of the force field?" he asked.

"It's worth a shot."

She tried to use an energy beam to grab the book and lift it out of the field. The book moved, but wouldn't come out of the field. It was trapped inside.

"We are going to have to shut it off." She said finally.

"There must be a switch or lever." Danior said.

"That's what I was thinking. But where?"

Týr looked up and tried to see into the rafters. It was too dark to see anything. It was then that Danior spoke up.

"Why are there two towers?"

"I'm not sure," Týr said, "what are you thinking?"

"What if the switch is in the other tower?"

"Varanus said there wasn't anything in there." Týr said.

"At least not that he could see."

"Are you suggesting that we go back down and reset all the traps again to try and find this switch that may or may not be there?"

"I'm suggesting that I go back down and try to find it. when I get out, Varanus can help me find my way to the other tower. He said that there was nothing inside so I should be able to feel around and find what we need. He can always stick his head in to help me if he wants."

"Can you find your way back down?"

"I'll be fine."

"I don't know." Týr said. "I worry about you."

"Trust me."

She pulled him close and kissed him on the mouth.

"You better come back to me."

"I'll see you in a little while." He told her.

Danior felt is way down to the second floor and then to the first. He managed to find the exit and came out alone, causing concern with the wyverns.

"Where is Tÿr'Ynyn?" Varanus asked.

"She is waiting up above. We believe that the switch to release the book may be in the first tower. Could you lead me to it?" Danior asked.

Varanus and Qaren'a led Danior to the other tower. Varanus stuck his head in the doorway. He looked around but didn't see anything.

"I didn't notice any switches, but you might be able to find something I missed," he told Danior.

Danior entered the tower and began to feel his way around the circular room. He ran his hands over every surface in it, feeling for any cracks or bumps or anything that was different. The walls were smooth and Danior didn't find anything out of the ordinary. That is when he tripped over a bump in the floor. It wasn't large but it was different from the rest of the smooth floor. He knelt down to feel it. It was a perfect square and inside the square was another square. A button. He was amazed that he found it at all.

He used his thumb to press in on the inner button which gave way. Then he pressed on the larger outside button. It depressed and locked down.

"That's it!" he heard Tÿr yell. "I've got it!"

Danior came out of the tower and waited by the wyverns for Tÿr to come out of the second tower. She came running out holding the book in her one hand, carrying hers and Danior's staffs in the other.

"Here's your staff." She said, passing it to him.

He took his staff back and turned to Tÿr.

"I told you I could do it."

"Yes, you did." She said, patting him on the back.

"I would have thought a kiss was in order," he whispered to her.

"Later," she whispered back to him, smiling.

"That's two books, one to go." He said.

Tÿr put the book in the bag on Varanus for safe keeping. Now they just had to figure out where the last book was located. That meant that Varanus would have to do some scrying when he got back to Ÿkkynnÿk. The third book had proven to be difficult to find thus far.

"If you two are ready to leave, we need to get this book back to Thunder Mountain." Varanus told them.

"We are ready," Danior said.

The two mounted up and the wyverns lifted off to begin their long journey back to Ÿkkynnÿk. They flew high and were buffeted against the prevailing winds. Still, they stayed high, flying throughout the days and resting at night. Tÿr and Danior spent as much time as they could together when they weren't flying. They loved being in each other's presence.

It took six days of hard flying to reach the shift. The wyverns were tired by the time they landed on the ground of the Kirin-Noirin shift. They decided that it would be best to take a day to rest before traveling on to Thunder Mountain. They still had four days of traveling to go with the winds against them. Tÿr and Danior were happy for the time together. They spent it walking around and talking together about life. They were serious about spending their time together. Each wanting to get more intimate but not knowing how to approach the subject.

That night they made a fire and sat and roasted some sausages and had some ale with them. The brown ale was smooth and went nicely with the sausages. When they were done eating, they got out their pipes and had a nice pipeful of rum flavored pipe weed. They both got light-headed from the thick smoke that they drew into their lungs.

"I love a good pipe after a meal." Danior said.

"I agree."

"It just tastes better after eating."

Tÿr nodded, drawing in another lungful of smoke.

"Can you blow smoke rings?" Danior asked.

"I don't know, I never tried."

Tÿr made her mouth a perfect circle and tried to blow a smoke ring. It didn't happen. She would need more practice. She tried again and again and still couldn't do it. Danior pursed his lips and blew. He blew out the perfect ring.

"How did you do that?" Tÿr asked.

"Did I do it?"

"Yeah. How did you do it? I tried but couldn't."

"I just went like this." Danior said, blowing another perfect smoke ring.

Tÿr mirrored what Danior was doing but just couldn't get the hang of it.

"Where do you put your tongue?" she asked.

"On the bottom kind of in the back."

She tried again with no luck. Over and over, she tried until finally she got a small ring to form.

"I did it. I don't know how, but I did it. Now I can quit," she said.

Danior laughed. "You're not going to try again?"

"Nope, I did it once and now I'm done."

"So, what are we talking about?" Varanus asked as he and Qaren'a walked up on the healers.

"Danior is trying to teach me how to blow smoke rings."

"Like this?" Varanus asked and then he blew a small flame which he extinguished and then he too blew a smoke ring.

"Show off." Tÿr said jokingly.

Varanus chuckled.

"Can you do it too Qaren'a?" Tÿr asked.

"I'm afraid I cannot."

Tÿr continued to try blowing smoke rings and talk with Danior and the wyverns. They discussed the possibilities of where the last book might be. Varanus told them not to be surprised if it was on Peyda Kirin. He would scry when they reached Thunder Mountain. If he couldn't find the book, perhaps the paragon, Ghra'zhenn would be able to locate it.

Danior reached out and took Tÿr's hand. She held on tight. The wyverns were ready for sleep and walked off to sleep in the clearing where they landed. Tÿr and Danior chose to sleep under a large tree in case it rained during the night. Tÿr got out their sleeping rolls and put them next to each other.

When they were finished with their pipes, they were ready to turn in for the night. It was still light out, but the tree shaded them from some of the light. Tÿr reached out and took Danior's hand. He rolled over and gave her a kiss. She kissed him back.

Progress for Kaistam-Laq was slow going as the winds were not in their favor. They had to angle the sails to catch the wind in order to move forward. It is not easy to sail against the wind, but the captains were experienced sailors, and they got the ships moving, zigzagging through the water.

Laq still didn't leave his stateroom. He remained in it, scrying the whole time. The book with the writing on it had become an obsession of his. He tried to figure out the writing on it but there was nothing in his books that had any reference to it. The language, he guessed must be Draconian or Cmok. Both languages were a guarded secret among the lizards. No human knew them to his knowledge. Even the sorcerers of old didn't know the languages as far as Kaistam-Laq knew. His mentor, the sorcerer called Kallistar-Lahm, never mentioned any human ever speaking the wyvern or dragon's tongue.

Kallistar-Lahm was a sorcerer that trained Kaistam-Laq in the ways of sorcery and magiq. He was well known in the lands as a dangerous man who had a no time for insolence from anyone. Kaistam grew powerful and greedy for knowledge. When he felt he had learned all that he could, he poisoned the sorcerer while he slept and took his place as the most powerful sorcerer on the planets.

Kaistam-Laq killed his mentor on the seventeenth of the month at the seventeenth hour of the day. From then on, he was obsessed with the number. He took seventeen rings off of his mentor's hands for himself, and then recruited seventeen people into his crew. Everywhere he looked, seventeen played a roll in his life. From then on, he planned everything around the sacred number.

The captains kept the ships moving as quickly as they could. Captain Harrow of The Savage Bateau was secretly thankful that the sorcerer had not boarded his ship. He had enough to deal with without having to keep the sorcerer happy at all times. Although Captain Black was a strong man, he was no match for the sorcerer if he got angry.

Time was running out for the captains to collect their bonus from the sorcerer. The seas were not being very obliging to them, and they fought the winds now as well. Swells as high as twenty feet made it hard to navigate with the wind in their faces. Still, they moved on toward the island with two towers. It made it difficult to navigate to the island because the sorcerer didn't have an exact location. The captains were forced to land on almost every island and send a landing party out to find the towers.

After floating around through many different islands and traveling a long time, they finally came to their destination. The towers loomed up above the island as the ships floated up to it. They cast anchor and sent a landing party to the towers led by the sorcerer.

Kaistam-Laq almost ran to the towers. He moved past the first tower which appeared to be empty and went to the second one.

There was nothing blocking the door but there was the symbol of the eye with the arrow piercing it. Kaistam looked at the symbol and tried to hit it with magiq.

"Step through the door." He instructed one of the crew members.

The man stepped forward with an apprehensive look and walked to the door. He got to the doorway and tried to get through. He was stopped dead in his tracks by an invisible force. He could not move forward. He tried to back up and found he couldn't move back either. Then suddenly an invisible force threw him violently from the spot he was standing. He landed hard on his back.

Kaistam called another crewman up to try it again with very similar results. Then he called another, and another. They all ended up flying violently onto their backsides.

The sorcerer was losing patience. He was so close to the book and this was causing him all of this trouble. Finally, he figured the symbol out to mean that they needed to walk in blind. He sent the next person in with their eyes bound with a cloth. He walked straight through and into the bottom level of the tower. Kaistam had several more bind their eyes and walk through, then he closed his eyes and walked into the tower.

There in the center of the room was the pedestal. The sorcerer figured out right away that it had to go into one of the holes in the floor. He just needed to figure out which one. He looked around the room and tried to figure out the most logical place to put the pedestal. The pedestal was quite heavy, requiring two men to lift it. Kaistam-Laq had them try holes at different intervals around the room. Eventually they found the correct hole and with a click, the stairs slid out of the wall.

Kaistam ascended the narrow stair to the floating floor and saw two stairways that went up to the next floor. From where he stood, he could see the plinth in the middle of the half floor. It had a glowing forcefield covering it.

This was surely where the book was. He had two crew members walk up either set of stairs to test them. He told them to stand back when they reached the top. Then, taking his staff of power with him he climbed the stairs and reached the top. When he arrived at the zenith of the stairway he looked at the plinth which held nothing on it.

He stared at it quizzically. What was he missing. Where was the tome? Did he have to get past the force field to get it? He moved forward and stuck the bottom of his staff in. The blue force field sizzled and burned the staff. He quickly removed it.

The sorcerer had an idea.

"Stand back, I'm going to blast the pedestal out from under the force field." He told his crew.

They all stood back against the walls and the sorcerer spoke some magiq words. A huge bolt of energy shot out from his staff and hit the plinth. Nothing happened. The energy bolt was actually absorbed into the plinth.

Kaistam-Laq roared with frustration. He didn't usually lose his composure in front of his crew like this, but he was beyond aggravated. The book wasn't where it should be, and he couldn't figure a way to turn off the force field.

"It must have something to do with the other tower." He said finally.

The sorcerer went back down the second tower and into the first tower. He looked around the dark tower. There were only spiraling steps going up around the walls. He cast a light on the end of his staff and searched for any other clues. There were no levers or switches on the walls. He couldn't figure out what he needed to do next until an idea came to him. He cast a spell that would help him detect magiq in the tower. The sorcerer looked around, trying to spot anything that looked out of place or glowed with magiqal light. He looked up into the rafters and all up and down the walls. There was nothing that glowed. He was even more frustrated because he didn't know what he needed to do. It was then that he tripped over something small on the floor. He glanced down and saw a small glowing square on the floor.

Kaistam bent over to inspect the button on the floor. He pushed it and nothing happened. Then after more inspection he pushed the inner button first and then the outer one. They stayed depressed. He walked back to the other tower and back up to the fourth floor. When he reached the plinth, he had a major meltdown. There was no book. He ranted and raved, shooting beams from his staff in all directions that he could. His crew ran for cover, fearing for their lives.

After his initial rant, Kaistam managed to calm himself down enough to think clearly. Where had the book gone? That was the big question. He tried to divine the answer but the magiq was strong around the towers and it kept him from seeing anything useful. Obviously there had been someone here recently, because the book had been here while he was scrying just a few days before. The answer was obvious to him. It had to be the healer, no one else was as powerful as she was.

Kaistam-Laq had no idea where to look for the book now. It could be anywhere. He had to find the healer and take it from her. He tried to scry again but without success. The book was in what appeared to be a vault of sorts, but he neither knew where it was nor how to get at it. It was still protected by strong magiq but the sorcerer didn't have any idea where. It was infuriating to him that he couldn't see it.

"What is the plan?" Renner-Van asked the sorcerer.

"We go after the healer. She has the book that I need, and I will take it from her." He told him.

"Do you now where she is?" Renner asked.

"I do not. I will have to consult my mirror. We are going to head back the way we came. Instruct the captains to sail back to the shift." He told Renner.

"Yes. Of course."

Renner went to the captains and instructed them to sail back the way they had just come. If they were confused by these instructions, they didn't show it. They prepared to weigh anchor and were ready to set off within the hour. Kaistam was back in his stateroom and told Renner that he was not to be disturbed.

The seas were much more agreeable on the way back, as were the winds. Though the waters were choppy, the winds were at their back and they sailed faster than they did on the way there. Kaistam's mood had lightened a bit now that their conditions were more favorable. Still, he couldn't see the healer in the mirror. She was protected by magiq of some sort. He needed to ask the right question of the mirror to get the response he desired. Of this he was certain.

The ships still needed to stop on certain islands to resupply with food and other necessities. People in the port cities were not pleased to see the assassins arrive. They were rowdy and caused many problems in the towns they visited. The magistrates were scared to refuse them landing privileges though for fear of what would happen to their towns.

Kaistam brought the crew to a halt on a small unnamed island. He decided that he would not move until he had more information about the healers. He needed to figure out where they were or at least where they lived. He would raid their home and hopefully find what he was searching for.

The sorcerer became so obsessed with finding the healers that he barely ate or slept. He spent his time scrying on his mirror for hours at a time. When he wasn't doing that, he would try to divine locations with a crystal ball. He preferred to use the mirror as the crystal ball was not as accurate. The mirror seemed to give more details than the ball did.

The mirror would flicker to life with scenes of a cavern. It was a place the sorcerer did not recognize. No matter what he did though, he didn't see the healer. She was absent from every scene that he saw in the mirror, nor were there any wyverns. The magiq that protected them was strong and no matter what he did he couldn't break through it. Then he remembered his candelabra. He still hadn't tried it. Perhaps its magiq was strong enough to break the magiq of the healers. He went to the side of his room and pulled the candelabra over to the table. With a wave of his hand he lit the candles and the incense in the center. He let the incense burn for a moment before blowing the flame out and letting the smoke fill the center of the candelabra. Speaking the words of divination, he waved his hands over the luminaire and it began to show a scene of dark figures. They were human and they were flying on the backs of wyverns. The two healers!

He watched closely as the figures flew through the air, trying to see if he could tell where they were. The candelabra didn't give details, but he knew the healers were on the move and traveling, which meant that they weren't in Vennex. He would be able to tell if they were there. He moved to the scrying mirror and ran his hand over the surface.

"Show me where the healer is going." He said.

There were visions of mountains and then a lake. He didn't recognize the place but now he had a picture of where she was headed. He just needed a name.

Kaistam went to his books and maps to look for the place he had just seen in the mirror. He unrolled the maps and placed them on the table in front of him. He began to search for places that had lakes surrounded by mountains. She had to be on the shift, he decided, but where? Soon he found out that there were several places that the healers could be. There were many mountains and lakes. This did nothing to improve his mood.

The sorcerer was in such a foul mood that even Renner-Van didn't approach him with any issues. He and his sister dealt with the crew and kept them from bothering the sorcerer. They didn't want him to get upset and harm any of them.

The crew could hear the sorcerer pacing back and forth in his chambers. He had gotten no closer to figuring out where the healers were. His maps had been no help and his divining instruments had proven to be useless as well. He had come close to smashing his mirror on several occasions, but he was superstitious and didn't want to risk bringing any more bad luck down upon his head.

Finally, after days of having no luck with finding the healers, the sorcerer decided it was time to leave the island and get back to the shift. He instructed the captains to sail again. The crew had been getting worried about the sorcerer's sanity. They were relieved to be on the move again and hoped that the sorcerer had ceased his relentless pacing and obsessing of the healer.

Four days later, they reached Thunder Mountain. Tÿr and Danior were greeted by Ghra'zhenn when they dismounted the wyverns.

"You have another tome to store here?" Ghra'zhenn asked.

"We do." Danior said turning to the wyvern.

"Excellent."

"Have you located the last book?" Tÿr asked.

The wyvern turned his massive head and looked at the healer. "We have been having issues trying to locate it. I had hoped you would be able to help."

"I will do what I can," she said.

The healers followed Varanus into his cavern. He went to the shelf where the huge scrying mirror was kept and lifted it down to the floor. Tÿr prepared to scry. She drew the proper glyphs on the mirror and then placed her palm on them. The mirror came to life.

Tÿr asked the mirror to show her where the final book was. The mirror dimmed for a moment and then flared back to life. It showed a mountainside cave in a desert. There was a small lake surrounding the mountain. Varanus looked and saw the mountain.

"That is located on the far side of Peyda Kirin." Varanus said. "Whoever separated these books, really made certain they were spread out."

"How long will it take us to reach it?" Danior asked.

"We should be able to make it there in five days of hard flying." Qaren'a said.

"Agreed." Varanus replied.

"I assume there will be protection surrounding it." Tÿr said.

"Most definitely."

"When do we leave?" Danior asked.

"I say we should go within the next couple days." Qaren'a offered.

"Yes. The sooner we get this book the better. The sorcerer could already know about it." Varanus told them.

"I'll be ready to go in the morning," Tÿr told them.

"Me too." Danior chimed in.

Varanus offer the beds in his chambers to the healers. He told them that they never get used and they should feel free to use them. Tÿr and Danior were grateful for the chance to sleep on a bed. They got their sleeping rolls and made up their beds. They slept for ten hours that night. Both were very tired and needed the sleep. The wyverns needed the rest as well.

When they got up in the morning, they rolled up their sleeping rolls and got ready to fly. They would be making several small flights to the mountain as it was in the desert, and they would need to stop and get water often. Tÿr helped Danior get packed up and they were ready to fly within the hour. Tÿr was grateful for the saddles that they had, they made travel so much more comfortable.

They traveled for the whole day before landing at a small lake. It was a small oasis in the desert. There were a few trees and plants surrounding the lake and they decided to camp there for the night. The suns were still up and beat down on them making it hard to get any sleep until they began to slowly dip down on the horizon. It was still too early for them to set completely, but it made for a nice change from the oppressive heat.

Tÿr and Danior snuggled close despite the warmth. They liked to be close together and wanted to spend their time as close to each other as they could get. Often times, the wyverns discussed the blossoming romance of the two healers when they were sleeping. Varanus was pleased that they had found each other, though he wondered if it would have happened if Gordian was still alive. Still, he was happy for them, and felt they deserved happiness. Qaren'a was concerned that they might not be able to complete the mission because one of them would be too concerned for the other's safety. Varanus assured her that they were both strong and would complete the mission no matter what it took.

In the morning, Varanus told them that the next stop would be a small village in the desert called Tyber. They would reach Tyber by late afternoon and would spend the night there. Both Tÿr and Danior were looking forward to spending time in town. It meant they could have a bath and a hot meal in the tavern. Danior also mentioned that they could have a cold ale which made Tÿr smile.

The winds were strong high up so the wyverns stayed lower than they usually flew. This meant that it caused them more energy to fly. They couldn't glide as far as they would have been able to up high. The wyverns were tired by the time they reached Tyber and were ready to rest and find a meal. While Danior and Tÿr went to the inn, the wyverns went out hunting. There was a small mountain range not far from the town that was home to a flock of mountain goats.

Tÿr led Danior to the inn and they booked a room with a bathtub. It cost extra, but they both agreed it would be worth it to soak some of the dirt and dust off. It turned out that there were two tubs in the room. They could both soak at the same time. There was a large curtain separating the tubs so Tÿr and Danior could each have their privacy. The innkeeper came in with hot water and filled the tubs for them.

Danior climbed into the tub and let the hot water ease his muscle aches. He could hear Tÿr sigh as she climbed into her tub.

"This is nice." He told her.

"So nice," she agreed.

They both sat in the hot water and soaked until it cooled off completely.

"Well, my water is cool now." Danior told her.

"Yeah, mine too. I suppose it's time to get out."

"Do you have a cloth to dry off with?" Danior asked.

"Yeah, I'm sure you do too. I'll come over and pass it to you."

Danior covered himself as best he could. Tÿr came around the curtain and grabbed the towel for him. She handed it to him and he took it with his one free hand, and waited for her to walk back around the curtain. When he was certain that she had gone, he got out of the tub and dried off. His clothes were right where he left them, so he got dressed and waited for Tÿr to come and get him.

"Are you dressed yet?" she asked.

"I'm ready," he said.

She collected him and they walked over to their bed feeling better than they had in a while.

"Do you want to go down and get something to eat?" Danior asked her.

"Sounds good."

"I could eat a horse," Danior told her.

"You're always hungry," she said.

They walked out of their room and down the stairs to the main room. There were a few guests there drinking and a couple eating a meal of roast meat and turnips. Danior almost began to drool. He was hungry and ready to eat.

They found a table near the bar and were waited on almost immediately. Danior ordered an ale and a short glass of rum. Tÿr opted to just have the ale while she waited for her meal. They sat and talked about the upcoming leg of their voyage and what they could expect to find. Danior's stomach was growling, and he had finished his rum when the innkeeper brought their meal. The plate was filled with meat and turnips and other roast veg. There was a custard of some sort for pudding.

Danior ate until he couldn't eat another bite. Tÿr was just as full. They thanked the innkeeper for the wonderful meal and then headed off to their room.

"I'm miserable," Dani said.

"I didn't think you could eat that much," Tÿr told him.

When they reached their room, they went to their bed and climbed in. The sheets were nice and clean. It had been a while since they had crisp, clean sheets. Tÿr pulled the covers up over them and rolled over to Danior. She kissed him on the forehead and then moved down to his lips. He kissed her back. They spent the night in each other's embrace. Danior didn't want the night to end.

Morning arrived and the healers went out to find the wyverns. They were right where they left them. The wyverns were ready to get going. They had a long journey to continue and wanted to get back in the air. When the healers were mounted in their saddles, the wyverns lifted off and headed toward the mountain in the desert.

The wyverns still flew fairly low since the currents were strong and buffeted them. Tÿr and Danior rode low on their backs to keep from being beat up by the winds. The trip lasted all day and they landed at an oasis in the desert. There was a small, shallow lake that kept the immediate area green. A few farmers had goats that grazed on the grass surrounding the lake. The farmers were very cautious of the new arrivals to the lake. Tÿr had to do some quick talking and negotiating to allow them to stay the night. The farmers were worried that the wyverns would run off with one of their goats. Tÿr assured them that th wyverns were completely safe and would do no such thing. Despite her assurances, the farmers posted armed guards on their flocks overnight. Tÿr didn't have the heart to tell them that the crossbows that they had would do little damage to a wyvern. The wyverns stayed on the outskirts of the area to try to ease the farmers' minds. Tÿr and Danior slept on a grassy patch that was near the wyverns, in case any trouble broke out. It was safe to say that nobody got much sleep that night. The farmers were glad to see the wyverns go and also relieved that none of their flock were gone. It was safe to say that they hadn't seen a wyvern before.

The wyverns flew the healers away from the oasis and on toward the mountain. They still had several days to go before reaching their destination. Varanus chose to fly lower than usual because of the wind currents. They were strong and hot, and he preferred staying low. This didn't bother Tÿr in the least. She still didn't like flying high, so when Varanus chose to fly lower she was more at ease in the saddle.

It was mid-afternoon before they came to another oasis-like area. Varanus brought them down to land and asked the healers whether they wanted to stop for the night, or if they wanted to push on and see if they could find another oasis farther on. Tÿr asked Danior what he wanted to do and he figured that they should push on a little farther. There could be a town farther on. Varanus wasn't too certain as he hadn't been through here for quite some time.

"Would you mind if we continued on for a bit?" Danior asked the wyverns.

"I am fine to continue." Varanus said. "Qaren'a?"

"I am fine. I think it would be good if we could find something to eat tonight though." She told them.

"I agree. We still have a long trip and nourishment would be useful."

"If you see a town or village, feel free to stop, even if its not far from here." Danior told Varanus.

"That is the plan then. If we don't find a town, we will stop at the next green area. There should be some wildlife there." Varanus told them.

The healers mounted up and they got back into the air. They flew on for another two hours before the ground became green and a small village appeared below them. A small river ran through the town and into the desert. It was what seemed to keep things green out this far.

The wyverns circled the town and landed. They stayed outside of the town so the healers could walk in.

The wyverns decided to hunt while the healers went into town. There were flocks of sheep grazing on the greenery around the village. The wyverns had to be careful where they hunted because there were shepherds watching the flocks and they were armed with heavy crossbows.

Varanus told Qaren'a that maybe they would have to wait to eat because there were so many shepherds in the fields, and they risked being shot at if they tried hunting the fields. Varanus also knew that they needed to eat. They might need to take a sheep from the flock, but if they were going to do that, it would have to be when they were leaving. That or they would have to buy a sheep or two from the shepherds.

The town was small, only seven main buildings, there were houses on the outskirts. Tÿr and Danior went to the inn and took a room there. They got a meal and ate it quickly before retiring to their room to sleep. They were both more tired than they thought they were. Both fell asleep quickly and slept through until the morning. Danior woke first and found Tÿr snuggled up next to him. He smiled and pulled her closer to him.

Tÿr woke up and found that she was nestled up next to Danior. He had his arms around her and his head on hers. She smiled as she rolled over.

"Good morning," she said.

"Hi. You're awake."

"Did we sleep like this the whole night?"

"I'm not sure. I'm just glad to wake up like this." He said.

She reached up and kissed him, and he kissed her back.

"We better get out to the wyverns." She told him.

They got out of bed and got their boots on. They walked out to the wyverns who still hadn't eaten and told them that they were ready to go. The wyverns asked them to talk to the shepherds about getting a couple sheep for them. So Tÿr and Danior walked out to the fields to see how much two sheep would cost. The shepherd that they spoke to wanted six silver pieces per head for the sheep. Tÿr paid him and they led the sheep back to the edge of town.

Varanus and Qaren'a told them that they might want to take a walk while they ate. Tÿr took Danior by the hand and they walked back into town to visit some of the shops. There was an herbalist and a bookstore that had very few books. Tÿr found several herbs that she couldn't find in Vennex so she bought them while she was there. There was a temple that no one seemed to visit for some reason and a tavern. They didn't visit the other buildings because Tÿr figured that the wyverns would be done eating by then, so they began their walk back to meet them.

Both Varanus and Qaren'a had gore on their faces when the healers met up with them. Both sheep were gone.

"Did you have enough to eat?" Tÿr asked the wyverns.

"We have eaten our fill for now." Qaren'a said.

"You have a bit of sheep on your faces." Tÿr told them.

Immediately the wyverns began to try to lick the gore off of their visages. Tÿr knew that Varanus was self-conscious about things like this. He liked to maintain a neat appearance.

The wyverns continued to clean themselves off while Tÿr and Danior waited to go.

"That's better," Tÿr told them.

They climbed aboard and were off again. There were still about three days left to reach the mountain.

The next three days went by quickly. When they weren't in the air, they were eating or sleeping. They needed to get their rest for the last obstacle on the journey. None of them knew what to expect when they reached the mountain. There were bound to be deterrents meant to keep them from reaching the book.

Finally, the mountain loomed before them. The wyverns had taken them low and were flying them close to the ground. Varanus chose to stay close to the ground despite the fact that it made gliding difficult. They moved to the base of the mountain and the wyverns landed. Tÿr could see the opening from where they were on the ground. It was about two thousand feet above them. There appeared to be a trail leading up to the opening.

"It looks like we are walking." Tÿr told Danior.

"Do you want us to go with you?" Varanus asked the healer.

"No, I think we will be okay. Besides, we have our whistles if we need you."

"Very well," Varanus said, "we will wait here for you."

"How far is it?" Danior asked.

"It's going to be a good little hike." Tÿr told him.

They got their staffs and began to hike up the side of the mountain. The trail was rocky and had several roots sticking out making it difficult to traverse. Danior held on to Tÿr's arm and did his best not to trip over the obstacles on the ground. It took them over three hours to reach the opening in the side of the mountain. Climbing had been tough leading Danior, but he was insistent that he go. He didn't want anything bad to happen to Tÿr if she was alone.

When they came to the opening, there was nothing to prevent them from entering. Tÿr searched the ground for any pressure plates or any trip wires. There were none. She led Danior into the chamber. It took her eyes a few moments to adjust to the dimness inside.

"Do you sense anything?" she asked Danior.

"I don't sense anything or hear anything."

"Yeah, me either."

"We should be careful." He told her.

"Agreed." She took his hand and led him forward.

The cavern broke into two separate caves. Both were dark and looked like they went back a good distance. Tÿr chose the left one first and they walked slowly down. Tÿr lit her staff so they would have some light. The cave looked like it went back for quite a long way. Tÿr suggested that they try the other cave before going all the way down this one.

They backed out of the cave and walked into the other cave. This cave had an eerie glow coming from the end of it.

"I think we're in the right one." Tÿr told Danior.

"Yeah, there's a humming sound coming from this one." Danior told her.

"Really? I can't hear it," she said.

"Yeah, it's very quiet but I can hear it. It's high pitched and it's getting louder."

Tÿr slowed them down. She tried to see around the cave with her staff. Whatever was making the noise and the light, was coming from in front of them.

Tÿr noticed an altar in front of them with tiles spread out around it on the floor. She stopped them and described the scene to Danior.

"Don't touch the tiles," he said, "I bet they are pressure activated."

Tÿr found a decent sized rock on the floor and picked it up.

"I've got a rock that I'm going to throw on the tiles," she told him.

She tossed the rock out in front of them, and it skidded over three of the tiles. There was a swishing sound and then a clattering as something hit the wall of the cave. Tÿr noticed that the three tiles that the rock had skidded across were slightly depressed. She showed her light toward where the noise of the clattering was. There on the floor were three deadly looking darts. They were four inches long and it appeared that they were tipped in some black substance.

"Poison darts." Tÿr said.

"How do we get across the tiles?" Danior asked.

"*We* don't do it. *I* have to do it." Tÿr said.

"How? Can you fly over there?"

"Not fly, but I can walk very lightly."

"Come again?" He said.

"I can walk without touching the ground. Varanus taught me how to do this when I first started to learn magiq."

"Well, be very careful, one wrong step and you're going to be in trouble. I think that poison is bÿchymme oil and that is very toxic."

"Understood. I will just need to concentrate. I can't levitate yet, but I can do this, which is close." Tÿr said. "I need you to stand back here and not move. I will come back and take your hand if I am successful. If I get hit, I will need you to heal me."

Danior stood back and let Tÿr walk forward. She mumbled some words and then stepped over the tiles.

She knew the spell worked immediately. Her foot felt like it was standing on a thin pillow. She stepped over the tiles and walked to the altar. The area immediately around the altar was not surrounded by tiles. It was smooth rock of the cave floor. She reached for the book and then saw that there were several strings of magiqal light connected to it. The light strings went from the book to the ceiling.

She tried to remove the book from the altar, but the strings held the book in place. She could move it but could not remove it. She tried pulling it away from the altar, but it wouldn't budge. She called back to Danior and explained what was going on.

"We have to find a way to sever the strings," she told him.

"Do you know a severing spell?" he asked.

"I know how to cut non-magiqal things, but I don't know if it will work on magiqal things."

"There is only one way to find out."

Tÿr spoke the words to sever. A small beam of energy shot out at one of the strings. Sparks flew everywhere, but the string remained intact. If anything, it almost looked like it grew in thickness.

"Nope, no luck. It looks like it got stronger." Tÿr said.

"What about a sphere of energy?" Danior asked.

"How do you mean? Shoot a sphere at them?"

"No. Create a sphere and surround the book with it. Let the energy beams penetrate the sphere and then remove the book from the sphere." Danior said.

"That might work," she said.

Tÿr crafted a sphere of blue energy that sparked and crackled and then she moved it to the book. She enlarged it to surround the book and then moved it into place. The energy strings were absorbed into the outside of the sphere, and they grew in thickness, but the book looked like it was able to be taken. There were no strings attached to it anymore.

"I need you to lift the book with your staff." She told Danior.

"Um, I can't see it.

"Just listen to my voice and try to lift the book. It is right next to me. I will guide you."

Danior pointed his staff at Tÿr, and she guided him to her left.

"Okay. Now lift it up. I just need you to lift it about two feet, then I will take it."

Danior concentrated and the book began to move.

"Higher." Tÿr told him.

The book rose higher. Finally, it cleared the energy sphere and Tÿr snatched it out of the air.

"Okay, I have it."

"Now you have to come back across the tiles. Please be careful!"

Tÿr cast the spell to walk lightly over the tiles again. She walked back over to Danior and took his hand to let him know she made it back safely. They now had to go back down the mountainside and find the wyverns.

The trek back down the mountainside was easier than the trip up. Still, it took the over two hours to reach the base. The wyverns were waiting patiently for them at the bottom of the mountain. Tÿr put the book in the saddlebag on Varanus.

"I see you had no issues getting the book," the wyvern said.

"Well, not too many issues. There were traps set to deter would be thieves."

"That was to be expected."

"At least we have all three books now." Tÿr said.

"We need to get this one back to Ÿkkynnÿk." Qaren'a told them. "I don't trust the sorcerer.

"He is bound to find out that we have them sooner or later." Varanus agreed. "We need to find out where he is so we can prepare for a fight."

The healers got their belongings packed in their saddlebags and then mounted their saddles and prepared to fly to Thunder Mountain. It would take them about three days from here with the winds at their backs again. Varanus and Qaren'a chose to fly high and fast. Tÿr, once again, was thankful that she had found her saddle. It made flying so much more comfortable.

The first night they spent in the wilderness, but on the second night, Varanus spotted a village below them and decided to land near it. It was getting late, and the healers were tired, so the wyvern thought it was a good time to take a break. The town they stopped in was called Miner's Locke.

Tÿr and Danior found their way to the tavern and inn which were connected making it easier for them. They took a room at the inn and then walked down to the tavern for a meal and a few glasses of ale. Danior had a small glass of rum first and then stuck with dark ale the rest of the night. They had roast mutton and veg for dinner which was cooked just how they liked it. There was a small gravy boat of the tastiest gravy that either of them had ever tried before. There were also little loaves of crispy bread that they used to sop up every bit of the gravy that they could. The barkeep offered them custard for pudding but neither of them could eat another bite. They complimented him on his incredibly tasty meal and tipped him generously. It was obvious that the barkeep wasn't used to receiving decent tips because he acted like he didn't know what to do when he got the tip from the two healers.

The healers left the tavern and retired to their room. They were both very tired and full from their meal and fell to sleep quickly. Danior wrapped his arms around Tÿr and held her tightly to him. She smiled as they snuggled together.

Morning came quickly for the two. They were still tired and full from the night before. Tÿr considered staying another night but knew that they needed to get back to Thunder Mountain. It was important to get the book back to the vault where it would be safe.

They were on their way back to Ÿkkynnÿk early in the morning. They wanted to get as much flying as they could by the end of the day. Each day the healers were together they felt closer to each other. If it wasn't for their mission, Danior would have already asked Tÿr to become his mate.

On the third night, the healers decided to sleep in the wilderness near a small lake. They were getting close to Thunder Mountain, but the wyverns were tired and needed to rest. Tÿr and Danior had some sausages that they had gotten in Miner's Locke so they roasted them over a fire. They both enjoyed them tremendously. Sausages were one of their comfort foods. They also had a bottle of wine to share which they drank slowly to keep from getting too intoxicated.

Varanus and Qaren'a went to hunt while the healers ate their meal. They returned an hour later after feeding on wild boars that they hunted out in the wilderness. Varanus made certain that he cleaned his face off before returning back to the healers. He knew that Tÿr would tease him about it, if there was gore on his face.

Danior and Tÿr slept, snuggled tightly together. They were so tired that they didn't say much to each other before falling asleep. Varanus smiled as he watched the healers sleep.

"I never would have thought those two would have ended up together," he told Qaren'a.

"Really? I could see how much they admired each other from the first time I saw them."

Varanus chuckled. "Must be woman's intuition."

"It is just like I knew we were meant to be together the first time I saw you hunt." She told him.

Varanus was at a loss for words. He turned to look at her and then turned away, smiling.

The two wyverns settled down to sleep as well. They had one more leg of the journey to complete the next day. The wind was at their backs, and they hoped to be at Thunder Mountain by the middle of the afternoon.

Everyone woke early in the morning to get ready to set off. Danior and Tÿr mounted their saddles and were off. The wyverns decided to fly high and use the air currents to their advantage. Tÿr really hated being this high up but knew it wouldn't be for long. They flew fast and were nearing Thunder Mountain sooner than they had expected. The currents were strong and pushed them toward the mountain at extremely high speeds. They landed in the early afternoon and by then Varanus was ready to rest.

Varanus took the tome into the cavern and placed it into the vault. He then told Tÿr that he would add a way for her to open the vault as well in case anything ever happened to him.

"I need you to be able to access the vault in case I am unable to do it," he explained.

"How do we do this?" Tÿr asked.

"We will imprint your hand into the wall below mine and then teach the vault to recognize your magiq. You will then be able to open the vault."

Varanus explained how to she would heat her hand hot enough to melt rock. She attempted it several times before she mastered the technique. Then Varanus walked her to the precise spot that she would need to make her mark in the wall. He put his winged hand over hers. Together they heated their hands until they glowed white hot.

"Place your hand here on the wall." Varanus said, moving her hand to the side of the cavern.

The wall began to glow red hot. Melted rock leaked out from around Tÿr's hand and fell to the floor. Her hand sunk into the wall making a perfect imprint of her hand. Varanus's handprint was imprinted over hers.

"Okay, now you can remove it."

Varanus told her the magiqal word to say to seal the charm. It was in Cmok, the word *Vraakchyck.*

"Commit that word to memory. You will use it to open the vault." Varanus told the healer.

Tÿr repeated the word several times out loud to make certain that she was pronouncing it correctly. When she was sure she had it memorized she told Varanus that she wanted to try it.

She put her hand on the indentation and spoke the word, "Vraakchyck."

The wall opened and admitted her to the vault.

"Okay, I think I have it."

Varanus made her practice it a few more times just to be certain that she could do it repeatedly. When she was confident that she could, the wyvern stopped her and told her never to forget the word and never to let anyone else know it.

"There are too many items in here that people like the sorcerer would love to get their hands on." He told her.

Tÿr swore that she would never let anyone even know about the place.

"Now that we have the books, I would like to continue my quest to defeat the sorcerer." Tÿr told the wyverns.

"I figured you would want to continue to search for him." Varanus told her. "Just remember that he is more powerful now than he has ever been. He has a whole new group of assassins that are more dangerous than the last ones. We must proceed with caution."

Tÿr nodded. "I understand. I just want to make them pay for Gordian, and I know that Dani can't do it by himself."

"I want them dead." Danior said with very little emotion in his voice.

Tÿr reached over and took Dani's hand. He squeezed it back. "We will make them pay," she said.

The sorcerer and his crew landed back on the Kirin-Noirin shift after almost five weeks of sailing. They were tired and seasick from the rough waters. Even the sorcerer was feeling ill from the effects of the choppy waters. He had remedies and took them, but they weren't helping like he had hoped they would.

Renner-Van and his sister were feeling the effects of the seas especially bad. They were cloistered in their cabin and feeling terrible. When they landed on the shift, they practically ran off the boat, as did the rest of the crew. None of them were used to sailing. An attack now would be very bad.

Captains Black and Harrow were not sad to see the assassins go. They were happy to get the sorcerer and his crew off of their ships. They had lived in fear for their lives from the time the crew boarded until they left. Their own crew was strong and could stand up to a fight, but not against a group of assassins.

Kaistam-Laq wanted to get moving the second his feet hit the ground, but he was still feeling poorly from the effects of the sea, so he had the crew rest for the night. He made potions for everyone that he forced them all to drink. They were potions that helped to calm their stomachs and stop their heads from spinning.

The sorcerer spent the evening on his mirror. He tried to figure out where the healers were. The mirror showed the unfamiliar mountain again. Still, he couldn't see the healers. He knew this mountain was important and he needed to figure out where it was. Kaistam scried every different way that he could think of, and still he didn't come up with anything.

By morning the crew felt much better and was ready to ride. The sorcerer's mood had not improved from the night before. He was still ranting about not being able to find the healers. The crew knew not to bother him when he was in one of his moods.

They rode on from the port where they landed and moved on toward the middle of the shift. The sorcerer didn't know exactly where they were headed but he had a feeling that they would find the healers somewhere ahead of them.

They came to a small town called Brÿsville and there they stayed for the night. The crew ran to the tavern for drinks while the sorcerer stayed behind to scry. He was not about to give up on finding the healers. He knew they were out there somewhere, but he didn't understand why he couldn't see them. There was some type of magiq protecting them, and he needed to figure out how to break through it.

Brÿsville was a town full of ruffians, and the tavern held most of them. Fights broke out almost immediately when the crew got to the tavern. Renner and Ollis-Van tried to break up the fights but were dragged into them as they had to protect half of the crew from the town ruffians. Renner went from one fight to the next trying to break them up. He found himself in the middle of several scraps as he attempted to stop the fighting before any law enforcement got there.

Ollis had to break the nose of one of the ruffians for touching her inappropriately. Whether it was on purpose or not, she didn't know. She didn't tolerate it either way. When some of the locals saw what she was capable of, they began to back down. She and her brother were beginning to overpower the locals with the help of the crew, when there was a shrill whistle from outside of the tavern.

"It's the law!" Renner yelled.

The crew scattered and ran from the place just as three constables ran in carrying short crossbows and yelling for everyone to stay where they were.

Kaistam was still trying to scry when the crew came dashing back.

"What is happening?" he asked Renner-Van.

"Trouble with the locals. We need to move."

The sorcerer was not pleased and cursed loudly. He put up his mirror and prepared to move on. The crew all mounted their rides and they left quickly before any law enforcement official found them. The sorcerer's palanquin jolted forward, and his mirror fell down to the floor. It cracked into several pieces despite being wrapped in a satin cloth.

The sorcerer screamed out in rage and shot beams of energy out in all directions hitting a couple of the crew members' horses, killing them instantly. The crew members fell to the ground, one of them trapped under his horse. Renner-Van jumped down and pulled the trapped assassin out from under the horse.

For the next couple of hours Renner and Ollis spent time trying to calm the sorcerer down. They explained that now they would have to travel even slower because they had assassins that would have to walk because they had no horses until they could replace them. The sorcerer was not easily calmed but eventually they managed to placate him. They made certain not to mention that it was his fault that they were down three horses.

The assassins began to move again, slower than before which displeased the sorcerer, but he knew it was his fault. Despite this he pressed them forward at a pace that caused those on foot to run to keep up. Before long those on foot were lagging behind and the sorcerer was forced to wait for them. He told Renner to search for the nearest town to acquire some new horses. He didn't care if they bought them or stole them. He wanted to pick up the pace.

By nightfall a small village came into view on the horizon. It was situated on a hilltop. The suns were still in the sky and so the sorcerer pressed the crew on to the village. He instructed the already weary assassins that they would not be stopping for long. They were there to appropriate horses and move out before anyone realized what was happening. The horseless assassins moved furtively into the little village and as cautiously as they could they wrangled three horses away from the local tavern where they were tied up. There were no saddles or any riding gear on them save for the ropes that tethered them to the post outside the tavern. It wasn't until they were riding away that someone noticed them stealing the horses. The alarm was raised, and the tavern emptied.

Men and women both ran at the assassins on the horses. The assassins drove the horses hard and sprinted to meet up with the others. Kaistam-Laq noticed the ruckus and prepared the crew to move off.

"We move now!" he yelled.

The caravan moved out as the three horsemen ran to meet up with them. The villagers were falling behind but still pursued the horsemen.

"Move! Move!" one of the horsemen yelled.

Kaistam could see the villagers in the distance but knew they didn't have much of a chance to catch them up. Bells rang from the village square, sounding an alert. There were some villagers on horses though, and they would be able to follow them. The sorcerer counted about twenty village horsemen, but the assassins moved forward at a higher rate of speed, trying to lose the villagers. The bells continued to peal loudly alerting the villagers of the thievery.

From his palanquin, the sorcerer threw up a shield of darkness. Instantly they were blocked out of sight from the approaching villagers. The sorcerer wanted to cast a spell of invisibility on them but there were too many of them to do it properly. He could cast on a few of them, but trying to cast on all of them was impossible, even for him.

Eventually the villagers gave up the chase and returned to the hilltop village. They were lucky that none of them had actually caught up to the assassins. They might have been angry and ready to fight, but they were no match for trained killers.

The sorcerer was forced to divine using his crystal ball, which was not as accurate as his mirror, but now that his mirror was in several pieces he was forced to improvise. He sat in front of the ball and asked it to show him the healers. All he got in return was dark shadows. He didn't get any places or any faces that he could recognize. He tried to divine the location of the book, and a vision of a mountain appeared and disappeared as quickly as it came. He tried to commit the vision to his memory. He didn't recognize the mountain. *This too must be protected by wyvern magiq*, he thought.

The sorcerer's mood did not improve as they rode along. The harder he tried to see where the healers were the less, he saw. He felt that he needed to ask the ball specific questions, but he was running out of things to ask. Once again he tried to see the mountain, and once again it flickered in the ball, but he could not get the vision to stay. He practically screamed in rage.

The assassins heard the commotion but didn't dare to see what it was. They knew better than to bother the sorcerer when he was in one of his moods. Renner-Van kept the caravan moving forward and his sister stayed at the rear to watch out for invaders. She had a small crew of three assassins that kept riding circles around the caravan to ensure its safety. The sorcerer wanted to ride on into the night, but the brother and sister convinced him that the horses needed to rest.

The assassins were glad for the respite. They had ridden hard all day and they needed the break. Kaistam-Laq stayed to himself and continued to use his crystal ball.

When morning rolled around the sorcerer got the crew up and moving again. They were moving faster than the day before because during the nighttime the sorcerer thought he had a breakthrough on the crystal ball. He was certain that he knew where the mountain was in the visions. It was a place called Thunder Mountain, but nobody had ever heard of it before. Renner and Ollis-Van thought that the sorcerer was beginning to lose his mind because of his obsession with the healers. They didn't like to question their leader, but he was starting to lose his grip on reality.

Kaistam-Laq had heard of the place called Thunder Mountain from one of the old tomes he had read in the past. He knew it was a place inhabited by wyverns and that it would be well protected. In fact, he had no ideas on how to infiltrate the mountain. When he told the brother and sister about it, they told him they would need more information about it, privately thinking that he had become too obsessed with the healers.

When they were together alone, the brother and sister talked about how obsessed the sorcerer had become. He was spending all of his time trying to locate the healers and neglecting everything else. Unfortunately, he was in such a foul mood that neither of them dared approach him about it. Though they could use magiq, he was still more powerful than they were.

The sorcerer spent all of his time on his crystal ball, and he wasn't taking care of himself. He wasn't eating or drinking except to grab a quick bite here and there. Even the other assassins were beginning to notice. Things were said in hushed voices as they traveled on. Renner told them to mind their own business.

They traveled on for three days before the sorcerer called them to a halt. He stopped them to admit he didn't know exactly where they were going. He asked if anyone in the crew had heard of Thunder Mountain before. There was muttering amongst the crew, but the sorcerer didn't seem to notice. When none of them came forward with a response, he got a bit more forceful.

"We *are* going to Thunder Mountain. If you cannot help to get there I have no use for you. You are relieved of your duties to me."

There was a lot more muttering. The crew knew that no one was just let go to carry on by themselves. When someone was let go from the crew, they met with horrible accidents and were dead within hours. They knew that Renner-Van or his sister was the enforcer of this, and no one wanted to be let go. They all muttered that they would assist the sorcerer in finding the mountain.

Kaistam-Laq was pleased with his little inducement. It had gotten the desired results that he had been going for. The crew now had new motivation.

Finally, Kaistam-Laq decided that he needed nourishment. He called the crew to a halt at the next small town that they came to. The sorcerer was weak from lack of food and drink. He told the crew before they entered the town that they were to conduct themselves professionally and to leave the rowdy behavior behind. He didn't want to have to leave in a hurry this time.

Renner and Ollis went with the crew into town and watched over them to make certain that no one got out of line. The tavern had a few rowdy townsfolk that were itching to start a fight with a stranger, but the brother and sister quelled any fight that threatened to break out.

The sorcerer stayed outside of town in his tent and finally ate a meal. He drank a bottle of wine that made his head spin. He didn't like the feeling. He preferred to be in control of his faculties at all times. Kaistam ate a lot of meat and bread and cheese with his wine. When he was finished, he went back to his crystal ball to try to divine any information that he could. He was becoming desperate for anything. Any piece of information that he could glean from the ball. All it showed was the mountain in brief glimpses. He still had no idea where to find it.

In the morning the crew reassembled, and they prepared to move on. Kaistam was feeling stronger now and led them forward. He was confident that they would find this mountain if they moved on toward the middle of the shift. Unfortunately, he had no landmarks to help him find the mountain, nor was he completely certain that it was on the shift. He just had to go with his instincts. He did not share his lack of knowledge with the crew. They were on a need-to-know basis, and they did not need to know right now. He would tell them if the need arose. Fear is what he would use to keep them in line.

"Where do you think the sorcerer is, Varanus?" Tÿr asked the wyvern.

"We can attempt to scry, but I am afraid that he will have protection around him that we can not break through," he told her.

"I would like to attempt to scry again," Tÿr said.

"We can definitely do that."

Varanus went over to the shelf where he kept his huge square scrying mirror. The obsidian mirror was heavy, so he lifted it down for Tÿr and put it on the cavern floor. The healer sat in front of the mirror and drew the future and seeing glyphs on the mirror and then placed her hand on the glowing symbols. She concentrated on what she wanted to see the most, the sorcerer. She needed to see where he was heading next.

An image of the sorcerer appeared in the mirror. He was sitting in an ornate palanquin. Tÿr tried to see if she could tell where he was, but she couldn't see any landmarks. She asked Varanus to look and see if he could tell anything. Varanus drew another glyph over the mirror and the scene changed. Suddenly the scene was wider, and they could see more, there were others with the sorcerer. It appeared that they were somewhere on the shift. Varanus pulled the scene way back to make certain.

"They must be on the shift. The sorcerer knows that the book is gone from the island. He doesn't know about the mountain book yet; I'm willing to bet. I also think that he is planning on taking the books from us." Varanus told the healers.

"The books are safe in the vault though, correct?" Danior asked.

"They are, but that won't stop him from trying to get them."

"He can't get into the vault, can he?"

"He cannot. Not unless he is escorted in." Varanus told him. "The vault is highly protected from outside and in. He would need to get past all of the wyverns of Ÿkkynnÿk before he even entered the cavern, and then there is the actual vault which he has no chance of breaking into."

"How many wyverns are allowed into the vault?" Danior asked.

"There is just me, and Tÿr." Varanus answered. "No one else. That way there is accountability. If something is missing or gets broken, I know it is either myself or her. I don't have to go looking for the culprit."

"Could you show me how to make a vault similar to yours?"

"I could. It would take some training on your part, but it is very teachable. Where would you like to make this vault?" Varanus asked Danior.

Danior turned to Tÿr. "I was thinking we could make a vault where we go camping back in Vennex. It is out in the woods, and no one ever goes there. There are caves near the campsite and we could use one of them."

"Or we could ask Varanus to store our things in his vault." Tÿr suggested.

"But it is so far from home. We need something closer." Dani said.

Varanus suggested that they make a vault in the base of their clinic back in Vennex. He explained that he could use magiq to remove the earth from the base of the building and they could use the empty space as a vault. He could then replace the earth with a façade making it look like the earth hadn't been moved at all. Then they would have a space to store their belongings and treasures. They could either do that or they could build a room onto the clinic that had no doors or windows and was solid stone. They would use a spell to open it and deposit their belonging in it. The only problem with that is that everyone would know where the room was. They just couldn't enter it. If the sorcerer found it though, he could use magiq to break into it.

"We will have to discuss this," Danior told Varanus.

"I completely understand."

Danior and Tÿr sat and discussed the pros and cons of each of the vaults. In the end Tÿr felt it would be best to have the vault under the clinic. Danior tended to agree with her, he felt that if they collected anything of importance, it would be best that they kept it close.

"So, do you want to head back to Vennex and build this before we continue our hunt for the sorcerer?" Varanus asked the healers.

"I suppose a small detour won't hurt us. It would be nice to go home for a little while. We could open the clinic while we build the vault and see patients." Tÿr said.

"Mum would like a visit too," said Danior.

"Then it's settled. On to Vennex!" Tÿr declared.

Vennex was a three-day trip from where they were. The wyverns stayed high in the air the whole time. Tÿr didn't enjoy the flight but she knew it would be over in a few days so she hung on tight and closed her eyes for a good deal of it. Once she felt the wyverns begin to descend, she would open her eyes again. She loved the ride down for some reason. Ascending was not her favorite by far but dropping down towards the ground made her feel safer.

It was the last day of flying for a while and Tÿr could see Vennex up ahead. She was excited to be going home despite the fact that her parents weren't there. They were still in Londstäc. She was looking forward to seeing the people she had known since she was a little girl. People that now trusted her to heal them.

The wyverns circled the village in large circles, spiraling in to land in the village center. Several people rushed up to greet them when they landed. They all had the same question for Tÿr and Danior.

"Are you going to open the clinic to heal?" they asked.

Tÿr told them that they had business to tend to, but they would see patients for the few days that they were in town. The people were very happy to hear this. Tÿr had a feeling that they were going to be very busy for the next few days. For now though, she wanted to head over to the pub and get a drink and a meal. She took Danior by the hand and they walked to the pub together. They wyverns told them that they would go out to hunt.

When they got to the pub, Tÿr recognized just about everyone there. There were a few new faces that the locals introduced her to. She was happy to meet them. She and Danior got a table to themselves though everyone kept stopping by to tell them how nice it was to see them.

The barkeep came by and took their order for two roast dinners. He gave them two glasses of ale on the house. Tÿr thought how nice it was to be back home. No matter how nice it was to travel, being home was just special. The people were so friendly and happy to see them.

Their meals came and they were about finished with them when the door of the pub opened, and a woman walked in. Tÿr didn't notice her because her back was to the door. The pub got quiet.

"What's going on?" Danior asked.

"I'm not sure."

Tÿr turned around and saw the woman walking toward them. It was Danior's mother. She had tears in her eyes.

"Dani, it's your mum."

Dani looked up. "Mum?"

The woman walked up to the table. "You can't even come to see your old mum."

"We were going to come and see you after we ate." Danior told her.

He stood up and reached out to her. His mother hugged him to her tightly.

"I have been so worried about you."

"We are fine, Mum."

"You are taking care of my boy." She told Tÿr.

"He's taking care of me as well," She told his mother. "Please, sit and join us."

"I don't want to be any bother."

"You aren't any bother. We are happy to see you." Tÿr told her. "Please sit!"

Danior's mother sat down with the healers and Tÿr asked the barkeep for another plate. At first his mum fussed and said she didn't want to be any trouble but then they two of them convinced her to join them for a meal. They got her a glass of dark ale to go with the roast and they sat and told her of their adventures. She listened to their tales as they went after the books and blanched as they told her how they had to get past traps and obstacles.

"It's a wonder that you're still alive," she told them.

"Not really," Danior told her. "Tÿr has been looking out for me."

Danior didn't bother to tell her that the sorcerer was probably looking for them as they sat there. He figured that she worried enough without letting her know about that.

They finished their meal and Mëyan Suttÿr told them that they were welcome to spend their time in

Vennex in her home. At first Tÿr was apprehensive, but Danior convinced her that it would be nice for his mother to have company.

"Well, if we stay at your house," Tÿr told her, "Then we buy your dinner every night."

Mëyan tried to argue, saying that she was happy to take care of them, but Tÿr knew that she didn't have much, and she didn't want to be a burden on her.

Finally, Danior's mother conceded and Tÿr and Danior went to fetch some of their belongings they would need. They returned to his mother's house with their healer's bags and a change of clothes. Tÿr was looking forward to taking a bath. It had been a while since they had been in a place with a nice tub. Mëyan was happy to heat some water for Tÿr. The healer sat and soaked for an hour, until the water turned cold. Danior's mum asked if she needed any more, but Tÿr told her to save it for her son.

Danior took his turn next. He didn't soak as long as Tÿr did, but he did enjoy a nice soak and then he scrubbed up and got out. His mother offered to clean their dirty clothes for them. Tÿr told her not to bother herself with them, but she told her it was no trouble and set out to wash their clothes. Tÿr told Danior to give some silver to his mother. His mother tried to refuse, but Tÿr told her it was for room and everything she had done for them.

The pair was tired and went to Danior's room to sleep. His bed was small, so they had to snuggle close which made both of them smile. Tÿr liked being close to Danior, and he liked holding her. They fell asleep in each other's arms.

When morning came Tÿr reached up and kissed Danior on the mouth. He stirred and kissed her back.

"Good morning," he said.

"Yes, it is. Any morning I find myself like this is a good morning," she told him.

He smiled and hugged her.

They could hear his mother in the kitchen preparing something to eat. They got up and walked out to greet her.

"Morning Mum!" Danior called out to her.

"Good morning. I made some Z-Tri and I have some berries to go with it."

"You didn't have to go through any trouble, Mum." Dani told her.

"It was no trouble. I'm glad you're here."

Danior wondered where she got the fruit from. She usually didn't splurge on fruit. He hoped she didn't waste the money he had given her on him, but he knew there was no use in arguing.

"Well, it looks delightful," Tÿr told her.

She beamed at the two of them.

They all say down and ate their Z -Tri with fruit.
When they were finished Tÿr helped Mëyan clear the table
and do the dishes. Then they told her that they had to get
to the clinic. She asked if they would be back that night,
and Danior told her that they would if it was okay with
her. He told her not to make anything for that evening
because they were going to go to the pub to eat again. She
started to argue, but Danior told her he insisted.

Tÿr and Danior walked to the clinic and met up
with the wyverns. They were greeted by a line of people
standing at the clinic door. News had gotten out that
the healers were back in town. This was especially good
news for the people of Vennex, because now they didn't
have to travel to another town to see a healer or wait
for a traveling healer to stop in Vennex. Yelliton was the
nearest town that had a healer and that was a day and a
half trip on foot.

The healers spent the entire day at the clinic. They
had mainly easy cases. No broken bones this day, just
fevers and the odd cold. The wyverns were there just in
case the healers needed them.

When they finished up at the clinic, they headed
back over to Danior's mother's house. She tried to argue
about going to the pub for dinner, but they talked her
into going.

"You need a break from cooking." Danior told her.

"You don't need to spend your hard earned money on me," she told him.

"Let's not get into that again," he said.

Tÿr smiled because it would have been the exact same conversation with her mum. They made it to the pub and took a seat at the bar. Danior got a glass of rum for himself and Tÿr and his mother both had dark ale. He drank his down quickly and then ordered a glass of ale for himself as well. The meal consisted of half of a roast rabbit and boiled turnips and carrots. For pudding they were served a rich custard with a fox cherry sauce. They sat and talked after they were done and Danior ordered them another round of drinks. His mum tried to object, but he finally talked her into it. His mother got a bit silly which is something Tÿr had never seen before, though she really enjoyed it.

When they were finished at the pub, they walked back to Mëyan's house and Tÿr and Danior went to his room to get some sleep. They had a busy day and were going to have another tomorrow. Tÿr gave Danior a kiss and got into bed. Danior joined her and they snuggled together in the small bed. They fell asleep and slept holding each other again.

"How many people do you think we saw today?" Danior asked.

"I would have to check the ledger," Tÿr told him, "But I bet it was over seventy."

"I think that's the most people we have ever gone through." Danior said.

"I think you are right. There were a lot of them. Did you have to mend any bones?"

"No, did you?"

"No, thank goodness." She said.

They talked about the cases that they saw that day as they closed the clinic and got it ready for the next day. When they were done, they walked back to Mëyan's house to bring her to dinner at the pub. She tried to argue that she would just make something to eat for herself at the house, but once again Danior won and she joined them at the pub. That night they were served a roast of wild hog and boiled potatoes with a rich gravy and a side of wild vegetables.

When it was time for pudding, none of them had room for anything else. The barkeep tried to get them to have some wild berries and cream, but the three of them had to decline. Danior had trouble finishing the last of his ale.

"I couldn't eat another bite even if I was forced at the point of a sword." Tÿr told the other two.

"Me either." Danior agreed.

"I haven't eaten that much in twenty years," Mëyan told them.

"Aren't you glad you decided to come with us instead of staying at home, mum?

"I am really enjoying my time with you two. I just wish Gordian was here to enjoy it."

This was the first time she had mentioned her dead son. Týr knew she was still mourning him and that the wounds were still deep. Danior got quiet for a moment.

"We are going to make the people who killed Gordi pay, mum!"

"Just don't get hurt trying to get revenge. I can't lose you as well."

"We are prepared. They will pay." He said with a determined voice.

"Promise me that you will bring him back to me." Mëyan told Týr.

"I promise. We won't do anything that will get him harmed." Týr said. She wasn't sure that she believed this, but she wanted to ease Mëyan's mind.

"Okay, I just can't lose another son." Danior's mum said, getting tearful. "It was the hardest thing I ever went through."

Danior felt guilty that he was preparing to fight the strongest sorcerer on the planets, and he couldn't tell his mother about it. She would literally have a fit. He did feel that they had an advantage with the wyverns on their side. The assassins' magiq wouldn't work on the wyverns.

When they were done eating, they left the pub and went back to Mëyan's house. They decided to stay and talk for a while but then they were going to go and get a room at the inn. The beds were larger, and they would be more comfortable. They sat up talking late into the night before Tÿr told Danior that she was getting tired. He was inclined to agree with her, so they told his mum goodnight and went to the inn and got a room. They were pleased to find that the bed was much larger in the room they got. They got ready and then climbed into bed.

"There is something I want to talk to you about." Danior told Tÿr.

"Yeah, what's that?"

"Well," he started, "I was thinking. Since we both, um, since we both…"

"Since we both what?"

"Well, I love you, and I think you feel the same way." He said.

"Are you asking what I think you are?"

"I, um though we should be mates." He finally managed to say.

Tÿr didn't say anything for a moment.

"You think we should be mates? Are you seriously asking me?"

"Um…yes."

"I thought you never would. Of course, I accept. When would you like to have the ceremony?"

"I thought we could do it as soon as possible."

Tÿr thought about it for a few moments and then said, "Do you want to do it before we go out to defeat the sorcerer?"

"I thought we would," he said.

"Then maybe we will stay for another day or two. I'm sure your mother will want to be a part of the ceremony."

"Or we could go to Londstäc and have your parents be a part of the ceremony too. We could take mum away from here and set her up with a home there for a while. She would be safer there than she would be here."

"Shall we go talk with her?"

"Do you want to go back tonight yet?" he asked.

"Why not?"

"We can go back and if she is still awake, we can talk to her. If the house is dark we will wait until tomorrow." He said.

Tÿr agreed and so they got dressed again and headed back out the Mëyan's house. Tÿr could see that there was still a light on in the house, so she led Danior up to the door and they knocked. Mëyan answered the door looking confused.

"Is everything okay?" she asked.

"Everything is great." Danior told her. "Can we come in?"

"Of course, of course. Come in." She led them into the living area with a confused look on her face.

When they all were sitting Danior explained what had happened back at their room. Mëyan was surprised by the news. Danior told her that he would like her to go to Londstäc with them to be with Tÿr's parents and then stay there for a while. He would put her up in a house and give her some money to live with for a while. She was not very receptive to the idea at first. But together the healers convinced her that she would be safer there and she would already know Tÿr's parents. Finally, after an hour of talking and begging and pleading with her, Tÿr and Danior convinced her to go to Londstäc. It would be a bit out of the way for the healers, but right now they didn't know where the sorcerer was anyway, so it didn't really matter.

They decided to leave in two days. They would get another horse for Dani's mum to ride and then they would leave Vennex to go the Londstäc. Tÿr knew her parents would be thrilled to see Dani's mum. They had made some new friends while they were there, but they would love to see a familiar face. Tÿr knew that her parents got along well with Mëyan and would be happy to see her.

The trip to Londstäc would take them several days. They had to travel the entire shift to get there. Dani and Tÿr went to the inn to get some sleep after they told his mum goodnight. She seemed pleased about them becoming mates, and it pleased Tÿr that Mëyan was happy about it.

The two healers slept well that night and spent it snuggled together. Danior was so happy that Tÿr agreed to become his mate. He had never felt this way about another person before. Tÿr too was happier than she had ever been.

In the morning they got up and went out to find a horse for Mëyan. It needed to be gentle and not too large, but strong and have stamina to carry her over a great distance. They had flied so far so they would have to walk and lead the horse carrying Dani's mother. She was older now and could not walk the distance that they were about to travel. It was possible that they could fly but the added weight would be a burden to Qaren'a.

After they located a horse, they went to let the wyverns know of their plans. Varanus told them that he and Qaren'a would fly up ahead of them and keep a lookout for any trouble. This was agreeable to the healers, so they took the horse back to Dani's mum's house and they prepared to leave the next day. Mëyan offered to cook them a meal that evening, but Dani told her that they would go to the pub for the meal. She didn't need to be doing that before their trip.

They ate another huge meal and drank a few ales. Danior paid and they left to go home for the night. They would need their rest for the next day. Mëyan finished packing her belongings and went to bed. The healers went back to the inn and enjoyed the large bed. It would be some time before they slept on a bed again. Tÿr pulled Danior close to her and wrapped her arms around him.

"I love you." She whispered to him.

"I love you."

She kissed his neck, and he got chills. He really, truly, loved her. He fell asleep thinking about how much he loved her and that he wouldn't let anything happen to her. Tÿr didn't fall asleep right away, she lay awake thinking about how much she wanted to be with Danior. She blushed. She shouldn't feel this way, it was perfectly natural. She rolled over and kissed him on his cheek. He sighed in his sleep, and she smiled. How she loved him.

In the morning Danior woke up first and found himself in Tÿr's arms. He hugged her to himself.

"Good morning." she said.

"Good morning."

Tÿr and Danior got up and moving and then made their way over to Mëyan's house. She was already packed and ready to go when they arrived. They got her belongings loaded on the horse and then they went to meet up with the wyverns. Varanus and Qaren'a were ready to go when they arrived. Mëyan was riding sidesaddle as they left the town of Vennex. Tÿr was leading Danior who in turn held the reigns of the horse. Both healers carried their staffs with them as they walked. Varanus and Qaren'a flew up high keeping an eye out for any trouble that might be approaching.

They continued like this for a week, moving slowly but steadily along. They stopped often to let the horse rest and get water. Mëyan needed to get down and walk around as well. She was not used to sitting on a horse all day. By night they were exhausted and needed to rest. Mëyan slept in the tent while the healers slept under the open sky.

They tried to stop by all the small towns that they had come to. It helped to break up the trip if they stopped and visited a shop or two. Mëyan hadn't really done any traveling in her life so this was a new experience for her. She was thoroughly enjoying meeting new people and seeing different cultures. Varanus and Qaren'a always scouted ahead for any danger.

One day there were a band of vagrants that thought they would attempt to harass the travelers as they made their way across the shift. They outnumbered them by four to one. Tÿr brought the horse to a stop and told Danior to prepare for trouble.

"What's up?" he asked.

"There are about twelve men that are going to cause trouble." She whispered to him.

The leader of the little group came forward and said, "What have we got here?"

"We are just poor travelers heading to Londstäc." Tÿr told him.

"You don't look poor." He responded.

"We have nothing to offer you." Danior said, trying to look in his direction.

"Oh, I think you have plenty, don't you little lady?"

The group of vagrants still hadn't noticed the wyverns circling high above them. Varanus was watching from above. He was waiting to see if Tÿr needed any help.

"Boys, why don't we relieve these poor travelers of their goods." The leader of the vagrants said to the group behind him.

Immediately the others began to step forward.

"I will warn you that might not be your best move." Tÿr told them.

Some of the men laughed, but continued to advance.

"I'll take my chances," the leader said. He had a big evil grin on his face.

"You can't say she didn't warn you." Danior said to him.

"Shut up, you." The man went to hit Danior, but Tÿr's staff shot up and caught his wrist before it reached Danior's face. There was a loud crack as it made contact.

"You bitch!"

"Oh no," Danior said.

Tÿr smiled. "I beg your pardon?"

"Get them!" the man shouted to his group of ruffians.

They began to converge on the three travelers. Tÿr and Danior raised their staffs, and they began to glow. Mëyan tried to stay as inconspicuous as she could. The ruffians paused when they saw the staffs glowing.

"Get them!" their leader shouted again. He stepped back to let his men do the dirty work. A typical coward thought Tÿr.

As a warning, Tÿr shot a beam of energy out at the closest ruffian. It hit him in the leg and he crumpled to the ground in pain.

The ruffians stopped moving as they saw what the staff could do. None of them wanted to be the next target.

"She can't hit all of you at once! Get her!" their leader practically screamed, yet he didn't move forward to help.

As the ruffians moved in to attack, the sound of wings became evident as Varanus and Qaren'a dropped from the sky to land right behind the group of attackers.

Danior chose this time to bring up his staff and smack the nearest attacker in the head. The man fell to the ground without a noise. The attackers looked around to see what had happened and realized that the attack had come from the blind boy.

When the attackers saw the two wyverns they knew that they were in trouble and they ran off as fast as they could go. They left the two that had fallen, not caring what happened to them.

Mëyan was shaken up by the experience. She had lived a quiet life and had never dealt with people like this before. In fact, she had never really dealt with a rowdy crowd in the pub. She preferred to live a peaceful life at home.

"Does this happen to you often?" she asked Danior.

"No not really." He told her. "But there was this one time that we met some assassins in the woods while we were camping."

"What?!"

"It was a long time ago and nothing bad happened."

"I swear, you're going to be the death of me."

"We never told you all of the stuff we got up to, because we knew you would have a fit." Danior said.

"I appreciate that." His mother told him.

They continued to travel on. The trip was uneventful from then on. They only passed a few travelers on their way. People like them, moving slowly on to the next town or village. They still stopped at every village that they came to so they could get water for the horse and to let Mëyan rest. The days were long, but she never complained.

When evening came, they stopped. They would make a fire and cook meat that they had purchased in a village that they passed through. This is how their days went until they came to Londstäc. When they reached the village they went to Tÿr's parents and told them of their plans to find Mëyan a home in town. Seryth and Elmky Tÿr were glad to help her find a place. They told her that there were several homes that were available near them. Then they insisted that she stay with them until she found a place to live. She tried to tell them that she didn't want to be any trouble, but they wouldn't hear of it. in the end, she agreed to stay with them. Danior and Tÿr told her that they would go out and look at houses the next day.

That night Elmky made them a huge dinner. Of course, she fretted that she wouldn't have enough for everyone, and she had plenty left over. After they ate, Tÿr and Danior went to the inn near her parents' house to sleep. They had a new, larger house, but it was cramped with everyone there, so they decided to go to an inn where it would be more comfortable. Before they left,

Tÿr told her parents that she had some news to tell them. She told her dad that he might want to have a pipe for it.

"Oh my, what news is this?" he asked.

Tÿr and Danior joined her da in a pipeful of pipeweed much to the chagrin of her mother. With pipes lit, Tÿr began.

"Well, you know I am not getting any younger."

"None of us are Lass."

"Anyway, Danior has asked me…"

"Are you two going to be mates?" her mother guessed.

"Um…yes."

"Oh my. That is big news." Her da said.

"When were you going to do this?" Elmky asked.

"We would like to do it while we are here." Danior said, "so you can be a part of it."

"I think a bottle of fox cherry wine is in order." Seryth said.

Fox cherry wine was a sweet wine and was very hard to come by as they berries grew in the wild and there weren't a lot of them. The berries had to ferment for a long time, almost a year and then had to be bottled for two years before the wine was palatable. It was a long process which most vintners didn't chose to attempt because the yield was so small.

Tÿr didn't like to think about how much her da spent on that bottle of wine. It probably cost him ten silver pieces.

Tÿr and Danior sat and had a glass of wine before going back to the inn. They both really enjoyed the wine. It was a special treat for them. Neither of them had ever had fox cherry wine before. Tÿr's da made a toast to the young couple and then they all continued to chat. Eventually it got late and Tÿr and Danior left to go to the inn. They made plans to have breakfast with Tÿr's parents and Danior's mum in the morning.

Between the wine and the long trip, the healers were very tired and both fell into bed and were asleep in just minutes. Danior held onto Tÿr as she slept. He enjoyed being with her so much and loved having her next to him in the bed. It just felt right. Tomorrow was bound to be another long day. They were going to go to the magistrate and ask to be a mated pair. Danior had never guessed when he was little that he would be with Tÿr for the rest of his life.

Tÿr was the first to wake in the morning. She stayed in Danior's arms until he woke up. Then she rolled over and kissed him on the mouth.

"Mmmm, good morning." he said.

"Are you certain that you want me as your mate?" Tÿr asked him.

"I have never been more certain about anything in my life."

"Me either." She told him.

"After today we will be bound forever."

He hugged her tight to himself. "I can't wait."

They kissed again and then got up and ready to go to Tÿr's parents' house. Today was a big day for them.

Elmky was already awake and had breakfast cooking on the fire. Seryth was in the living room with a pipe and Mëyan was in the kitchen trying to help with breakfast but Elmky kept telling her that she had it taken care of.

The two healers sat in the living room with Tÿr's da and chatted with him about their journey so far. He asked about the clinic and how it was coming along. Tÿr told him that they had opened it for a few days while they were in Vennex.

"We saw over three hundred people in three days." She told him.

"That is a lot of people. Were they all from Vennex?"

"Some came from neighboring towns I think."

"I am very proud of you and Danior. You have made your town and your parents proud."

Elmky came into the room and told them that breakfast was ready. The three of them got up and joined the two women in the kitchen. Elmky had prepared

Z-Tri and wild hog strips with some wild berries that Tÿr didn't recognize.

"Where did you get the berries, mum?" Tÿr asked.

"They had them at the market. I thought I would try them. They are tart and go well with cream and honey."

"I'll take mine without honey," Tÿr said. She hated everything to do with honey.

Tÿr put her berries in the Z-Tri and ate them mixed together. Her mum was right. The berries were tart, but they were a good tart. She cut up her hog strips and ate them separately. It was a good meal and she wanted to know where to get some more of those berries. They were small and red and yellow in color. They would make a delightful little snack on the road. She enjoyed tart things and bet that the fruit would make an excellent wine.

When they were finished eating Tÿr helped her mum with the dishes and then they prepared to go to the magistrate's office. The little group walked to the office and Tÿr and Danior told the magistrate that they wanted to become mated. He told them that they would have to fill in the required documents and pay the fee of one silver piece to cover the cost for his officiating the ceremony.

Danior paid the fee and Tÿr filled in the document. The magistrate looked over the document and then put a wax stamp on it, giving his permission. He rolled it up and put a silk ribbon around it to be filed in the archives of the city. He then filled out another document which he gave to Tÿr.

"This is your copy of the agreement. You keep it and file it in your city of residence. Do you have any witnesses with you?" he asked.

"Our parents will be our witnesses." Danior told him.

"Very well. Then let us collect them and move into my chambers."

Tÿr went and called to the parents. "We are ready for you now."

Mëyan, Elmky and Seryth all followed Tÿr to the magistrate's chambers. It was a very ornately decorated room with documents on the walls and large paintings adorning the spaces that didn't have any documents. There were two large sconces on either side of the huge desk. A silk carpet covered most of the hardwood floor. The office screamed opulence. The magistrate had elegant tastes and liked to flaunt them.

The ceremony was simple and there were no frills. The magistrate asked the two if they were willing to be committed mates and then he declared the union. It was short and sweet and then they were mated. Tÿr reached forward and kissed her new mate. Danior kissed her back.

"Now you're stuck with me," he whispered to her.

"Nah, I am very pleased to be mated with you. I could not have chosen better."

Danior blushed. "Awe shucks."

Their parents clapped and gave them wishes of congratulations. Both Tÿr and Danior were as happy as they had ever been in their lives.

D anior and Tÿr spent another three days in Londstäc before they decided that they needed to be moving on. Their need to find the sorcerer was growing. Rumors of his movements were spreading throughout the land, and they wanted to meet him on their terms.

They told their parents goodbye and then they mounted the wyverns and took off in search of the sorcerer. Varanus suggested that they head toward Peyda Noirin. There were rumors that the sorcerer had been on the water planet recently and the wyvern thought it might be a good place to start. Varanus also thought that they might travel back to Ÿkkynnÿk for him to consult with Ghra'zhenn again.

The paragon might have new information for them regarding the sorcerer or maybe how to destroy the books in the vault. If there was a way to destroy them, they had to try to find it. The books were too dangerous to have where someone might come across them.

Varanus asked the healers what they wanted to do. Whether they wanted to go to Peyda Noirin or to Thunder Mountain. Tÿr thought it would be best to go and talk with Ghra'zhenn first. He might have some insight on what to do about the sorcerer. Danior agreed with his partner.

They flew hard for several days to get to Ÿkkynnÿk. Ghra'zhenn was there to greet them when they landed. He congratulated the newly paired mates when he found out that they were joined as mates. He brought the healers and the other two wyverns aside and told them that he had some news for them.

"I have been doing some research on how we can destroy the books," he started. "There is a fable of a scepter that is so powerful that it is said that it can destroy anything. I understand that it can even destroy the books if used properly."

"Where do we find it?" Danior asked.

"Well, that is tricky, there aren't any records of its exact resting place. Some say it is in a tomb and some think it is in a cave surrounded by traps. Wherever it is, it will not be easy to obtain."

"Of course, it won't." Danior said.

"I will need to do more research on it. If it does in fact exist, we must try to retrieve it. The books must be destroyed. They are too dangerous."

"I will assist you in your endeavor," Varanus told the paragon.

Ghra'zhenn nodded his huge head in agreement and the two wyverns walked off to begin their research. They had a lot to do and the healers didn't want to get in their way so they stayed back and talked with some of the younger wyverns.

The younger wyverns were very congratulative about the healers becoming mates. Some of them even brought them little gifts of crystals. Tÿr and Danior thanked the wyverns for their generous gifts. Qare'a explained to them that crystals were an appropriate gift for becoming mated. It signified the union of two individuals becoming one. She explained that each crystal they received would be a perfectly formed crystal with no imperfections.

Tÿr went to look at the crystals they received and noticed how they were perfect double terminated crystals. They were beautiful amethyst and citrine and other crystals that she didn't recognize. She also noticed that each of them had a record keeper used to record information inside the crystal should they choose to use it for that purpose. These were very valuable crystals.

Danior and Tÿr thanked the wyverns for their generous gifts again and again. The wyverns seemed very pleased that the humans liked their gifts so much. It wasn't often that they celebrated a union of mates in the dynasty since wyverns lived so long and births were few.

The healers spent their time with the wyverns for three days and nights. They used this time to learn customs and rules of the dynasty. Both knew much about the dynasty, but there was still a lot to learn they found out. Qaren'a spent a day going over the policies and the laws. Some of the younger wyverns sat with the healers to learn with them. The second day the younger wyverns taught them some of the traditions of the dynasty. On the last day, Varanus and Ghra'zhenn came back from their research and explained what would need to take place to retrieve the scepter.

As Tÿr figured, it was going to be a lengthy and involved process. Nothing was going to be easy about this.

"You are going to have to retrieve a tablet that is hidden in a cave on Peyda Noirin. Once the tablet is found it will need to be placed in a pilaster in the palace in the city of Vorräs."

"Where is the city of Vorräs?" Tÿr questioned them.

"From what we can tell, it is located on another island." Ghra'zhenn told her. "Once the pilaster has received the tablet, it should open a door to a room that contains the scepter."

"And we just walk in and take it?"

"Not exactly. There will be preventatives; things meant to keep you from just walking out with it. You will need to disarm the traps. Then you will be able to claim the scepter. The scepter itself is said to be able to destroy any object. We are hoping that you can use the scepter to destroy the books. Then we will return it to the palace before anyone realizes that it is missing."

"Shouldn't we just take the books with us and destroy them at the palace?" Danior asked.

Varanus shook his head. "No, we run the risk of them falling into someone else's hands if we bring them with us. If they stay on Thunder Mountain, we know they are safe."

"We also run the risk of Kaistam-Laq attacking us if he finds out about our plan. He wants those books I believe and would do almost anything to get them. He has the ability to divine the future and can see what we are doing." Tÿr voiced her concerns.

"The sorcerer has a limited ability to divine your movements while you are with us," Varanus told the healer. "Wyvern magiq can block out his ability to see us the same as his magiq has blocked him from our sight."

"So," Tÿr started, "we need to go back to Peyda Noirin to an island with a cave. Do you know the island?"

"We believe we do." Ghra'zhenn cut in. "it will take you to the far side of the planet and you will need to be cautious as usual. The cave is not in the side of a mountain. You will have to find it in the ground somewhere on the island. We believe that the entrance could be overgrown by now so it will not be an easy feat."

"Nothing on this adventure has been easy." Danior said.

"We will begin our quest after resting tonight." Varanus told the healers. "Ghra'zhenn plans to accompany us on our journey to the island and then to the palace. He feels that it is important that he come along to show his support."

This news gave the healers a boost of confidence. The paragon was a huge wyvern and very skilled in battle. If any trouble arose, he would know how to deal with it. Varanus was a very good diplomat and excellent fighter, but having the paragon along on the trip was a huge boost of confidence to the healers.

The wyverns had a huge fire for the healers to sit around that night. They roasted meat and drank wine. The healers knew about the wyvern's wine and only sipped theirs. Tÿr could tell that some of the wyverns were succumbing to the effects of the wine. They were getting silly, and their speech was slurred. Both Danior and Tÿr thought it was very amusing but tried to keep their laughing to a minimum. They didn't want to offend anyone.

In the morning Danior and Tÿr were awakened by Varanus. He and Ghra'zhenn were ready to go. Qaren'a was near their saddles and waiting for them to come and get them on. Tÿr and Danior got their saddles on the wyverns, and they loaded their saddlebags with what they would need for their journey. The wyverns took off and headed for the water planet. It would take them several days, possibly a week or more to reach their destination.

The currents were in their favor, and they flew high and fast. They stopped in the evenings to let the wyverns rest and hunt for food. Danior and Tÿr had packed sausages for their trip so they planned on having them when they weren't in any village. Luckily for the healers, they really liked sausages, so this wasn't a hardship for them. The wyverns tried to stop on the larger islands along the way as there was more wildlife on them to eat. The larger islands had wild hogs and some goats which the wyverns preferred. There were more trees on the larger islands to build fires with as well.

One day the wyverns landed on a small island to rest in the middle of the afternoon. It didn't have many trees or large animals, but it did have an abundance of serpents. There were vipers everywhere. Tÿr and Danior had to be careful where they walked because there were so many dangerous snakes. Varanus and Ghra'zhenn spent several minutes snatching snakes up and eating them. Their venom didn't affect the wyverns like it would the humans. Qaren'a wasn't fond of snakes, so she just stepped on them for the other two to snatch up.

When the wyverns were done with their snack, they prepared to take off again. The healers climbed aboard, and they were off.

It took nearly a week of hard flying to get to the island that Varanus had told them about. It was a uniquely shaped island. It looked like a horse's head from the air. The wyverns circled the island in large arcs, spiraling in and finally landing in the raised center.

"Now we search," Ghra'zhenn told them. "Look for any opening in the ground big enough to fit in.

Tÿr took Danior's hand and they walked to the mounded center of the island. She figured that they would walk in an outward spiral towards the edge. They had their staffs to poke in the undergrowth. After their encounter with the snake island, she wasn't going to risk anything. The wyverns were going to start on the edge of the island and work their way inward.

The healers walked in a gradually widening circle around the center of the island. They poked every nook and cranny they came upon. The undergrowth was fairly dense, and their feet got tangled in the weeds. More than once they had to stop to retrieve Danior's boot.

Then without warning Danior stumbled and began to fall into a hole in the ground that was covered by the thick undergrowth.

"Dani," Tÿr yelled and grabbed him by the hands, dropping her staff. She pulled him up and moved them back from the hole. Then she retrieved her staff and called the wyverns over to them.

The three wyverns came over to where the healers stood and Tÿr pointed to the hole in the ground.

"Is this our place?" she asked.

Varanus moved over and clawed the undergrowth away from the opening. When Tÿr saw how large it was she realized how lucky Danior had been that he didn't fall all the way in. The hole was actually quite large.

"I believe this is the place." Varanus told them.

Tÿr lit the end of her staff and put it inside the opening. She could see there were easy footholds to get down to the floor which was only about ten feet down.

"I think I am going to go down by myself. It will just be easier than trying to get us both down."

Danior began to argue but he knew she was right.

"Okay, but I want you to tie a rope around your waist. If anything happens, we can pull you out fast."

Tÿr thought about it for a moment and then agreed. She went to her saddlebag and got out some rope. There were about seventy feet, which she hoped would be enough. She tied one end around her waist and the other around Danior's waist. When she was secured, she began to lower herself down into the hole. Her staff was still lit so she could see.

She reached the bottom of the cavern and looked around it only went back about fifteen feet in all directions.

"It's not very big in here." She yelled up to the others.

She searched around the cavern for anything resembling anything that looked like a tablet.

"How big is this thing supposed to be?"

Varanus stuck his head down the hole and said, "It could be any size. Search the walls and the floor. Look for any straight edges. Things that don't look natural."

Tÿr spent an hour running her hands over the walls and trying to clear dust off of the floors. She didn't see anything, and was beginning to worry that it wasn't there anymore. She looked up to call out to Varanus and tell him of her suspicions when a shape on the steps caught her eye. She had looked everywhere but, on the steps, so she brought the light in closer to investigate. There on the second step was a small rectangular shaped object. She would need something to pry it off of the steps, so she used her knife to pop it off. There was writing on the backside of the small tablet.

"I think I found it," she yelled out.

"Okay, we'll bring you up." Ghra'zhenn said.

She moved to the center of the cavern below the hole and the wyvern took the rope and pulled her up with one easy movement.

Tÿr brushed the tablet off so she could see the writing better. It was carved into the stone.

"Can you read this?" she asked Ghra'zhenn.

"It just says that this tablet must be placed in the pilaster in the throne room of the city of Vorräs. Then you can retrieve the Scepter of Kebnor."

"Who is Kebnor?" Danior asked.

"I believe he was a sorcerer that lived several hundred years ago. He created this scepter to destroy his opponent, a powerful wyvern. The wyvern was supposed to have found a source of everlasting life. He, according to legend, kept it hidden away from everyone and used it to keep himself alive, but the sorcerer created the scepter to destroy the wyvern and take his source of everlasting life."

"Whatever happened to the wyvern?" Danior asked.

"We don't know. He disappeared. He took his knowledge of everlasting life and was never seen or heard from again. There are some that say he hides on Peyda Kirin in the mountains somewhere, but no one has ever found him. If he is still alive, he would be over one thousand years old."

"So, this Kebnor fellow made the scepter to destroy the wyvern, but now it can destroy anything?"

"That is correct, Young Master." Ghra'zhenn told him. "Which is why we must obtain it to destroy the books."

"What will we do with it once we are done using it?" Tÿr asked.

"We will keep it in Ÿkkynnÿk. It will stay there until we can find a better resting place for it." Ghra'zhenn told her.

"That is if it is still in the palace in Vorräs." Danior said.

"We have no reason to doubt that it isn't there. At least not yet." Varanus said.

Tÿr turned to the wyverns. "We haven't talked about where this Vorräs is. Do you know where to find it?"

"It is more than likely on the other side of this planet. I don't believe that it is on Peyda Kirin. I believe we have a long flight. From what I can tell, it is about on the exact other side of this planet. There is a small drawing on the tablet which shows two locations. One on one side of the planet and one on the other. This means we must travel a great distance to reach it. The good thing about that is the likelihood of running into the sorcerer before we are ready is very slim. This gives us time to prepare for battle." Ghra'zhenn told the healers.

With the tablet in their possession the healers and wyverns were ready to go in search of the city of Vorräs. Tÿr placed the tablet in her saddlebag and Varanus led the way with the paragon in the rear.

Varanus flew them high for two days landing only to eat and sleep. On the third day he flew lower and began to search for the city in earnest. Whenever they came to an island that was inhabited by a large population, the wyvern would land and ask if they knew of the city of Vorräs. At first no one had ever heard of the elusive city, but as they neared the far side of the planet, there were more and more rumors about it. Eventually they found a city that traded with Vorräs and was able to tell the wyvern how to reach it.

"We are nearing the city." Varanus told the party. "From what I can tell, we are not going to have any company. The city is abandoned. There may be a few people left on the island but from what I was told, the city is mainly uninhabited."

"So, we should be able to walk in and out with no issues?" Danior asked.

"Nothing has been that easy so far. It probably won't be that simple when we get there, but I just don't know." Varanus said.

It still took two more days of hard flying before they reached the city. Vorräs was a sprawling city on a large island. It looked like it had been abandoned several years before. Buildings were falling into disrepair and the roads were overgrown with vegetation. It appeared that no one had been there for at least a year. The palace sat in the middle of the city surrounded by many ornate buildings and statues. The buildings would have been beautiful when the town was in its prime, but now they too were crumbling and falling apart.

The travelers walked the streets cautiously, moving toward the palace. The palace was a large structure that spread out over several blocks of the city. It was by far the largest building that the travelers had ever seen. They walked through the entrance which was fronted by huge pillars leading into the main chamber. The pillars were at least three feet across and decorated with small tiles of turquoise and silver.

The main chamber was decorated with frescos that were faded with age but still beautiful. Scenes of pastoral landscapes of distant lands with tall trees and beautiful birds. Places that the travelers had not visited. The main chamber was large enough for the wyverns to enter but they were not able to enter the throne room which was much smaller. Tÿr retrieved the tablet from her saddlebag.

The healers proceeded into the throne room cautiously. It was just as ornately decorated as the main chamber. They both had their staffs lit and at the ready for any unexpected attack, but none came. Tÿr located the pilaster which was in the center of the room behind the thrones. It was huge and had many indentations in it. She had to figure out which one of the slots to put the tablet in.

Tÿr shined her staff over the face of the pilaster. All of the slots looked the same. She went around the huge object looking carefully. Finally she spotted one of the slots that was different from the others. One of the slots had the same unusual writing above it. The healer took the tablet and inserted it into the slot. She assumed it needed to be face up since the writing was above the slot. She pushed the tablet into the slot, and it clicked when it reached its limit.

There was a grating sound from behind her as the dais that the thrones sat on began to move away from the pilaster. When they finally stopped moving they revealed an opening beneath the thrones with stone stairs leading down into a dark room.

"I think I should go down alone," Tÿr told Danior.

"You aren't leaving me up here by myself. I'm coming with you."

Tÿr tried to argue that it would be safer for him, but in the end, he won the argument, telling her that he could help with whatever they came across in the room below.

Tÿr led the way down holding Danior's hand in one hand and her staff in the other. The room below was not very big and when she got halfway down she could see the scepter lying in a cradle on an altar of stone.

"What do you see?" Danior asked.

"It's here." She told him. "There is writing on the wall."

"Can you read it?"

"It says that to take the scepter you must prove your worth."

"What does that mean?"

"We will find out," she said.

Tÿr took the scepter and waited for something to happen, but nothing did. The scepter was golden with a crystal in the center. Tÿr put it in between her belt and tunic and then took Danior out with her. They met the wyverns at the main chamber of the palace and Tÿr showed the scepter to Ghra'zhenn. Upon closer observation there were crystals on either end of the scepter as well as the one in the middle.

"You use this by grasping it between the crystals on either end and aim the middle crystal at the item you wish to destroy." Ghra'zhenn told her.

"Then what?" Tÿr asked.

"Then it will produce a beam of light that will shoot out from it and destroy the item you wish to destroy."

"Can anyone use this?" she asked.

"Only a magiq user can use this," Ghra'zhenn said, "at least that is how I understand it to work."

"Shouldn't we try it first to make certain that it works?" Danior suggested.

"What do you suggest we destroy?" Varanus asked.

"Something simple. Just to make sure that we can use it."

"That is a good idea." Tÿr said. "What if we get it back and it doesn't work?"

"Very well." Ghra'zhenn told them. "Let us find something that we can destroy."

Tÿr looked around the area for something and found a large rock. It was made of kyanite or lapis lazuli or some other blue material that Tÿr didn't know. She lifted it over and sat it down in front of them. The rock was dense and heavy so it would be a good thing to test the scepter on.

The healer took a step out in front of everyone else and held the scepter in front of her. She pointed the middle crystal at the rock and thought of what she wanted it to do. Without any warning, the crystals on the end began to glow and then a bright yellow beam of light shot out of the middle crystal and hit the rock. The rock splintered into a hundred pieces and exploded. Tÿr took a step back as debris flew out at her. In the spot where the rock had been sitting was a small pool of blue melted rock. The scepter had worked.

"Well, now we have our answer."

"What happened?" Danior asked.

Tÿr explained what had just taken place. Danior asked if he could try it so Tÿr found another rock and set it up in front of them. She helped to aim the scepter for her blind mate and told him what to do. She took a step back and told him to fire the scepter.

Danior thought about what he wanted the scepter to do and then again, the crystals on the end began to glow. ZAP! The scepter shot out at the second rock and completely destroyed it too.

"Did it work?" Danior asked.

"It did." Varanus told him. "It completely decimated the rock."

"Wow, it didn't even move when it fired." Danior said.

"This is something that will need to be kept from the sorcerer." Tÿr said.

"He could do some real damage with it," Ghra'zhenn agreed.

"That is why it will remain on Ÿkkynnÿk when we have finished with it." Varanus said. "It is too dangerous for it to be out in the world. The wyverns will guard it until a new resting place can be found."

Tÿr put the scepter in her saddlebag and then they prepared to fly back to Ÿkkynnÿk. She kissed her mate quickly before they took off.

"What was that for?" Dani asked.

"Just because." Tÿr told him. She mounted her saddle and then Varanus and the other wyverns took off for Thunder Mountain. It was going to be a long trip. Ghra'zhenn figured it would take about eight days. Seven if the winds were in their favor. They would visit several villages on their way back home.

The sorcerer spent his time on his crystal ball trying to divine the location of the fabled Thunder Mountain. He was certain that it existed, and that there would be the odd wyvern or two there, but he didn't realize that the whole wyvern dynasty of Ghra'zhenn lived there. No matter what he did, he could not find the correct incantation to divine the position. It was while he was divining that something happened. A quick flash of a golden scepter popped into the images he was seeing.

Kaistam didn't know what this meant, but he knew that it must be important. He stopped what he was doing and concentrated on the image he had seen. The scepter appeared in the ball again. He froze the image in the crystal. What was this scepter? He began to believe that it had to do with the healers and that they must be in possession of it.

Renner-Van came to see when they were going to move on.

"Not now!" the sorcerer bellowed.

Renner took a step back. His sister looked at him with concern on her face.

Ollis-Van took her brother aside. "This has got to stop!"

"What can we do?"

"We can always break away and form our own enclave."

"You need to be careful speaking like this, someone could overhear you." Renner told his sister.

"I'm sure we could recruit over half of the crew right now, maybe more." Ollis said.

Renner looked around to make sure that they weren't being overheard. The two sat and talked in hushed voices. While they were talking, the sorcerer managed to sneak up on them and surprised them.

"I hope I am not disturbing you." Kaistam-Laq said.

"Not at all," Renner stuttered.

"What is our next move?" Ollis-Van asked the sorcerer.

"We are still going after the healers. I believe they now possess something of great value."

Both the brother and sister knew better than to ask what it was. They simply said that they would get the crew ready to travel. Both hoping that the sorcerer had not heard anything that they were just talking about. They were fairly certain that he hadn't because they were both still alive.

"Okay, let's get ready to move out!" Renner shouted to the crew of assassins.

The assassins all began to move and get their belongings together so they could leave. They knew the sorcerer was not a patient man so they hurried and were ready within a half hour. Renner-Van checked with the sorcerer to make certain that he was ready, and then he pulled the crew out. They moved as fast as they could with the sorcerer still able to utilize his crystal ball. He was not about to lose the vision of the scepter now.

Kaistam sat and continued to divine on his crystal ball. The ride on his palanquin was not as bump free as he would have liked but he managed to utilize the ball and see the scepter in glimpses. He knew that the healer must be in possession of this mysterious scepter because of the shrouded images surrounding it. He seemed to have forgotten about the books for the time being.

The assassins continued to move forward on the shift. There were some that doubted their mission. They didn't know why they were headed on to the shift again.

Only Renner and his sister were the ones to encourage them and keep them moving forward. The sorcerer continued to remain in his palanquin away from the rest of the crew. He was obsessed with the scepter now and spent every waking moment trying to divine its location.

The assassins approached a small village as night fell. Though it wasn't dark on the shift the crew was tired and ready for a rest. They had been pushed hard and needed to sleep. Renner called for them to halt at the village and the crew all took rooms at the inn. Kaistam-Laq stayed in his tent at the edge of town once again. He would spend his time on the crystal ball.

The assassins went straight to the village tavern to blow off steam and have some ale. There were several local townsfolk there that didn't like that the strangers were there. Some of them attempted to get rough with them, but Renner and Ollis quelled those incidents as soon as they began. One of the locals came up to Ollis and told her to mind her own business. She gently told him to take his business elsewhere by throwing him across a table.

There were other little incidents but nothing too severe. The assassins were way more prepared to deal with any altercations than the townsfolk were. Still, the townsfolk tried to press the assassins' buttons and make them fight. None of the assassins wished to incur the wrath of the sorcerer so they ignored the townsfolk for the most part.

Renner and Ollis had to break up a few different spats that the townsfolk attempted to start, but once they saw that the brother and sister meant business, they backed down. In the end, the assassins got to drink their ales and glasses of rum in semi-peace. When they were done, they went back to their rooms and fell asleep. In the morning they met back up with the sorcerer who was still sitting in front of his crystal ball.

"Where are we headed?" Renner asked the sorcerer.

"We are going on to Thunder Mountain. Maintain the same heading that we have been on. We should reach it within four days according to my calculations." The sorcerer told him.

Secretly Renner doubted that the sorcerer knew the location of Thunder Mountain. It was a highly guarded secret, and he didn't think that any wyvern had disclosed the location to Kaistam-Laq. He didn't know of any human alive that had been there. If any human had been there, it might have been the healer girl. She continued to surprise him with her abilities and knowledge. He understood why the sorcerer was so desperate to bring her into the crew. She was definitely a dangerous enemy, but would make a powerful ally.

Kaistam-Laq tried to ride the crew hard and fast but with as much riding as they had been doing the horses were just not up for a lot of galloping. The most he got out of them was a good trot and that lasted for half of the day before they became tired and needed to rest. The sorcerer was not happy about it and was prepared to get new horses, but Renner and Ollis-Van convinced him to let the crew rest for the remainder of the day.

Kaistam began to grow impatient, he wanted to be farther along than they were. Luckily for the crew he was busy on his crystal ball most of the time, so he wasn't yelling at them to move faster. Renner kept them moving fast enough though.

They traveled as fast as their horses would go during the day and spent the nights in tents wherever they happened to be. Kaistam forbade them from entering towns now because he wanted the crew to be fresh to travel and didn't want them to be suffering from the effects of alcohol. The crew's morale had dipped but no one dared to say anything to anyone for fear of retribution.

The horses were tired by the end of the third day. The sorcerer was certain that they would reach Thunder Mountain by the end of the following day, so he rode them harder than he had been. Several of the horses dropped from exhaustion which made the sorcerer furious. It took an hour to calm him down after the last horse dropped.

He was ready to kill all of the horses and make the crew walk, but Renner-Van talked him out of it.

The next day after a long rest, the crew took turns riding the horses that remained. It was much slower going, but no horses were killed. The sorcerer planned on having his crew steal horses at the next few towns that they came to. He could do that, or he could buy a couple of wagons for his crew to ride in. In the end he chose to buy some wagons and hook them up to some of the larger horses. If he got a wagon that two horses could pull, he could put five or six assassins in the wagon. They could store some of their belongings in it as well.

In the end, they bought two wagons that were pulled by two horses each. Each wagon held six assassins. They couldn't move quite as fast as they had been able to before, but it was better than walking. The caravan was underway again and by the sorcerer's estimation, they should be reaching the mountain by the next night.

The next day turned out to be disappointing for the sorcerer as Thunder Mountain was nowhere in sight. He was furious with everything and everyone. He took it as a personal affront that they had kept him from reaching his goal. What he didn't realize was that Thunder Mountain was on an island many miles away from them and couldn't be reached by wagon. In fact, it wasn't even on the shift, it was on Peyda Kirin.

Renner and Ollis were beginning to become concerned with the sorcerer's behavior toward the crew. They were worried that he might snap and harm one or more of the assassins for some small reason. He had become obsessed with so many things lately and they were worried that it might be affecting his state of mind. They began to tell the assassins to come to them with any issues that they might have. The assassins were happy to capitulate because they too, were beginning to see the difference in the sorcerer.

The assassins moved out again not knowing exactly where they were supposed to be going. Kaistam-Laq was still in his palanquin and not really paying much attention to them. He gave the marching orders but then went back to his crystal ball.

The assassins and sorcerer traveled many miles over the next day and still didn't come to the mountain they were seeking. The sorcerer finally brought the group to a halt so he could use his crystal ball to attempt to divine the location of the mountain again. He sat in front of the ball for an hour while the crew rested and tried everything he could think of to divine the mountain. He got glimpses of wyverns but no location. Overall, this soured his mood once again and he refused to speak to anyone.

Tÿr and Danior arrived at Ÿkkynnÿk and went straight to the vault with Varanus and Qaren'a. They retrieved the books and brought them out to the surface.

"Is there something we need to do first before we destroy the books?" Tÿr asked.

"No, we should just do it and be done with it." Varanus said.

They had the wyverns clear an area so no one would accidentally get harmed by the scepter. Varanus brought the books over to the area and set a rock on top of them to keep them from blowing away. It was windy on Thunder Mountain this particular day.

Tÿr had everyone stand back as she raised the scepter. With both hands on the rod, she aimed the crystal at the books and she fired a beam of energy at it. The books caught fire and began to burn a red angry fire which burned for a few seconds before extinguishing. The books were damaged but needed to be hit again.

"You will have to use the scepter again, only this time concentrate the beam on the books and leave it there for as long as it takes to destroy them." Varanus told Tÿr.

Tÿr nodded and stepped forward again. She held the scepter out and fired it in a steady beam. The red fire licked at the books, it took over five minutes to completely destroy them, but the task was finally accomplished. The books lay in a pile of ashes which the wind was blowing away.

Varanus put the scepter in his vault. He felt that it was too powerful to be left to be used by just anyone as did Ghra'zhenn. It would stay in the vault until such time as it would be needed again.

Tÿr talked to Varanus about getting back on her quest to find the sorcerer. Both she and Danior wanted to exact revenge on him for Gordian and they wanted to strike while they were prepared. They had both been practicing spells and using their staffs in preparation for their showdown with the sorcerer and his crew of assassins. They knew that they would be outnumbered but they were certain that they were more prepared to deal with the sorcerer now than they had ever been.

Ghra'zhenn agreed to let the healers continue their quest for revenge. It was hard for Tÿr to tell if the paragon agreed with them continuing their quest. He didn't say that he did not approve, but he did not say that he supported them either. She felt that it would be best if he had his blessing, so she grabbed Danior and approached the paragon.

"Ghra'zhenn, you haven't said much about us going to find the sorcerer. I wanted to know that we had your blessing before we left."

"Ghra'zhenn thought about it for a moment before speaking. "I know how important this is to you both. I believe that I would do the same if I were in your position. I only ask that you use caution when confronting these people. They are trained assassins and very skilled at killing. They also know magiq and can employ it as quickly as you. Just be careful!"

"We will, I promise," Danior told him.

"We have been practicing our magiq during our down time and I believe we are ready to face them." Tÿr told the paragon.

"Then there is nothing more to say, other than good luck. May fortune be with you."

"Thank you, Paragon." Tÿr told him.

Varanus and Qaren'a prepared the healers to fly. The healers climbed aboard and then they were off to find the sorcerer and his assassins. The wyverns flew lower than they normally would have because they were searching for any signs of the sorcerer. Because they were flying lower than usual, the wyverns had to beat their wings more to stay aloft. This made for a rough ride for the healers as there was very little gliding at this altitude.

The healers flew for most of the day before deciding to rest for the night. The planets were making their way to their farthest point from the three suns so on parts of the shift it was constant twilight now. They came to a medium-sized village called Caspirum which was situated all alone on the shift and hundreds of miles from any other village or town.

Being a decent sized town, Caspirum boasted all of the amenities that any larger town had, several inns and taverns, a chapel, a large marketplace and its own constabulary. It was a modern and thriving village despite being so secluded from everything. Even though Caspirum was so progressive, the wyverns still got strange looks as they landed outside of town. Many of the townsfolk hadn't seen a wyvern before.

Tÿr chose a small tavern to visit and when she and Danior entered the whole place got quiet. They weren't used to having strangers there so this was a bit of a novelty. There were only about ten people in the tavern including a serving maid and the barkeep. Tÿr led Danior to a table and the two sat down as the locals stared at them.

"Be prepared for anything?" Tÿr whispered.

The two had their staffs with them which is something that was unusual for the locals as well. They placed their staffs at the table near them so they were in arms reach and sat down. The barmaid came over to them and asked what they would like to order.

"What would you suggest?" Tÿr asked.

"I would suggest a glass of our brown ale, but I am partial to brown ales. The porter is also nice." She said.

"We will start out with two glasses of brown ale." Tÿr told her.

The barmaid returned a few moments later with two huge mugs of the richest brown ale the two of them had ever tasted.

"Who brewed this ale?" Danior asked the barmaid.

"That would be our brew master. His name is Gareth. He's right over there." She pointed to a stocky man with a mug of the brown ale in front of him. He was talking animatedly to a couple of the other patrons.

"Well, could you please let him know that this is the best ale I have ever tasted?" Danior requested.

"I will let him know." The barmaid assured him.

Tÿr and Danior finished their mugs and then ordered another along with a roast dinner. They were serving lamb chops with roast vegetables and gravy. Both of the healers ate heartily and ordered another ale. By the time they were on their third ale, the stocky brew master walked over and joined them at the table.

"I understand you are enjoying the brown ale." He said.

"Very much," Tÿr replied.

"I haven't met a person who didn't like it yet." He smiled.

"It is the nicest brown ale I have ever tried," Danior told him.

"Well thank you very much. The next one is on me."

"Oh, I don't think I could drink another." Tÿr said.

"There's always room for one more." The brew master chuckled.

By the time Tÿr and Danior had finished their fourth ale, they were feeling little to no pain. Tÿr repaid the kindness of the brew master by buying the tavern a round of ale before they left. Everyone thanked her and Danior as they left to find a room for the night. They took their staffs and walked out of the tavern and to the nearest inn.

The inn was a neat little place that offered them a large room for a single room price. They hadn't been busy and were glad to have any visitors. Unlike many of the inns they had stayed in, this room was immaculate.

Tÿr planned to leave a nice tip to the landlord when they left in the morning. So far, the hospitality in Caspirum had been second to none. They would have to remember this town and stop in again on their way through.

This was the first night since they had been a mated pair that they had shared a nice large bed. In the past they had been forced to cram together in small beds meant for one person. This bed was big enough for three people. The two healers spent a very comfortable night together snuggling in a bed meant for two. In the morning they were both on either edge of the bed, but they had gotten the best night's sleep that they had ever had. The ale probably had something to do with it. Before they left, Tÿr tipped the landlord two silver pieces. He was flabbergasted by such a generous tip and told them to come back any time.

When they woke, the healers went out to join the wyverns. Varanus and Qaren'a were ready to go when the healers found them. Some of the villagers had even turned up to wish them well. Tÿr thanked them all for their hospitality before mounting her saddle. Danior climbed aboard his and then they took off. Once again they flew low and slow keeping their eyes open for the sorcerer's caravan.

Varanus wasn't certain that the sorcerer was on the shift at the moment. He thought that he might still be on one of the planets. The healers had flown for three days and had not seen any sign of the assassins. Tÿr suggested that they try the backside of the shift. They had only been on the front of the shift this whole time. This would take them way out of their way, but something had to be done. They were not finding the sorcerer where they were searching.

The wyverns flew higher as they made their way to the back side of the shift. Tÿr had to rely on the wyverns' eyesight to see down to the ground. She couldn't see that far down from the height they were flying. Varanus and Qaren'a scanned the ground for any signs of movement below them. There were some travelers on the ground but none the size of the assassins' group. Tÿr was glad that she didn't have to watch the ground because looking down that far made her stomach sink and her feet tingle.

Two days later they were on the backside of the shift. They began to fly the length of it, going lower so Tÿr could watch for any sign of the sorcerer's crew as well. Towns were few and far between. They passed on town in the morning and didn't see another until they were ready to land for the night. Varanus brought them in close to the town so the healers could get a room. Tÿr helped take off the saddles when they landed like they did each time. It was just more comfortable for the wyverns not to have to sleep with the saddle on.

Tÿr and Danior walked into town while the wyverns went out to hunt. Varanus placed a cloaking spell over the saddles to make certain they didn't disappear while they were out hunting. The wyverns caught wild goats near the town and had a nice meal while the two healers went to the local tavern to eat.

The tavern was a small building with only seven tables and a bar. The barkeeper was an old lean man with wispy white hair around the crown of his head. He wore an old green striped apron over his stained white shirt. Tÿr and Danior sat down at the bar as all the tables had patrons sitting at them. They both ordered a glass of ale and a shot of rum. The rum was a high proof rum and the ale was strong as well. They ordered food before they got another round of drinks. They hadn't eaten since the morning so they were feeling the effects of the alcohol.

The barkeeper brought out two plates with some roast meat of some sort covered in gravy and some boiled vegetables and roasted asparagus spears. The meat turned out to be venison and was cooked to perfection. It was tenderloin and so very juicy, especially with the gravy.

Tÿr and Danior ate quickly and then ordered another round of ale. They wanted to finish eating so they could get to bed. They were tired, flying all day was wearying and they wanted to get a good night's rest. Beds were few and far between while they were out, so they cherished them when they got to sleep in them.

They went to the inn and got a room. It was a small room with a decently sized bed. They started to get ready to go to sleep when Danior had an idea.

"How would you feel about a pipe before bed?" Danior asked Tÿr.

"I think that sound like a fantastic idea."

The two went out and sat on the stoop of the inn and lit their pipes. They drew in the velvety smoke and exhaled, enjoying the experience of smoking together.

"There is nothing better than a good pipe of pipeweed at night." Danior told Tÿr.

"I totally agree. This was a great idea."

"You know what would make this even better?"

"What?"

"Another glass of ale."

"It would, but I better not. It is getting late, and I don't want to end up with a headache in the morning."

"Yeah, you're probably right." Danior said.

"Maybe tomorrow night, if we start earlier."

The two sat and chatted for a while as they finished their pipes. When they were done, they slowly walked back to their room and went to bed. Tÿr snuggled tight with her mate and best friend. Danior fell to sleep with a big smile on his face.

Both healers were awake early the next morning. They went out to the wyverns and got the saddles back on them to prepare to fly.

As they were leaving the town, Tÿr told the wyverns that she didn't even know the name of the town.

"It is called Orvol, I believe," Varanus said.

"It was a lovely town," Tÿr told him, "So many of these little towns remind me of Vennex."

"Do you think we are ever going to find the sorcerer?" Danior asked.

"We will find him. It just may take some time. It will give you a chance to be more prepared."

"Do you think that if we practice more magiq it will draw him to us?" Tÿr asked Varanus.

"It may, but I think he would have found you by now. You haven't kept your magiq a secret."

With the saddles on the wyverns, the healers prepared to fly again. They lifted off and the wyverns chose to fly high again. Higher than Tÿr preferred but she knew they could see more of the country this way.

Several times the wyverns dove down to see groups of travelers moving across the country, but none of them were the sorcerer and his assassins. The groups were either too big or too small. Danior enjoyed the times when the wyverns dove. He found it fun to dive fast and then level out. It was very exciting for him. Tÿr on the other hand did not enjoy it as much, though she did like flying lower when they did dive. Unfortunately for her, they usually climbed back up and flew high again.

The trip to the next town took all day. The wind was in their backs, and they stopped twice to take rests on the way there. While the wyverns were resting, the healers practiced their magiq. They worked on defensive spells and spells to attack. They had done these over and over, but they wanted them to be second nature. When they faced the sorcerer they would need to be fast and not waste energy on spells that would not be effective against him. He and his assassins would be trying to kill them, and they needed to be just as savage.

Tÿr and Danior practiced using magiq in tandem to each other. They learned to strike out at the same place. Tÿr would use her voice to tell him where she was and he would calculate where to aim from her voice. She would direct him to shoot left or right at a moment's notice and they were getting very good at communicating with each other. They barely needed to use words, many of their cues were just grunts or shouts.

Varanus and Qaren'a animated objects like sticks to fly at the pair as if they were being attacked, and the two defended themselves with their staffs. The wyverns would shoot three and four objects at a time at the healers, and nothing would get through. They were hitting or blocking everything. It was hard work which made them tired, but they felt good about their chances with the sorcerer when they were done. He might be able to attack them using magiq, but he was only one person, they doubted that the assassins would use much magiq to attack them. Most of them would try using brute force. At least that was the consensus. Varanus was certain that the assassins would take their cues from the sorcerer.

Tÿr and Danior's magiq was at a place that they were ready for a showdown. The wyverns told them that they had improved by leaps and bounds from even a few months ago. They told them that there was not much more that they could teach them.

"You have learned all that I can teach you." Varanus told them one night. "I am very proud of you both and I know that you will be able to hold your own against Kaistam-Laq when you face him."

When they were done practicing technique, they decided to find a place to stay for the night. The wyverns flew them on for about another hour until they came to a small town called Vrysdale. It was so small that it only had one tavern and an inn that was connected to it. There was a small market and a healer's hut but there was no healer in residence. When they landed, Tÿr talked to the magistrate and told him that she and Danior were healers and they could open the healer's hut for a day or two if he was agreeable.

The magistrate was grateful to have the healers in town and he opened the healer's hut the next day. People came from all over to be seen. Tÿr was worried that they might run out of herbs that they had collected for their own kit. The pair of them healed over sixty people in the town that day. Tÿr didn't even think that there were that many people in the town. She was sure that some of them had come from neighboring towns. Whatever the case, the people were happy to pay for their services and Tÿr and Danior's dwindling coffers were replenished.

The healers were given a room at the inn that night free of charge. Both Tÿr and Danior were tired that night. They had healed many people and they slept very well that night. The room was a neat and tidy room with a large bed and two chairs.

When they awoke the next day they had all intentions on leaving Vrysdale, but there were more people waiting to be healed, so Tÿr talked to Varanus and they decided to stay one more day to heal those who hadn't gotten the chance to see the healers the day before. In the end, they saw over one hundred and thirty people in the town between the two days. Most were just minor complaints, but a few needed mended bones or more serious work.

The people were very grateful that the healer had stopped in their town.

On the second night on Vrysdale the healers decided to go to the tavern for an ale or two before retiring for the night. No one in town would let them buy their own drinks. Before they knew it, they were on their fourth ales.

"I really need to get to bed." Tÿr told Danior.

"Me too, my head is spinning. I think that last ale did me in."

"If I don't leave now, I'm not going to be able to fly tomorrow."

"I agree."

The healers thanked the locals for their hospitality and then walked back to their room. The locals were sad to see them go, but understood that they needed their rest. Many of the locals followed them back to their room. They were treated like celebrities.

Not wanting to be rude, Tÿr and Danior chatted with some of the locals until late into the night. They were so impressed with how kind the people were. Finally, Tÿr said that she needed to get to bed, and excused herself from the group of people. Danior too excused himself and the pair went into the room to get some sleep.

They took their boots off and then climbed into bed, not bothering to get any further undressed. They were exhausted and ready for sleep. The pair fell into a deep dreamless sleep and slept until late the next morning.

Varanus and Qaren'a were waiting for the healers when they finally showed up.

"I'm sorry we're so late," Týr told Varanus. "We were up much later than we planned on."

"Yeah, the locals kept buying us ales and we just couldn't say no." Danior said.

Varanus chuckled. "I understand."

Qaren'a seemed to be amused as well. "Are you going to be able to fly?"

"We'll be fine." Týr assured her.

With the saddles back in place, the wyverns were ready to take off in their search for the sorcerer. Týr and Varanus took the lead with Qaren'a and Danior in back and to the left a bit. They spread out to cover more country. Still, there were no signs of the sorcerer. They flew all day with very few breaks and when Varanus saw a town in the distance he signaled Qaren'a that he was going to land.

The town turned out to be an idyllic little haven called Quantimo. It was a picturesque town straight out of a picture book. Týr took Danior by the hand and led him to the nearest tavern. Not unlike many of the towns they had been to, the tavern got deathly quiet when the healers walked in. the patrons all stopped and stared at them and immediately Tÿr could sense that something was off.

"Stay close to me," she whispered to Danior.

"What's up?"

"I'm not sure."

One of the larger patrons got up from their chair and approached the healers.

"You are not welcome here."

"We just want to get something to eat and have a glass of ale." Tÿr said.

"I don't think you heard me. You are not welcome here!" he said.

"We don't want any trouble," Danior started, but the man cut him off.

"Get out!"

"Whistle," Tÿr whispered.

Danior reached down and put his whistle in his mouth.

"That's a nice staff." The man sneered. "I've been needing a new one." He reached out to grab Danior's staff. Danior blew the whistle. The man laughed. "Seems like you need a new whistle, that one doesn't work."

Danior then brought his staff up and cracked the man in the face with his staff. The grin disappeared from the man's face.

"You son of a…"

Tÿr and Danior began to back out of the door as several of the other patrons began to stand. *This is not going to be a fair fight,* Tÿr thought.

"Please take your seats before anyone gets hurt." Tÿr said to the men. She put her own whistle in her mouth and blew.

The tavern erupted with laughter.

Tÿr and Danior made for the door. The men all tried to stop them but were not fast enough. Tÿr pushed Danior out of the door and she followed him close behind. Tÿr could hear the man who had grabbed Danior's staff roar with fury as he came after them. He was fully expecting to come out and find the healers helpless and cowering, instead he ran out to the healer and two wyverns. The blood drained from his face as he saw the two large creatures standing in front of him. The others came running out and stopped dead in their tracks when they saw the wyverns.

"Is there a problem?" Varanus asked the man.

The instigator stood there without saying a word.

By this time, both Danior and Tÿr had drawn on the power of their staffs and they were glowing with energy, ready to strike out at a moment's notice. Energy crackled from the top of each staff as the healers stood there waiting to see what the men would do.

"I ask again, is there a problem?" Varanus said.

The man stuttered a bit and then said, "no, there is no problem."

"We are going to go in and have a meal and a drink. Is that okay with you?" Tÿr asked.

The man didn't say anything but just nodded.

"Thank you. Does anyone else have a problem with us eating here?" Tÿr looked around at the men gathered at the door.

None of them really answered, but they did shake their heads in unison.

Tÿr and Danior walked back into the tavern and sat down at the bar. The barkeeper watched them with a wary eye but served them none-the-less. He brought them each a plate of roast meat and turnips with a thin gravy and a small fruit tart for pudding. The meal was excellent and Tÿr tipped the barkeep generously for it. Then she offered to buy the room a round of drinks. The men in the room warmed up to the healers after that. When they were finished eating the healers went out and decided to camp at the edge of town with the wyverns. Tÿr felt that they would be safer with them than if they stayed in an inn.

"Are all of these small towns going to treat us like this?" Danior asked.

"These are close minded people who are very wary of outsiders." Varanus told him. "They don't trust what they don't know."

"But we could have helped them." Danior said.

"True, but like I said, they just don't trust outsiders." Varanus articulated.

Danior asked if it would be alright if they had a fire that night. Varanus told him he didn't see any reason why they shouldn't. Tÿr went out and collected a bunch of wood for a fire and the wyvern lit it for them. The humans and wyverns enjoyed the fired long into the night. On the back side of the shift it got darker than the front, it was nice for camping out under the open sky. The suns almost set at night, and it almost got dark.

Tÿr sat in front of Danior who rubbed her back while they enjoyed the fire. He leaned forward and kissed her on the neck. It sent chills down her back. She turned to kiss him on the mouth. Then she remembered that the wyverns were still there.

"Oops sorry." She told them.

"It's nothing we haven't seen before." Qaren'a told her.

Tÿr smiled and turned and hugged Danior. He hugged her back. They truly loved each other.

It was then that Tÿr noticed something that she hadn't noticed before. Varanus and Qaren'a were laying closer to each other than she had seen them before. She didn't know if she was imagining it or not, but she was certain that there was something going on between the two wyverns. She would bring it up to Danior when they were alone. Was there a romance brewing between Varanus and Qaren'a, or was she imagining it? Did wyverns even have romances?

The healers sat and enjoyed the fire well into the night. It wasn't until Tÿr was yawning that she suggested that they go to sleep.

"We are doing the right thing aren't we?" Danior asked.

"What do you mean?"

"Going after the sorcerer."

"Definitely. I would have gone after him even if you wouldn't have come with me." Tÿr told him.

"I just don't want either of us to get hurt." Danior continued.

"We have been preparing for this fight for a long time. I believe we are ready." Tÿr said.

"I know, I just don't want anything to go wrong."

"Besides," Tÿr said, "We have the wyverns on our side." Then Tÿr got very quiet. "Have you noticed anything unusual with Varanus and Qaren'a?"

"Like what?" Danior whispered back.

"I think they are…" Tÿr paused.

"Are what?"

"A couple."

Danior snorted. "Really?!"

"Yes."

"They are laying closer together than they usually do. Plus, they sit and talk quietly when we are doing things. I've been watching them. I think they are pairing up."

Danior didn't know what to say.

"I mean, can you imagine?" Tÿr said.

"Yeah, think of the size of their children." He snickered.

"Oh my."

They heard Varanus stir in his sleep, and they decided to go to bed themselves.

Tÿr gave Danior a quick kiss goodnight and the pair laid down on their sleeping rolls and went to sleep for the night. The weather was cool and nice for sleeping out in nature.

In the morning the pair was awakened by the chirping of birds. Tÿr got up and saw that the wyverns were already awake and talking quietly together.

"Good morning!"

"Good morning to you." Varanus told her. "I trust you slept well."

"Very well, thank you."

Danior got up and joined Tÿr. They decided to eat a bit of cheese and bread before they continued on.

Kaistam-Laq's mood still had not improved. He was nowhere closer to finding Thunder Mountain because he was looking in the wrong place. His crew was getting restless by just moving between small towns with few people. The sorcerer spent his time on his crystal ball attempting to divine the mountain. He had given up on trying to find the healer.

Renner and Ollis-Van were both very concerned about their leader. He was neglecting everything but the crystal ball, and the other assassins were beginning to take notice. There were murmurings amongst the other assassins about the sorcerer, questions being asked.

The sorcerer was so certain that the mountain was somewhere on the Kirin-Noirin shift that he had not bothered to look anywhere else. The mountain was on

Peyda Kirin and the sorcerer was looking in the wrong spot altogether. No one dared to ask him about the mountain for fear of retribution. They had almost finished searching the front side of the shift and the sorcerer was ready to move them to the back side. The one thing that the sorcerer was no longer doing was putting up a shield of protection on the crew. They could now be divined if anyone chose to look for them. He was so concerned about finding the mountain that he had forgotten to put up the shield.

The crew did not stay in any towns now. They camped in the woods or near a town, but the sorcerer kept them out of the towns. He felt that they would get into unnecessary trouble. Morale was dipping to an all-time low in the crew with no way to blow off any steam other than to fight with each other. Renner-Van had to pull more than one crew member off the other for fighting because they were so bored. Instead of training they spent their time fighting each other.

As they moved toward the back side of the shift, the sorcerer continued his search for the healers. He sat in front of the crystal ball night and day, moving only to answer nature's call and to eat when he got hungry. He barely slept and got moodier with everyone in the crew. Soon, even Renner and Ollis only spoke to the sorcerer when they absolutely had to. If they could handle the questions of the crew, they did and left Kaistam-Laq alone.

Travel was slow, as the sorcerer would get upset if his crystal ball was jostled while they were traveling. He still had no idea as to where the healers were nor where the infamous Thunder Mountain was. His frustration grew with each day.

Finally, one day after not finding any information that he was seeking, the sorcerer stopped the crew in a town that they had come upon. The town was the village of Nyburg. It was a fairly large village for being out in the middle of nowhere. There were two inns and three taverns, a large chapel and several shops.

The crew had been away from people for so long that they didn't know how to behave when they got to the tavern. Renner-Van had to break up three fights almost immediately. The crew became drunk and disorderly very quickly and more fights broke out that the local constable had to intervene with. Four of the crew members were taken in for fighting with locals.

When Kaistam-Laq was told about this he became furious. Renner had to duck a book being thrown at him by the sorcerer. He tried to explain that the constable had arrested the locals as well, but the sorcerer didn't want to hear any of it.

"These idiots should know better than to act this way!" the sorcerer ranted.

"I agree. We need to get them out of the jail. How are we going to do that?" Renner asked.

"We are going to walk in and get them and walk out again. It's that simple. Anyone that gets in our way will pay the price." Kaistam said. "Now get your sister and let's go."

Renner went and fetched Ollis and the three of them walked to the constable's office and prison. When they entered, the constable was just finishing up locking the last of the sorcerer's crew. The assassins looked up and saw their leader walk in. They stood back from the doors of their cells. The sorcerer walked up to the constable.

"I am here to collect my men." The sorcerer said.

"I'm sorry? What men?"

"The men you just incarcerated. I am here to collect them and take them out of your town."

The constable laughed. "I am afraid not. They will be staying with us for a while."

"On what charges?"

"I will think of some. Right now, they are drunk and disorderly."

"Actually, constable, I wasn't asking, I was telling you. I am taking them. Now!"

The constable's cheery disposition disappeared. "No wait just a minute. You don't tell me what goes on here. I am the law and I say what happens in this village. Your men will be staying with us ubtil I decide they are ready to leave. Do you understand me?!"

Kaistam-Laq got an eerie grin on his face. The constable was obviously used to getting his way, and the sorcerer was about to disappoint him. The sorcerer raised his staff, and it began to glow. Renner and Ollis-Van prepared to fight, but they didn't see any other law enforcement officials in the prison.

"What do you think you are doing?" the constable asked the sorcerer.

"Like I said before, I am taking my men with me. You can either stand back and let that happen or you can get hurt."

The constable took two steps towards the sorcerer with his hands balled into fists.

The sorcerer sent a burst of energy from his staff at the constable, and it hit him directly in the chest. The energy picked him off of his feet and blew him back against the jail cells. He dropped to the ground, knocked unconscious. With his staff still raised, Kaistam turned and aimed it at the cell door. With a pop, the door fell off its hinges and clanged on the floor.

The crew filed out of the cell and left the prison with the sorcerer and the siblings. The sorcerer ranted at the crew the whole way back to their caravan.

The caravan moved out of the town as quickly as they could. They were gone by the time the constable had awakened. He was furious with the whole incident. They had made him look foolish and inefficient. He thought of going after them, but nobody seemed to know where they had gone.

The sorcerer was skeptical about letting the assassins go into the next town that they came to. He was busy on his crystal ball and left it up to Renner-Van and his sister. The two of them had a talk with the crew before they allowed them into the town of Carlisle. Carlisle was a tiny town and only had one pub and inn combined. The sorcerer told the crew that they would be spending the night in tents that night. The inn was not large enough to accommodate the entire crew. The pub was busier than it had ever been with the crew invading it. The barkeeper was worried that he would run out of ale. Renner and Ollis made sure that the crew behaved and didn't drink too much. That night was the most profitable night in the pub's history. The assassins almost drank the barrels dry. The barkeeper would have to make a trip to the next town over to get another barrel of ale.

If anyone in the pub tried getting rowdy with the assassins, the brother and sister put a quick end to the altercation. The locals could tell that neither of them were people that they wanted to mess with. Renner-Van was a big man, standing taller than the tallest local by at least six inches. His sister, Ollis, was just as tall as any man in the pub.

After every assassin had gotten enough to drink, the crew made their way back to the sorcerer's palanquin and their tents. They were given specific instructions to be back early so they could leave early in the morning. None of them wanted to incur the sorcerer's wrath so they returned earlier than they normally would have.

Kaistam-Laq had the crew up early the next morning and they were moving before the residents of the town were awake. He was on a mission to find Thunder Mountain again and nothing was going to disrupt it. He was going to search every square mile of the shift to find the mystical mountain.

The horses were all rested so the sorcerer moved them out at a fairly quick pace. They moved fast enough to keep the convoy moving, but slow enough to give the sorcerer a smooth ride. If he couldn't use his crystal ball, he would not be happy. The two-horse palanquin moved over the terrain as smoothly as was possible. The crew members that led the horses made certain to avoid rough and uneven ground.

They only traveled about twenty miles that day, which was about average. At the end of the day they pitched their tents and camped in the wilderness. They were still miles away from the nearest town. They would check out the next town to see if anyone knew of the place called Thunder Mountain. The assassins didn't know what the sorcerer would do if they made it all the way to Peyda Kirin without finding the mountain. Would he turn them back around? Would he make them travel the desert planet? None of them knew what was going on in the mind of the sorcerer anymore.

The next day they came to a small town which was so small that it didn't even have an inn. The only pub was so small that there wasn't enough room for the crew to sit. There were only three tables and a very short bar with five barstools. There were seven locals in the pub at the time so there wasn't room enough for the crew to visit. They had to take turns drinking.

Luckily the pub was well stocked and there was plenty of ale and rum to go around.

Kaistam left his palanquin and walked around the small town asking people if they knew anything about Thunder Mountain. He had talked to practically the whole of the town or at least it felt like it and he had almost given up when he came to the healer's shop.

The healer was an old woman who was nearing ninety years old. She was hard of hearing and her eyesight wasn't the best, but she managed to hear the sorcerer's questions and answered them all. When he asked about the mythical Thunder Mountain she got quiet for a moment and then she said that he was looking in the wrong spot.

"Thunder Mountain is not on the shift young man," she told him, "It is hidden away on Peyda Kirin. I can't give you the exact location because I don't know it, but I do know that it is not here on the shift."

"You are certain?" Kaistam-Laq asked her.

"Oh yes. Be warned." She said seriously, "It is guarded by wyverns."

"I thank you for your information." Kaistam said. He handed her two silver pieces.

"Thank-you kind sir." She replied and put the silver somewhere in the folds of her tunic.

Kaistam left the old woman, and he was elated. He had not been this excited in a long, long time.

The sorcerer practically ran back to his palanquin. "Get everyone ready to leave!" he yelled to Renner-Van.

Renner was confused. They had not been in the town for very long and had not even had time to rest.

What was the sorcerer up to? None the less, he called everyone back and told them to prepare to leave within the next few minutes.

The assassins gathered back at the palanquin and prepared to move out. If any of them were confused by the sudden departure, they kept it to themselves. The sorcerer rode on one of his horses for the first time in a long time. He led the way toward Peyda Kirin. They still had a long voyage ahead of them but at least now they had a destination in sight. Thunder Mountain was on Peyda Kirin and even though he didn't know exactly where, he now had an idea of where to begin looking.

If he had asked the old woman for more details, she may have been able to tell him that he could follow the Ajenti River to the Keltainyn Sea and then he would be able to find the mountain in the middle of the sea. The Ajenti River ran from Peyda Kirin all the way to Peyda Noirin and through the shift. It was the longest river on the planets. The river could flow in either direction depending on the position of the planet at the time. It was a very unique river. A sacred river.

With the sorcerer in the lead, the assassins moved quickly towards Peyda Kirin. They still had over two weeks before they would reach Thunder Mountain at the rate they were going. Unfortunately, the sorcerer didn't have the exact location of the mountain, so it was bound to take them longer. They would have to make frequent stops to water the horses because the planet was so hot and dry, and water was scarce.

The assassins noticed a change in the sorcerer's mood. He was now happier than they had seen him in many weeks. It was almost unnerving to see him this way. Renner and his sister were on their guard because they didn't trust the sorcerer. His mood could change in an instant, but for now they followed him cautiously.

Despite his good mood, the sorcerer pushed the assassins hard. He made them ride faster than they had been in the past few weeks. Their horses were not used to the new schedule and tired easily. Renner and Ollis had to calm the sorcerer when they had slowed down to water the horses. They had to explain that the animals weren't used to the hot climate and needed to be hydrated or they would not make it. Kaistam-Laq didn't seem to like it, but he accepted it and quit griping when they did stop. He was still too excited about the news of Thunder Mountain and not much could dampen it.

When the assassins came to a small town on the shift, Kaistam-Laq told them to enjoy a night of drinking and carousing. He even sent them to the local pub with some silver from his own coffers. Something that he usually never did as he was greedy and kept as much silver to himself as he could. This night, however, he sent the crew to the pub with a handful of silver coins and told them to have a nice time.

Some of the men were leery. They saw this as a test, a way to see if they would get in trouble with the locals. Many of the crew only had one ale and were done for the night. Others, however, saw this as an opportunity to blow off steam and get rowdy. They had many glasses of ale and got loud. Some of the locals wanted to start trouble with them. A big mistake.

One of the bigger local men got right in the face of one of the smaller assassins.

"You come to our town and think you own it. You need to take your friends and get the hell out of here." He said the smaller man. He figured that because the man was smaller than he was, he wouldn't be able to stand up for himself. That was his first mistake. The second mistake was to assume the fight would be fair.

"You need to go sit down big man, before you get hurt." The smaller man said. The smaller man's name was Qualin-Loe.

The bigger man seemed to find this to be very amusing. He laughed at the smaller man and said, "Maybe you didn't hear me. Get the hell out of here." He reached out to grab Qualin-Loe by the front of his tunic.

Qualin moved so quickly that the bigger man was caught off guard. He side-stepped the big man and then punched him in the kidney a couple of times, causing the man to grunt in pain.

The pub got deathly quiet and watched as the altercation developed.

The larger man tried to catch his breath and swung at Qualin-Loe. The smaller man easily ducked the attack and then landed three more punches to the lower abdomen. Qualin backed up signaling that he was ready to end the altercation, but the big man was angrier than before. He was being made to look foolish by the smaller man. The large man lunged forward, trying to grab Qualin-Loe, but the assassin was too fast. He had employed magiq to move out of the way. The assassin knew that you didn't win fights by fighting fairly.

The big man roared in frustration. He was big and muscular and shouldn't be losing a fight to such a small man. He turned and tried to hit Qualin again, but the little man was just too fast. Qualin stepped behind the larger man and hit him in the lower back several times in quick succession. No matter what the large man did, he could not make contact with the smaller man. Finally, Qualin stepped directly in front of the big man. He balled up his fist and jumped up while he punched the man on the chin. The man made a sound of surprise at the sudden attack and then he dropped straight down to the floor.

The pub was quiet for a few moments and then a cheer went up from some of the locals. Two of the local patrons ran out and held up Qualin's hands as a champion.

A couple others helped to drag the big man from the pub.

"That man has been terrorizing us for weeks. He comes in and tries to challenge everyone. No one is big enough to stand up to him." One of the patrons said.

"He doesn't look that tough now." Qualin-Loe said.

The barkeeper came up to Qualin and brought him an ale. "This is for getting rid of that oaf."

Qualin-Loe nodded to the barkeeper and took the drink.

The rest of the evening passed quietly enough at the pub. The assassins got drunk on many rounds of ale, but none of the townsfolk wanted to mess with them after they had seen what Qualin-Loe could do. When the pub closed in the early morning hours, the assassins staggered back to their tents at the edge of town. The sorcerer was in his palanquin and for the first time in a long time, he was not on his crystal ball. He was actually sleeping.

The next few days were spent traveling in the wilderness with no towns in sight. Finally on the fourth day they came to a village called Widlowe. Widlowe was a small village without many amenities. The assassins didn't care about much as long as there was a pub or a tavern.

The sorcerer was still in a decent mood and didn't care what the assassins got up to as long as they didn't get into trouble with the law in town. Kaistam hated to go up against the law. It took up valuable time and energy. It also made them unwelcome to go back to the town in the future.

While they were in Widlowe the sorcerer decided to go to the tavern for a glass of rum. He was joined by all of the assassins who hoped that he would pay for their drinks as well. He did end up buying a round of drinks for them and then he sat in the back of the tavern and drank his rum alone.

While the assassins were drinking a small group of people walked into the tavern. They had traveling cloaks on and were acting strangely. They kept watching the door and the barkeeper as he put money in his cash box. The strangers were hiding something under their cloaks, but no one seemed to pay them any attention at first.

The assassins were busy drinking and talking to each other when one of the strangers walked up to the barkeeper and pulled out a crossbow from under his cloak. He pointed it straight at the barkeeper and told him to hand over all of his cash.

Suddenly the tavern erupted into chaos as the other strangers pulled out their crossbows and began aiming them at different people.

"Okay, everybody freeze! We are here to relieve you of your purses. When we come around you will put them in this bag!"

Kaistam sat in the back of the tavern and grabbed his staff. He brought it to life.

"You really don't want to do this." A female assassin called Xanuk said.

"Shut up! You will give us what we want, or you will die."

There were seven of the robbers and they all carried crossbows. The leader of the robbers came around to the first assassin and told him to put his coin purse in the bag. He pointed his crossbow directly in the assassin's face.

"You are making a big mistake." The assassin told him.

"I said shut up!" the robber yelled.

The other robbers had their crossbows drawn on the other assassins. The assassin looked at the others as if he were giving them a signal. He gave them a quick wink and then with the speed of a cobra he snatched the crossbow out of the robber's hands and turned it around on its owner. The other assassins had done the same.

Kaistam-Laq had gotten up by this time and had moved to the middle of the room.

One of the robbers grabbed a knife from his belt and threw it at the sorcerer. The sorcerer moved with the speed of a much younger man, bringing his staff up and the knife stuck into the middle of the staff. The sorcerer removed the knife from the staff and held it by the blade. With one quick movement, he threw the knife back at the robber. It hit him in the neck. The surprised robber pulled the knife from his neck but the damage had been done. The knife had severed an artery and the man began to bleed out. He put his hand up to the wound and blood poured through his fingers. The sorcerer then took his staff and shot a beam of energy at the man, hitting him in the chest and blowing him off his feet.

The man lay on the floor and blood pooled under his neck. The other robbers raised their crossbows, but the assassins were way too fast for them. One by one, the assassins disarmed the robbers. After they had seen what happened to their leader they surrendered immediately. The assassins held the robbers at the points of their own crossbows until the local constable could show up. He thanked the sorcerer and his assassins for helping to disarm the robbers and bring them to justice.

Upon returning to the tavern, the barkeeper rewarded the assassins with free drinks for as long as they stayed that night. They were happy to take him up on his generous offer.

The healers were on their way to the next town in their search for the sorcerer. They flew throughout the day and landed outside a small town just about dinnertime. Týr asked Varanus if he knew what town it was. The wyvern told her that he thought that it was the town of Drydon. A town known for its several small lakes surrounding it.

The tavern in Drydon boasted several different types of fish on their menu. Many of the fish that neither Danior nor Týr had heard of before. They both ordered a couple of different types of fish for their meals with a nice big glass of ale.

The fish turned out to be excellent and they sampled each other's fish. The healers ate until they couldn't eat another bite.

"This was incredible." Danior told Tÿr.

"Yes, it was."

"I've never had so many different types of fish before." Danior said.

"Me either. I really liked the one with the batter."

"The breaded one was really good too."

They sat and chatted about the different types of fish that they had eaten and then the topic switched to their upcoming confrontation with the sorcerer. Danior was worried that he wasn't prepared to take on the sorcerer and his minions but Tÿr assured him that they were ready.

"We have done everything that we know of to prepare. There is nothing more to do, other than wait." She said.

"Do you really think I am ready for this?" Danior asked.

Tÿr took his hand. "Dani, you have done everything you know of to prepare. You know your spells, and you have mastered your staff. You are ready. Besides, I will be there with you, and so will the wyverns. We have this!"

Danior smiled. "I'm just worried that I'll forget something."

"You know everything like it is second nature to you. I have seen you attack things like you have sight. You've got this!"

"Thanks."

The two sat and held hands for a while. They didn't say much, they just sat, enjoying each other's company. Tÿr kept thinking about how much she loved the man sitting across from her. She never in a million years would have imagined that they would have ended up together, but there they were, and she was happier than she had ever been.

"What's up?" Danior asked after Tÿr had been quiet for a bit.

"I've just been thinking about how happy I am."

"Me too. Who would have believed that you and I would end up together?"

"I know, but here we are." She said.

"How about another glass of ale?" Danior suggested.

"Sounds good."

The barkeeper brought them each another large glass of dark ale. They sat and nursed their drinks for another hour before deciding to go back to their tents. When they arrived, the wyverns were already snuggled up and getting ready to go to sleep.

"Hey Varanus," Tÿr started, "I have a question for you."

"Very well, you may ask." The wyvern told her.

"What is the deal with you and Qaren'a?

Both of the wyverns' heads lifted in unison. Tÿr could tell that they had not expected this question.

"What do you mean?" Varanus asked trying to play coy.

"You know what I mean. Are you two…together, or what?"

"Ah…" There was a long pause. "Yes, we have chosen each other to be mates."

"That is great!" Tÿr said.

"Congratulations!" Danior added.

"In fact," Varanus continued, "we have been keeping something else from you."

Tÿr was pretty sure she knew what it was.

"When?" she asked.

"In fourteen months."

"What?!" Danior asked, completely confused now.

"Qaren'a is pregnant!" Tÿr said.

"Oh."

"If you look at the scales around Qaren'a's neck," Varanus said, "You can see that they are turning a different color. A sure sign of pregnancy."

"Oh yeah I see that," Danior joked.

"Oh shush." Tÿr told him.

Tÿr could see the scales around Qaren'a's neck were changing color to a pale yellow-orange. If Varanus hadn't said anything she might not have noticed it for a while.

"Are you going to be able to continue on our mission?" Tÿr asked the female wyvern.

"I will be fine. I will be able to do anything I want up until it is time to give birth."

Tÿr couldn't believe it, Varanus was going to be a father. He was so young for a wyvern. She didn't even know how old Qaren'a was. She didn't know if it was rude to ask. She did know that in wyvern years, Varanus was as old as she was or maybe even younger. A wyvern could live to be 700 years old or even older.

"Qaren'a is it considered rude to ask your age?" Tÿr probed.

"Not at all." The wyvern told her. "I am two hundred and seventeen years old."

Tÿr tried to do some quick math. She knew that Varanus was about 84 when she met him. That would make him about 85 now.

"Whoa, Varanus, you like your older woman huh?" Danior teased.

"Yes, it would appear so, young master." Varanus chuckled.

"Well congratulations from us!" Tÿr told the wyverns.

"Thank you." Said Varanus and Qaren'a.

"Come on, let's let them get some rest," Tÿr told her mate.

She took Danior's hand and led him away. He was still chuckling.

They left Drydon the next day and flew on to find the sorcerer. The wind was at their back and they were making good time. Tÿr was not pleased to be flying as high as they were, but she knew that they would make better time the higher they were. The air currents were stronger higher in the sky.

They flew all day long only landing at night for the wyverns to rest. They landed at a lake in the country away from any city or town. The healers pitched a tent, and the wyverns went off to hunt. Tÿr built a fire to cook over. The healers still had some sausages to eat so they decided to have a few of them with some crusty bread and a bottle of wine.

"Do you ever think that we will have children?" Danior asked Tÿr.

"Whoa, what brought that on?"

"I just wondered if you ever thought about it."

"I do, occasionally. When this is all over."

"How many do you want?" Danior asked.

"I don't know. How about you?"

"Two, I think. A boy and a girl."

"That would be nice." Tÿr agreed.

The healers were just finishing their meal when the wyverns returned. They still had the remnants of their meal on their faces. Tÿr pointed this out to them and they quickly cleaned themselves off. The healers sat out with the wyverns until it got late and Danior began to nod off.

"I think I am going to take him into bed." Tÿr told the wyverns.

"He looks like he could use the sleep." Varanus agreed.

Tÿr took Danior by the hand and led him to the tent.

"Why did we leave? I was fine?" Danior said.

"You were practically sleeping sitting up."

"I was fine."

"Come on, let's go to bed." Tÿr said.

"Okay, if you insist."

Danior laid down and was asleep in less than two minutes. Tÿr laid next to him smiling. She held his hand as he slept.

It took Tÿr a little while before she fell asleep. There were many things going through her mind. She was concerned about the upcoming showdown between them and the sorcerer. They were grossly outnumbered. She knew they would have to strike hard and fast to win the confrontation. She too, was worried about Danior. He would be at an obvious disadvantage against the sorcerer and his assassins, but his magiq was strong and he was fast. Things like this plagued her mind almost every night before she fell asleep. She knew that they had the magiq of the wyverns and their brute strength. Now she was concerned about Qaren'a and her unborn baby. One more thing to worry about. Finally, Tÿr took a deep breath and tried to relax. These were all things that they would have to deal with in the future. Worrying about them now would not do any good. Finally, after an hour or so, she drifted into a dream filled sleep. Images of fighting and young wyverns assaulted her dreams as she slept. When she awoke in the morning, she couldn't remember her dreams from the night before.

"You must have been having one hell of a dream." Danior told her.

"Yeah? Why is that?"

"You were tossing and turning and mumbling in your sleep."

"I honestly don't remember anything of my dreams."

"That's a shame I might have been in them."

"I would have remembered you." She smiled.

"Are you getting nervous about meeting up with the sorcerer?"

"Yeah, I am kind of nervous. You?"

"A little." He admitted. "I don't want to be the one to screw up."

"You won't." she assured him. "We have practiced over and over. We are ready for this."

"We're probably going to get hurt."

"Probably, but we are healers, and we can take care of each other. We just can't be afraid of being hurt. Living in fear will make us weak." Tÿr said. "It's better to get our doubts out now than when we are fighting."

"I'm just scared of losing you, Tÿr." Danior said.

"Well, you won't be getting rid of me that easy. I'm with you to the end. We will be growing old together."

"I sure hope so. I love you."

And I love you." She responded.

They sat and snuggled together for a while. Tÿr laid her head on Danior's chest and listened to his heartbeat. There was no place on the two planets that she would rather be at the moment.

In the morning the healers continued their pursuit of the sorcerer. They began to land at every town that they came to. They couldn't take the chance that the sorcerer was hiding out in a town and holding its people hostage.

There weren't many towns and villages in the area they were flying, but it helped to break up the long flights. Tÿr and Danior met many new people on their trip, and were able to warn them about the sorcerer and his assassins. They told them that the sorcerer was trouble and that chaos and danger erupted wherever he went. Most of the people were very grateful for the warning, but a few told them to mind their own business and that they were more than capable of dealing with a sorcerer and a few assassins. Tÿr felt bad for those towns because they had no idea of what they were dealing with.

At one town, a place called Danosburg, Tÿr spent over an hour with the magistrate arguing that the sorcerer would be through his town and wreak havoc there if he didn't do something to stop it. The magistrate assured her that his town's militia was strong and could deal with a simple sorcerer and his cronies.

"But, Magistrate, you don't understand, this sorcerer is very powerful and can make almost anything you can imagine happen."

"I'm sure, but we have a crack team of crossbows who can take him out as soon as he tries anything. We don't tolerate any nonsense here in Danosburg. Our militia is world class and has been trained by me, myself."

Tÿr did everything she could to keep from rolling her eyes at the magistrate. He just wasn't getting it. She was reminded of her uncle who was so sure of himself at one point that it led to his downfall.

The two sat and argued for over a half hour before Tÿr got frustrated and left his office.

"There was nothing more you could have said." Danior told her.

"He was just being pig-headed."

"Sometimes people just don't want to hear the truth,"

Varanus could tell that Tÿr was upset when she approached the wyverns.

"What seems to be the problem, young mistress?"

"Oh, that magistrate is a pig-headed ass."

"He wouldn't listen to you?"

"No, and he made me feel like I was paranoid."

"Well, sometimes people won't see the truth despite the fact that it is right in front of their eyes."

"Yes, and what happens when Kaistam-Laq comes to this town? They could be in real trouble!"

"That is very true," Varanus said, "but they will have to figure it out for themselves."

Tÿr was frustrated as they left Danosburg. She was certain that the town would fall if the sorcerer found his way there. They were weak and overconfident, two things that were bound to cause them to lose in a quick battle with the magiq of the sorcerer and his assassins.

The next towns they visited were more receptive to their warnings. The magistrates thanked the healers for letting them know about the sorcerer. Many of the towns put their militias on alert immediately which helped to ease Tÿr's mind.

Towns were farther apart now. They were scattered among the hills and small lakes of the shift. Tÿr and Danior warned everyone that they could about the sorcerer. When people were apprehensive, Tÿr brought the wyverns in to help convince them. For some reason, people seemed to believe wyverns over humans when it came to dire warnings.

It was as they were moving on to the next town and they were quite high in the sky that Tÿr spotted a speck in the sky moving toward them on an intercept course. She yelled out to Varanus, and he dove to the ground. The speck grew larger as it moved toward them.

"What is it?" Tÿr asked and then she heard a high-pitched shriek.

"It is a säqyr wyvern," Varanus said. His eyesight was much better than hers. "I believe it may have a message for us."

They waited as the little wyvern approached. It circled them once and then landed in front of them. The little creature walked up to Varanus and waited.

"Tÿr, would you do me the honor of reading the message?"

Tÿr bent down and took out the rolled up parchment from the tube that was hanging around the säqyr wyvern's neck. She read the message:

"What do we do?" Tÿr asked the wyverns.

"We go to their aid. They can hold the sorcerer off for a few days, but if he begins to kill wyverns, there will be a problem. We can not let him infiltrate Thunder Mountain!" Qaren'a said.

"We need to get in the air as soon as possible." Varanus agreed.

Tÿr and Danior got their belongings together and loaded on the wyverns and then they took off for Ÿkkynnÿk. The wyverns flew as high as Tÿr had ever flown. She was not enjoying the flight, but she knew that they needed to get back to the mountain as quickly as possible. She also knew that the fight that they had been dreading was about to happen.

Varanus figured that they had about three days of hard flying before they reached Ÿkkynnÿk. Luckily the wind was with them, and they were able to fly fast. Still the wyverns chose not to glide like they normally would at these heights. Tÿr hung on as tight as she could and hoped that the ride would be over quickly.

In order to gain more speed, the wyverns used the air currents to dive up and down, speeding them along at speeds Tÿr and Danior were not used to. Both humans had to hold tight to their reigns as the wyverns performed these maneuvers over and over again.

Tÿr's arms were tired and sore from holding on so tightly. She was glad when they finally landed at the end of the first day. She was not looking forward to two more days of this, but she knew that they must get back to Thunder Mountain in order to save it from the sorcerer. She didn't want to think of the lives that could be lost at his hands.

The wyverns followed the Ajenti River to the Keltainyn Sea and Ÿkynnkÿk. When they were still a long way off Varanus landed and told the humans that he could see wyverns fighting up ahead. He told them that the attack had begun and that they should be prepared to fight the moment that they landed. Both Danior and Tÿr took a deep breath and then told the wyvern that they were ready to face the battle ahead of them. Varanus wished them good luck and then they took off for the final bit of their destination.

As they neared Thunder Mountain, Tÿr could see assassins casting spells at the wyverns in the air. Most of them were missing the wyverns and going wide, but some were hitting them in their most vulnerable areas, their wings. There were shrieks of rage coming from the wyverns as the healers were nearing the mountain. Tÿr scanned the ground for any sign of the sorcerer. At first, she couldn't find him. She did find several of his assassins shooting spells at the wyverns and she directed her staff at the nearest assassin.

Tÿr shot several beams of energy at the assassin on the ground. Some of them hit the ground around him throwing up dirt and rocks in all directions. Then, one well directed beam hit the assassin in the mid-section and he doubled over and fell backwards, incapacitated.

"Stay with Qaren'a!" Tÿr told Danior. "I'm going to find the sorcerer."

Together, Tÿr and Varanus moved forward blasting their way through assassin after assassin. Varanus used his incredible fire breath to down two assassins that tried to attack him and Tÿr at the same time. They used some type of magiq spell to attempt to disarm the healer, but Varanus was too fast and the assassins were both set on fire and running away.

There were fireballs flying through the air sent by the flying wyverns. Many of them hitting the assassins who tried to extinguish them using magiq. Several of the wyverns had large holes that had been torn in their wings from the magiq spells cast by the assassins and the sorcerer.

Tÿr was riding on the back of Varanus who was breathing fire at most everything that moved in front of him. The mountain was on fire and assassins were running around, trying to avoid the fires and hit the wyverns with their spells and crossbows.

Qaren'a and Danior were staying high up above the fray. Still there were crossbow bolts flying up at them. The wyvern had to duck and dive several times to avoid being hit. Magiq spells were being sent up at them when the assassins had a chance to cast a spell, but they were mostly being kept busy by the wyverns on the mountain.

Tÿr finally spotted the sorcerer. He had been casting spells of invisibility on himself to pop in and out of view. She yelled to Varanus and told him where the sorcerer was. The wyvern whirled around and flew directly for the sorcerer. Kaistam-Laq saw the wyvern coming for him and disappeared from view again.

Varanus landed on the mountain in the spot where the sorcerer had just been standing. He let out a shriek that called Qaren'a down from the air to join them. Both Tÿr and Danior dismounted the wyverns and took their staffs, preparing to fight.

"Kaistam-Laq was just here!" Tÿr told Danior. "Be prepared!"

Danior called up the power of his staff. The top glowed with magiq. Tÿr did the same.

Varanus and Qaren'a turned to fight. Three assassins had snuck up on the four of them. Tÿr struck out first and hit the first assassin in the head with an energy beam. He didn't even have a chance to blink. He simply toppled over, dead. The power that she had used was more than the assassins were expecting.

"Kill the bitch!" the next assassin yelled, reaching to his belt for a throwing knife.

Danior heard the voice of the assassin and gauged where he was standing. Before the assassin had the chance to throw the knife, Danior shot a beam of pure energy at him. It hit him in the chest, causing him to drop the knife before he flew back twenty feet, crashing to the ground in a heap.

During the fight, the third assassin had drawn his knife and had prepared to throw it. Danior heard him yell before he released it, but it was too late for him to move out of the way. He had turned toward the sound of the assassin and in that moment, the knife that the assassin threw embedded itself in Danior's left arm. Had he not turned at that moment it would have hit him in the chest.

"AH!" Danior cried.

"Dani!"

Varanus saw what had happened and shot forward and used his giant tail to swat the assassin off of his feet. The powerful blow knocked him thirty feet away from the group. Tÿr, who still had her staff raised, used it to shoot four quick bursts of energy at the fallen assassin on the ground. She was madder than she had ever been in her life. When she saw that the assassin wasn't moving she ran to Danior's side.

"Are you okay?"

He had his hand on the handle of the knife and was trying to pull it out.

"I will be fine. You may need to heal my arm. There's been damage to the muscle."

"It will have to be quick, there is still a lot of fighting going on, and the sorcerer is still out there."

"Okay. I'm going to remove the knife. You will have to stop the bleeding."

Danior pulled the knife out and blood poured from the slit in his arm. Luckily the knife didn't hit any arteries. It was just muscle damage which Tÿr could fix fairly easily. Tÿr used her staff's magiq to mend the cut in Danior's arm and the bleeding stopped almost instantly.

"How's that?" she asked.

"It's better than it was. Still sore, but better. Now let's kill these bastards!"

Danior's staff was crackling with energy. He was listening for any sound of the enemies around him. Whenever he heard one of the assassins in front of him, he shot out a beam of energy. Not a small narrow shot, but a large burst meant to take down anything in front of him. Both his and Tÿr's arms glowed as they used their staffs because of their intercalation. It gave their magiq a huge boost of energy which the assassins were not prepared for.

During the fighting Tÿr and Danior became separated. Danior was near Varanus and Qaren'a and Tÿr had run off to search for Kaistam-Laq. The sorcerer was not staying in one place as he fought. He would appear in one place, fire energy at a wyvern and then disappear only to appear in another place.

Tÿr saw the sorcerer doing this but he was too fast to follow. She took aim at him several times but by the time she would fire at him, he would be gone again. Finally, the healer decided to go after some of the assassins. They were much slower with their magiq and they didn't seem to be able to just disappear.

Tÿr took out three assassins before they took notice of her on the ground. Suddenly the assassins stopped firing at the flying wyverns and began to aim for the healer. Tÿr put up a shield around herself to protect from magiq and from throwing knives. When Varanus saw that the assassins were going for the healer, he called to Qaren'a to go to her aid with him. The two wyverns took to the air and dropped down in between the healer and the assassins.

Tÿr was fast with her magiq and hit several of the assassins, wounding them. They were very wary of the staff that she carried. The assassins threw knife after knife at the healer but between her shield and the wyverns, none of them got through. Many of them switched to magiq then. They tried using spells to disarm her. They were trying to get the staff out of her hands.

Varanus and Qaren'a blew fireball after fireball at the assassins causing them to take cover. Still there was no sign of the sorcerer. The assassins tried everything that they knew to harm the healer, but the wyverns were there to protect her. She managed to take out two more of the attackers, killing them outright. Kaistam's crew was becoming exiguous.

As they were fighting Varanus suddenly perked up.

"Danior!"

"What is it?"

"His whistle!"

Tÿr turned around from what she was doing and began to run back to where she had left her mate. Varanus and Qaren'a lifted off the ground to find the other healer.

Tÿr spotted Danior about fifty feet away from her. Her blood froze in her veins. Standing across from Danior was Kaistam-Laq. He had his staff pointed at the healer and he was laughing. Tÿr could see that Dani's staff was still at full power and he was trying to hit the sorcerer with an energy beam. The beam had gone wide and exploded on the ground about ten feet from the sorcerer.

"Left Dani!" Tÿr screamed, but it was the sorcerer's turn to attack.

Kaistam-Laq shot out a beam of red energy from his open hand. It hit Danior in the chest, causing him to take a few steps backward.

That should have killed him. Tÿr thought to herself. Then she realized that Danior had a shield up as well. Yes, the energy beam had gotten through, but it only knocked him back. If he hadn't had a shield up, it would have definitely killed him. He must have known that the sorcerer was coming.

Danior didn't waste any time attacking this time. He shot three beams of his own red energy in the direction of the sorcerer. He shot three times in case he missed with one. Luckily the second and third shot hit home, knocking the sorcerer off of his feet. The sorcerer was not amused. He tried to get up, but he was wounded. His legs did not want to work.

Tÿr ran up to Danior to make sure that he was okay. When she saw that he was still on his feet and smiling, she turned to face down Kaistam-Laq. She saw that he was down on the ground and not able to stand. It was then that three assassins jumped out from behind a rocky outcropping and began to fire their crossbows at the healers and wyverns.

Tÿr threw up a quick shield again and the crossbow bolts shot off harmlessly into the air. One of the assassins came running forward with a knife trying to cut Tÿr, but Varanus was so quick with his tail spike and he smashed into the assassin throwing him into the air. The man came falling down with a sickening thud. One of his arms was severely broken and sticking out at an unnatural angle.

The other two suddenly stopped what they were doing and turned to run. Tÿr turned to see the sorcerer was back on his feet and casting a spell to open a portal. She shot a blast of energy at the sorcerer, but he had already stepped through the portal and vanished. The assassins followed their leader through the portal and as soon as they were through, the portal closed.

Tÿr and Danior sat down and took a deep breath. The sorcerer had gotten away again and they had no idea where to look for him.

"Are you alright?" Varanus asked the healers.

"We are okay." Danior said. He was still holding his arm.

"Let me see your arm." Tÿr told her mate.

"It is fine." He told her.

There was blood on his arm from the wound. Tÿr went over to inspect his arm. He tried to pull away from her, but she held firm.

"Just let me look." She told him.

Eventually he relented and let her look at his arm. She gently prodded his arm where he had been stabbed.

"Does this hurt?"

"Not too bad. You healed it pretty well."

"I'd like to try to heal it better. I didn't get a chance to heal it properly."

Danior moved his arm around. He grimaced a bit when he moved his arm over his head.

"Here," Tÿr took his arm in her hands and with her staff she healed the wound better. She could feel the flesh knit beneath her hands.

"Okay, try it now." She told him.

Danior moved his arm around in a large circle. This time he didn't grimace. Tÿr was satisfied with her work.

"You're still going to have a scar." She told Danior.

"It will remind me to duck in the future." He joked.

"Hopefully you won't get hurt in the future."

Tÿr hugged him close to her. "Don't ever do that to me again."

"I will try, but you know it wasn't on purpose."

"I know silly."

The two of them sat there with the wyverns and discussed how they were going to find the sorcerer. "While we are here on Ÿkkynnÿk I can try to scry again and see if Kaistam-Laq shows up anywhere. I can also try to see if I can track the portal that he created. I believe that we should try to attack while he is still injured."

"Do you think that he was injured seriously?" Danior asked.

"You gave him quite a shot." Varanus told him. "He was incapacitated for quite some time. We need to strike while the iron is hot."

Tÿr sat and told Danior everything that she did while she fought the assassins. He listened attentively to every detail. He loved to hear war stories. Especially ones that Tÿr was part of. She also told him about his battle with the sorcerer and how he caused him to fly off of his feet.

"It's too bad that we didn't kill him when we had the chance." Dani said.

"He'll be back." Varanus said. "His kind never stay hidden for long."

"We will be prepared." Tÿr said.

"I know you will."

"They will pay for Gordian." Danior said. "I want to take out as many of those assassins as I can."

Tÿr hugged Danior. She knew he was still hurting from the loss of his brother. She also knew that she would do anything to help him get revenge for Gordi. Tÿr too, missed his brother.

The four decided to spend the night on Thunder Mountain. Tÿr told Danior that there were some injured wyverns that they could heal. Varanus gathered those wyverns that had been injured during the fight with the assassins and brought them to the healers. Tÿr and Danior spent several hours healing wyverns. From fractured and ripped wings to lacerations and burns from the energy beams. For the most part, the wyverns were in pretty good shape. They had tough skin and spells were hard to get through their defenses.

Tÿr and Danior slept well that night. They were tired from the fight and from all of the healing. That night they forgot all of their worries and cares and slept deeply.

Kaistam-Laq was furious that they had not found the scepter when they were on the wyvern's mountain. He was also in a foul mood because he had been injured. He thought that he was above being injured by a lowly healer.

He gathered the assassins that we left together and told them that he was planning on going back to Thunder Mountain.

"We have not completed our mission and we now have a vendetta to exact against them."

"Will we be recruiting more members?" Renner-Van asked. He was concerned that they were going to be running into a very unfair fight.

"We will be going back with the members who remain." Kaistam-Laq said. "They will not be expecting another attack so soon."

Renner looked at his sister with doubt in his eyes. This was going to be a suicide mission.

Of the original seventeen assassins, Kaistam only had twelve left. It was not a reassuring number.

"What will our plan of attack be?" Renner asked. He didn't know if he was pressing his luck by asking. The sorcerer seemed to be in a decent mood, so he dared to ask.

Kaistam's eyes flashed to the assassin. "We will be taking a portal to the sea, and then another portal to the mountain. The wyverns will not be expecting us to just walk straight into their home. We will attack hard and fast, killing as many as we can. We will not be trying to injure any of them! This is a mission to slaughter the beasts. Anyone who kills a wyvern will be given a bonus."

This caught the attention of the assassins that were gathered around the sorcerer. Not only did they enjoy killing but they were also greedy, a combination that the sorcerer coveted.

The sorcerer prepared for the attack on the wyvern mountain. He had the assassins make certain that they were carrying two knives with them in case they lost one. Plus, each assassin was to carry a crossbow. He would have had them tip the bolts in poison, but he knew that wyverns were immune to most forms of poisons. He did have them increase the pull of the crossbows so that the bolts shot faster and harder. This would slow the loading of the crossbows but he hoped that they would do more damage when they hit their targets.

Kaistam-Laq gave the assassins a couple hours to rest before he called them to prepare for the attack.

Renner and Ollis-Van were surprised that the sorcerer was attacking again so soon after the first attack. They knew that the other assassins had barely had a chance to catch their breath from the first attack. This was just another sign that the sorcerer was losing his grip on reality.

Kaistam cast a portal and told everyone to get prepared. He yelled for everyone to run through. The portal opened on the shores of the Keltainyn Sea. When the entire crew was gathered on the shore, Kaistam-Laq cast another portal to open on the top of the mountain. He rushed the assassins through it.

Tÿr and Danior were just waking up when they heard the commotion outside of the cavern.

"We are under attack!" Varanus yelled to them.

Tÿr dared a glance out of the cavern and saw the sorcerer and the assassins attacking the wyverns. She ducked back into the cavern and told Danior what was going on. They both grabbed their staffs and headed for the entrance.

"Be careful," she warned Danior, "they have crossbows."

"We need the scepter." Danior said. "That's how we can destroy the sorcerer."

Tÿr stuck her head out of the cavern and located Varanus. She put her whistle in her mouth and blew.

Varanus was in the air trying to avoid crossbow bolts when he heard the whistle. He turned and headed back to the cavern.

"What is it?" he asked Tÿr.

"Danior has an idea. We can use the scepter to destroy the sorcerer."

Varanus thought about it for a moment and then nodded. "I will fetch it from the vault."

The wyvern hurried through the entrance and went into the vault. He returned a few moments later holding the scepter in his wing hand.

"Here," he said, handing it to Tÿr.

Tÿr took the scepter from the wyvern and ran out to join the battle. She held her staff in one hand and the scepter in the other. Danior was already out in the middle of the battle shooting energy beams in all directions. He wasn't hitting anything, but no one dared to get close enough to take a shot at him.

The sorcerer was popping in and out of portals, shooting at wyverns with his staff and then disappearing again. He was making it difficult to take an accurate shot at him.

Wyverns were diving at the assassins, shooting fireballs at them. The fireballs were exploding all around the mountain. Assassins had to throw up shields to protect themselves from the fireballs and the energy beams coming from Danior's staff. The air was full of raw energy.

Tÿr yelled to Danior that she was coming up behind him. He stopped shooting the energy bolts for a moment while she caught up to him. This gave the enemies time to regroup for a moment.

"Attack the healers!" Kaistam-Laq screamed amid a barrage of fireballs.

The sorcerer had his shield up and the fireballs were veering away to smash into the ground around him.

The assassins doubled their attacks on the wyverns. Crossbow bolts flew through the air at the creatures hitting some in the wings and tearing the thin membranes. Some hit the soft underbellies and stuck. The wyverns continued their attack with a ferocity that the assassins were not accustomed to. Fireballs exploded all around the mountaintop.

Tÿr searched for the sorcerer. She knew that he was somewhere on the mountain, but she didn't see him. She wanted to give Danior a chance to attack the murderous coward.

Kaistam-Laq stood on the top of the mountain shooting at the wyverns as they dove after his assassins. The wyverns were not doing any damage to him due to his shield. The fireballs were still not hitting him.

The wyverns were taking little damage thanks to their thick hides and their magiq. So far, they had managed to take out three more of the sorcerer's assassins. One of the wyverns dove down and grabbed an assassin by the head and lifted him off the ground. The assassin's neck had broken as he was yanked into the air. The wyvern carried him up about a hundred feet and then let him go. If he wasn't dead from the broken neck, he would have been dead from the fall.

Two more of the assassins had died from being hit by powerful fireballs which had completely engulfed them and burned them in just minutes.

Tÿr had the scepter and used it to take out one more of the assassins. The woman snuck up on her and tried to grab her from behind. Tÿr spun around and smashed the scepter into the temple of the woman who was standing at her back with a knife drawn. The woman never saw it coming. Tÿr had spun around so quickly that she had completely surprised the woman who crumpled when the scepter made contact with her skull.

The sorcerer saw what had happened and saw that the healer had the scepter. He cast a portal to appear right in front of the healer. Danior heard the energy forming and told Tÿr to give him the scepter. The girl handed the scepter to Danior. He held it at the ready, and told Tÿr to be prepared. She called up the power of her staff.

At that moment, the sorcerer appeared out of a portal in front of the healers. Tÿr shot three beams of energy at him as soon as he appeared. The sorcerer tried to avoid them but couldn't avoid them all. He was hit in the hip by the last beam and spun around completely.

Danior stood and listened closely to the fight, he needed to hear where the sorcerer was so he could aim the scepter properly.

The sorcerer still didn't realize that the blind boy had the scepter. He spun back on the girl.

"Give me the scepter!"

Tÿr shot out at him again. This time he was ready and blocked the shots, sending them wide and into the rocks beside him.

It was the sorcerer's turn to attack. He used his staff to produce a ball of red energy that shot at Tÿr and Danior. Tÿr was too fast and blocked the shot with an invisible shield that absorbed the ball. The sorcerer struck out again. he picked up several rocks from the ground and hurled them at the healers. Again, Tÿr's shield blocked the attack.

Danior was getting a grip on the scepter and listening to hear where the sorcerer was. Tÿr saw what he was doing and stepped behind him. She put his hand on his shoulder and whispered in his ear.

"He is right in front of us."

Danior held up the scepter and shot three bursts. He was concentrating on the sorcerer's voice. The three shots went wild and missed the sorcerer, but only by a little.

"Give me the scepter, boy! You don't know how to use it." the sorcerer taunted.

Danior was able to tell where the sorcerer was now. He adjusted his fire and shot out again. The first shot hit the sorcerer's staff and it broke in two. The sorcerer screamed out in rage.

Kaistam-Laq tried to cast at Danior but his spell was weak because his staff was broken now. The spell still had enough power to cause Danior to wince.

"You killed my brother, and now you will pay for it." Danior told Kaistam-Laq.

"You will find that you will be the one who suffers boy." The sorcerer said. He began to attempt to cast a spell at the blind boy.

Danior heard him begin to mutter something and then he used the scepter. He shot at the last place he had heard the sorcerer's voice coming from. He shot four times in quick succession. Each energy beam struck out and hit the sorcerer before he even fell forward. The first three beams hit the sorcerer in the chest and caused a huge black mark to appear. The fourth beam burned straight through the sorcerer's chest and out the other side.

Danior heard the sorcerer's body hit the ground.

"Is he dead?" Danior asked.

"He is dead." Tÿr told him.

Danior handed the scepter back to Tÿr. She took it from him and stepped out to see if she could help the wyverns with the rest of the assassins. There were still a few assassins fighting, they didn't realize that their leader was dead.

Tÿr used the scepter on three more of the assassins before they realized that they were fighting a lost cause. In the end there were only five assassins left and they ran from the battle. Renner and Ollis-Van had called a retreat and they went into hiding. After waiting for several months, they realized that the sorcerer was not coming back for them, and they split up and went their separate ways.

Danior and Tÿr spent many hours treating wounded wyverns. They had to remove crossbow bolts and mend wings. This helped to win hearts in the wyvern dynasty.

Tÿr asked Varanus if he thought it was safe for her parents to come back home to Vennex. The wyvern speculated that the assassins had all fled and the sorcerer was dead so the threat to them was minimal.

"You can probably return to your clinic as well." He told the healers.

"Could you fly us to my parents' house in Londstäc so we can tell them in person?" Tÿr asked.

"We can do that."

"Then on to Londstäc!" Danior said.

"We should probably return the scepter to the vault." Tÿr told the wyverns. She handed it back to Varanus who took it and went back to the vault. Danior collected his belongings and put them in his saddlebags. Tÿr went around and picked up some of the knives that were on the dead assassins. She figured that she could never have too many knives. Many of them were made of lachtrys.

When Varanus returned from the vault he told them that he was ready to fly whenever they were ready. Tÿr and Danior climbed up in their saddles and they were off.

It took the several days to fly to Landstäc. The weather was good, and the wyverns chose to fly high and fast. There was much gliding and smooth sailing. They stopped in several small towns along the way where news of the sorcerer's demise had already reached them. There was much celebrating in the taverns. People were glad to hear that they wouldn't be bothered by the sorcerer again. Tÿr and Danior celebrated along with the people. They listened to wild tales about how two healers killed the sorcerer and ended his reign of terror. Many of the tales were exaggerated, but the healers didn't correct any of the people. They enjoyed hearing of their exploits.

Finally, after a long flight on the final day, they landed in Landstäc. They had flown through the night and landed in the morning around mealtime. Tÿr knocked on her parents' door. Her father opened the door and stood there in shock.

"Tÿr?"

"Hi Da!"

"Elmky! Tÿr is back!" he called out to his wife.

Elmky came running to the door. "Oh my!"

"Hi Mum!" Tÿr said cheerfully.

"Are you back to stay?"

"No, but you can go home now!"

"What?!"

"It's over." Tÿr said. "The sorcerer is dead. You can go back to Vennex!"

"Truly?"

"Yep. Truly." Danior told her.

Elmky told them to come in and have something to eat. She told them that she had just finished making the morning meal and they should stay and eat.

"Where are my critters?" Tÿr asked.

"Oh, they are around here somewhere."

About that time Tÿr heard a bunch of scurrying on the floor from the back room. Sëvyq and Rævii came running out to greet her. She dropped down and hugged her little friends to her chest.

"Hi, my Lovelies!"

The shift fox practically purred as Tÿr petted her. Sëvyq sat patiently and waited his turn.

After greeting her little animal friends, Tÿr's mum told her that it was time to eat.

"I hope there is enough." She said.

"Tÿr and Danior laughed at this. They knew that there would be leftovers.

The four of them went to eat while the wyverns went out to hunt.

Elmky and Seryth asked the healers about their journey. They wanted to know how they defeated the sorcerer. News about his defeat had even made it back to Londstäc. Her parents figured that Tÿr and Danior had something to do with it. The healers told them as much as they dared about their adventure. They left out the bits where they had come close to getting hurt. Tÿr knew her mum wouldn't like those parts. Her father seemed to guess that they were leaving out bits of the story. Tÿr gave him a look that said that she would fill him in later.

When their meal was over Tÿr helped her mother with the dishes and then she and Danior went out to have a pipe with her father. He had some new pipeweed that he thought they would like. They weed was soaked in rum and vanilla. It was very pleasant and an enjoyable smoke. He told Tÿr that before they left, he would give her some to take with her.

Elmky convinced them to stay for the night. She told Tÿr that she would make roast chops of wild hog and something new that they had learned to like while they were in Londstäc. Rice. Tÿr couldn't resist, she went out to talk with the wyverns to see if they would mind staying for the night. Varanus told her that they would be fine here for the night so Tÿr told her mum that they would stay.

"What is rice?" Tÿr asked her mum.

"It is a grain that you cook in water and then you can add things like mushrooms and onion to it. I think you might like it better than Z-Tri."

Tÿr had never heard of rice before and was anxious to try it. Z-Tri was not her very favorite thing. Rice definitely sounded interesting.

Tÿr and Danior helped around the house that day. Elmky was anxious to begin packing up so they could go back to Vennex. Tÿr helped her get some of the smaller items put away in boxes. Danior helped Seryth in his shop. They began to pack up some of his tools. Seryth knew that his wife wanted to get back to Vennex as soon as possible. Their friends were there and so was their home. They had left everything behind when they fled.

When dinnertime came, the four of them sat down and enjoyed the roast hog and rice. Tÿr and Danior really liked the rice. It was something different from Z-Tri. Elmky told them that she would be bringing some back to Vennex with her.

When their meal was finished Elmky told the two healers how glad she was that they were together. Then she brought up the uncomfortable subject of when they were going to make her a grandmother. Danior's face got bright red and Tÿr told her mum that they didn't know yet.

"We've only become mates. We have time mum."

"I'm not getting any younger lass." Elmky told her.

"Well, I'm sure it will happen in time." Tÿr assured her.

Danior tried to change the subject. "So, when do you think you will be ready to move back to Vennex?"

"I would like to leave within the week," Seryth said.

"That soon?" his wife asked.

"Definitely. The sooner the better."

"If you want," Tÿr said, "we can stay and help you pack up."

"We will be fine, there isn't that much to pack, really." Her da said.

"Really Da, it wouldn't be that much of a problem."

"Nonsense, you need to get home and open your clinic."

"Danior, tell them." Tÿr said.

"Really, we would be happy to help you." He said.

Seryth shook his head. "You two need to get back and start your lives together, not stay here with us. Besides, there are people who will need to see you at the clinic.

"If you're certain."

"Of course, we are," her mum said.

Tÿr and Danior did stay for another two days and help pack things for her parents. At the end of the two days, her parents told them thank you for their help and then told them that they could handle the rest. The wyverns were ready to fly and so they took off for Vennex. Tÿr's parents promised to be right behind them and bring the animals with them. It would be easier for them to travel with the critters than for Tÿr to fly with them.

EPILOGUE

Tÿr and Danior had gotten back into their regular routine at the clinic since their adventure. It had been a year since they had returned, and many things had changed. Tÿr's parents had returned to Vennex and her father had reopened his furniture shop.

Varanus and Qaren'a had gone back to Ÿkkynnÿk for a little while. They wanted to have their baby at Thunder Mountain. Qaren'a was getting large and Varanus was a doting mate. It was about this time that Tÿr and Danior found out that they had their own news to share.

One night they went to gather their parents together for a meal. Elmky and Seryth were there along with Danior's mother, Mëyan Suttÿr. Tÿr had cooked a wild boar roast and rice with mushrooms. She loved this dish and couldn't seem to get enough of it. Tÿr's mum had brought a custard and berries for pudding.

The meal was delicious and when they were finished eating and it was time for pipes, Tÿr told everyone that she had some news to share.

She lit her pipe and began. "Danior and I have some news."

"Well, what is it?" her da asked.

"You are going to be grandparents." Danior blurted out.

"Tÿr'Ynyn! Put that pipe down immediately!" her mum shouted.

Everyone about jumped out of their skin.

Tÿr put her pipe down and Danior laughed.

The rest of the night went off without a hitch. Everyone congratulated the two soon-to-be parents and Tÿr's da brought out a bottle of wine for them to toast the happy occasion. Tÿr took a small sip from Danior's glass when her mum wasn't looking.

Nine months later Tÿr gave birth to their first child, a healthy baby girl. They named the girl Riel and she grew fast and strong. Danior was concerned that she might have inherited his blindness, but Tÿr assured him that she had not. She did inherit his blue eyes and his father's curly hair.

Danior and Týr lived a happy life at the clinic and people came from all over to see the hero healers. Varanus and Qaren'a visited often to make certain that the healers had everything that they needed. The wyverns doted on the little girl, and she loved them. She looked like a doll next to them, she was tiny compared to the huge wyverns. They brought her toys and treats whenever they visited.

Soon after the wyverns had a young one of their own. Qaren'a gave birth to a female wyvern in the spring the next year. Varanus and Qaren'a called her Xera. Xera looked just like a miniature version of her mother with light blue, almost translucent scales. Her wings spread out as if she wanted to fly, but she wasn't strong enough yet. Varanus told the healers that it would be about a year before she would be able to fly well enough to leave them.

Týr and Danior found out that the baby wyvern had a taste for fresh fish, and so they would often go fishing and bring back an extra fish or two for Xera. The little wyvern learned that when the healers came to visit, they often brought treats and she would run up to greet them. Rævii and Sëvyq soon made friends with Xera and they would romp and play in the fields like they were old friends.

Riel grew to be an independent little girl who loved to spend time with her extended family. The animals had a sixth sense about them, and they knew to be gentle to her. Tÿr and Danior were as happy as they could possibly be.

"I don't think I could be happier than I am right now," Danior told his mate.

"Life is good, isn't it? I do have something to tell you though."

"What now?"

"Well, you know how we have been trying to…"

"Again?! Really?!"

Tÿr laughed. "Yep, again. I'm already three months."

"Does anyone else know?"

"Nope."

"Good, let's keep it a secret for a while."

"Why?"

"Because I'm going to need about a month to wrap my head around this."

Tÿr walked up and hugged Danior. "You'll get used to it."

He hugged her back and thought about how long it was going to take him to get used to the fact that they were going to be parents again. They would need a bigger house. Their cottage was fine for the three of them, but with another child in the house they would need another room. His mind was spinning. At least his was good news and he had a while to plan. He could hear Riel calling for food. It was his turn to feed her. One of the many chores they divided between them.

"Coming my dear," he called to his daughter. She waited patiently for him to bring her the food and then he sat down to feed her. Life was good and he couldn't wait to see what else was in store for him and his family.